Senegalese Stagecraft

performance works

SERIES EDITORS
Patrick Anderson and Nicholas Ridout

This series publishes books in theater and performance studies, focused in particular on the material conditions in which performance acts are staged, and to which performance itself might contribute. We define "performance" in the broadest sense, including traditional theatrical productions and performance art, but also cultural ritual, political demonstration, social practice, and other forms of interpersonal, social, and political interaction that may fruitfully be understood in terms of performance.

Senegalese Stagecraft

Decolonizing Theater-Making in Francophone Africa

✦

Brian Valente-Quinn

NORTHWESTERN UNIVERSITY PRESS
EVANSTON, ILLINOIS

Northwestern University Press
www.nupress.northwestern.edu

Printed in the United States of America

10 9 8 7 6 5 4 3 2 1

Library of Congress Cataloging-in-Publication Data

Names: Valente-Quinn, Brian, author.
Title: Senegalese stagecraft : decolonizing theater-making in Francophone Africa / Brian Valente-Quinn.
Other titles: Performance works.
Description: Evanston, Illinois : Northwestern University Press, 2021. | Series: Performance works | Includes bibliographical references and index.
Identifiers: LCCN 2020047319 | ISBN 9780810143654 (paperback) | ISBN 9780810143661 (cloth) | ISBN 9780810143678 (ebook)
Subjects: LCSH: Theater—Senegal—History. | Theater and society—Senegal. | Senegalese drama (French)—20th century—History and criticism. | Senegalese drama (French)—21st century—History and criticism.
Classification: LCC PN3000.S38 V35 2021 | DDC 792.096630904—dc23
LC record available at https://lccn.loc.gov/2020047319

For Rita

CONTENTS

ACKNOWLEDGMENTS

The long research project that eventually led to this book has at various moments been enriched and even salvaged by the many kind souls, or *borom baax*, who offered their guidance and support throughout the years. First, warm thanks go to the members of the Kàddu Yaraax theater company for making their corner of the world my home away from home in Senegal these past years. Artistic Director Mouhamadou Diol simply cannot be thanked enough, and I am equally grateful to the company's vice president, Leïty Kane, and to Abdoulaye Karel Dieng, director of the Salon Africain des Langues et Cultures. From the project's beginnings, dear friend Ousmane Guèye has provided invaluable research assistance as well as countless hours of peerless *teraanga*. My understanding of the many cultural worlds of Senegal benefited tremendously from conversations with the late Yelimane Fall, Cheikh Ibrahima Fall of the *Bamba Mos Xam* troupe, Abdou Diaw of Daaray Kocc, visual artist Viyé Diba, master percussionist Oumar Thiam, stage director Seyba Traoré, and popular theater activist Maguette Thiam of Thiès. Warm thanks also go to the members of the wonderful Compagnie Sant Yàlla of Yeumbeul, and particularly to Adama Gueye, Fallou Diop, and Moussa N'Diaye, who graciously agreed to collaborate with Gino Canella and myself on a short documentary film. Thanks also to Gino for embarking with me on that adventurous journey. Lastly, I had the great fortune of conversing at length with several luminaries of the Senegalese theater world who have since passed on, and each of whom was most generous in sharing their insight and experience. These include former minister Assane Seck, stage director and choreographer Mamadou Diop, director and playwright Oumar Ndao, playwright and filmmaker Massèye Niang, and director and performer Macodou Mbengue.

This project began under the guidance of Dominic Thomas and Allen F. Roberts of UCLA. My deepest gratitude goes to Dominic, Al, and to the dearly missed Polly Roberts for their unwavering support and invaluable mentorship. The Department of French and Francophone Studies at UCLA provided a rich and dynamic intellectual environment for the project to take shape, and I am grateful for the early guidance of Andrea Loselle, Alain Mabanckou, and Andrew Apter. I also thank all of my colleagues and friends at the University of Colorado Boulder, especially those in the Department of French and Italian, for making our institutional home such a pleasant and supportive one. I am grateful to Elizabeth Rose and Sara Fischer for their research assistance. A number of scholars have kindly offered valuable guidance and support by reading drafts, writing letters, or providing feedback in multiple forms. I would especially like to acknowledge the assistance and collaboration of David Murphy, Ferdinand De Jong, Fallou Ngom, Judith Graves Miller, Hélène Neveu Kringelbach, Souleymane Bachir Diagne, Christopher Braider, Suzanne Magnanini, Warren Motte, Ruth Bush, Claire Ducournau, Charles Forsdick, Cheikh Anta Babou, Glenn Odom, Ousmane Diakhaté, Ndiouga Benga, Joanna Grabski, Frédérique Louveau, Andrew Sobanet, and Aun Hasan Ali. I am also grateful to Patrick Anderson and Nicolas Ridout for their interest in the book, as well to Trevor Perri, Anne Gendler, and the entire staff at Northwestern University Press for their timely and attentive guidance through the production process.

My research for this book has benefited from the support of the Mellon Foundation, the Center for European Studies, and the Lennart Grant at UCLA, as well as the Fulbright and Foreign Language Area Studies (FLAS) programs. I also received funding from the Eugene M. Kayden Award and the Graduate Committee on the Arts and Humanities at the University of Colorado Boulder. I enjoyed a productive year spent as a *pensionnaire étranger* at the École Normale Supérieure in Paris, as well as a year's affiliation with the West African Research Center in Dakar, thanks to the support of the center's president, Ousmane Sène. I am grateful to both of these institutions for the time and resources necessary to complete this long project. I also wish to thank my talented Wolof teachers, including Mohamed Camara, Oumar Diallo, and Lamine Diallo of the Dakar Language Center. A special word of gratitude goes to Paap Alsaan Sow, whose tremendous spirit of generosity and kindness led to, and provided, some of the most generative insights in my study of Wolof-language theater.

On a personal note, I am grateful to the many people who have offered enriching conversation and friendship these past years. These include Séverine Awenengo Dalberto, Ndèye Diop, and everyone I had the pleasure of meeting over the years in Zone A and then in Amitié 3. Personal thanks also go to Jen Lazuta, Lauren Honig, and Ashley Fent, as well as to old friends Chris Seehase, Nathaniel Armstrong, Mark Rendeiro, Malik Soares, Tom Narins, Howard Padwa, and Duncan McEachern Yoon. Lastly, I warmly thank my wonderful Lisbon family, who have provided support in ways too numerous to count.

This book is dedicated to the memory of my father, Dennis Patrick Quinn, who is dearly missed each and every day. It was made possible by the endless love and support of my mother Nancy and brother Timothy. Finally, my deepest gratitude goes to my partner Rita and our children Dennis and Adelaide, for all the joy they bring and with love forever.

Writing a book on Senegal in English poses a particular spelling conundrum. For Wolof terms and names, one must choose between a colonial orthography based on French phonetics and an academic Wolof orthography. For cities and names, including their own, most people in Senegal use French spelling, and so do I in this book. However, when citing Wolof sources or terms, I opt for Wolof spelling and follow Jean-Léopold Diouf's French-Wolof dictionary. I also take the liberty of using Wolof spelling when discussing certain historical figures and places such as those connected to the Murid Sufi brotherhood.

Senegalese Stagecraft

INTRODUCTION

In Senegal, the word "theater" applies to a wide range of cultural and performance practices. The term recalls a series of historical moments when theater-making, or the work of crafting the stage space through the use of text, place, and embodied performance, offered an opportunity for creators to respond to and act upon the political forces of the day. The first major experiment with original works of Western-style stage performance took place in dialogue with the demands of life under French colonialism. In the interwar context of the 1930s, on the picturesque island of Gorée, just off the coast of Dakar, students at the École Normale William Ponty, French West Africa's elite training ground for indigenous teachers, doctors, and clerks, took the stage to enact African myths and customs and to tell the stories of local rulers and their confrontations with colonial forces. These original creations, which became known as *théâtre indigène* (indigenous theater), combined French-style dramaturgy with African forms of music, ritual, and dance. They enjoyed an enthusiastic reception among colonial educators, administrators, and visiting dignitaries, who saw the staged works as heralding a new Franco-African creative spirit. The performances also offered the young students a means of writing and performing their way into the cosmopolitan cultural spheres of the colonies. Buzz around the students' work even earned them a trip to Paris, where they performed as living demonstrations of the supposed benefits of France's civilizing mission in West Africa. In the Ponty stage, students saw more than a simple tool for colonial interests. They used the stage to project themselves beyond the limited roles assigned to them as colonial intermediaries. The practice of staged enactment inherent to the theatrical space offered a means of actively defining their place and identity under French colonialism rather than figuring as passive objects of colonial policy.

From the "Ponty" experience onward, theater served as a privileged space of negotiation between colonial authorities and a group of Africans who were deeply invested in the promises of a French education. A rising French-educated elite called (in the colonial terminology of the day) the *évolués*, or the "evolved," stood out for their commitment to French culture, their mastery of the French language, and their eagerness to envision political enfranchisement in an African context through the lens of French republicanism. Since they lacked the authority to make their voice heard in the political sphere, these African intellectuals turned to culture. This was notably the case in the French *centres culturels* (cultural centers) of West Africa in the 1950s, where theater provided a platform for contemplating the potential benefits of a region-wide Francophone African identity. Writers and creators in search of a deeper connection with the globalized postwar world turned their gaze toward new forms of citizenship as the model of a French Empire shifted to that of an ill-defined and ultimately short-lived "French Union." Culturally, their performances evoked discourses of both the traditional and the avant-garde, delving into precolonial performance forms and, in so doing, inspiring major figures of European experimental theater who applauded the rise of indigenous theater from as far away as the international Theater of Nations festival in Paris.

The first generation of Ponty performers came of age in time to become the most prominent politicians and intellectuals of their respective West African countries in the era of independence that began in 1958.[1] In Senegal, as elsewhere in the former colonies of French West Africa, the seasoned stage performers put culture at the heart of their political projects. With the establishment of robust national cultural institutions, African directors and performers sought to employ stage performance as a means of direct encounter with the African world. The stage served as a site from which the Western outsider and African artist could come together to reimagine Africa, its culture and its history, as an integral and constitutive part of a shared human heritage. Theater artists proved eager to situate new African stage works within a global theatrical canon. The large-scale productions of Senegal's new national theater, Le Théâtre National Daniel Sorano, inaugurated in 1965, included original creations employing dramaturgical techniques developed by the students of the Ponty School, along with "Africanized" adaptations of such Western classics as Shakespeare's *Macbeth* and Molière's *The Imaginary Invalid*. Always an outward-looking institution of international focus and scope, the Sorano Theater placed Dakar at the forefront of global experimentation in performance forms coming from Africa and the African diaspora. It also facilitated sustained cultural engagement with France as the country's first president, Léopold Sédar Senghor, sought to forge a close relationship between national cultural institutions and the state, much as his friend André Malraux had begun to do in France as that country's first minister of cultural affairs.

For Senghor, as for the stage artists of the Ponty generation, theatrical creation in Senegal went hand-in-hand with the conceptual configuration of a transnational *Francophonie*, or a community of nations united by their attachment to the French language and French culture. Senghor and his fellow "men of culture," the elite French-educated writers and bureaucrats now charged with running the country, saw Francophonie as a means of deepening Senegal's cultural and political connections with European powers under a model that placed the formerly colonized on an equal footing with the colonizers. For the notion's defenders in Senegal and elsewhere in

Africa, Francophonie was an indelible aspect of their respective countries' histories. It was what had been co-created via sites of exchange such as the Ponty stage. Yet, the theatrical stage also hosted the work of artists and intellectuals who were far less sanguine about the promises of a purportedly shared Francophone identity. Chief among these was Senegal's first theater scholar, Bakary Traoré, whose work reminded the spectators and performers of "indigenous theater" that theatrical forms and practices had existed in Africa long before the arrival of European colonizers. In his 1958 study *Le Théâtre négro-africain et ses fonctions sociales* (*Black African Theater and Its Social Functions*), Traoré ardently defended the theatrical status of what French observers considered precolonial rituals, pointing out that many such performance practices had very little to do with ritual or religious beliefs but rather responded, like all theater and art, to a number of fundamental societal needs.[2] Traoré underscored how the continent's Francophone theater resulted from the particular historical conditions of colonialism and did not reflect the introduction of theater to cultures in which no such practice had existed beforehand.

Today, the theatrical stage in Senegal reflects its history as a site of exchange for both partisans and detractors of the notion of Francophonie. However, it has also hosted forms of performance heritage rooted in alternative temporalities, ontologies, and expressive cultures. One illustrative example of this is the stage's use to recount the Sufi histories of this Muslim-majority country, most notably in the reenactment of the life of Shaykh Amadu Bamba (written as Cheikh Amadou Bamba in the French orthography), founder of the Senegalese Sufi order of the Murids. The dissemination of Sufi narratives via the stage required a reworking of theatrical convention in order to accommodate the performed embodiment of a religious figure whose very image is considered sacred. By introducing an element of performed religious fervor to the national stage heritage, director Tamsir Ndiaye and his troupe crafted a new and profoundly Senegalese theatrical experience which they called *Bamba Mos Xam* (Wolof for "to taste Bamba is to know"). The production had such an impact on popular audiences as to contribute, up until its closure in the 1980s, to the spread of today's most visible Sufi order in Senegal. Drawing primarily from the canon of nineteenth-century Wolof-language religious poetry in Ajami, the term for African-language writing in Arabic script, *Bamba Mos Xam* offered a new Senegalese vision of stage performance that relegated to the periphery debates around the cultural heritage of Francophonie.

In the contemporary Senegalese context, theater is used as a vital tool in processes of community formation, as well as in grassroots initiatives connected to forms of Global South activism. Popular theater organizations offer the primary means of contact for most Senegalese with the performance stage. Yet the creative work of such organizations is rarely the focus of scholarly or critical attention either from Senegalese critics or foreign researchers.

The diversity of post-independence stage sites, while emerging from a shared Senegalese performance heritage, is often lost as the study of performance practices is parsed out among academic disciplines. Thus, disciplinary boundaries separating scholarly approaches and methods can pose a considerable challenge to the study of theater-making and its specificities as a craft. In the field of Francophone studies, scholarly appreciations of theatrical production in Francophone Africa tend to limit themselves to published plays. Yet recent studies of contemporary African playwrights often omit Senegalese creators altogether, since the most active stage artists today have taken a largely collective approach to crafting informal and untranscribed theatrical texts.[3] The field's blind spot to alter-textual practices risks giving the erroneous impression that theater has ceased to play an important role in the national cultural imaginary of Senegal.

This book explores the craft of theater-making in Senegal through a focus on the stage spaces that have allowed performers to engage with the social, political, and cultural spheres of their day. Theater's diverse contemporary landscape here attests to a history of context-specific efforts of stagecraft that address local concerns while also taking part in broader theoretical discussions of theater within a global and experimental framework. Throughout this book, I use the term "stagecraft" in order to focus on the contextual work of stage artists as they contend with, respond to, and reconfigure the implicit rules and expectations of the theatrical stage. Working through a range of historical performance contexts, I explore how Senegalese theater-makers have transformed and deployed the theatrical stage as a variety of decolonizing stage spaces capable of producing real-life, functional criticism of and responses to the realities of colonialism and its aftermath. These decolonizing stage spaces make full use of their interaction with audiences to reimagine and rehearse new forms of social, economic, and intercommunal relations among performers and audience members. I describe the stage space as decolonizing rather than as decolonized because visions of what, precisely, decolonizing entails vary with each newly crafted stage space. However, a decolonizing effort is central to each of the stage histories presented here.

The contextual approach of this book serves at least three interconnected purposes. First, it approaches theater as an inherently sited expressive practice.[4] This study emerges from the field of Francophone studies, which favors techniques of literary analysis. Within that field, discussions of cosmopolitan and transnational texts and performances originating from Francophone Africa often come at the expense of an exploration of local uses of theater in Francophone African contexts. A focus on sites of performance will resituate the function of the playwright as one tool of stagecraft among many others. Second, a sustained focus on theater as a sited expressive practice will underscore the political, social, and economic stakes involved in any form of innovative stagecraft. Such stakes highlight the stage's role in facilitating rehearsals of, and innovative responses to, emerging discursive, relational, and embodied scripts taking shape in the social context of a given performance. At the heart of this project lies the conviction, eloquently expressed by Ngũgĩ wa Thiong'o in response to Peter Brook's book *The Empty Space*, that the performance space is never empty. "Bare, yes, open, yes, but never empty. It is always the site of physical, social and psychic forces in society."[5] Ngũgĩ points out the role of such wide-ranging forms of discourse in creating the performance space, or what he calls "a magnetic field of tensions and conflicts" and considers a crucial piece of any theorizing of theater, particularly in a postcolonial context.[6] In my approach, I conceptualize these magnetic fields as generative sites of exploration for new forms of social critique and activism. Lastly, my focus on sites of performance seeks to build on the scholarship, most notably in anthropological discussions of African expressive cultures, challenging assumptions that, while local customs and conditions may vary, culture and performance, in their essence, remain constant across contexts.[7] Rather than analyzing theater as a self-evident form of expressive practice, this study will focus on how and why certain expressive practices are made into theater—thus the emphasis on "theater-making"—and are used to craft or recraft stage spaces that willfully occasion new configurations of the role and essence of culture and performance.[8]

Theater in Francophone Africa: Approaching the Field

The theater of Francophone Africa, whether in French or in African languages, has received little scholarly attention compared to the continent's French-language literature. This imbalance largely reflects the inevitably sited and contextual nature of theatrical performance, and is compounded by the specific challenges of conducting site-focused research in a country of the Global South. Literary scholars focusing on Francophone African contexts frequently find themselves limited to addressing the role of playwrights in the craft of theater-making. The difficulties and cost of long-distance travel and extended research stays hinder Western scholars' ability to explore the local lives and uses of the texts they study. Meanwhile, persistent inequalities in resources and access to scholarly publishing have limited scholarly output on theatrical production by researchers based in universities in Francophone Africa.[9] As a result, a disproportionate share of the scholarly writing on this theater originates from European or North American institutions. These studies tend to focus on published plays that have garnered international attention and which receive stage productions among the limited number of European performance platforms dedicated to French-language work from Africa—leaving unanswered the question of whether such works also represent theatrical culture *in* Africa.

North American and European studies of Francophone African theater have productively explored the emergence of a cosmopolitan and experimental trend among Francophone African playwrights. Focusing on the work of authors like Koffi Kwahulé, Kossi Efoui, and Caya Makhélé, among others, Sylvie Chalaye has identified a dramaturgical movement beginning in the 1990s characterized by a certain experimental aesthetic. Through a poetic hybridization of African and Western mythologies and rituals (most notably by Kossi Efoui in plays such as *Le Carrefour* or *Io*), or through an intrinsically musical approach to the French language as characterized most notably by the work of Koffi Kwahulé (as in *Jaz* or *Misterioso—119*), these playwrights have developed what Chalaye calls "an avant-garde chimerical theater of collage where forms and ideas are borrowed and transplanted to reflect postcolonial hybridization; what one may call a form of 'Frankenstein' theater."[10] Proposing the terms "Frankenstein syndrome" and "alien generation," Chalaye describes the aesthetic approach of a group of playwrights who assume fully the "profoundly monstrous nature" of a dramaturgy which unapologetically splices cultural references and traditions together without any regard for where such traditions should "naturally" occur.[11] The theater Chalaye describes proves every bit as site-specific as any performance form, with key historical and geographical touchstones such as Radio France Internationale's African radio play competition, which once shed light on an innovative generation of post-independence playwrights that included Sony Labou Tansi and Sénouvo Zinsou.[12] A similarly generative site can be found in the annual theater festival "Les Francophonies en Limousin," which focuses on the work of non-European French-language playwrights and has provided an important breakout venue for a number of innovative theatermakers from Africa.

Notwithstanding the value of such a hybrid theater and its impact on the global theatrical landscape, from a critical standpoint it proves a problematic entry point to theatrical production in Francophone Africa. Its main sites of cultural production such as the RFI radio play contest and Les Francophonies en Limousin maintain, despite their best efforts, France and the West as the authoritative center of discussions around theatrical performance. In terms of reception, Judith Miller, in her work on Francophone African theater, has observed: "We can ask rightly just how 'African' . . . this theater [is] when performed before a non-African audience—a question which itself occludes the obvious existence of several different kinds of African publics."[13] Miller's observation puts the reader on guard against conceiving of African, or Senegalese, theater audiences as monolithic. She also indicates the processes of production and cross-cultural translation that are necessary to bring such stage works to European venues.

Certainly, the challenges of a decontextualized theater present themselves with any play or production that attains transnational status. Yet, within scholarly discussions of Francophone African theater, one must consider the degree to which Western venues contribute to framings of what Valentin Mudimbe has identified as a discursive and Western "invention of

Africa," or an image of the continent that forever determines and distorts understandings of its peoples and cultures.[14] Judith Miller raises a similar concern when she addresses Koffi Kwahulé's worry that the work of African playwrights, despite their experimental and dynamic contributions to what Miller describes as an emerging Francophone African stage textuality, may serve simply to reinforce received ideas and stereotypes.[15] In order to address what John Conteh-Morgan has called the need to develop a "fuller picture of theatrical activity in Francophone Africa," literary scholars must seek out the role of place and context in the emergence and success of African stage practices.[16]

Beyond concerns of access and cost, literary studies' disciplinary lacunae are also reminders of the field's former tendency to declare, from a position of institutional authority, what constitutes "real" dramaturgical writing, "good" stage performance, or even "authentic" African theater. The patriarchal tone that pervades much of the foundational European writing on theater in Francophone African contexts reflects the status of the European cultural expert sent to Africa to consult with local artists on the development of their craft. The Martinican poet and playwright Aimé Césaire thoroughly lampoons the cultural consultant figure in his play *La Tragédie du Roi Christophe* through the character of a clownish master of ceremonies, whom Césaire describes in a footnote as a white man sent by the "Technical Educational Scientific Cooperation Organization (TESCO) as a technical consultant to under-developed regions."[17] The character busies himself with the rigorous instruction of frivolous courtly manners. Vastey, the secretary to Christopher, the Haitian King and title character of Césaire's tragedy, remarks bitterly: "Have you seen who Europe sends us when we ask for help from international aid organizations? Not an engineer, a soldier or a professor, but a master of ceremonies! That's civilization, my friend. All a matter of form."[18] Here, Césaire broadly mocks European arrogance, but also refers to a specific French initiative by which France once professed to assist the continent in its cultural development. With African independence looming, the French government found itself eager to maintain its influence through soft power and diplomacy. The French Ministry of Cooperation, created in 1959, deployed a number of French *coopérants*, or foreign consultants; these were usually young men, sent on mission to assist their African counterparts in a variety of domains.[19] Some of these *coopérants* arrived to work in the cultural field. Eager and willing, though sometimes with limited training in their assigned fields, these consultants helped to train a new generation of cultural professionals and made a lasting impression on their Senegalese counterparts in a number of artistic fields, including theater.[20]

One result of the *coopérant* model was the conferral of a special status, that of exceptionally qualified experts, on French teachers and performers. This status extended to scholars sent to Senegal to observe and write about the state of African theatrical performance. Coming from fields still attached to Eurocentric literary canons and hierarchies, these scholars applied the same comparative and hierarchical lens to the performances they observed.[21] Their site-based studies of African theater conclude with sets of recommendations pointing toward the possible "evolution" of African theater toward the standards of European stage traditions. Such a result to what was nonetheless a locally situated approach indicates that the sited perspective, while offering many advantages, does not eliminate the risk of falling into a certain paternalism that runs through much early scholarship on African cultural forms. Such paternalism is rare in writing on Francophone African theater today, since scholars no longer see their role as that of a consultant to the theater professionals whose work they study. However, a satisfactory method of engagement with theater-making in African contexts has yet to step in to replace the scholar-consultant model. A silence persists when scholars are faced with theatrical performances in African contexts that do not correspond with their own localized notions of what stage performance is supposed to look like and accomplish.

This book highlights the need to meet stage performances in African contexts on their own ground through a multidisciplinary approach that includes field methods to complement more familiar textual ones. My integration of experiences in the field, or what James Clifford described as "embodied activities pursued in historically and politically defined places," situates this project within an emerging trend whereby literary scholars adopt fieldwork methodologies in order to approach objects of study pertinent to their disciplines, though slightly beyond the scope of their conventional methodological toolkit.[22] Acknowledging the considerable challenges this move presents for literary scholars without specific training in field methods, Shalini Puri highlights how the use of fieldwork can, at the very least, help indicate which media are available to literary approaches and which lie outside of their scope. Moreover, without fieldwork, scholarship simply cannot address manifestations of theater, dance, or performance that deeply inform the novels and published texts that are more apt to arrive at the shores of foreign researchers. Drawing on the text-as-migrant metaphor, Puri states that, in the absence of fieldwork, "drama and performance are the stay-at-home country cousins of the novel or cinema; they are unable to cross borders with the same ease."[23] Not only does fieldwork take the trouble to meet theater and performance on its own ground, but sustained fieldwork also invites a broader interrogation of the cultural categories and criteria foreign researchers inevitably bring to their research encounters.[24] What is gained when expressive forms are explored through their own local frameworks justifies, in my estimation, the methodological discomfort caused by attempts to render the processes of creating scholarly knowledge more collaborative and dialogical.

The field of performance studies has fostered a rich theorization of at least two aspects of critical engagement with performance and fieldwork that tend to fall outside the scope of a literary approach. First, scholars of performance concern themselves deeply with embodiment and its role not only in performance and social relations, but also in approaches to critical fieldwork. In his writing on methodological approaches in performance studies, Dwight Conquergood foregrounds the many advantages of performance as a theoretical paradigm, since it "privileges particular, participatory, dynamic, intimate, precarious, embodied experience grounded in historical process, contingency and ideology."[25] The lens of performance and its integration of embodiment and the particular do not supplant the study of texts but rather complement it. "The Performance Paradigm," as Conquergood argues, "will be most useful if it decenters, without discarding, texts."[26] In the framework of Francophone African theater-making, therefore, Conquergood's methodological approach, along with that of performance studies in general, presents less an alternative to textual analysis than an adjustment of critical framing. The undergirding critical objective, between the textual and performative paradigms, remains "the excavation of the political underpinnings of all modes of representation, even the scientific."[27]

The second way performance studies can help fill in the lacunae of text-centered approaches is through the field's consideration of the researcher's place within the theoretical framework being applied. In this, theorists of fieldwork have pointed out that academic writing, the end result of field research, has the secondary effect of denying coevalness to its object of study. In other words, fieldwork may grant the advantage of placing the researcher and the researched in a coeval and perhaps dialogical and collaborative relationship. However, the writing-up of research is not only done in solitude, but is also framed in an anthropological discourse that places the other in an eternal, timeless realm.[28] For Margaret Drewal, field methodologies in the domain of performance must account for the fact that, in the process of creating knowledge, "performers and scholars alike are engaged in representation."[29] The scholar leaves an indelible mark on the knowledge being produced irrespective of any attempt at objective scholarly distance. "Neutrality," Drewal insists, "is an impossibility."[30]

Although Drewal's remarks refer specifically to research resulting from field methodologies, they also lay out a challenge to any scholarship on an expressive cultural form in which performance plays a central role. If scholarly approaches determine the limits of knowledge produced by research, a purely textual approach to theatrical performance disembodies the scholar's analytical outlook on a profoundly embodied art form, therefore reproducing the very text/body dichotomy that the field of performance studies has sought to deconstruct. A focus on literary writings, anthologies of published plays, and their performance within the context of European-sponsored venues or festivals highlights the work of a select group of authors and creators operating within a specific transnational framework. Such an approach often fails to examine its own role in the creation of its object of study, and tends, furthermore, to overlook the multiple variations and uses of the stage in local African contexts. This point is highlighted by Catherine Cole in her groundbreaking work on the history of the concert party form in Ghana, wherein she points out that, despite the ample theorizing employed in studies of postcolonial theater: "What has not yet been fully accounted for in scholarship on West African popular theatre is historical change, both within particular traveling theatre traditions and in the theatre's relationship to transformations in society at large and to the audiences it serves."[31]

More recently, Maëline Le Lay has echoed the call for a focus on African performance contexts in her field-based study of theatrical production in the Katanga region of Congo. She underscores the limitations of literary approaches that fail to integrate field methods. For Le Lay, this scholarship "has the effect of focusing the public's attention on writing by diasporic Africans." The result is that "today's average readers will believe they know about 'African literature,' even though they know nearly nothing about the real literary activity taking place on the African continent."[32] Such an observation does not necessarily imply or impose a stark division between a diasporic realm of literary or theatrical production and a local one. The two indeed intersect and influence each other at strategic convergence points. A Francophone author is rendered no less local or, to employ an even more treacherous term, less "authentic" for successfully exporting work abroad. Nor do local uses of the stage cut themselves off from global and cosmopolitan views on performance. The anthropologist Hélène Neveu Kringelbach points out in her study of Senegalese dance and self-fashioning the adeptness with which Senegalese performers engage their audiences in a double perspective, with one eye fixed on local concerns, and the other "turned to the wider world . . . concerned with individual success and participation in global cultural production on equal terms with artists from other parts of the world."[33]

A study of decolonizing performance stages in a postcolonial context need not erroneously pit the local against the global or seek truly African performance traditions in contrast with Europeanized cultural products for export. Scholarship in both literary and field-based disciplines has illustrated the complex and hybrid processes that belie such rigid and simplistic categories. From a methodological standpoint, it is also possible to integrate fieldwork into a study of theatrical performance without entirely surrendering the analytical lens offered by literary studies as a discipline. As a response to tendencies in performance studies to associate theater with ritual in a manner that framed the two practices as manifesting the same performative essence, Alain Ricard described the place of theater as situated primarily within a system of poiesis. Ricard outlines his argument in contrast to the more anthropological approach to performance pioneered by Richard Schechner, which extends the domain of theater to forms of ritual, ceremony, and folklore.[34] Ricard's approach, which nonetheless defends the importance of observing the lives and work of performers through fieldwork, does not frame itself as fundamentally anthropological, but rather conceptualizes the stage as a space of composition, writing, and poetic construction where, through a series of conventions, art reflects on itself and on the world around it, resulting in a sophisticated and compositional form of dramaturgical expression.[35]

Within this broader theoretical perspective, my own approach represents an attempt to bridge the apparent divide between literary studies and fieldwork-based disciplines. In committing to a sited approach—that is, one that focuses specifically on theatrical practices as they emerge, innovate, and thrive in a Senegalese context—I look to explore the processes of production, performance, and reception which define a given performance space and frame that space's ability to host a certain kind of embodied, performed behavior. I employ the term "stagecraft" to refer to the nuts-and-bolts work that goes into the craft of theater-making from conception to reception. I also stretch the term to highlight, on a more theoretical level, the intangible and dynamic processes forever attached to these "magnetic fields of tensions and conflicts," to return to Ngũgĩ's definition, or to highlight how historical memory, politics, and local social structures come to inform their creation and parameters. These processes involve the active participation of performers and audience; they engage deeply with the social and political and make do with multiple restrictions of space, customs, and resources while occasionally positing innovative new ways of being together as an audience-community.

On Reading Decolonizing Stages

In *Decolonizing the Stage: Theatrical Syncretism and Post-Colonial Drama*, Christopher Balme explores the strategies of what he calls "syncretic theater," an approach which uses indigenous performance elements within the framework of Western theatrical and dramaturgical conventions in order to respond to the legacies of imperialism, colonization, and decolonization.[36] Acknowledging the wide range of scholarship on performance iconographies of "the East" in the work of European stage directors (Peter Brook and Ariane Mnouchkine are among the most frequently cited in this regard), Balme points out how syncretic models have also served playwrights, directors, and theorists from throughout the formerly colonized world. In light of this observation, Balme explores, in one of his chapters, the presence of Yoruba ritual in the dramaturgy of Nigerian playwright Wole Soyinka, which, he argues, exemplifies the potential of such a syncretic approach by suspending at strategic moments conventional Western and Aristotelian rules of drama. Through his reading of Soyinka's writing for the stage, Balme underscores how "syncretic theatre often attempts to reinvest theatre with a communal religious spirit, the long-cherished desire of several generations of Western theatre-reformers, which they very seldom achieved in practice."[37] This study adopts a similar outlook on stage artists' ability to appropriate and deconstruct performance forms through syncretic means and also seeks to place these achievements in dialogue with the ambitions of Western theater-makers. However, rather than framing such stage innovations within a global dialogue held largely between the former colonized and colonizers, I focus on a single national context in order to address theater practitioners' engagement with specific and locally situated debates for which the West, or a broader transnational audience, is not always the primary interlocutor. I also deemphasize the nonetheless undeniably syncretic nature of the forms studied by granting that once stage spaces and practices emerge in Senegalese performance contexts, they become sites of African or Senegalese stagecraft, and no less so for originating from an encounter with French colonial discourses.

Throughout this book, I adopt an approach that conceptualizes the work of stagecraft at the convergence of three deeply imbricated elements of performance: text, embodiment, and place, each of which takes on a literal meaning along with a more theoretically construed level of interpretation. "Text" can, of course, include written texts in the form of plays but need not refer to plays, literature, or any form of writing at all. Such a view of text as it relates to performance resonates with attempts, most notably in France, to establish what Anne Ubersfeld called in her 1977 book *Lire le théâtre* (*Reading Theater*) a theater semiotics.[38] This movement took root in a reconsideration of the concept of dialogism developed by the literary scholar Mikhail Bakhtin.[39] In her use of dialogism as a critical approach to theater and performance, Ubersfeld departs somewhat from Bakhtin's own understanding of the concept, since the Russian critic argued that the dialogical effect emerged by way of a narrative voice—present in the novel though unavailable to embodied stage performance—that is able to absorb and reflect the framing social reality, or the multi-vocality of discourse, in which any utterance arises.[40] While theater indeed seems to lack such a framing narrative voice, Ubersfeld counters Bakhtin's exclusion of the stage by exploring how the interplay of text and performance generates a semiotic relationship and multiplicity of voices similar to those Bakhtin identified in the novel. If theater lacks the discursive foundation offered by the narrative voice, the very nature of the stage space is to absorb the social heteroglossia that is central to Bakhtin's model.

Among the processes of stagecraft which constitute the theatrical stage, the textual element also includes what in literature one might call the "paratext." These are utterances and ephemera leading up to or framing an event, as well as the artists' or audience members' personal narration prior, during, or after the event. In their essay bringing theater studies into dialogue with the genetic criticism of literary texts, Almuth Grésillon and Jean-Marie Thomasseau call for the analysis of "peritexts" (*péritextes*), or the ensemble of documentation produced by a performance, including programs, reviews, interviews, and so on.[41] The genetic approach indeed relies on a semiotic reading of performance that goes beyond the written text, underscoring how, in performance, "everything hinges on the in-between of the text and the stage, on the complex and delicate movement between the space of the page and that of the stage, on a continuous and reversible back-and-forth between that which can be read, heard and seen."[42] Although this study integrates a discussion of such peritexts, my view of text and its place in performance aligns more closely with Karin Barber's notion of "entextualization," which displaces writing as the sole means of conferring textuality on discourse. Barber's definition of text includes forms of language, action, and speech acts, casting a wider net in order to conceptualize as text that which "is created when instances of discourse, by being rendered detachable from their immediate context of emission, are made available for repetition or recreation in other contexts."[43] This more "neutral" view of text lends itself more freely to cross-cultural analyses, as Barber argues: "Instead of trying to export a culturally-loaded category ('literature'), we can use an entextualisation perspective to develop a more neutral comparative sociology and history of textuality, oral and written."[44] Barber could very well have included "theater" as another example of such a culturally loaded category, a fact that makes her model of textuality particularly well-suited for a study of stage performance in African contexts.[45]

The second element, embodiment, encompasses many different concerns, recognizing, first and foremost, the degree to which performative analysis benefits from an embodied approach that does not limit an understanding of knowledge and heritage transmission to questions of rhetoric, trope, and conceit. Highly instructive in this regard is Diana Taylor's concept of the "scenario," which she describes as "a paradigmatic setup that relies on supposedly live participants, structured around a schematic plot, with an intended (though adaptable) end."[46] Embodiment includes the semiotic value of the body on stage as a signifier at the same level as the text, the set, costumes, and so on.[47] However, embodiment in performance may also produce, as well as reflect, social relations, on stage as in social life. In her study of African performance and audiences, Barber draws out the role of performances in constituting their own audiences through the performative act of convening them: "Performances do not just play to ready-made congregations of spectators which are out there awaiting address; they convene those congregations and by their mode of address assign them a certain position from which to receive the address. Thus performances, in the act of addressing audiences, constitute those audiences as a particular form of collectivity."[48] Part of performance's strength thus lies in its use of embodiment as a means of rehearsing new and innovative social models, or reinforcing existing ones. Such embodied interventions employ inherited scenarios to interact with the limits and discourses governing their stage space, potentially remolding the space into something new.

Socially situated forms of discourse through performance left a profound mark on the early years of theatrical creation in Senegal, and continue to influence the ways in which contemporary performance spaces are perceived and crafted. As the early performers of this theater sought out rhetorical and performative space on the stage of the William Ponty School to respond to the demands of colonial pedagogy, they also employed their embodied enactment as a meaningful dodge of racial discourse, stepping out of their own role and into that of another. The stakes of embodiment also rise with the decision to don a role or to embody a character in a manner that runs counter to the socially or culturally acceptable, a central issue in chapter 4's discussion of Sufi stage performances. Contemporary performers on the Senegalese stage contend with the functions of a performance space left behind by the elite of a previous generation and employ embodied performances to trouble old narratives in ways that text cannot. Lastly, my own role as a foreign researcher bringing attention to these performance practices is not neutral within the processes of fieldwork and knowledge formation, a fact I attempt to foreground particularly in areas where fieldwork has played a prominent role in my research methods.

Place, the third element of this study's analytical approach, refers on the most obvious level to the place where a performance occurs. Whether a staged piece will be presented in the streets of a popular neighborhood in plain view of public onlookers or on the stage of the Daniel Sorano National Theater for ticket-holding spectators clearly has an effect on the piece's creation and reception. Moreover, place is of primary concern to directors and performers who craft their work with the implications, limitations, and potentialities of place at the forefront of their minds. Discussions of place can also take into account stage artists' ability to appropriate or evoke sites of memory connected to a collective remembering of the past or an imagining of the future, and often both simultaneously. "Place" therefore can refer to both a physical location and its weight within social discourses of cultural memory. Place plays a prominent role in my examination, in chapter 1, of the special status of the William Ponty School in narratives of Senegalese cultural history. It also informs the function of the French *centres culturels* in instantiating new Franco-African identities during the late colonial period.

The three elements of performance described above do not fit neatly within discrete and mutually exclusive categories, and the creative processes I wish to examine operate within a fluid and interweaving dynamic. Yet, as creative notions, text, embodiment, and place are among the principal concerns and creative tools at the disposal of theater artists in Senegal as elsewhere. This study places a sustained focus on the act of putting these three elements into play with one another. In focusing on such acts of stagecraft, I aim to highlight the means by which theater artists in Senegal have recrafted the theatrical stage into a variety of decolonizing creative spaces that serve to articulate expectations of the political realm, constitute new social relationships, and re-narrate forms of historical and cultural heritage. The stage spaces and innovations that result from such processes do so in dialogue with what preceded or coexists with them. They comment simultaneously on the past and present. Theater-makers imbue them with hopes and concerns for the future and craft them to propose, by performance, a certain vision for moving forward.

Exploring Histories of Senegalese Stagecraft

The goal of this book is not to provide a comprehensive history of theatrical performance in Senegal, but rather to focus on sites of stage innovation that fall into the blindspots of strictly literary or field-based approaches. The following chapters are loosely structured in two parts and, for the sake of clarity, follow a historical chronology; however, I do not wish to suggest the existence of rigid boundaries between the stage spaces and artistic movements I explore. The first part addresses sites of performance generally understood as being part of the "official" history of theatrical production in Senegal. In chapter 1, I revisit the use of the theatrical stage space at the French colonial school called the École Normale William Ponty. I read against previous critical assessments of this "teachers' theater," which has been frequently dismissed as the product of colonial pedagogy and discourse, in order to focus on the performances' embodied function within a colonial social space. Chapter 2 explores a subsequent adaptation of the colonial, "Franco-African" stage space for the *centres culturels* of the 1950s. The cultural centers' performance stage and theatrical competition, called "La Coupe Théâtrale," led to a post-war and post-Ponty theatrical renewal allowing creators to reimagine their roles as potential citizens of the French Empire under the terms of the newly established "French Union." Chapter 3 continues to explore the stage as a space of dialogue and engagement between the country's political elite and an audience at once local and global by addressing the stakes of the Premier Festival Mondial des Arts Nègres (or First World Festival of Negro Arts) in Dakar in 1966. I argue that the festival served as a key site for imagining a range of Pan-African approaches to culture and stagecraft, which the event framed as an integral part of the statecraft expected of the *hommes de culture*, or men of culture, who were tasked with leading the continent's newly independent democracies.

The second half of the book adopts a more field-oriented approach, making greater use of oral histories and fieldwork to address underexplored or unexplored aspects of Senegal's theatrical heritage. Chapter 4 delves into the hitherto unwritten history of a traveling Murid performance called *Bamba Mos Xam* which, from its opening in 1968 until its closure in the 1980s, chronicled the life and miracles of the Sufi order's founding saint, Shaykh Amadu Bamba. I argue that *Bamba Mos Xam* laid the groundwork for de-secularizing what had been an inherently secular stage space in order to speak to the Sufi religious sensibilities and morality of a broader Senegalese public.[49] Chapter 5, in its exploration of the widespread success of telefilms and televised series beginning in the 1980s, continues an examination of Senegalese stage artists' alternative means of interacting with large, popular audiences that were not likely to meet them in the confines of the country's few professional performance venues. By teasing out the central themes and narrative techniques employed by the most in-demand television troupe of the time, Daaray Kocc, I underscore the medium's ability to address, in the intimacy of domestic spaces, topics deemed inappropriate for public airing. Television proved particularly adept at giving voice to the disenchantment and grievances of an ever-emerging, though hardly thriving, Senegalese middle class in the era of post-independence neoliberal reform. My final chapter explores the emergence and use of the most widespread approach to stage performance in Senegal today, that of popular theater. I focus on the work of one prominent theater company of the Dakar region, Kàddu Yaraax, as it embraces, sometimes defies, and most often contends with its status as a leading "popular" troupe. I discuss popular theatrical approaches as a form of stagecraft that is adept at navigating the demands and interests of a limited range of funding sources while creating new spaces of contemporary social and political criticism addressed to the collectively imagined Senegalese masses.

The different stage sites addressed throughout this book call for varying and flexible research methodologies. They align themselves with a diverse range of performance traditions and historical temporalities, activating narratives rooted in the country's multivalent heritage as a crucial player within African histories, the Muslim world, a transnational Francophonie, the Global South, and the cultural avant-garde. Each of these facets informs, to varying degrees and in a broad range of tonalities, the stage spaces addressed herein. The stage work I explore consists not only of the production of theatrical content, but also the crafting of stage spaces that recall, reinvent, and connect the above-listed facets through dynamic approaches to representation, activism, and embodiment. Therefore, to study stagecraft and theater-making is to focus not only on what theater says, but also on how theater artists turn the stage space into a platform for productive and participatory social dialogue.

Chapter 1

✦

Colonial Pedagogy and Creative Enactment

The Theater of the École Normale William Ponty

For Maurice Sonar Senghor, longtime director of the Daniel Sorano National Theater and one of Senegal's leading theatrical figures in the twentieth century, the École Normale William Ponty (William Ponty School) represented the birthplace of an African theater to come. In his memoir *Souvenirs de théâtres d'Afrique et d'Outre-Afrique* (*Memories of Theaters from Africa and Beyond*), he casts the interwar theatrical productions of that French colonial school as no less than an originary moment for theatrical creation in Africa, asserting that "it is indeed out of this tradition that the contemporary African theater was born."[1] His statement willfully confuses commonly accepted notions of African and European theater. He employs the term "tradition," typically associated with images of a timeless African culture, to describe European stage spaces and dramaturgical approaches that were passed on to African students. And although in artistic circles the word "contemporary" more commonly connotes avant-garde performance styles associated with the West, Sonar Senghor describes as contemporary the theatrical movement that spread as a result of African students appropriating, innovating, and repurposing European traditions to their own context and artistic proclivities. His portrayal of "Ponty" (as the school came to be known) as the birthplace of African theater serves primarily to acknowledge the school's role in facilitating the emergence of an enduring and innovative stage space.

Originally designed to host colonial representations of an enrooted African subaltern class, the Ponty stage was quickly repurposed by a group of academically gifted students as a tool to define and defend their special status within colonial society. These students later went on to serve as the first leaders and public intellectuals of their respective West African nations.[2] Among the rising figures was the Ivorian Bernard Dadié, one of the most prominent authors of his country's history and, through the Ponty performances, the first African face, as well as the first published playwright, of sub-Saharan Francophone African theater. Before attending Ponty on its Gorée Island campus, Dadié had attended the French colonial school (L'École Primaire

Supérieure) at Bingerville, Côte d'Ivoire, where he studied under school director Charles Béart, the French pedagogue most publicly associated with the rise of the school-performance tradition in French West Africa. When Béart received a transfer in 1935 to the William Ponty School, of which he quickly became the director, he oversaw the same kind of theatrical exercises he had initiated at Bingerville and allowed Dadié, who went on to attend Ponty during Béart's tenure, to shine as the school's star dramatist. Press publications and ephemera related to the school's original theatrical creations, which combined dance, music, enactments of ritual, and performances of scripted drama, credited each piece to the collective authorship of the students from a given colony. However, they listed the Ivorian entries as having been written by Bernard Dadié, a distinction that placed Dadié squarely in the spotlight, particularly in such high-profile occasions as when the *pontins*, as the students were called, toured France and performed at the Théâtre des Champs-Élysées in Paris as part of the 1937 international exhibition there, called the Exposition Internationale des Arts et Techniques dans la Vie Moderne.

More than his country's first playwright, Dadié also served as the first French West African theater critic, having been invited to publish a text titled "Mon pays, son théâtre" ("My Country, Its Theater") in the colonial teachers' trade journal *L'Éducation Africaine*. The young student reflected upon his French superiors' and instructors' probing queries regarding the authenticity of the Ponty theatrical performances or, as he asks in his own words: "Is this theater truly indigenous and of our own making?"[3] Dadié responds by pointing out that theater, strictly in the European sense of the practice, implying regular rehearsals, designated performance spaces, paying spectators, and paid actors, did not exist in the African context. Its closest equivalent is the storytelling he describes as inseparable from all African culture. Among the challenges of translating the universe of the storyteller for a European audience, Dadié cites the need to cut down texts and repetition for the sake of Western tastes: "When something pleases us, its repetition pleases us even more."[4] Dadié also mentions the need to explain and contextualize his myths for Western spectators, a need that does not arise in African storytelling since the stories appeal to a collective memory. The young Ivorian ends his piece with a subtle reflection on such collective memory, explaining that, according to his culture's mythology, the first man sent to the world by God was named Ezohiré, and that each time a son of Ezohiré dies it rains, just as it did the day God sent the first man to Earth. "As for myself, a second-generation Catholic, I know that the legend of Ezohiré is just a legend. Yet if I saw a man of my family die on a sunlit day, I would feel as though he had committed a faux pas, or an error of taste."[5] This, Dadié states, is crucial to keep in mind if one wishes to understand what he calls "our theater."

Dadié's understanding of the Ponty performances and their significance as examples of an emerging *théâtre indigène*, or indigenous theater, clearly indicates the world of traditional African storytelling as a major source of inspiration for the new practice of theatrical representation in French West Africa. However, it also marks a fundamental difference between its stage space and the realm of ritual, given the cultural, spiritual, and historical distance that often separated the Ponty students from the "traditional" worlds they found themselves called upon to represent. Although Dadié frames the Ponty plays and their aesthetic landmarks in terms of a preexisting storytelling tradition, he also excludes the kind of invested belief required for the plays to take on a fully ritualistic value for the students. His stated Catholicism indicates his own sense of distance from the world of myth and legend associated with the storyteller, but does not prevent him from taking inspiration from his community's collective memory. In acting out the stories of African legend and lore, the *pontins* do not perform *as* the characters on stage (as one might perform a ritual), but rather *as if* they were them. The resulting embodied role-play, as the students shifted their comportment from that of "modern," French-educated subjects of colonial society to that of a collectively imagined traditional past and back again, constituted the specificity of the Ponty stage and its singular value to the students who performed upon it.

My analysis of the stage of the William Ponty School and its lasting relevance to Senegalese stage culture builds on previous scholarship by considering that performance space as an innovative site of embodied role-play.[6] The stage allowed students to step out of the roles assigned to them by colonial society, if only temporarily, and offer creative renderings of local legend and ritual, along with discursive reenactments of historical encounters between African culture and European colonialism. As Bakary Traoré points out, the Ponty stage was far from the first such African performance space to fulfill a mediating social function by facilitating forms of productive role-play not necessarily tied to ritualistic practices.[7] Histories of African performance in the region indicate that the Ponty theater was not even the first instance of "indigenous theater" per se, given the preceding use of the stage by French missionaries, in addition to earlier, short-lived attempts at school productions.[8] The distinction of the Ponty stage lay in its inclusion of the colonial encounter in its diegetic world in order to renegotiate the terms of a shared future within an expanded range of cultural expression. To this effect, the Ponty performances made use of several different modes of performance, African and French, and seamlessly shifted in and out of each at key moments.

The question of whether the Ponty theater constituted a tool of colonial domination by cultural means runs through the scholarship on this syncretic stage tradition. The complex realities of colonial life complicate any simplistic pronouncement on the repressive or emancipatory nature of such performances.[9] Ben Jukpor responds to early analyses by pointing out the gap between the performances' meaning for educators and their use by students.[10] Not only did the Ponty plays serve as a useful tool in the creation of new identities within the emerging colonial order of the day, as Jean-Hervé Jézéquel argues, but in terms of their "meaning" they also facilitated what Harry Gamble calls "complex semiotic arenas where a profusion of signs circulated and where divergent meanings could be constructed."[11] Indeed, colonial audiences, which were attached to the notion of theater as a Western art to which African populations were slowly evolving, proved blind to the nuances of the Ponty performances, seeing in them the emergence of a new African mind resulting from concerted efforts of colonial conquest and policy. The *pontins*, however, immediately began using the stage to envision their future within the beginnings of a new cosmopolitan and Pan-African reality.

Stages of Pedagogy and Conquest at the William Ponty School

The Ponty stage and its performances emerged within, though were not fully determined by, the historical conditions of attempts, since the mid-nineteenth century, to put pedagogical initiatives to work in facilitating the conquest, pacification, and profitability of France's West African colonies.[12] By the interwar period, the École Normale William Ponty represented the summit of a colonial hierarchy of educational offerings for the region's indigenous male population. The gradual articulation of its mission can be traced, in part, back to that of its oldest institutional predecessor, founded in 1855 in Saint-Louis and known as L'École des Fils de Chefs (School for the Sons of Chiefs), or L'École des Ôtages (School of Hostages).[13] Educating the sons of defeated chiefs along with young men often sent willingly, the institution at first played a role in negotiating and enforcing local treaties during the French military conquest by ensuring good faith and a commitment to cooperation with the encroaching French presence. As French military domination of the region became a reality, the school enacted shifts in its purpose and student population. In 1903, changes in colonial policy's approach to young African elites led to the creation of the École Normale de l'Afrique Occidentale Française (Normal School of French West Africa) in Saint-Louis. This school's mission was to produce young African teachers and interpreters able to promote, by example, the perceived benefits of French culture and reason, characterized in this context by an amenability toward compromise and collaboration with colonial authorities. The director of the École Normale at the time described his graduates' role in the post-military French conquest of the region through the following declaration: "Called to live among exceedingly backward populations, it will be the teacher's duty to mix with them so as to infiltrate new habits and ideas likely to improve their material situation, to increase well-being and to elevate the moral level of their inhabitants."[14] While the military conquest of the region was mostly complete, colonial authorities saw local educational institutions as key to the next phase of colonial control: domination through softer, cultural means.

In 1913 the school was moved closer to the colony's new capital of Dakar, to the island of Gorée, just four kilometers offshore from the main port. One of the French Empire's earliest holdings in the region, Gorée had changed hands several times between the Portuguese, British, and Dutch, and played an important role in the early stages of the transatlantic slave trade.[15] At the start of the twentieth century it, along with Saint-Louis, Rufisque, and Dakar, had the special administrative status of a *commune*, which granted its male indigenous population citizenship in Third Republic France, as well as voting rights allowing the communes to send representatives to the French Assembly. This special status, along with centuries of trade and European presence, gave rise to a cosmopolitan *métis*, or mixed-race, cultural hybridization through which Gorée natives often sought to differentiate themselves from their fellow Senegalese of the countryside, who were considered "subjects" under French law.[16] It was specifically during its tenure on Gorée Island that the Ponty School became known as a *pépinière*, as it has often been called, or "nursery," for an emerging generation of African elites.[17] In 1915, two years after its transfer to the famed island, the school was rebaptized L'École Normale William Ponty, in honor of the former governor-general of French West Africa, who had served from 1908 to 1915. Within the local and regional imaginary, the school's image was closely connected to the spirit and culture of its site and became known unofficially as *l'école de Gorée.*

Teaching the Pontins *to Be "Natives"*

Admission to Ponty was only granted to the highest results-earners of an annual region-wide exam, or *concours*. The school's curriculum consisted of three years of full-time study, with specialized tracks preparing students for careers as teachers, administrators, or doctors through additional training at the Dakar School of Medicine. By many of the students' own accounts, the ambience of the Ponty campus was that of a harmonious cross-section of the region's brightest young minds.[18] Despite the occasional strike led by disaffected African employees, as well as frequent student forays to the nearby capital, the students generally maintained respectful and often warm relations with their French teachers, who bestowed upon them no small measure of pride in their elevated status within the emerging Franco-African society.[19] Later testimonies of the *pontins* suggest that the students were often reluctant to leave the Ponty campus after their three-year stay for a post in a remote village among a population to which they often felt no particular affiliation or connection.[20]

The Ponty School proved a useful symbol for the perceived success of new approaches to colonial education and administration. From the perspective of French administrators and visiting observers, Ponty offered a poignant illustration of the possibilities of Franco-African collaboration.[21] Furthermore, the school placed itself at the cutting edge of new initiatives in *enseignement indigène*, or indigenous instruction, offering workshops in artisanal crafts and agriculture alongside coursework in French literature and history. The future and self-image of the school's students were of central importance to a colonial administration seeking to steer an African elite of its own making away from global, cosmopolitan ambitions and toward a more local and traditionalist understanding of their place in colonial society.[22] As the historian Boubacar Ly notes, the Ponty schoolmasters sought in all disciplines to bring students in direct contact with African life, an objective clearly expressed in the published commentary of a colonial educator reporting on a Ponty performance gala held before a mixed audience of students, colonials, and administrators. The unnamed educator reveals the underlying pedagogical impulse of the event as he imagines the delighted audience's collective reaction: "All were able to take note of how these educated and well-mannered young people were in no way uprooted [*déracinés*], and how closely they associated school with indigenous life."[23] Reflecting on the desired outcome of such cultural events, he goes on to explain: "Above all, we want them to remain African, and to be educated and taught bearing always in mind the life they will lead back in their countries."[24] Ironically, therefore, among the school's chief objectives was not only to promote the French part of the Franco-African equation, but also to denote Africanness for the sake of its students, and to ensure that the *pontins* remained steadfastly within it.

In effect, colonial education at Ponty was envisioned not as a step toward French culture, but as a further enrooting, or *enracinement* into African life.[25] This was part of what Jean-Hervé Jézéquel has highlighted as the working misunderstanding of the colonial promise with regard to education.[26] The students of Ponty often came to Gorée with the ambition of helping to promote France's "civilizing mission," or the notion that, in its colonial endeavors, France was accomplishing a moral duty by bringing civilization, of which France retained the highest form, to the indigenous populations of its overseas territories. The students soon discovered, however, that colonial pedagogy actively sought to prevent any potential alienation or "uprooting" from native customs and beliefs. Amid a deeper sense of doubt regarding the feasibility and wisdom of molding foreign populations in France's own image, colonial educators found the recognition and instantiation of profound differences between Africans and the French to be useful, if not even indispensable. Supposedly objective notions of cultural, historical, and philosophical difference—most notably that of an African mind innately tied to tradition and impervious to abstract thought or even objective reason—provided the authoritative ground from which the French administrator could rule, the ethnographer analyze, and the educator instruct.

Staging Colonial Authenticity

Ponty's theatrical experiment began in 1933 and is closely associated with Charles Béart, a French teacher who had previously worked as the director of the École Primaire Supérieure de Bingerville in Côte d'Ivoire. Having experimented with the use of theater in colonial education at his previous post, Béart became deeply involved with a similar exercise upon his arrival at Ponty. The initiative won him a reputation, which lasted throughout his lifetime, as the educator behind the highly successful Ponty performances and, by extension (and however erroneously), behind the birth of theatrical performance in Francophone Africa. Béart himself shunned the distinction, explaining that the performances originated from an impromptu comedic moment when his students in Bingerville began to satirize the gait of a "*garde-cercle*," or local police officer, an anecdote also recounted by Béart's former student Bernard Dadié in his semi-autobiographical novel *Climbié*.[27] Seeing an opportunity to instill camaraderie among students through theater, Béart had a stage space cleared where they could rehearse freely and on their own time. He then established a regular Saturday-evening event allowing students to perform for their classmates and teachers.

A similar practice was already in place at the École Normale William Ponty when Béart arrived there in 1935. Two years prior, the school had begun hosting performances by its students from Dahomey. The Ivorians soon contributed as well, eventually leading to theatrical performances presented by each colony and meant to reflect something of that particular colony's culture or history. Just as had happened in Bingerville, Béart's scheduled performances became a perennial event, this time steeped in the cosmopolitan culture of the small island of Gorée. Interest among colonial authorities and foreign residents in Dakar soon led to an annual evening gala at the capital's opulent Chamber of Commerce building. There, the program included words of welcome to the audience, and of encouragement to students, from officials as high up as French West Africa's governor-general. At each performance, the *pontins* regaled audiences with comedic sketches, reenactments of African customs and traditions, and stage adaptations of historical African chiefs' encounters with French colonial forces.

Béart's theatrical initiative no doubt emerged from a desire to foster an esprit de corps among students, but above all it allowed educators to see in the theatrical stage a conduit for what they considered to be the students' authentic African identity. More than a simple distraction, the stage served as a pedagogical and administrative tool whose use aligned with a decades-long initiative to steer the colonial administration away from earlier goals of assimilation, or of turning African colonial subjects into "Black Frenchmen." As an alternative to assimilative models, administrators began adapting a newer, slightly protean objective termed "association."[28] Theories of association formed a mixed group of ideas rather than a fixed school of thought, and arose following a late nineteenth-century assault on assimilation as a functional concept for the French colonies. Once a central tenet of the civilizing mission, assimilation's usefulness was put in doubt as early as 1899, with Léopold de Saussure's *Psychologie de la colonisation française dans ses rapports avec les sociétés indigènes*, which depicted France's impulse to assimilate foreign populations as part of a misguided, inherited belief in universalism and the equality of races.[29] Jules Harmand's *Domination et colonisation*, published in 1910, argued that, justified though French colonization might be in his view, it was naive to expect sympathy from a population that remained, despite all rhetoric, dominated by an unwanted conquering power. Harmand's argument also arose out of increasing pressure to extract economic and financial benefits from the colonies, a concern highlighted in an influential 1923 book by Albert Sarraut which called for greater economic development, or the *mise en valeur* of French investment in the colonies.[30] Out of these debates sprang a range of new approaches grouped under the category of "association" and committed to the preservation of the institutions and customs of the native, who was seen as a potential associate in the colonial project rather than an equal collaborator, much less as a future citizen.

From the outset, association proved elusive as a concept, and even more so as a directive. During the interwar period of the Ponty plays, French instructors across French West Africa struggled to adapt their pedagogical approach to an administrative imperative to produce culturally rooted, practically minded Africans.[31] In the context of the Ponty School, instructors mainly sought to combat a rising sense of elitism among the student population which, in the administrators' view, was fed by the emergence of a politically active class of educated French West Africans. The figurehead of such a group was the Senegalese assemblyman Blaise Diagne, the first Black African to serve in the French National Assembly, who fought to solidify citizenship rights for residents of the four communes. For the purposes of the colonial administration, the example of Blaise Diagne, or what was often called *diagnisme*, proved doubly problematic. First, indoctrination with French culture and republican ideas through schooling risked leading to a disavowal of local customs and beliefs, rendering tenuous the relations between young African teachers and bureaucrats and the communities they were to serve. Second, with the growing political influence of French-educated Africans, the colonial authorities became increasingly concerned with the potential perils of producing an entire class of politically conscious individuals who would be eager to use the tenets of French republicanism to secure expanded rights for indigenous African populations.

In their efforts to implement a new, adapted form of instruction, French educators turned to the contemporary work of scholars and ethnographers. The most cited of these, such as Henri Labouret and Maurice Delafosse, were part of a new turn in ethnographic thinking defending the inherent value of African civilization, which they saw as every bit as worthy of the name as that of the French, although it was grossly misunderstood or ignored by colonial authorities. For these thinkers, the key to a more efficient and harmonious Franco-African future lay first in a deeper understanding of, and respect for, African customs and beliefs. These "colonial humanists" thus believed that the successful integration of local religion, agricultural practices, artisanship, and performed folklore into French colonial society might lead to a functional Franco-African society in which the natives nonetheless remained "authentically" African.[32]

A colonially imagined sense of authenticity served to instantiate not only the formidable difference perceived between Africans and the French, but also, by depicting Africans in a favorable light, suggested that they might nonetheless catch up with the French in some eternally deferred, politically enfranchised future. This is what historian Gary Wilder describes as the double-bind in which native Africans found themselves caught, but on which hinged the administration of the French imperial nation-state: "Although administrative racism functioned to disenfranchise even educated Africans, it operated within a republican idiom. Colonial humanism was a historically specific racial formation that was self-consciously anti-racist."[33] Colonial humanists' antiracism was thus part and parcel of a broader republican endeavor to restrict full citizenship privileges for Africans, and "ultimately worked to separate and fix natives within a confining cultural tradition largely constructed by French ethno-administrative practices."[34]

Colonial education's attempt to enclose interpretations of the Ponty plays and their social meaning within colonial humanist discourse reflects the event's place within the contradictions of interwar colonial administration. To again quote Wilder: "A new colonial rationality placed subject peoples in a politically effective double-bind that racialized them as minor members of the French nation. But it was also self-undermining and created possibilities for critical political intervention."[35] In the case of the Ponty plays, these possibilities took shape in the elite status granted to the very space of Ponty and its performance stage. One colonial administrator would reflect, in a 1936 speech, how the actual space of the school site had become deeply problematic for colonial officials, symbolizing for students the promise of cultural elitism through French education. In a paternalistic appeal for students to follow the example of the "forward-thinking races," the administrator asks his young interlocutors to lend him, in effect, their unpretentious, African ears:

> To remove any hint of pretense in the word, let us banish right away the term conference . . . Let's say from the start that a colonial administrator is speaking to you as a bush administrator who, by way of chance, happens at this moment to be assigned to Dakar . . . My friends, we are quite simply going to hold a palaver. With a bit of imagination, we will picture ourselves far away from Gorée.[36]

The rhetorical gesture here is symptomatic of a move in colonial pedagogy to associate the space of a specialized school like Ponty with the customs of a rural environment. Similar framing gestures proliferated in the case of the Ponty plays and were, moreover, instrumental in the campus's 1937 transfer away from the problematically cosmopolitan site of Gorée Island to the bucolic and remote fields of Sébikotane, some thirty kilometers removed from the temptations of Dakar.[37]

"Parole aux Acteurs!": The *Pontins* Take the Stage

Most of the extant written versions of the Ponty plays are accessible today thanks to their publication in *L'Éducation Africaine: Bulletin de l'enseignement de l'A.O.F.*[38] In 1937, the journal published a special issue dedicated to the Ponty performances, titled *Le Théâtre indigène et la culture franco-africaine* (*Indigenous Theater and Franco-African Culture*). The issue framed the plays through the rhetoric of the associative and colonial humanist models examined above. In a prefatory text, Charles Béart contextualized the plays and their creation as "an excellent French lesson, but, and even more so, . . . one of the rare occasions when French thought has been able to mix intimately with indigenous thought."[39] This meeting of minds and mentalities, however, would not, in Béart's view, lead to an assimilation of African tradition, but rather an affirmation of it, since, as he asserted, "nothing will help them more to preserve within themselves the poetry of their ancestral land than indigenous theater with its music, dance, and choruses."

The special issue of *L'Éducation Africaine* commemorated two editions of the annual *fête d'art scolaire*, or school art festival, held at Dakar's Chamber of Commerce in February 1936 and 1937. In his introductory remarks in the journal, Béart argued that the current iteration of indigenous theater served as a useful pedagogical exercise, one that brought the students in contact with African ritual and myth while also helping to create a sense, among students, of a common French West African identity. Still in an educational vein, the journal contextualizes chosen texts of the Ponty plays with ethnographic and historical commentary, while also including reactions offered by attending administrators and intellectuals such as the colonial administrator Robert Delavignette and the author Denise Moran. The issue includes a statement given by one of the *pontins* immediately before one of the performances. His closing words to the audience seem to run counter to colonial framings of the event, especially in their depiction of his classmates' status as performers, since he concludes his remarks by thanking people of note in attendance and then declaring: "*Parole aux acteurs!*" ("And now let's hear from the actors!").

The sample of plays published in the special issue offers a view of the diversity of genres and approaches adopted by the Ponty students. Some of the performance pieces, such as the Guinean students' *Un mariage chez les Mandégnis* (*A Mandegni Wedding*) and the Senegalese presentation of *Trois scènes Sérères* (*Three Serer Scenes*), took on an explicitly ethnographic approach, focusing mainly on staged reenactments of African customs and ceremonies. Others reflected the *pontins*' desire to revisit key episodes of

African mythology or history, particularly those they judged to have been neglected or misrepresented in their colonial education. In his reading of one such historical reconstruction, *La Ruse de Diégué* (*Diegue's Ruse*), by the students from French Sudan (today's Mali), Stephen Bulman points out the Ponty theater's role in transmitting oral practices of epic narrative.[40] Indeed, the Sudanese students' original theatrical creation placed on stage a key episode of the Mandinka epic tale of Sunjata, a fact that curiously goes unmentioned in the otherwise extensive commentary in the special issue of *L'Éducation Africaine*. The presentation of *Retour aux fétiches délaissés* (*Return to the Abandoned Talismans*) by the Dahomean students took a different tack, appearing to challenge the dominance of French-fashioned logic and science by staging the story of an African man who brings ill fortune upon himself by abandoning the fetish objects of his ancestors, a crisis quickly resolved once the character returns to his traditional practices. The play offers a possible cautionary tale against giving up one's own cultural practices. However, it also implicitly reinforced colonial discourses of the day, which tended to point to what many educators and social scientists considered the stubborn persistence of a "prelogical" African mind.[41]

In their exploration of native African life, the Ponty plays resonated with the pedagogical goals of another exercise, emblematic of the school and implemented in the same year as the performances. As a means of enrooting students in their native culture while also developing a sense of observation and objective analysis, the school inaugurated a capstone writing exercise that had students play the role of the ethnographer by carrying out a study on a specific local custom, such as marriage rites, religious practices, or agricultural customs. They then filled a small notebook with a description and analysis of their findings, often concluding with suggestions on how certain problems might be better addressed or how lands might be cultivated more efficiently. Soon referred to as the *cahiers Ponty* (the Ponty notebooks), the written exercises, hundreds of which are housed today in the archives of the Institut Fondamental d'Afrique Noire in Dakar, were meant to serve as a test of each student's reasoning capacities, with the goal of developing an appreciation for man's direct intervention on his surroundings in the form of efficient labor and social organization.

In his study of the vast archive of Ponty notebooks, Tobias Warner examines the self-reflexive and often contradictory stance that Ponty students were expected to maintain in writing their assignments. Warner demonstrates how, through the *cahier* exercise, the *pontins* performed their own modern subjectivity vis-à-vis colonial society while foregrounding how they came to become modern subjects in the first place (that is, through the French colonial school). Thus, through the *cahiers* "a Ponty student was asked not only to see the world with new eyes, but also to tell the story of how those eyes came to be theirs."[42] Such discursive performances of modernity involved frequent recourse to literary genres and devices, with forays into novelistic language or occasional adaptations of the European form of the bildungsroman. Yet, as Warner points out, the *pontins* could not venture too far onto the terrain of the literary or else they would risk the admonishment of their graders for flowery language or authorly pretensions.

Colonial framing around the theatrical performances did not manage to contain those events quite so easily, though it was not for want of trying. If the pages of the *cahiers* or of *L'Éducation Africaine* could serve to police creative pretenses and orient interpretations of the students' work, the stage offered an array of ephemeral, embodied means of artistic agency. Though the full range of educational discourse surrounding the event insisted that the *pontins* were not, properly speaking, creative artists, in the midst of performance the stage was theirs. Thus, while Warner convincingly demonstrates the peculiar "para-literary" character of the Ponty notebooks, the students' plays were fully and unabashedly theatrical despite colonial claims to the contrary. This perhaps explains in part why the students seem to have taken up the stage performances with greater enthusiasm than they did the *cahier* assignment. Generally describing the *cahier* work as dry, tedious, and uninspiring in later oral histories, the *pontins* saw in their theatrical performances a means of stepping into their role as the future elite leaders of the West African region, while also creatively recasting their cultural heritage to suit the needs of that future.[43]

Interweaving Modes of Performance

In the special issue the contribution of Bernard Dadié, the school's already prominent young playwright, includes a number of stylistic and dramaturgical devices that illustrate the degree to which the performances allowed for creative license in both staging and script scarcely afforded by the *cahier* exercise. Dadié's play, *Assémien Dehylé, Roi des Sanwi* (*Assemien Dehyle, King of the Sanwi*), reflects the Ponty students' overarching claim to the status of stage artists rather than mere artisans of representativity.[44] Colonial framings of the performances interpreted their value altogether differently. In a preface written by Charles Béart, the headmaster refers to the authenticity and representational value of *Assémien*: "Bernard Dadié and his classmates have managed to render with rare perfection all the flavor of the barbarous civilization that exudes from these tales . . ."[45] Yet Dadié's own writing, and indeed the performance by the group of Ivorian students, highlight the artistic interpretation at the root of their work.

The play is structured around three "tableaux" and tells the story of the rise of King Assémien of the Sanwi. In his staging of this story of war and succession, Dadié allows the plot to unfurl against a tapestry of interwoven voices combining historical reenactment, depictions of myth, and expressions of popular opinion and discourse. The first tableau opens with a musical introduction, a chorus sung amid the animated ambience of a public square in Krinjabo, capital of the Sanwi kingdom. In this scene, a diviner named Ezan reads his cowrie shells and advises the young Assémien to run to the side of his uncle the ailing king, Amon N'Doufou. The remaining performers, labeled "the people," then engage in a series of riddles and games. When they call for a tale, a storyteller figure enters and recounts the legend of Queen Pokou with the help of a chorus, which accompanies him with popular folk songs. This central story of Baoulé lore tells of the founding young queen's sacrifice of her own son to satisfy the gods and secure safe passage westward for her people in search of a new home. The queen's cry upon the death of her son, "*baoulé*" ("The child is dead"), gives that tribe the name by which it is known to this day. In the second tableau, the play returns to its titular character as the young Assémien is initiated to the throne by Amon N'Doufou. Their consultation then requires the execution, off stage, of the surrounding captive-servants, who have heard (along with the audience) the contents of their conversation, which no uninitiated ear must hear. The enemy tribe, the Dankira, attack shortly after the king's death. Assémenien departs to war to the sounds of the vigorous war songs of the Sanwi tribe. In the concluding tableau, Assémien returns victorious from battle and learns that the tribe's council of elders has confirmed his status as the rightful heir to the throne. The play ends with a musical celebration of his coronation.

Dadié's approach represents an attempt to take advantage of the full range of performance modes at his disposal. Placed upon the stage of the Ponty School, whose students had studied French classical drama, the story of Assémien seems to have resonated with the themes of valor and honor typical of works by Pierre Corneille or Jean Racine. Reflecting on the apparent influence of these canonical literary figures on the young playwrights, Ponty headmaster Charles Béart once stated (in reference to Corneille's drama *The Cid* and Racine's *Andromaque*): "It provided a seed, and at times a mold. I always feared we would see a Rodrigue-Soundiata or a Bineta-Andromaque, but we never did."[46] In *Assémien Dehylé, Roi des Sanwi* the lessons of dramatic convention learned through the *pontins*' French schooling interweave with African worlds of performance. The stage is used to host community word games and riddles, traditional songs and dances, as well as the narrative work of the storyteller, and his evocation of the realm of mythology. The presentation of the Queen Pokou legend particularly highlights the diegetic complexity of Dadié's play. Staging through the storyteller a form of play within a play, Dadié places on stage, and for a colonial audience eager to behold a reenactment of authentic African myth and folklore, a community as it reenacts such myths for itself. This slight narrative and staged distance from the realm of myth, which is always evoked through an act of performance and never fully assumed by the *pontins*, reflects something of the students' own stance as artistic interpreters. In weaving such staged tapestries or "tableaux" of French and African performance traditions, they act as creators rather than in the capacity of faithful native informants for the ethnographic record.

Recasting the Colonial Encounter

The *pontins* also used the stage to revisit and revise what they saw as failed early encounters with European colonialism. They especially sought to alter the recurring depictions in French colonial literature of early African leaders, most notably Guinea's Samory Ture, Béhanzin (now a national hero of Benin), and Lat Joor (a national hero of Senegal), as illogical, untrustworthy, and war-hungry chiefs. These figures reemerge in what later came to be known as the *pièces historiques*, or history plays, of the Ponty School, a genre that would operate to a far more pointed and political effect in the nationalist theater of the post-independence years. In the case of the Ponty plays, such works use the stage primarily as a performative tool to re-adjudicate the historical roles, and restore the dignity, of nineteenth-century African chiefs and leaders.

A prominent example, *L'Entrevue de Samory et du Capitaine Péroz—1887* (*The Conference of Samory and Captain Péroz—1887*), was published in the 1937 special issue of *L'Éducation Africaine* and performed by the students from Guinea. The play imagines a decisive encounter between its titular characters Samory Ture, an African military leader and intractable resister to European encroachment, and Marie-Étienne Péroz, the French captain tasked with securing Samory's allegiance. The Guineans, in the staging of their locally born hero, do not utter a dissident cry against the conquering French, but rather present a Samory Ture who is forced to concede to the threat of French military might. However, there are nuances in Samory's capitulation which suggest that the authors were not merely concerned with showing deference to the strength and will of the colonizers. They also sought to counter French notions of the prelogical African mind as reflected in the educators' commentary in *L'Éducation Africaine*. The *pontins* depict Samory as conceding to Péroz in the name of his own strategic self-interest, thus behaving logically and with the understanding that he and his people will have something to gain from the exchange with the French.

The play begins with Samory's son, Karamoko, who delivers a speech after returning from France, where the colonizers had arranged for him to attend military parades and battle simulations. The young prince urges his father and the court to acknowledge that they are no match for French military might and therefore must agree to sign a peace treaty with Péroz, who is fast on his way to Bissandougou. "I saw their soldiers, I watched their combat simulations. In truth, nothing equals their strength," Karamoko declares, to the ire of his father.[47] Following the loud protest of his *sofas*, or Malinke warriors, Samory concedes that defeat may well be inevitable this time should he decide to take up arms. The king is aware that his army would follow him to their death, "but," he tells them, "despite your unshakeable courage, despite your impetuousness in combat, I fear for you and believe that I would do well to make peace with these infidels" (42). Samory exercises his powers of reasoning to recognize an opportunity to benefit politically from a treaty with Péroz. Speaking of the potential advantages of such an agreement, Samory reasons, "It will allow us to expand our states gradually at the other end" (43).

I contend here that the staging of an African leader such as Samory laying out a rational assessment of his political and military options represented a meaningful symbolic act in the context of colonial education at the time. The students pointed out through this play that African minds did not require French influence in order to appreciate the benefits of rational decision-making. The play's title points to the centrality of the encounter between Samory and Péroz. Yet Samory's final decision leading him to concede to French forces has largely taken place before the *entrevue* in question, thus diminishing Péroz's importance in the culminating moment of the story. At the end of the first scene, Samory repeats aloud his conclusion on the action to be taken, stating that although his warriors are ready to fight, "this time I prefer peace, for now I am loath to spill the Whites' blood. We will use this peace with them to make war with our enemies in Ouassoulou" (43).

In the Samory-Péroz encounter depicted in the subsequent scene, the French captain begins by warning his counterpart of the importance of his decision on whether to ally with or fight the French: "The situation is critical. You must choose between peace and war." He then accuses Samory of failing to follow through on earlier agreements with French forces. "You pillaged Bidiga. You took captives in Niagossola. You destroy the regions you promise to respect. You mistreat the populations that you swore to leave in peace" (44). Péroz seeks to get the better of Samory by agitating him through insults in front of his court and warriors, and even questioning his legitimacy as ruler and his royal lineage. Samory at first responds to Péroz's provocations, calling him "forked-tongued man," but, upon a further dressing-down from Péroz, he shows himself capable of introspection and self-criticism, stating, "I admit that I was carried away by an anger that is beneath my dignity" (45).

With the stakes of the encounter established, and the conditions of a dialogue set mostly by Samory's ability to respond calmly to Péroz's provocation, a negotiation can take place that reflects the historical importance of this exchange, but which above all would, for the audience of the time, resound clearly as an echo of contemporary concerns of governance in the colonies. Appealing to Samory to accept peace with the French (which he has already decided to do), Péroz states that this is his last chance to enter into good relations with the French colonel Louis Faidherbe by allowing the French access to the Niger River so that they may provide supplies to the famished region of Bouré. "Moreover," Péroz adds, "you will join in our work [*oeuvre*] and you will help bring prosperity to this desolate region by granting our merchants open access to Kankan and Ouassoulou" (45).

The "work" here is that of the civilizing mission, and what is at stake is a partnership that will allow the French to expand their presence throughout the region. The young *pontins* staging this play are indeed quite aware of the commercial interests at stake in such a process. Just as colonial authorities had at this point emphasized the importance of a greater economic return, or "*mise en valeur*," on their colonial endeavors, the *pontins* recognize that their relations with the French must involve a facilitation of their commercial activity. However, the quid pro quo for such an agreement, as they saw it, was greater authority for their people within the new local political configuration. Péroz thus makes an offer to Samory: "France is willing to recognize your authority over the sofa states you have assembled, but she wants to see these peoples enjoy the fruits of their labor in peace" (45). Samory accepts Péroz's terms: "Chief, you are right. I will sign your treaty of friendship because you are strong and good" (46). The play ends with the king calling his court to celebrate the newly forged friendship with a dance.

While making no revolutionary political statement in its text, *Entrevue* is exemplary of the Ponty plays in that it describes the contours of still unsettled hegemonic and political points of contention. The reconciliation resulting from the encounter, based on reason, between Samory and Péroz reflects the kind of partnership that French colonials hoped to establish with the *pontins*. In their performances, as in their comportment, the students show that they are willing to enter into such an agreement. However, they also look to establish their right to tell their own stories and histories, seeking to argue, through acts of embodied performance, that behaviors of logic and reason are by no means foreign to the African mind. Lastly, the plays point out that the proposed Franco-African partnership with the young students toward a greater capitalization of the colony must involve more serious roles of authority for the African elite.

The scholarship on the Ponty theater and firsthand accounts of *L'Entrevue de Samory et du Capitaine Péroz—1887* suggest the existence of several different versions of the play. In his study of youth culture, revolution, and nationalism in Guinea, Jay Straker explores the role of *Entrevue* in the later emergence of a Guinean tradition of drama and performance.[48] Through oral accounts of a performance said to have taken place as part of the Ponty students' participation in the 1937 international exhibition in Paris, Straker considers a revised version in which Samory storms off at the end of the play, refusing to enter into any agreement with Péroz.[49] Likewise, Céline Labrune-Badiane and Étienne Smith, in their discussion of the Ponty plays, consider the protests of the Malian (then Sudanese) writer and former *pontin* Fily Dabo Sissoko in *Dakar-Jeunes* regarding a "grotesque" theatrical depiction in Paris of a Samory who bears no resemblance to the actual historical figure.[50] Whether or not the alternate version in question was actually seen on the stage of the Théâtre des Champs-Élysées in Paris in 1937 is unclear. Programs and documentation from the tour, including those aiming to give a full report of the *pontins*' program, make no mention of this particular play.[51] It is conceivable that a collectively shared/invented memory of the play's performance in Paris persisted among those who were not part of the tour but perhaps saw a revised version of the staged Samory story in Dakar, just as it is possible that the performance indeed took place during the international exhibition but somehow escaped documentation.

What one might ask regardless of any uncertainty over the play's performance in Paris is whether the alternate, pugnacious Samory represents, as Straker suggests, a revolutionary and proto-national contrast to the more irresolute figure presented in the original framework of the Ponty event. I would argue that the Samory of the Ponty stage also allows for an analysis of the character's logical realpolitik through which he would have sought to gain maximal advantage from a position of inferior military strength. In contrast, the alleged Parisian depiction, while perhaps flattering for later claims to a revolutionary bent in the Guineans' stage work, coincides tellingly with French colonial notions of an irascible, prelogical African chief. Another notable *pontin*, Bocar Cissé of French Sudan, recounts having composed a play of his own based on the same theme only to see it rejected by his teachers, who insisted he take as his reference the original Ponty play by the Guineans.[52] Cissé's Samory also faced his adversary with fearless aggression, leading the young playwright to take the rejection of his play as an act of colonial censorship. Yet the same Cissé glows with pride at his later uses of the Ponty repertoire. In his memoir he recounts the experience, as a young soldier in the Second World War, of forming a troupe with his fellow enlisted *pontins* while stationed in Fez, where the seasoned West African performers' rendering of the Queen Pokou myth drew larger crowds than their French companions' staged excerpts of classical French theater. Such accounts indicate a cultural phenomenon that corresponds, as Labrune-Badiane and Smith write, with "neither a simple 'pro-colonial spectacle' nor mere 'cultural proto-nationalism' . . . The Ponty theater is an ambiguous genre that the authorities (by giving its official and authorized meaning at the time) and the students (in their commentary or memories after the fact) attempted to interpret and orient in diverging ways."[53]

In the context of this study, I would like to suggest that the subtle decolonizing function of this particular stage space lay in the *pontins*' attempts to assert their role as actors on at least two levels. First, by way of the Western stage they took advantage of the creative and rhetorical liberties afforded by the gesture of role-play. The act of incarnating characters understood to be other than themselves facilitated a brief though powerful respite from the burden of representativity, at least in the *pontins*' understanding of the event, if not in the colonial framings of it. Second, the *pontins* were able to make the case, in front of an audience of administrators and instructors, for their own role as actors within future plans for an emerging Franco-African society. Where the colonials saw profound cultural and intellectual differences with regard to African cultures, the students portrayed the possibilities for greater interconnectedness and collaboration. Where educators sought to diminish the role of intellectual abstraction in their programs, the *pontins* embraced the abstraction of embodying the other in staged pieces that were inspired by their native cultures, but which included a degree of creative alienation from those same cultures. This view of alienation as a productive technique of performance differs from that often used to discuss the "malaise" of the African creator within a Francophone African context. Instead, it refers to the potentially positive side of alienation explored provocatively by Abiola Irele, who writes: "we need to take charge of our objective alienation, but assuming it as an *intention* so as to endow it with a positive significance."[54] While the *pontins* may not have articulated their stage gestures in such terms, I argue that their performances represented a means of stepping into a stage space rife with colonial discourse in order to enact such a creative alienation.

Colonial Framings of the Ponty Stage

Colonial reactions to the Ponty shows were generally marked by enthusiasm and praise. Commenting on the first performance held at the Chamber of Commerce in Dakar, one journalist admired "the gripping truthfulness of the reenactment . . . The actors' performance is remarkably natural," and he further remarked that their performance evinces nothing "of the artificial creation of a role"; rather, he states, the African students appeared to reenact for their audience an authentic scene of indigenous life and history.[55] The performance consisted of two separate parts, one a staging of classical European works, and the other inspired by the students' original writing and based on indigenous culture. The first, it seems, was marked by a dry "classroom feel," while the second, which included "local songs and choruses and two indigenous plays," was seen by the same journalist as "the symbol of a long-pursued evolution," nothing less than "the sign of a new African mind." Also laudatory, if somewhat less enthusiastic, was the response in a 1937 edition of *Afrique Française* written by the colonial administrator and author Robert Delavignette, then director of the École Nationale de la France d'Outre-mer (National School of Overseas France), who saw in the Ponty plays the beginnings of an emerging African literary movement. "We are not claiming a masterpiece," he wrote, "but if an African dramatist emerges one day, he will come from this educators' theater," a rather prescient statement in response to what Delavignette called "an indisputable testament to a happy colonization."[56]

Although colonial figures and writers recognized in their commentary on the Ponty performances the novelty and innovation behind the works, this did not translate into an acknowledgment of the students' role as artists or actors. In her reaction to the performances, Denise Moran argued that it was with the dances that the pieces demonstrated their "art value," and she suggested that the students, in their dramatic writing, were mostly either mimicking French literary styles from their coursework or merely reflecting the mores of their native performance cultures.[57] As Moran's view suggests, the *pontins* were seen less as performing artists and more as the product of a new approach in colonial administration based on the notion of adapted indigenous instruction. The newness, as it were, was occasioned by astute colonial policy, which allowed the French to note what was seen as an emerging Franco-African mind. The plays provided authorities with a fitting opportunity to declare the success of their preceding associative efforts. Surely, it was thought, these students would not fall into the trap of *diagnist* political activism. For admiring French spectators, the *pontins* represented the emergence of a long-awaited enrooted, French-educated African elite.

The colonial administration was quick to appreciate the potential utility of such an event not only within the colony but also in the *métropole*, the term for mainland France in the days of the empire. The Ivorian playwright François-Joseph Amon d'Aby recounts how, at the curtain of the premiere of Dadié's play at the Chamber of Commerce, the Ivorian performers received a handwritten note from the colony's inspector-general of education, Albert Charton, who was in attendance with the governor-general, stating, "Keep it up, my children: this play will perform in Paris next year. So the governor-general has just decided."[58] The request was subsequently made to the Ministry of Colonies to permit the students to participate in the 1937 Exposition Internationale des Arts et Techniques dans la Vie Moderne. Thirty *pontins* (*sans* Bernard Dadié, who was no longer eligible, since he had graduated by then) thus embarked on a tour that included a performance at the exhibition's Île des Cygnes on the river Seine and another at the opulent Théâtre des Champs-Élysées in Paris, with an additional concert given at the Congrès International de l'Enseignement and a visit of the École Nationale de la France d'Outre-mer accompanied by the school's director, Robert Delavignette. The production at the international exhibition provoked lively reactions from critics and the press, which praised the students' performances, with some considering the implications that such theater had for the productions being staged in Paris at the time. Artistically, the Ponty School and its "*théâtre indigene*," or "indigenous theater," made a lasting impression in Paris. In the context of the exhibition, the original Ponty plays seemed to correspond neither with the objectifying framework of the event, nor with the exoticizing plays about colonial Africa that had been regaling French audiences for decades.[59] The result was an awed reaction in the French press, with inquisitive observers marveling at the emergence of this new type of African performer and writer. Writing about the *pontins*' performance at the Théâtre des Champs-Élysées, Robert Delavignette praised the students' work, declaring: "this theater is no longer a local form of entertainment and has taken its place within the universal theater . . . It is no longer exoticism for our sake, nor a European imitation for theirs. In a synthesis of dance, song, music, and literature, a dramatic art awakens, stemming from their country and ours, from our language and theirs."[60]

Delavignette's statement occludes the great concerns surrounding the event from the perspective of the colony. For the Ministry of Colonies, it was of utmost importance that the event not run counter to contemporaneous political objectives, that is, to a long-standing pedagogical effort to ground students in local, African traditions. A primary worry of the higher-ups was how the young Africans would react to their first encounter with the "intoxications of the stage" (*les griseries de la planche*) and the temptations of Parisian society. It was specified that the students must not see themselves as fulfilling the role of performers, but rather were to understand the tour as an opportunity to demonstrate the fruits of colonial education, a mission described as purely educational in character. The Ponty plays were not viewed as "theater" in the proper sense of the word, nor were the students viewed as actors. If the colony wished to go to such lengths and expense to facilitate a trip to Paris, it was, as Albert Charton reassured the governor-general in his correspondence, solely to demonstrate to metropolitan France "the existence of an indigenous civilization that we can bring up to our level."[61]

Colonial officials' insistence that these students not consider themselves proper artists as a result of their Parisian tour reveals the central political stake of the Ponty plays. Though performing in such worldly venues as the Théâtre des Champs-Élysées, where professional artists like Josephine Baker were taking the Parisian performance world by storm, the *pontins* were held to the status of representatives of ways of indigenous life. In contrast to the students' foray into creative stage performance, colonial framings enclosed the works within the confines of pedagogical innovation in the colonies. It is thus in reference to the plays' pedagogical value that Robert Delavignette discusses the event, explaining that, following such an experience, the *pontins* will return better prepared to serve the colonies as teachers and administrators. He cites Denise Moran, who declared: "When they return to their village to cure and to teach, they will not be foreigners unable to understand or to make themselves understood . . . Thus will emerge a modern Africa that, far from losing its own genius, will see it flourish." [62] In his closing analysis, Delavignette traces the plays' raison d'être back to an approach to colonial pedagogy that circumscribed African students within the limits of a laboring subclass irrespective of their academic or artistic achievements. The Ponty stage, he declared, did not facilitate theater merely for theater's sake: "It is enrooted in the soil and it will ceaselessly instill the sense of an evolving Africa that nonetheless remains essentially attached to farming."[63]

✦

The Ponty stage and the performances upon it facilitated multiple possible framings of the same cultural phenomenon. The colonial reception and subsequent exploitation of the Ponty plays saw in the students' creations a tool to instantiate the performers' inalienable Africanness. The projection upon the students of an innate African identity served to indicate to both African and French audiences the subaltern role in which even the intellectually elite members of African society were to remain as indigenous doctors, teachers, and clerks. Such uses of the Ponty theatrical performances reflected a particular moment in the shifting policies of the colonial administration, when an intellectual tone of colonial humanism allowed for a general appreciation of African culture without going so far as to push for meaningful political enfranchisement according to a French republican idiom.

Another diverging yet concurrent reading of the event was that of the *pontins*, many of whom saw in the Ponty stage a new kind of cultural platform. The stage space provided a certain degree of elasticity in dealing with African ritual and legend on the one hand and colonial ethnographies and histories of conquest on the other. The Ponty stage allowed the students to engage in traditional African cultural practices such as dance, music, and storytelling as a form of theatrical performance. The distance from the performance spaces in which such practices typically did the work associated with their form allowed the students to step in *as if* doing the work of the traditional storyteller or dancer, rather than as native informants or representatives of such practices, a distinction largely lost on colonial audiences. Moreover, the ability to step out of one's own personal role and into that of another character provided the *pontins* with the opportunity to reenact and reassess key historical encounters between African populations and the French during the period of colonial expansion in the nineteenth century.

The dramaturgical approach and themes of these historically inflected performances carried over into later understandings of an independent African theater as the same *pontins* of the interwar period became the first elite *hommes de culture*, or men of culture, of their respective independent nations. However, just as the style of the Ponty plays became established and recognized for a certain originality, the space of performance absconded under a new shift in pedagogical initiatives. The Ponty performances were discontinued after World War II in part to make room for a more rigorous curriculum that hewed closer to the one used in the schools of metropolitan France. School performances were no longer an accessible means of demonstrating an elite status or reworking one's position within the French hegemonic system. However, the rise of another colonial initiative, the French cultural centers, soon provided a space from which to recuperate debates around the role of the French-educated African within colonial society.

Chapter 2

✦

A Political Theater for a New Elite

The French Cultural Centers of the 1950s

The period after the Second World War saw the emergence of a new institutional stage space in French West Africa for an educated elite that was ready to reimagine its place within Franco-African society. The postwar context brought with it a new set of possibilities and expectations for a population eager to claim full rights as citizens, not subjects, of the French Empire. New political demands emerged following a war in which large numbers of African infantrymen called *tirailleurs* had fought and died alongside French soldiers. The need for a postwar renegotiation of the colonial order proved all the more pressing after the official abolition of the status of the colonial "subject" in 1946, following the passage of the Lamine Guèye law, so named for the socialist Senegalese deputy who spearheaded the legislation. The law effectively turned all residents of the French territories into legal citizens, although the specifics of how this new citizenship might resemble or differ from that of the metropolitan French remained unclear. In the same year, the French Empire was renamed the French Union and formed a reconfigured entity that united as French citizens a vast grouping of peoples throughout France's overseas territories.[1] A time of great uncertainty followed as the negotiating parties of metropolitan and overseas France explored new and ill-defined federalist possibilities, while also debating the extent to which the European French would be willing to concede rights equal to their own to millions of new fellow citizens.[2]

Stage artists of the time used performance culture to experiment with an expanding and transnational notion of French identity according to which an expression of one's "Africanness" could also stand in as, or at least was not mutually exclusive from, an affirmation of "Frenchness." Many members of the French-educated elite who had taken the stage to claim a place for themselves in shifting Franco-African social structures did so again to explore the possibilities of the French Union. They proceeded this time without the platform of the Ponty stage, which had fallen victim to an educational reform shortly after the war. The reform was led by Senegal's future first president

Léopold Sédar Senghor, who, as a young African deputy and participant in France's Constituent National Assembly in 1945, fought to pressure the French government to reassign the administration of African education away from the Ministry of Colonies in order to integrate it into France's own national education system.[3] His effort was an attack on the kind of adapted education pursued by colonial curricula of the interwar period. Senghor hoped to bring about a model closer to curricular equivalency with the intellectual training grounds of metropolitan France; this was a central cause among the elite of French West Africa, whose degrees did not give them access to further study at European institutions of higher learning.[4] The call for reform led to a rigorous new program that eliminated the time once set aside at the William Ponty School for its signature performances of "teachers' theater."

In the absence of the Ponty stage, an opportunity to create a new stage space arose. Once again, the colonial administration proved eager to employ theatrical performances to demonstrate the cultural synergy between France and Africa, particularly with regard to the region's French-educated cultural elite. Such discussions took on new meaning during the years of the French Union which, by its rhetoric if not by its actions, represented a step toward reenvisioning the French Empire as an egalitarian gathering of peoples rather than a manifestation of the relationship between colonizing and colonized populations. The French *centres culturels*, or "cultural centers," were part of an initiative of the early 1950s that quickly took hold throughout the French West African region. The centers provided a platform for reprising debates around the role of African administrators and cultural leaders within a changing colonial and institutional context. This chapter explores the creation and use of this platform as an experimental space for rehearsing and imagining the new possibilities of identity and citizenship offered by the postwar period. The theater of the cultural centers, which is often judged harshly when read according to strictly aesthetic or dramaturgical criteria, has been largely overshadowed by the independentist productions associated with the anticolonial or nationalist movements of the following decade.[5] However, its stages left a lasting mark on the political uses of theatrical performance in Francophone Africa, in addition to serving as a generative means of exchange with a globally minded experimental theater movement then taking place in Europe.

The Cultural Centers of French West Africa

The cultural centers of French West Africa hosted an amateur theatrical practice that became the site of interaction of a group of elites, many of them graduates of the William Ponty School, with the shifting political and social landscape of their time. The first of the cultural centers in the region opened in 1953 under the impetus of French West Africa's high commissioner Bernard Cornut-Gentille who, much like the Ponty educator Charles Béart, played a decisive role in the initiation and promotion of a colonial stage space that was quickly appropriated by African playwrights and performers. As a French administrator, Cornut-Gentille had launched a similar effort in 1946 in French Equatorial Africa, and he brought the experiment with him to his new position in Dakar. He saw in the cultural centers a means of promoting unity and cohesion among the diverse populations inhabiting the region's urban and rural environments. The centers were also designed to appeal to a small group of French-educated Africans who were assigned to occasionally solitary positions as rural teachers and administrators. These elites often expressed a sense of isolation from their peers, but nonetheless proved quite eager to take on new positions of leadership locally.

The initiative met with immediate success, and by 1957 French West Africa counted as many as 107 cultural centers in both urban and rural areas. The centers placed a strong emphasis on the practice of team sports, with a coordinated effort to transmit the rules and techniques of major European sports. Each center included a library with offerings generous in their depiction of French colonial efforts in Africa and beyond. They chose their periodical publications carefully, favoring magazines such as *Paris Match*, which glorified metropolitan French life but made no mention of the more turbulent aspects of French political life at the time, and certainly not of the growing unrest in Algeria. Cinema was central to the institutions' cultural life, and at least seven cinema vans toured continually from center to center, projecting films that romanticized the French presence abroad. As the testing grounds and rehearsal sites for a newly modified form of Franco-African identity, the centers served the dual purpose of offering institutional recognition and visibility to the African leaders who managed them, while also providing a means of familiarizing rural populations with metropolitan customs and cultural practices.

Claiming the Social Space of the Cultural Centers

The locally managed cultural centers soon became active social spaces in their own right, rife with the intercommunal and political tensions of the day. Among the colonial administration's primary concerns was the threat of an enduring rift between urban and rural populations, which had come about due to the concentration, over several centuries, of European influence along the coastal cities and former trading hubs.[6] Cornut-Gentille called for the cultural centers to serve primarily as "halls of friendship" (*foyers d'amitié*) for all citizens of West Africa. In an impassioned call published in the inter-center newsletter *Traits d'Union*, he entreated his readers to think of the cultural centers as spaces of equal exchange to help ward off the interpersonal conflicts that might arise as Africans began to take on roles of responsibility. Notably, he singles out his "metropolitan collaborators," or fellow European Frenchmen and women, directing at them the following rebuke: "cease entirely at the Cultural Center behaving like a superior who deigns to mingle with his subordinates, repress any temptation to supervise them, and do not treat Africans as if they should be grateful to you simply for showing them a modicum of respect."[7] The high commissioner sought instead to use the centers as a space for inverting entrenched colonial social dynamics: "it is necessary that, in the Management Committees, the major roles go to Africans alone: it is they who must take responsibility and lead the initiatives."[8]

The young elite formed by African schoolteachers and clerks proved crucial to the centers' management and comprised the bulk of the institutions' staff. By relying on the leadership of French-educated Africans, the colonial authorities supervising the centers attempted to navigate between two potentially contradictory objectives. In the centers' administration, they sought to avoid creating cultural sites exclusively run by and made for a select group of "westernized" Africans. However, the centers' initiatives also relied heavily on this group to model and promote a certain image of Frenchness so that it might appeal to the populations of the West African territories.[9] As with the Ponty theater, the colonial authorities missed the mark in their attempts to limit the elitist air surrounding the centers' activities. The appointed editor-in-chief of *Traits d'Union* and former Ponty student from Upper Volta (today's Burkina Faso), Lompolo Koné, described his vision of the centers' main purpose in a series of editorials placing at the core of their mission the elite class of which he was a member, those he called with some self-deprecating irony the "*Noirs toubabisants*," or the "toubab-ling Blacks" ("*toubab*" being the term in French West Africa for white Europeans).[10] For Koné, the centers served primarily as "a tool that, on the one hand, allows the African elite to educate and improve themselves while also enjoying themselves. On the other, it allows them to attract and educate the masses from which they should never feel too removed."[11] In his first contribution to *Traits d'Union*, Koné describes a feeling of isolation often experienced by the French-educated African elite destined for positions far from the cosmopolitan hubs of the coast. To be "in the bush," he explains, "often means being on the margins of whatever is taking place, cut off from all things cultural at the very moment one is thirsting for culture. It means, with few exceptions, being at the mercy of the pull of influences that, far from favoring the elevation and growth of a human being, actually destroy the little predisposition one may have to elevate oneself and to grow."[12] The centers could therefore serve, in Koné's view, as a "sanctuary of culture," as he solemnly describes them, or a balm for the soul of the cultural elite who were otherwise forced to endure a definitive separation from the cultural practices to which they had become so attached during their French schooling.[13]

Koné's language certainly reflects a paternalistic vision of French culture as a benevolent force that elevates the soul. However, he and the African elite did not hesitate to use that domain of culture, and especially stage culture, to participate in the ongoing debates on the political and social implications of the French Union. Indeed, the inter-center activities and newsletter provided a valuable opportunity for far-removed, often like-minded aspiring writers

Figure 2.1. A 1955 performance by the Centre Culturel et Folklorique de la Côte d'Ivoire (C.C.F.C.I.) at the Dakar final of La Coupe Théâtrale. Photograph by Georges Galmiche.

Figure 2.2. François-Joseph Amon D'Aby receiving the first prize of La Coupe Théâtrale for the C.C.F.C.I. Photograph by Georges Galmiche.

and intellectuals to form a network of community leaders who were eager to turn the French notion and practice of culture into a political tool for debate and local mobilization. In the words of one prominent center participant, the Ivorian François-Joseph Amon d'Aby, the centers served, above all, as a space for the elite to gather and discuss the roles of their own customs and institutions in order to decide how one could go about being both African and French. He described the centers as the sites where elites gathered to ask: "Should we preserve as they are the institutions, habits, and customs inherited from our ancestors, or should we instead see them as ways of thinking and being from a bygone era and, therefore, replace them with Western civilization?"[14] The centers allowed the new elite to serve as active participants in such discussions and to come up with answers for, by, and among themselves.

Crafting the Centers' Performance Stage

The theatrical stage provided the basis for what quickly became the key cultural event linking the entire network of centers. In an editorial in *Traits d'Union*, Cornut-Gentille announced his decision to inaugurate a region-wide theatrical tournament called La Coupe Théâtrale (The Theatrical Cup).[15] La Coupe was organized into a series of competitions in which amateur performance groups presented original ensemble pieces that were expected to represent the culture of their home region. Each cultural center selected a troupe from among its membership to compete with neighboring centers in an eliminatory contest. The winning troupes advanced through a series of local and regional face-offs, with the final for each territory taking place in its *chef lieu*, or hub. In the inter-federal rounds, Cornut-Gentille matched territory against territory in line with the colonial cartography of the day, pitting Dahomey against Niger, Upper Volta against Sudan, Côte d'Ivoire against Guinea, and Senegal against Mauritania. The tournament eventually concluded with a final competition for the cup and first-place title of all of French West Africa at the Théâtre du Palais in Dakar. Cornut-Gentille laid out the specifics of who would serve on the presiding juries. Jury members would include a local French public servant, one member of the academic association IFAN (or Institut Français d'Afrique Noire, today's Institut Fondamental d'Afrique Noire), and a representative of Youth and Sports Services. The troupes were to perform in French in order to make the pieces intelligible to the members of all centers. This stipulation came with the "natural exception" of any songs, dances, or folkloric elements that troupes wished (and indeed were encouraged) to include and which were to be performed in the appropriate African language.

One frequent jury member, the Senegalese stage director Maurice Sonar Senghor, became a key partner in Cornut-Gentille's theatrical efforts. Sonar Senghor had spent his formative years training as an actor in Paris, largely under the mentorship of the Algerian-born Sudanese actor Habib Benglia—to whom the young Maurice had been sent by his influential uncle Léopold Sédar Senghor—as well as in the company of Senegalese performer Féral Benga. While in Paris, Sonar Senghor met and performed alongside such international stars as Josephine Baker and the Guinean dancer Fodéba Keïta. His rising artistic profile in France and political connections back home led to an eventual invitation to take up the directorship of Dakar's Théâtre du Palais, which he accepted.[16] In the early 1950s, the Théâtre du Palais benefited from the enthusiastic support of High Commissioner Cornut-Gentille, whose plan to develop the 500-seat theater into the premier performance venue of French West Africa was of a piece with the promotion of the French cultural centers' amateur theatrical activities.

Under the direction of Sonar Senghor, the stage of the Théâtre du Palais reflected the political concerns of the postwar context while participating in the debates around the place of Africa's cultural traditions and institutions within the French Union. One particularly illustrative event in this regard was the performance of a stage version of the Senegalese author Birago Diop's short story "Sarzan," which was directed by Sonar Senghor and adapted for the stage by the Senegalese playwright Lamine Diakhaté.[17] "Sarzan" famously tells the story of a character named Thiémokho Kéita, who after fifteen years spent serving in the French military returns to his native village of Dougouba. Determined to civilize the population by ridding it of its "savage ways," Thiémokho is the prototypical tragic *déraciné*, or uprooted African. His demise would clearly resonate in the late colonial context as a cautionary tale for the French-educated Africans of that time. However, Diakhaté's stage version also inserted into Diop's tale an impassioned defense, for its mainly African audience, of both the French Union then taking shape and Africa's place within such a union. This defense was voiced on stage by the character of the wise Veterinary Inspector, who replaces the narrator of Diop's original story and serves as Thiémokho's guide through the latter's re-initiation to his native culture. The Veterinary Inspector explains to Thiémokho the importance of the "community" of peoples that the French Union represents:

> For the moment, we need to be held up by the community. The same community took us in at our birth: it supports us, we feel the need to exchange with it and to do so throughout our existence. Can we deprive ourselves of this past and this wealth of works, institutions, habits, language and methods that we have found here?[18]

In response, Thiémokho emits a resounding "No, we can't!" The "here" that concludes the Veterinary Inspector's appeal is as ambiguous in the play as it was in the context of the French Union itself. Even in Thiémokho's remote village, the sense of a "here" could include, the play implies, a connection to a broader French identity. Thiémokho's affirmation of this notion constitutes an avowal of what West Africans stood to gain from an alliance with

France. It also revealed, in the context of the play's performance, the political concerns and expectations that underlay both the professional stage of the Théâtre du Palais and the amateur performance spaces of the cultural centers.

As the director of the Théâtre du Palais, Sonar Senghor presided over many of La Coupe's high-stakes performance-matches, and he returned reports to the colonial administration about the content and quality of the presentations.[19] His reports highlight the highly competitive nature of the event, which established a grid system of allotted points. Although the troupes performed in the style of "total theater," meaning music, dance, poetry, and drama interwoven in a multidisciplinary piece, determining a "winner" required breaking up the total theater form into discrete evaluable categories. Thus, troupes could earn up to twenty points for each category in direction (*mise en scène*), diction (an assessment of the actors' French pronunciation and ability to project their voices), and presentation, which included the seamlessness with which troupes tied together sections of drama and folkloric elements such as dance and musical performance. The final forty points fell under the category of "execution," which allowed jury members to assess each troupe's overall level of talent and skill. Finally, troupes received penalties for each violation of competition rules; for example, if they exceeded the set length of ninety minutes (with a two-point penalty for each additional minute) or included more actors than the maximum of twenty-five.

The competitive spirit encouraged by the presence of a jury and the use of a formalized point system resonated with what Dale Byam has called a tendency toward forms of competition that has pervaded much of African performance since the stage of the Ponty School.[20] Indeed, the French-sponsored tournaments of the cultural centers, perhaps more than the Ponty performances, represented a formative moment in what eventually became a common association, present to this day in popular ensemble performances, between community-based theatrical work and the drive to compete among groups. La Coupe Théâtrale was plainly steeped in such a spirit of competition between troupes who acted as representatives of a community with much to gain from a successful outcome. A victory in La Coupe Théâtrale, especially in the final in Dakar, ensured a lasting reputation for that particular troupe or center with stakes that included a monetary prize of 75,000 francs CFA. Moreover, by taking home the cup in a given year, centers, and particularly their leaders, stood to gain considerable prestige as cup laureates.

The cultural center in the city of Banfora, the capital of Gouin country in the territory then called Upper Volta, provides an illustrative example of the lasting cultural capital earned by successful troupes. In a short time, the center managed to generate a remarkably high level of activity, with performances that drew large numbers of local spectators.[21] In 1957 the center presented a stage adaptation of a familiar narrative, *Les Paysans noirs* (*The Black Peasants*), a novel written by French administrator Robert Delavignette and known locally for portraying the conflict between the Gouin and

Dioula peoples.[22] Adapted by Lompolo Koné, the play, titled *Au pays des paysans noirs* (*In the Land of the Black Peasants*), met with considerable success and went on to win the cup in that year's final competition in Dakar. In an ethnographic study exploring the contemporary memory of the production and its legacy in Banfora, Michèle Dacher remarked on how the text of Delavignette's novel had become an object of prestige connected to a history of theatrical production in French West Africa, from Ponty to the cultural centers.[23] As a staged narrative, the performance and victory at La Coupe Théâtrale constituted a landmark moment for the local identity of Banfora, as well as for the collective sense of belonging to a larger Francophone West African community.

Critical assessments of the cultural centers' theater tend to describe a generally low level of dramatic quality in the scripted plays. Even the jury members of the first edition of La Coupe Théâtrale in 1955 wrote in their report to the administration that most of the plays lacked any kind of artistic or compositional sophistication. They found that the works failed to meet the expectations set by the considerable monetary prize being offered, and so they suggested that, in future competitions, submissions be divided into categories by genre, in part to encourage more formal structure within the works, but also to allow the jury to distribute the award money more widely. Yet the performances attracted large and energized crowds and took on such local importance as to incite one administrative higher-up to complain that, in the weeks leading up to the competition, African public servants often abandoned their offices to focus their efforts entirely on rehearsals.[24] In fact, the centers' troupes did not aim to create the kind of works sought out by those accustomed to Western conventions of stage drama. The troupes' directors and playwrights did not see themselves as aspiring stage artists but rather as an aspiring leadership class. Thus, the stage space they crafted served primarily as a forum for political discussion among African cultural leaders and their communities. In this sense, the performance practices hosted by the centers far exceeded the limited function ascribed to them by the colonial authorities. The centers' performances played an openly political role, most notably by addressing the possibilities and problems of a Franco-African citizenship that was promised though never delivered by the fledgling French Union.

The Success of the C.C.F.C.I.

By far the most successful of the cultural centers, the Centre Culturel et Folklorique de la Côte d'Ivoire (the C.C.F.C.I.) proved a standout organization whose example illustrates the political and social ambitions often tied to participation in this amateur theater. The group had a cenacle of Ponty graduates as its founders: Bernard Dadié, François-Joseph Amon d'Aby, and Germain Coffi Gadeau, each already a member of a French-educated elite destined to work in the public service of colonial society in their native Côte d'Ivoire.[25] Thanks to the success of their performances with the C.C.F.C.I., these former *pontins* were able to conjoin their artistic and political activities, solidifying their status as both public figures and cultural leaders. The center began its activities by reprising some of the better-known works of the Ponty stage before deciding to address more directly the shifting preoccupations of a new leadership class eager for a transition to a future of equal political, economic, and social exchange with metropolitan France. Through stage performance, the same group of elites also expressed their anxieties regarding the effect such changes could have on local traditions, or, more polemically, the degree to which African customs risked hindering the region's shift toward a system of citizenship similar to that of Europe. To a greater extent than with the Ponty plays, the center's playwrights used the stage to explore the political ramifications of their place within the French Union, sometimes doing so down to the minutiae of addressing the need for reform in local succession and inheritance customs.

In its 1955 entry to the centers' theatrical competition, the Ivorian troupe performed a staged piece titled *Kwao Adjoba, ou procès du régime matriarcal en basse Côte d'Ivoire* (*Kwao Adjoba, or Lower Côte d'Ivoire's Matriarchal System on Trial*), a play by Amon d'Aby that addressed what the author saw as the problems caused by Akan laws of inheritance. In a note appended to his submission, Amon d'Aby traced understandings of Akan lineage customs to accounts of myth, pointing out the continued legality of a system he hoped to expose through the play's narrative, and which he saw as antiquated and ill-suited for a modernizing society. The play tells the story of a devoted wife, Kwao Adjoba, who finds herself destitute due to the machinations of her husband's brother and sister. The two siblings conspire to take advantage of their priority in Akan lineage over their brother's wife and son in order to inherit the household's property and reap the benefits of the brother's labor and that of his family. Amon d'Aby's tale presented African audiences with a social reality that he deemed unacceptable, and its author intended to use the play to incite reform within the local legal system. This socially engaged approach led African critics of the time to consider *Kwao Adjoba* a turning point in African drama in that it sought to do more than merely document the history or customs of African society; the play addressed directly the shifting realities and anxieties of its diverse audience.[26] In his later recollections of the production, Amon d'Aby names as the crowning achievement of the work not the cup, which his center took home that year, but rather a government decree of 1964 that reformed the country's inheritance laws.[27]

Amon d'Aby and the C.C.F.C.I. did not focus solely on what they saw as necessary reforms from within African society, but also addressed the damage done by French interference in local customs. In the following year, the C.C.F.C.I presented *La Couronne aux enchères* (*The Crown up for Bid*), a play that told of a succession struggle following the death of the king of the Massa country. The topic would be familiar to former spectators of the Ponty stage, but it invited a different approach in the context of the cultural centers. In Amon d'Aby's play, the dignitaries of the kingdom come to a satisfactory and widely accepted agreement designating a nobleman named Mian Aoussi as the rightful heir to the throne. However, sensing an opportunity to seize power by sowing confusion, a small group of counter-aspirants comes forward. Each presents his own spurious claim, with two insisting falsely that they are the rightful heirs through lineage. Another, despite being a foreigner to the Massa country, claims a right to the throne by virtue of his knowledge of the social and economic needs of the time, declaring: "It is to infuse the Massa kingdom with the invigorating air of modern progress that I oppose the nomination of Mian Aoussi."[28] The French administrator in charge has no understanding of the matter at hand and, hoping to resolve the dispute democratically, calls for a decision by popular vote. The election allows the false aspirants to form a bloc to influence the vote in favor of one of their own ranks, thus resulting in a charlatan ascending to leadership. The play does not present a successful and modernizing form of democratization, but instead depicts a colonial system running roughshod over an otherwise effective political system in place. It concludes with the lamentations of an elder, who directly addresses the cultural center audience: "Must we force ourselves to resemble as much as possible the Whites by neglecting, disdaining, renouncing even our own civilization and by sweeping away all of our institutions? Or must we instead learn to appreciate and preserve our cultural heritage while keeping it permeable to the daylight of progress?"[29]

The C.C.F.C.I. represents an important case not only due to its success in winning the first two of the three competitions that ultimately took place for La Coupe Théâtrale (the center was officially disqualified from the third in order to make room for another winner). It also offers the clearest expression of the political ambitions at the core of nearly all of the centers' performances. The small regional cultural centers used the stage to intervene in local and regional debates in the context of a French West Africa now understood as part of a Union rather than an Empire, and did so among a diverse population that was hesitantly considering how it might reimagine itself as somehow both African and French. The invention of such a multifaceted identity and the exploration of its implications formed an integral part of the political and performative contours of the centers' stage space. This political function failed to travel, however, when the centers' troupes found themselves called upon to represent something of an authentic African culture and folklore to audiences and fellow theater-makers abroad.

Projections and Legacies of the Centers' Stage Space

In its interaction with, and impact upon, the social sphere of the emerging French Union, the theater of the cultural centers also proved useful in a metropolitan context, though for different purposes. In 1956, through an editorial in *Traits d'Union*, Bernard Cornut-Gentille announced that the tournament champion of that year would receive the additional prize of a performance tour in France funded by the office of the high commissioner. In his correspondence with the administration of the French Union, Cornut-Gentille suggested that the event could serve to mark the transfer of the Union's Assembly to Paris from its original location in Versailles. Convinced that the students would win over a metropolitan audience and thereby demonstrate the benefits of the high commissioner's cultural approach to Franco-African relations, Cornut-Gentille issued a special request for the support and attendance of the Assembly's president Albert Sarraut.

The resulting month-long tour offered a certain visibility to the work of the cultural centers while catering to a shift in metropolitan tastes and expectations regarding the presentation of African culture. The organizers had settled on the Théâtre de l'Étoile as their Parisian venue, deeming the grandiose Théâtre des Champs-Élysées once used to host the *pontins* too large for the expected audience, a sign that the brand of colonial exoticism that once filled the theaters of Paris had lost its appeal.[30] Rather than a display of African kings encountering the onslaught of the French civilizing mission, spectators watched what they considered a respectful demonstration of African customs and folklore that removed any overt sign of French influence or intervention. Although the C.C.F.C.I. had won La Coupe Théâtrale that same year with a work of total theater that included the play *La Couronne aux enchères*, which criticized the effects of colonial policy, in Paris the troupe performed the award-winner from the previous year, *Kwao Adjoba*, a social critique that focused on the need to reform African society from within. François-Joseph Amon d'Aby, director of the cultural center's performance, suggested that the theater marquee read "Le Folklore d'Afrique Noire" ("Black African Folklore") in order to speak plainly to the expectations of their Parisian audience. The troupe delivered with folkloric elements of dance and music tied together by the total theater aesthetic developed on both the Ponty stage and that of the cultural centers.

The Paris tour of the Ivorian troupe proved to be Cornut-Gentille's final feat of cultural diplomacy as high commissioner of French West Africa. By the time the C.C.F.C.I. performed in France in December 1956, he had already accepted a new position as French ambassador to the United Nations. The theatrical initiatives continued under the mandate of the new high commissioner, but African theater had lost an important ally, one that Maurice Sonar Senghor went so far as to credit in his memoir with having single-handedly facilitated a theatrical renewal in French West Africa.[31] Sonar Senghor also describes a more tumultuous relationship between African theater artists, both professional and amateur, and the new administration, which did not grant the same degree of importance to theatrical performance as a matter of diplomatic statecraft. The change was felt most keenly by the budding professional theater world in Senegal, which had begun requesting funding for a permanent theatrical troupe and a structure with salaried administrators and artists. Sonar Senghor's vision of such a professional troupe would have to wait for the cultural policies laid out by his uncle after independence.

In 1956, the same year as the C.C.F.C.I.'s performance in France, the "*loi-cadre*," which granted greater legislative autonomy to the territories of the French Union, brought a sudden end to the theatrical space of the cultural centers by placing their activities under the budgetary purview of the individual territories rather than that of the Union's larger general budget. The cultural centers organized a final tournament of La Coupe Théâtrale in 1957, which marked the end of this short-lived stage space but not of its legacy. The performers and playwrights who had gained prominence through La Coupe Théâtrale went on to influence local approaches to community performance in the decades that followed. They were also called upon to provide a projection of African theater abroad, and took part in discussions of that performance tradition's potential place within an emerging, globally minded notion of the theatrical avant-garde.

Debating African Theater at the Theater of Nations Festival

In March 1960, the year that saw all the former colonies of French West Africa fly the flag of independence, the members of the C.C.F.C.I. served once more as representatives of African theater for the sake of a European audience. This time they took the stage as part of an event that envisioned a reconfiguring of global theatrical practices (which included non-Western traditions) within a cosmopolitan and avant-gardist framework. Although largely forgotten today, the Festival International d'Art Dramatique de la Ville de Paris, later known as Le Théâtre des Nations, or the Theater of Nations, provided an artistic meeting point for theatrical approaches from throughout the world, bringing together non-Western forms with the work of such key figures of twentieth-century experimental theater as Peter Brook, Julian Beck, and Joan Littlewood.[32] Founded in 1954 with the support of the cultural impresario Claude Planson, the event took place annually at the Théâtre Sarah Bernhardt in central Paris. The festival brought together representative demonstrations of national performance cultures from throughout the globe, an approach that took on a markedly political tone in that time of decolonization.[33] The French theater scholar Odette Aslan, in her 2009 study of the event, which she calls "the most complex and singular of all the festivals established in France throughout the twentieth century," summarizes the place of the independent nation within the festival as a performance-sign in its own right, which facilitated a form of global tourism, providing spectators with the broadest possible selection of nationalist performance forms: "Rather than shows or troupes, [the festival] invited countries to the point of boasting of the number of flags gradually planted upon its map of the world."[34]

In 1960, the Theater of Nations event included a special focus on the performance cultures of Africa. The festival made a conscious attempt to denounce previous exoticizing treatments of African artists in France, such as the one extended to the Ponty students in their 1937 tour as part of that year's international exhibition. As Odette Aslan states, "the Theater of Nations put other cultures on display but asked the audience to watch and listen differently than with a curiosity for the 'exotic' or for the repetitive swaying of an African tribe or the piercing sonorities of oriental music."[35] In their interest in Africa's theater, the organizers nonetheless needed an institutional means of locating an "authentic" representation of African performance. For this, they turned to the former leaders of the French cultural centers, nearly all of whom were serving among the political elite of their respective independent nations. The festival thus featured a presentation from the National Troupe of Mali, as well as one from the National Ensemble of Côte d'Ivoire, newly formed by the members of the former C.C.F.C.I.

The Ivorian performance, directed by C.C.F.C.I. founding member Germain Coffi Gadeau, consisted primarily of displays of dance and folklore, with the exception of a short piece by Gadeau titled *Yaounda*, a single-act comedy about a mother who imposes on her son a divorce from a woman who is unable to bear him children. The presentation earned the festival's award for best traditional ensemble, further bolstering the reputation of an already heralded group of theater-makers. However, the evaluation of the performance as essentially traditional in nature and of an ensemble-based aesthetic reflected the organizers' eagerness to applaud a timeless image of African performance, one understood as emerging from an almost unconscious collective spirit rather than as the fruit of a poetic construction, much less an act of syncretic artistic experimentation. The festival did not take into account the degree to which the performers had developed their craft within a global aesthetic and political mindset, or how, by interweaving performance traditions, they aspired to take part in a creative spirit of activism and experimentalism on an equal footing with their European peers. In short, it reflected what has since been criticized as the Eurocentric flaw underlying Western avant-gardist discourse of the twentieth century, which made ample use of the work of non-Western performance forms, claiming to acknowledge (i.e., discover) such forms' inherent art value, while denying non-Western actors any role as agents in the same experimental creative discourse.[36]

African theater's place in the aesthetic imaginary of the European avant-garde movement came to focus in the festival's public discussions on whether traditional performance forms could be considered "theater" in the same vein as a European performance based on a written work of drama. Festival organizer Claude Planson defended the ethos of the event by insisting that the non-Western forms of traditional performance or folklore constituted examples of total theater far more vibrant than conventional Western theater because they were unencumbered by what he saw as the West's excessive attachment to the written word.[37] Planson therefore channeled an already established sentiment in the world of experimental theater, beginning with Antonin Artaud, that European theater must untether itself from its conventional deference to dramaturgy and the written word.[38] He also projected onto a theater championed by the educated elite of the African continent—men very much attached to the function of text and the written word—a timeless, ahistorical quality that was more consistent with ethnographic and colonial understandings of African culture than reflective of the creative process of the writers and intellectuals at the cultural centers' helm.

The festival envisioned African performance within its own experimental framework as an example of pure total theater, in contrast to what participants understood to be the moribund theatrical tradition of the West. However, it also denied African stage artists any poetic voice or agency in conversations around what total theater meant or the forms it should take. Thus when, during a festival debate, African participants expressed an interest in artistic exchange with their European peers, Claude Planson interjected: "I fear that your theater, by looking for authors, and out of a desire to create plays, will fall into the same error into which we have fallen. That is, that your theater, instead of being a *total theater* that includes dance, song, and music as well as words, will become a withering theater like our own, which has become nearly incapable of producing anything at all."[39] Present at the debate were key figures in the emergence and theorizing of a syncretic theatrical stage in Francophone West Africa, including the Senegalese theater scholar Bakary Traoré, the author Alioune Diop (of the famed literary magazine *Présence Africaine*), and the stage director Maurice Sonar Senghor. The discussion also included Charles Béart, the former director of the William Ponty School, who had by then established a reputation as a leading figure in the promotion and development of *théâtre noir*.

Béart's remarks at the conference debate reflected the concerns of early colonial humanists who sought to preserve the authenticity of African culture, thus resonating with a widely shared opinion among festival participants that any mutual artistic exchange with African creators risked furthering a deviation from the pure form of their performance practices. He contextualized the beginning of this relationship by stating: "The colonizer neither 'imported' nor 'inserted' theater into Africa. Colonization merely pushed along an evolution. It did so while also diverting and distorting it through the imposition of its Western criteria, which took away any spontaneity or liberty and therefore any authenticity. And African theater was built on the foundations of these imported theatrical forms."[40] Bakary Traoré, on the other hand, focused on the function of theater as a "social fact," one that should be considered for its everyday uses more than for its adherence to a certain aesthetic or form:

> One can say that African theater goes as far back as African civilizations. Inasmuch as theater is a social fact or, even better, a social

> representation, it is exclusively linked to everyday life and becomes a daily manifestation. Therefore, it translates the emotions, hopes, joys and sorrows of man. That is how we might generally characterize Black African theater.[41]

Claude Planson responded to the discussion by pushing back vehemently against the slightest exoticizing of the African performances in question, even if it meant protecting such forms from their own creators. Thus, when Maurice Sonar Senghor suggested that workshops be established to help young African authors create in accordance with their own folkloric customs, Planson reacted immediately to the mere mention of the term "folklore," insisting that the very term was inappropriate, since the forms to which Sonar Senghor referred constituted a kind of theater in their own right.[42]

Planson's objections reflected a certain idealized vision of an untouched African theater standing in as a foil to conventional Western approaches to performance and dramaturgy. But notwithstanding Planson's efforts to leave African theater unmarked by European influence, the Theater of Nations indeed provided a useful new cultural framework for its African guests. In its festivalization of cultural nationalism, the Theater of Nations sought to instantiate and assemble a new understanding of a global theatrical heritage. As such it prefigured the stagecraft of later Pan-African festivals, especially that of the 1966 First World Festival of Negro Arts held in Dakar, which I explore in the next chapter. That Amadou Cissé Dia, politician and author of *Les Derniers Jours de Lat Dior* (*The Last Days of Lat Joor*), the Senegalese contribution to the 1966 festival's theater program, sought, at the behest of Léopold Sédar Senghor, to present his play at the Theater of Nations festival suggests the importance of this event in the imagination of a new political class trained in the art of theatrical performance.[43]

Total Theater and the Nawetaan *Competitions*

The performance paradigm of the French cultural centers forged an enduring stage legacy that continues to hold sway over Senegalese models of community-based culture and theatrical activity. In terms of performance style, the system of criteria used by La Coupe Théâtrale led to a formalization in French West Africa of the total theater approach, which has certain elements in common with notions of total theater explored in a Western theatrical framework but takes on a localized meaning in the case of African performance. Like their European counterparts, African practitioners of total theater aspired to present pieces that made full use of the skills of their performers, employing forms of music, dance, and folklore as integrated parts of the entire whole of the dramatic performance. However, as the theater scholar Praise Zenenga points out in his writing on total theater in Africa, the African version of the form emerged from a particular relationship between histories and philosophies of performance that often run parallel to the avant-gardist European movement. Zenenga writes that, unlike in Western forms of total theater, in African contexts "the interaction of multiple texts and multiple modes of expression and performance reflects the sum total of the African historical experience."[44] The multidisciplinary performance results in what Zenenga calls a "unified, holistic aesthetic of experience" designed to delight popular audiences who are, in turn, able to recognize in the piece signs of their collective cultural and historical heritage.[45]

The channeling of a collective cultural heritage through total theater constitutes a central aspect of a contemporary form of community-based theater in Senegal known as the *nawetaan* performances. *Nawetaan*, a Wolof word meaning "to pass the rainy season," refers to a series of summer vacation activities organized for youth groups through athletic and cultural organizations called the Associations Sportives et Culturelles (ASC). In a similar spirit to the French cultural centers, which catered to a French-educated elite, the ASC arose as a means of channeling the energies of what was seen as a potentially troublesome youth movement. Since the 1950s, groups had gathered informally during the summer, especially around Dakar and its then new and poorly serviced outer districts populated by migrant workers, to compete in youth soccer tournaments.[46] In 1970 these groups, which had become critical of the government, were formalized in the current ASC structure by a new organization funded by the Ministry of Youth and Sports called the Organisation Nationale de Coordination des Activités de Vacances (ONCAV). The overall goal of the initiative was to promote among the nation's youth a sense of civic consciousness and moral fortitude, qualities that Senegalese political discourse of the 1970s and '80s often described as lacking in the country's youth population.[47] In an attempt to expand its scope beyond the young male population, ONCAV included cultural activities in the yearly competitions, organizing competitive encounters between theatrical troupes originating from the various urban neighborhoods of the Dakar region and beyond.

The *nawetaan* competitions have since expanded broadly throughout the country's urban and rural regions. The theatrical performances take place within a tournament structure connecting neighborhoods, cities, and regions, and eventually ending in a nationally televised event called Les Oscars des Vacances (The Vacation Oscars).[48] The performances can draw large crowds and often benefit from the moral and financial support of their home neighborhoods.[49] Troupes must create original, multidisciplinary pieces addressing a chosen theme for a given year. In 2014, I attended a number of *nawetaan* performances around the Dakar area. The theme for that year was "citizenship," a topic that encouraged the young troupes to consider the meaning and importance of civic responsibility. Most of the performances attracted large crowds of young spectators who applauded their friends and participated by chiming in with the expressions of citizenship written into the play. In their form, the *nawetaan* performances are something of a descendant of the former French cultural center productions. They have adopted the jury evaluation system once used by the centers, inviting local leaders and cultural figures to assess performances based on a set list of criteria. Like the performances of the cultural centers, the *nawetaan* productions are judged by the "discipline" demonstrated by the performers on stage. They are also evaluated based on what jury members perceive as the overall authenticity of folkloric representations, as well as the seamlessness with which creators have integrated the various required elements of the show into a coherent framing narrative. *Nawetaan* performances are expected to reflect an aspect of local identity and custom while including in their compositions examples of theater, poetry, folklore, and dance.[50]

Nawetaan performances are often used to highlight local folklore or to pay tribute to key figures in local or national history. Successful troupes can become a source of great pride for their respective neighborhoods, and their leaders often earn reputations that help them to transition to later careers in local government or administration. Aside from serving to instill a sense of civic responsibility among young performers, the performances also constitute the primary means of encounter, for the vast majority of Senegalese, with theatrical practice. However, their status as a form of poetic stagecraft is rarely acknowledged by the professional theater community, which tends to praise their contribution to the popularization of theater while cautioning against taking them as representative of a national theatrical culture. As the late Oumar Ndao, then director of culture for the city of Dakar, said in a 2012 interview: "Everyone has participated in these competitions at one time or another," said Ndao, himself a playwright and theater director. "That means we must have the greatest number of actors per capita in the world! And yet we don't produce *good* theater."[51] The debates around what, precisely, constitutes "good" theater in a Senegalese context will inform the acts of stagecraft explored in the second half of this book. Ndao's provocative assessment underscores the ambivalence that many conventionally trained theater artists feel with regard to the dominance of popular theater in Senegal. His view of the ASC performances also resonates with critical stances toward the theater of the cultural centers of the 1950s, both of which occupy a cultural space whose primary purpose is not just poetic but also social and political in nature.

✦

Though ultimately short-lived, the cultural centers constituted an important stage space in the continuation of the theatrical experiment begun at the Ponty School, where African students had contended with historical encounters with the civilizing mission writ large. The theater produced by the cultural centers did not find itself praised for dramaturgical excellence, either by its contemporary juries, or by later critical assessments. Moreover, the tournament structure which the centers applied to theatrical performance led to questionable results in instantiating any form of unity among the territories. The structure enabled the maintenance of a network of elite cultural leaders but, on the popular level, it pitted communities against one another in a form of status-seeking competition. However, the cultural centers did not serve merely as an instrument of colonial interests in French West Africa. Both the performance spaces and the cultural model they promoted proved useful, in the end, to an African leadership class that was keen on defending its interests in dialogue with, rather than in opposition to, the French project to revise the tenets of empire into the more federalist notion of a voluntary union of peoples. The theater-making that went into preparing the centers' activities led to the crafting of a new stage from which an emerging leadership class could try its hand at managing local cultural institutions and mobilizing communities through cultural activity. The experience helped to forge, in the Francophone African context, the performance style of total theater now practiced throughout the continent. It also fostered a mode of local intervention in the cultural and political sphere that would greatly serve the popular theater movement initiated shortly after independence by those who felt cast aside by national cultural institutions.

Chapter 3

✦

The 1966 First World Festival of Negro Arts

Hommes de Culture and the Epic Pan-African Stage

The 1966 Premier Festival Mondial des Arts Nègres (First World Festival of Negro Arts) in Dakar took place amid the excitement of newly gained independence for dozens of former African colonies. The event projected to the world the image of an artistically and intellectually vibrant African continent that was eager to talk back to centuries-old forms of racist colonial discourse. The idea to mount such a festival emerged before independence and out of discussions that took place at the Congresses of Black Writers and Artists in Paris in 1956, as well as in Rome in 1959. It was at the Rome Congress that the Société Africaine de Culture (African Cultural Society) led by Alioune Diop, Senegalese author and editor-in-chief of the literary magazine *Présence Africaine*, committed to taking on the organization of an international event in Africa that was meant to bring together Black artists and intellectuals from throughout the world. The early stages of the festival's planning owed much to Diop's tenacity as an organizer and his respected status among a rising global Pan-African movement.[1] However, in the era of independence, Léopold Sédar Senghor, the French-educated poet and first president of Senegal, became the festival's primary figurehead and turned the event into the large-scale global gathering that eventually took place throughout most of the month of April exactly six years into Senegal's existence as a nation.

Senghor saw in the festival an opportunity to display the cultural wealth of an African continent as it "rises slowly out of her ruins," as he stated in the festival program, in what he called a "testimony of faith in Man."[2] He also saw the festival as a vivid illustration of the triumph of Negritude, a cultural and political movement he helped found as a student in Paris that offered a full-throated defense of African civilization and its contribution to humanity. Senghor framed the festival as the dawn of a new future for what he called the Black soul and its new, self-determinant role in the world: "Surpassing apparent contradictions, the tangle of complexes inherited from colonialism, deeply felt in the heart and brain of Negritude grappling with primitive fears and today's nuclear threat, this appeal comes as an assertion, without arrogance, of the African ontological reality."[3] In fact, the festival, which attracted representatives from thirty African countries as well as from the African diasporas of France, the United Kingdom, the United States, Brazil, Haiti, and Trinidad and Tobago, had a far broader reach than that of any single Pan-African ideology. As a celebration and concerted melding of political and cultural identities forged in the long process of decolonization, the festival played a decisive role in recrafting post-independence culture to reflect the diversity of global Pan-African visions.

The theatrical stage of the Dakar festival hosted high-profile cultural events to match the fame of the eminent artists, intellectuals, and statesmen in attendance.[4] Since its independence from France, and thanks in large part to the sweeping cultural policies carried out by President Senghor, Senegal represented for many global onlookers the frontier of an African political and cultural renaissance.[5] Senghor used his position as a prominent African head of state to negotiate the financial and logistical support of foreign governments, including a U.S. delegation that secured the participation of such globally renowned figures as Duke Ellington, Louis Armstrong, Katherine Dunham, and Langston Hughes.[6] Alongside academic conferences, concerts, and exhibits ran a robust theatrical program featuring a combination of stage plays, dance pieces, and traditional performances. These included a presentation by the Alvin Ailey American Dance Theater, the original production of Nigerian playwright Wole Soyinka's *Kongi's Harvest*, and a performance of the Martinican author Aimé Césaire's best-known theatrical work, *La Tragédie du Roi Christophe* (*The Tragedy of King Christopher*), which was staged by French director Jean-Marie Serreau.

Though less heralded by the international press, the performance of *Les Derniers Jours de Lat Dior* (*The Last Days of Lat Joor*) by Amadou Cissé Dia, a Ponty School graduate and a government minister at the time of the festival, nonetheless captivated local audiences. The play highlighted the festival's interaction with a regional theatrical stage heritage that undergirded the event's Pan-African rhetoric and framing. At the large, open-air stadium venue of the Stade de l'Amitié on April 4, Senegal's national day of independence, spectators rallied around the production of Cissé Dia's tragedy, which included hundreds of performers and musicians, some on horseback, in a triumphant retelling of the life of one of the nation's most revered heroes. The performance marked the apotheosis of a theatrical genre born out of the work carried out both on the Ponty stage and in the French cultural centers. *Lat Dior* consecrated an epic stage space that made use of the dramaturgical material of African histories of encounter with colonial forces in order to provide a platform for envisioning new Pan-African futures in an era of political independence.

This chapter explores the 1966 Dakar festival as a site rich with overlapping local and transnational heritages. The festival constituted a tour de force in claiming collective cultural agency for the African continent. Senghor, in his own ambitions for the event, maintained a globally interconnected vision of culture that surpassed national boundaries. His model for culture reached beyond the moment of African nationalism or anticolonialism to dialogue with similar redefinitions of culture then taking place in Fifth Republic France. This interconnectivity deeply informed one of the primary stakes of the festival: instantiating the figure of the statesman as *homme de culture* (or "man of culture"), a wielder of the forms of stagecraft necessary to meet the contemporary demands of statecraft. In Dakar in 1966, debates around the role and reach of such stagecraft frequently evoked the place and meaning of "Culture"—a term Senghor often capitalized to emphasize its cross-cultural and transnational scope—as a politically legitimizing, community-forming agent. The stage performances of the festival played an important role in performing this new vision of culture which, in the Senegalese context, included a repurposing of historical narratives and a recasting of African resistance figures as both epic heroes and prototypical men of culture for an imminent and radically emancipatory African renaissance.

Defining Culture at the Pan-African Festivals

Recent scholarship on the World Festival of Negro Arts has examined the event's role as a defining moment for emerging models of Pan-Africanism. Energized by global discussions of the uses of culture by the newly independent African nations, the festival sought, as David Murphy writes, "to situate culture at the heart of the post-imperial world."[7] Thus, an effort of world-making, perhaps more than the nation-building typically associated with the event, drove the political and cultural impulse of its program. Of course, pride of place was granted to a specific ideological form of world-making, that of Senghor's Negritude. However, the festival proved highly generative for both its ideological allies and opponents. This comes to light particularly in the event's "aftermath," a term Christina McMahon uses to explore the national and transnational communities that often result from the contesting energies of events such as the cultural festival.[8] In its contribution to solidifying culture's role in political imaginings of post-independence Pan-African futures, and through its resuscitations via subsequent attempts to address its legacy, the Dakar festival constitutes a major site for reenvisioning culture as a collective tool of eminently political force.

As an event of cultural stagecraft, the 1966 Dakar festival served at least as often as a foil as it did as a model. The equally ambitious Premier Festival Panafricain d'Alger (First Pan-African Festival of Algiers) of 1969 offered, in many ways, a scathing ideological critique of its predecessor by presenting attendees with a more militantly revolutionary vision of cultural Pan-Africanism. The Algiers approach to culture reflected an unshakeable commitment to meeting all forms of European dominance with a spirit of revolutionary resistance.[9] By its very location, the 1969 event highlighted the cause of the Algerian nation which, unlike Senegal, had earned its independence from France by way of a protracted and bloody war. Moreover, many critics of the Dakar festival pointed out in Algiers the incongruity of any celebration of the defeat of colonialism at a time when the armed independence movements in Lusophone Africa raged on.[10] The 1966 Dakar festival did not include a delegation from Algeria or Guinea-Conakry, both of which abstained in protest, nor of Lusophone Africa. The latter omission led the Algiers organizers to draw a pointed contrast by foregrounding the ongoing struggle of Amílcar Cabral's African Party for the Independence of Guinea and Cape Verde. In Algiers, the anticolonial figure par excellence was then-deceased Martinican revolutionary Frantz Fanon, who had taken part in the armed movement for Algerian independence and was a vocal critic of Senghor's particular brand of cultural policy, which he considered fundamentally elitist and removed from the concerns of the nation as expressed by its people.

The debates that circulated amid the "aftermath" of both events, each of which staked a claim to the title of the "first" collective manifestation of Pan-Africanist energies, underscore the many political factors at play. Andrew Apter brings these to light in his study of the 1977 Pan-African festival in Lagos known as FESTAC.[11] This event first billed itself as the second edition of the Dakar festival until disputes with the festival committee's Senegalese representatives, most notably Alioune Diop, led to the progressive isolation of the proponents of Negritude. The inclusion in FESTAC '77 of a North African delegation in the festival's colloquium caused the deepest rift. For Senghor, the North African world belonged to a separate, Arab cultural zone, and thus its people could not speak with authority on the Black cultural forms the colloquium was to take as its theme. This stance reflected a position also held by Senghor and his organizers at the Dakar festival in 1966. Apter suggests, however, that in the context of FESTAC, the Senegalese delegation's insistence that North African representatives not participate, and its threat to boycott the event if they did, was also a response to the sting of relentless criticism aimed at Senghor in Algiers in 1969.[12] Moreover, the festival's organization inevitably reflected a struggle for cultural influence on the continent between the two countries, one of which found itself newly awash in petrodollars and positioned to usurp its Francophone rival as the cultural and political leader of the region.

For all of their ideological differences, what these dueling festival events shared proved more substantive than their disputes. They each, at their core, responded to a pressing need to weave the notion of a Pan-African culture into the political struggles and debates of the moment. As a practical matter, they also conceived of culture as a shared, democratizing heritage that spanned multiple artistic and intellectual disciplines and fields. In their oral history project on the major Pan-African festivals of the twentieth century, among which they include the Zaïre '74 festival which famously hosted the

"Rumble in the Jungle" bout between Muhammad Ali and George Foreman, Dominique Malaquais and Cédric Vincent point out that, disputes aside, the Pan-African festivals indeed displayed some striking similarities.[13] Most notably, the festivals showed remarkable consistency in organizing themselves around familiar cultural touchstones, such as colloquia, exhibits, and large public performances. This point converges with the argument of David Murphy who, in the introduction to his edited volume dedicated to the Dakar event, highlights subtle continuities that are often concealed by a rigid focus on the ideological differences used to frame these major Pan-African festivals.[14]

Negritude at the Dakar Festival

For Senghor, the 1966 First World Festival of Negro Arts in Dakar was to serve above all as a performative celebration of "the sum total of the values of Black civilization," his shorthand definition of Negritude.[15] However, and despite the centrality of Negritude to the festival as a whole, attendees and participants did not unanimously accept a single vision of cultural Pan-Africanism and its uses, nor was participation in the festival tantamount to falling in line with a Negritude worldview.[16] In fact, some of Negritude's most vocal critics—Wole Soyinka, filmmaker Ousmane Sembène, and scholar Cheikh Anta Diop among them—not only participated in the 1966 event but also received festival prizes for their work.[17] The festival also wound up facilitating popular forms of participation that ran counter to the charge that the event fostered an overly "bookish" elitism. Tsitsi Jaji, in her work on the coverage of the festival in the popular press, suggests that popular magazines like *Bingo* provided a way for readers to engage in a form of non-elitist participation from their own homes. These diverse forms of popular participation demonstrate above all that, rather than a monological assertion of a certain ideology, "the cultural festival is a form that is necessarily noisy, crowded, and contentious."[18] In a similar vein, Hélène Neveu Kringelbach explores the popular street dancing events that took place in spite of the organizers', and especially Senghor's, low esteem for and limited interest in such forms. For Neveu Kringelbach, "the dancing that went on at the 1966 World Festival of Negro Arts demonstrates the limits of attempts by state-led ideologies to control people's bodily and creative engagement with the world."[19]

Descriptions of the 1966 festival as merely a carefully curated stage for Negritude ideology also reflect a lopsided critical reception of Senghor's thought and legacy. Much of the scholarly opinion on Senghor's cultural vision came to echo the repeated condemnations of the president's most vocal critics, most notably those of the Beninese philosopher Stanislas Adotevi, who declared at the 1969 Algiers festival: "The current Negritude movement sets and coagulates for its own shameful purposes the most threadbare of theories on African traditions of which it claims to be the literary reflection."[20] Among the most savored grist to the mill of anti-Negritude commentators one finds an oft-cited phrase, written in one of Senghor's early essays titled "Ce que l'homme noir apporte" ("What the Black Man Contributes"), which states that "l'émotion est nègre comme la raison est hellène" ("emotion is Negro as reason is Hellenic").[21] Herein lies the proof, for Senghor's critics, that at the heart of Negritude one finds the reflection of the colonial notion, put into words by the philosopher Lucien Lévy-Bruhl, of the prelogical primitive mind that is fundamentally alienated from the powers of reason and rational thought.

The philosopher Souleymane Bachir Diagne has responded to such criticism by placing Senghor's claim in the context of the latter's broader philosophical project.[22] Diagne argues that Senghor sought to make visible an alternative way of knowing that emerged particularly from African works of art, which he saw as the African world's primary contribution to humanity. This reading of Senghor's thought thus begins with the president's attempts to reorient, in favor of African politicians and artists, the invisible dynamics governing the fields of culture, philosophy, and politics. The historian Gary Wilder also considers Senghor's view of art as central to the president's particular political philosophy, which is often interpreted as favoring an aggressive form of cultural nationalism. Wilder instead frames Senghor's approach as a practice of world-making that was envisioned in response to "the problem of freedom" at the end of empire.[23] Reading Senghor's poetry, Wilder underscores the driving force of forgiveness, which, he argues, deeply informed Senghor's political commitment to sustained connectivity with former colonial powers. For Wilder, this comittment was "entwined with [Senghor's] view that despite the boundaries created by sovereign states and recognized by international law, former imperial powers and former colonized peoples had no choice but to create a new set of arrangements *together* since they would remain entangled on this shared earth."[24] Wilder further characterizes Senghor's political model as beginning "with social interdependence and cultural reciprocity as the basis for new forms of transcontinental solidarity and postnational democracy," an approach, he argues, which has proven more fundamentally innovative than the appeals to cultural nationalism launched by contemporaneous (and rival) intellectuals such as Sékou Touré and Frantz Fanon.[25]

Senghor was not alone among African leaders in envisioning the arts as playing a determinant role in the emerging relation between new states, their populations, and the nation's identity within a global geopolitical context. However, his performance of the erudite statesman or *homme de culture* offered a nuanced contrast to the models of Guinean president Sékou Touré's populist militancy, and Ivorian president Félix Houphouët-Boigny's liberalized economics. In his essay "On National Culture," Frantz Fanon used the figure of the "man of culture" as a symbolic stand-in for the colonized African intellectual left "hypnotized," in his words, "by mummified fragments" of a long-gone version of African culture and blind to the pressing contemporary stakes at hand in what Fanon called a true national culture.[26] At the Dakar festival, Senghor readily assumed Fanon's prototypical figure of such a man of culture, making use of a scholarly image earned by way of his studies and teaching career in France. The poet-president, as Senghor was often called, stood as the figurative intellectual benefactor of the 1966 event. However, his perceived elitism also served as a key piece of a larger geopolitical and cultural strategy, reflecting, as Joshua Cohen has argued in the context of state-funded visual arts, a desire to form transnational modes of "worldly participation" through politics, "whereby modern art was envisioned to build international bridges through high-profile channels."[27] In embodying the role of the nation's founding father and man of culture, Senghor endeavored to perform a productive figure for the nation. He had, moreover, crafted his approach in a process of dialogue and contrast with other prominent statesmen, including France's first minister of cultural affairs, André Malraux, who was also trying to adapt to the political needs of a changing post-imperial world.

Senghor and Malraux: Embodying the Homme de Culture

The fact that André Malraux, because of his participation in the Dakar festival, became for many the bête noire of the 1969 Algiers festival hints at the French statesman's function and role as part of the broader spectacle of 1966. In Algiers, many expressed their vehement opposition to Malraux's presence within any Pan-African framework by signing a text that denounced his speech at the Dakar colloquium.[28] Malraux also appears in the documentary film on the Algiers festival by the American filmmaker William Klein, in which the statesman's image accompanies the words of Stanislas Adotevi's fierce criticism of Negritude. For post-independence African leaders defending the idea of a revolutionary Pan-African cultural movement, the seemingly innocuous participation of the French minister amounted to a politically insidious move to maintain French influence over the continent. However, his presence, most notably as the guest of honor at the 1966 festival colloquium, also indicates the transnational framework through which Senghor envisioned the double role of the statesman as a leader of state affairs and a man of culture, an actor of cultural stagecraft as well as statecraft.

Malraux's own double role as both prominent intellectual and leading statesman has often been evoked to highlight the neocolonial interests underlying his actions. France's commitment to a *rayonnement culturel* (or cultural radiation) served to justify the colonial power's continued cultural engagement with its former colonies. In an essay on Malraux's diplomatic and political ties to Africa, Catherine Coquio underscores the subtle role the minister played in ensuring France's continued economic dominance over its former colonies by operating in tandem with the interventionist schemes of his contemporary, Jacques Foccart. The latter orchestrated the rise of what became known as *françafrique*, the systematic corruption of new

African nations through direct support to autocratic regimes in exchange for access to resources.[29] For Coquio, "Malraux's 'lyrical' speeches capped off 'with a flourish' the operation which consisted of accepting the end of an empire in order to pass on the baton to another system of domination, efficient to the extent that it hid behind a series of agreements granting 'assistance' and 'cooperation,' ensuring France's support to its African 'friends' and vice versa."[30] The two power brokers of such an exchange, Foccart and Malraux, represented two aspects of the selfsame political process: enforcing alliances with the former African territories, either through direct economic means in the case of Foccart, or, in that of Malraux, by promoting a model of *rayonnement culturel*, as Coquio writes, "by a France called to play its emancipating and 'fraternal' role within a 'universal civilization' of which it is understood to hold the key."[31]

Malraux's mission to redefine culture came with his 1959 nomination as the head of France's new Ministry of Cultural Affairs, the first of its kind, created under President Charles de Gaulle. The ministry had as its goal to democratize culture, disseminate works, and foster cultural activities among the provinces. It took on the double task of deciding which works to establish in the pantheon of a cultural heritage of humanity while facilitating a more democratic interaction between such a heritage and the greater public.[32] Malraux compared his role, in nature and scope, to that of Jules Ferry, who enacted sweeping national educational reforms at the beginning of France's Third Republic, making the republican schools of the nation free, mandatory, and secular. Malraux's ministry aimed, in his words, "to do what the Third Republic accomplished, in its republican spirit, for education: we must ensure that each French child has access to paintings, theater and cinema, just as he has to the alphabet."[33]

A newly inaugurated network of *maisons de la culture* (or culture houses) constituted a key tool in accomplishing Malraux's goal, but these also shared a formative connection with the *centres culturels* of the French African colonies discussed in chapter 2. Many of the former colonial administrators of the French colonies, having found themselves in search of employment in the wake of decolonization, came to play an essential role in pursuing the goals of Malraux's decolonization of culture in France.[34] The skill set required to establish and promote the African cultural centers of the 1950s corresponded to that sought out by a new ministry which at the time was struggling to recruit graduates from the traditional channels of France's prestigious *grandes écoles*. Malraux's first right-hand man in implementing his ministry, a former colonial administrator and director of cultural initiatives in Africa named Émile Biasini, recalls his first directive from Malraux as: "I want you to do for me in France what you have done in Africa."[35] Under Biasini's supervision, the ministry soon became what one collaborator, Jacques Renard, called "the scraps of the AFOM, the administrators of the French colonies, made redundant by decolonization."[36] Biasini later remarked that he applied many of the same "bush methods" in both the French and African contexts. For him, both required a sense of entrepreneurialism mixed with a willingness to collaborate with and lead negotiations among diverse populations that often held confrontational stances toward government bureaucrats. More importantly, as Herman Lebovics points out in his chapter on this bridge between the rise of the cultural technocrat in Africa and France, Malraux's ministry represented a continuation of colonial efforts in Africa, since "what was not fully carried out in far off Africa could be done for the regions of the European land—and for the same reasons: to cultivate loyalty to France."[37]

A concern for Africa's loyalty to France certainly motivated many of Malraux's official functions in the early 1960s, when he traveled to a succession of former French colonies to represent France at the celebration of their independence.[38] In his later writings on the era of decolonization in *Le Miroir des limbes*, Malraux focused on the immense task that lay before the continent's new heads of state, seeing the popular masses as a force to be channeled by their leaders rather than as a democratizing agent. Of his experience in Chad, he wrote: "From what savanna emerged this crowd in Africa and Asia that seemed to jump out from all sides? With his blue dancers, his mask-bearers, his Carolingian cavalry, President Tombalbaye . . . was supposed to form a state."[39] Standing at the podium of the Dakar festival's colloquium in 1966, Malraux expressed a similar concern for the work to be done not by the masses but by the leaders, in this case his fellow man of culture Léopold Sédar Senghor, in language imbued with a solemn sense of a historic present. "Here we are in history," he declared. "For the first time, a head of state takes into his mortal hands the spiritual destiny of a continent."[40] Malraux shared a vision with Senghor of the role of the cultivated statesman for whom the affairs of culture appeared necessarily indissociable from affairs of state. In fact, culture and the state proved as mutually informative for both men as did the co-emergent notions of culture they developed in the respective contexts of post-independence Senegal and Fifth Republic France.

Crafting a Post-Independence Theatrical Heritage

The performing arts were a central part of Senegal's cultural policy from the moment of the country's independence from France in 1960. And while the founders of the new nation's cultural institutions were intent on highlighting the contribution and value of "traditional" forms to Senegal's cultural heritage, they also made ample use of a stage heritage passed on from the performances of the William Ponty School, where Senegal's homegrown "men of culture" had first learned to use the theater to respond to policies and initiatives imposed by French colonialism. In the context of the Dakar festival, these same elites now found themselves charged with the task of fostering, through the stage, a sense of shared identity within and across the national boundaries of an independent Africa. They turned largely to the historical material that had once animated the Ponty stage, this time in order to develop the figure of the epic and often tragic African historical hero as a proto-nationalist leader and *homme de culture*.

Thus, the Senegalese stage epic became a featured genre of the Daniel Sorano National Theater, which was inaugurated in Dakar in 1965 in order to serve as the main stage venue of the following year's festival. The theater's national company housed several distinct troupes. The Ballet National du Sénégal grew from the former Ballet Africain de la Fédération du Mali, which specialized in African dance forms and had performed at the Theater of Nations festival in 1960. The Sorano company also launched the Ensemble Lyrique Traditionnel, a separate troupe specializing in "popular" performance forms that was conceived to represent, for Senegalese audiences, the country's long history of traditional music and praise-singing. The national theater's Troupe Nationale Dramatique carried on the practice, initiated at the William Ponty School and revived at the French cultural centers, of appropriating the stage as a space for interweaving Western and African theatrical traditions. Along with its productions of original Senegalese plays, such as Abdou Anta Ka's *La Fille des dieux*, which inaugurated the theater and had debuted in 1956 at the Théâtre du Palais, the troupe soon produced several adaptations of works from the Western canon, such as a production of Molière's *The Imaginary Invalid* as well as an adaptation of Gogol's *The Government Inspector* titled *Monsieur Podevin*, a satire on the problem of government corruption among independent African nations.

Through Sorano's global profile, national stage culture served as a diplomatic tool, much as the Franco-African stage had done in the interwar and postwar performance tours of *théâtre indigène* in metropolitan France. In the new era of political independence, the Senegalese national troupes often traveled in tandem with President Senghor, embarking on international tours meant to promote Senegalese culture abroad while contributing to the development of a tourism industry back home. In 1969, the dramatic troupe toured to France to perform an "Africanized" version of *Macbeth* based on an adaptation by the Belgian playwright Maurice Maeterlinck. In Paris, the company performed at the prestigious Théâtre National de l'Odéon in a production that counted among its audience members President Senghor himself, as well as then French Minister of Cultural Affairs Edmond Michelet. French reviews of the performance remarked extensively on the suitable nature of Shakespeare's world to what reviewers saw as the African "mentality," an assertion that recalls similar reactions to the Ponty students' Paris performance in 1937.[41] In the case of this production, the "savagery" of the sorcery and clan warfare of medieval Scotland found a fitting embodiment, in the French observers' estimation, in the worldview of African performers who, one journalist further argued, must feel far closer to Shakespeare's world than might any overly Cartesian French performer.[42] While French audiences contemplated the compatibility of Shakespearean dramaturgy with their own exoticized notions of African rituals and sorcery, Sorano's artistic director, Maurice Sonar Senghor, instead saw the production as a symbol of the troupe's engagement with a global theatrical heritage. His stance reflected the urgency of what he saw as Sorano's two primary goals: "We must first educate a people that finds itself confronted with the problems of its young independence. We then must restore our national heroes and bring to life an epic theater that is African in its essence."[43]

Lat Joor as an Epic National Hero and Man of Culture

The staging of the historical narrative of Lat Joor, or Lat Joor Ngoone Latiir Jóob, a major historical figure in Senegal remembered as both a great opponent of colonial rule and the unifier of the kingdoms of Kajoor and Bawol, responded to the need, expressed by Sonar Senghor, to found an epic stage while addressing the challenges that lay before the young Senegalese nation. As Ruth Bush points out in her reading of the play as one of the major "performances of the past" that ran throughout the Dakar event: "A dramatic reconstruction of Lat Joor as hero and anti-colonial martyr sat comfortably within a certain narrative of post-independence Senegalese nationalism oriented around recuperation of a shared past."[44] Lat Joor's story also proved particularly useful at the Dakar festival in supporting President Senghor's mission to assert a sense of cultural independence that would unite the country's diverse communities while encouraging continued exchange and connectivity with the former colonizer. Like Senegal's first president, Lat Joor served an important unifying role as a decisive leader of an emerging Senegalese nation. However, he is far from the only such foundational figure. The Senegalese historical epic at the Dakar festival stage situates the hero's resistance narrative within a constellation of fellow founding fathers, thus envisioning a Senegalese identity forged in the frictional and at times antagonistic moments of contact between these figures.

Performed twice during the festival, with a triumphantly received debut at the Stade de l'Amitié (today's Stade Demba Diop) on Senegal's national day of independence, *Les Derniers Jours de Lat Dior* took up the stage heritage of the William Ponty School—of which its author, Amadou Cissé Dia, was a graduate—by revisiting the encounter of a regional African leadership with encroaching colonial forces. The heroes of the Dakar '66 stage were posited as such by virtue of the sacrifices they made for the free African nations to come. Their actions gave body and voice to the anticipatory vision needed to recast the regional leaders and dissidents of the nineteenth century in a founding-father role to the nation-states not yet imagined on the stages of Ponty or the cultural centers. Cissé Dia's play also included popular performance forms via musical and dance interludes. The production offered its festival audience an open-air spectacle, with a cast of over two hundred and

Figure 3.1. A rehearsal of *Les Derniers Jours de Lat Dior* at the Stade de l'Amitié. Film still from *African Rhythms*, directed by Irina Venzher and Leonid Makhnatch.

the appearance on stage of Lat Joor's cavalry, which rode into the stadium grounds. The nature of the performance, which mixed drama, music, dance, and spectacle for an in-the-round setting in a venue that permitted forms of verbal audience response to the stage action, set it apart from the festival's other theatrical offerings. As a point of contrast, Jean-Marie Serreau's staging of *La Tragédie du Roi Christophe*, which featured Douta Seck, one of Senegal's most iconic stage performers, remained ensconced in the proscenium format of the national theater, which was located in the wealthy neighborhood of Plateau. At the popular site of the Stade de l'Amitié, a stadium which was typically used for sporting events, *Lat Dior* proved far more accessible to a local Senegalese audience.

Sonar Senghor commented in his memoir on the significance of the *Lat Dior* performance to the Senegalese public. He pointed out that this production not only attracted the greatest number of spectators but also included the participation of multiple layers of Senegalese society: "There was a wonderful surge of participation: the National Army, the students of the National Institute of Arts, the great traditional griots, and above all the tremendous enthusiasm of masses of spectators who seemed electrified."[45] The performance's success in bringing together such a broad sample of Senegalese society ensured the production's status as a watershed moment for local theatrical performance. In an interview, the festival attendee and Senegalese stage director Seyba Traoré spoke to the importance of the *Lat Dior* production to later performers and artists: "People often remember that at the First World Festival of Negro Arts in Dakar, the triumph was *La Tragédie du Roi Christophe*. But what they forget is that the most popular play, the one that brought out all the Dakar locals, was not *Christophe*. It was *Lat Dior*!"[46] Indeed, the legacy of having mobilized a large local audience rather than just an elite upper stratum of Dakar society made the festival performance of *Lat Dior* one of the touchstone events of the later popular theater movement, which I discuss in the final chapter of this book.

In his staged reconfiguring of historical narratives in *Les Derniers Jours de Lat Dior*, Cissé Dia begins with a reenactment of the encounter between his protagonist, Lat Joor, and the figurehead of French colonial encroachment at the time, General Louis Faidherbe. In contemporary commemorative practices, depictions of and performances featuring the French general have long played a prominent role in popular representations of Senegal's history and cultural heritage.[47] In Cissé Dia's play, Faidherbe figures as a nineteenth-century agent of modernization. Among the better-known aspects of Faidherbe's career of colonial conquest and administration in the region is his plan to create a railway connecting Senegalese cities and ports of trade, an initiative to which Lat Joor famously launched a tenacious and ultimately successful resistance effort. Yet, Cissé Dia depicts the agonistic relationship of these two figures of Senegalese history as reflecting two complementary contributions to the shared project of the nation to come. Faidherbe represents the modernizing initiatives that the independent Senegalese nation aspired to implement at the time of the Dakar festival, while Lat Joor embodies the popular acceptance and national symbolism needed for such a project to claim political legitimacy.

Cissé Dia portrays a Faidherbe frustrated by Lat Joor's resistance, yet deeply respectful of the man himself and what he has come to represent for the Senegalese people. Faidherbe initially affirms the progress made by French military encroachment in the region: "Jolof has finally been pacified and Siin and Saalum are at peace! And Waalo has been pacified! . . . Everywhere there reigns a relative calm, but it is enough for us to bring to fruition our great plans for creating a highly developed Senegambia." He then enumerates the modernizing initiatives he hopes to lead for the good of the population: "[The region] would benefit from secular schools, an efficient health system, and prosperous agriculture and livestock farming! It would above all benefit from a railway that would serve as the lifeline for this country!"[48] His project would certainly resonate with the one awaiting the political leaders of a now-independent Africa in search of modernization. Yet the national hero, or the legitimacy of acting in the name of a national character, frustratingly eludes the French general: "And all of that, once again, risks being completely ruined by one man alone: Lat Joor!" (26). And further on: "Lat Joor is always present, everywhere present, using our own guerilla methods . . . As soon as he appears, his ceddos [a local warrior caste] ignite like dry grass; all he has to do is speak and they return to the fight!" (26–27).

Though purporting to act for the good of the Senegalese population, Faidherbe will never benefit from the degree of loyalty that Lat Joor inspires, thus making his mission a modernizing one devoid of political legitimacy. Cissé Dia's Faidherbe forcefully imposes an attitude of respect toward Lat Joor on his subordinates and expresses his own admiration for the man: "And the paradox, Lieutenant, the paradox is that I will never be able to hate this man! I will always respect him!" (27). He even engages in the kind of anticipatory imaginings of the future nation characteristic of the epic heroes of the independent African stage at the Dakar festival, speaking of Lat Joor as a symbol for the ideal of a future nation and evoking such an ideal to justify his own actions: "In building up Senegambia, is it not for Lat Joor, that is, for the idea he represents, am I not working to achieve the same goal?" (30). Yet without the political authority of one like Lat Joor, the general's actions fall short and must await the emergence of a national hero to legitimize his modernizing projects. In the framework of the Dakar festival, such a depiction served to recuperate Faidherbe as a useful national symbol for a desirable modernization, but one that required the Senegalese, and thus independent African, leadership for its proper execution.

In the epic hero's journey through the historical and cultural touchstones of a brewing national and Pan-African character, Cissé Dia includes a fateful encounter between Lat Joor and the founder of the Sufi order of the Muridiyya, Shaykh Amadu Bamba. The Sufi saint here represents the spiritual character of a nation where an overwhelming majority of the population is Muslim, with most adhering to one of four major Sufi orders. Cissé Dia takes something of a risk in including Bamba in his stage production. Images of this local Sufi saint play a central role in the spiritual lives of Murid devotees. Reproductions of the single photograph taken of Bamba by colonial authorities in 1913 allow Murids to disseminate the Islamic figure's *baraka*, or aura, not only for themselves but for all who lay eyes on the image.[49] A powerful iconography of Bamba has thus emerged, but one that is not to be used lightly. Although reproductions of the saint's image abound, the act of embodying Bamba as a stage role was an unprecedented move in the performing arts, and one reprised to great effect shortly after the festival by a traveling popular theater from Kaolack, as discussed in the next chapter. On stage, the performed image of Bamba would enact, for the Muridiyya, the same ocular transmission of *baraka* that takes place via visual reproductions of the saintly figure.

Cissé Dia depicts these two foundational national heroes at a pivotal moment when the king, in a period of brief retreat from military activities, consults with the renowned spiritual teacher.[50] Cissé Dia's staging depicts the moment as a strategic crossroads in Lat Joor's response to French forces which has, furthermore, sparked a personal crisis of faith in the main character.

Lat Joor expresses a sense of battle fatigue along with doubts regarding the purpose of his resistance, declaring: "the warrior in me has died. My wish, Bamba, is to embark with you on the conquest of souls for the glory of Islam . . . and of God" (41). Bamba delivers to the king a message of perseverance in the face of adversity, born out of a sense of serving a grander, sacred purpose. Lat Joor responds to Bamba's encouragement by asking: "Will it be possible, then, for other generations—for my son, for our grandsons—to understand your great message . . . and to carry it out?" (46). In the published version of Cissé Dia's play, the otherworldly quality that the Bamba character must transmit on stage is expressed by printing the figure's lines, which consist solely of verses of the Koran, in italics. On stage, Lat Joor's question posed to the Sufi master echoed the earlier musings of General Faidherbe, both of which project the values of modernity and spirituality through the vision of a future nation to come for which the epic hero Lat Joor will serve as a cohering symbol.

The nature of Lat Joor's authority in Cissé Dia's play is military, but also, and perhaps primarily, cultural. He serves not only as the protector of his people but also as the guardian of its cultural identity, interweaving his role as chief with that of man of culture. Thus, when the *almamy*, or king, of the neighboring Tukulor kingdom sends a messenger to propose an alliance against the French, he sends with them a chorus of slaves who use the occasion to perform a song before Lat Joor's court and attendant soldiers. The song has an intoxicating effect on the soldiers. Cissé Dia indicates in his stage directions that they are almost possessed by the sound and noisily express their admiration. Recognizing the ploy of the *almamy*, Lat Joor puts a stop to the music, declaring, "That's enough! . . . So, Amadu Séexu intended to degrade our souls, to weaken our hearts and our arms, in order to defeat us!" (20–21). He dismisses the Tukulor soldiers and calls his own griot, who takes center stage to lead the assembly, as well as the audience at the festival, through a didactic rendering of the individual elements of a traditional musical ensemble of Kajoor and Bawol. A progression builds, with each instrument adding its sound to the final crescendo. In a statement to the king, the griot declares: "Dammel-Teeñ Lat Joor, when each of these voices resounds together . . . when all at once we hear the rhythm of our joy, our anger, our Negritude, then, Dammel-Teeñ Lat Joor, nothing, nothing can resist the People of Kajoor and Bawol" (23).

The cultural expressions of the visiting Tukulor are not innocuous in the world of this staging, but rather come with the power to diminish the resolve of Lat Joor's soldiers, who rediscover their strength in the source of cultural "Negritude," a term whose use reminds audience members of the contemporary founding figure present at the Dakar festival. In the spirit of Senghor's event—and as many of Senghor's most ardent critics would agree—culture proves a high-stakes affair. It provides a vehicle for the sense of loyalty Lat Joor inspires among his people, which Faidherbe tries in vain to channel for the good of his modernizing mission. It grants Lat Joor the legitimacy to carry forth the message of Bamba as the representative of a proleptically imagined Senegalese nation. Culture provides the link between a historical legacy reenacted on the theatrical stage and the concerns of what Sonar Senghor called "a people that finds itself confronted with the problems of its young independence." Culture is the business of chiefs and, by extension, of the heads of state now recasting their role, in line with Senghor's vision, as that as of modernizers, moral authorities, and leading men of culture in their respective countries.

Cheikh Aliou Ndao and the Revolutionary Epic Stage

The dramaturgical model of the African epic continued to serve at the Daniel Sorano National Theater and on the stage of the Pan-African festivals as a form that allowed a cultural elite to pose the most challenging political and cultural questions of its time. Senegal, home of the Ponty stage, proved the pioneer of the historical epic, winning the prize for drama at the second ("first") Pan-African festival in Algiers, despite the event's anti-Negritude tone. The Senegalese entry in the theatrical program, Cheikh Aliou Ndao's best-known stage work, *L'Exil d'Albouri* (*The Exile of Albury*), shifted away from the Negritude-friendly, "man of culture" model espoused by Cissé Dia. In his prologue to the published version of *Albouri*, Ndao declares his view of the advantages and goal of the epic form: "A history play is not a history thesis. My goal is to contribute to the creation of myths that galvanize the people and point the way."[51] Ndao's view embraces the inevitably political element of theater, and his refusal to engage in art for art's sake corresponds tellingly with the overall tone of the Algiers festival where his play received its first accolades. The past does not serve to validate the political realities of the present, as it seems to do in Cissé Dia's *Lat Dior*. Rather, it is evoked to transform the present and reimagine radical new futures, or, as stated in the Algiers festival booklet: "Culture has for its starting point the people as a self-creating transformer of its surroundings. Culture in its largest and fullest sense allows men to take control of their lives."[52]

In his historical epic, Ndao stages the story of another of Senegal's historic resisters of colonial expansion: Albury Penda Djeme Njaay. A key figure in the history of the Jolof kingdom whose territory extended north of the Senegalese nation, Albury fought French colonial forces until his death in what is today Niger.[53] Ndao focuses his play on a fateful decision made by the king when, upon learning of the arrival of a French battalion that he could not hope to overcome, he elects, against the wishes of his own army, family, and supporters, to retreat into exile in the northern city of Segu. He thus breaks with traditional expectations to stand his ground to the death, but he does so in anticipation of a greater conflict to come. Justifying his actions, Albury declares to his entourage: "My gaze does not stop at our small kingdom; it

Figure 3.2. Doura Mané as the lead character in *L'Exil d'Albouri* at a rehearsal in Algiers. Film still from *Festival Panafricain d'Alger*, directed by William Klein.

embraces the entire future" (34). Just as with Cissé Dia's use of historical time in *Lat Dior* to speak to the present, Ndao depicts a protagonist whose vision holds implications for those united around the stage of the Algiers event. Through his actions, Albury articulates a belief in the possibility of a future movement of Pan-African unity and resistance. But whereas Lat Joor defines his role through consultation with his fellow founding members of the Senegalese nation, Albury reflects a longer Pan-African struggle marked by a drastic break with tradition. Instead of negotiating with colonial forces or standing his ground as custom would have it, the king discerns a third, uncharted way, that of dissident noncompliance with what is expected of him.

In his reading of Ndao's play, John Conteh-Morgan considers *Albouri* to be one of the more sophisticated African history plays because it shows "a refreshing concern with plot structure," as well as "a desire to craft an absorbing story that is often absent in French African history plays."[54] The play also includes a revolutionary element that echoed the tone of the Algiers festival in 1969. In one of its more remarkable scenes, the play depicts with chilling clarity the importance of an unshakeable solidarity within the revolutionary Pan-African cause. As Albury and his followers are preparing to leave for exile, his attendant halts the action abruptly by throwing on stage a man who has been tied up, explaining: "This man is a traitor. He was dissuading people from following you." "Let him die," Albury replies. "Rather than shoot him, slit his throat; let his blood water the land . . . May his entrails provide a feast for the thieving hyenas" (80). The execution of the traitor serves no obvious purpose in the overall arc of Ndao's carefully crafted stage narrative. It stands in contrast to other stagings of collective violence that are likely to shock Western audiences. In Wole Soyinka's *Death and the King's Horseman*, for example, the titular character's (failed) act of ritualistic suicide is central to the story's progression. What Ndao's execution of the traitor does accomplish, however, is the depiction of an uncompromising collective commitment to the cause of radical social change. As a vocal critic of Senghor within the poet-president's own country, Ndao, who is also known for his later contributions to the production of Wolof-language literature, presents a level of commitment to anticolonial revolution that stands in stark contrast to the more reasoned approach of *hommes de culture* like Cissé Dia.

Moreover, Ndao's stage narrative resonates with a larger discussion around the use of violence in resistance to colonial encroachment. Although the king goes into retreat in order to avoid a violent conflict, Ndao posits through his play that revolution and resistance cannot take place without acts of violence, sometimes severe, wrought upon the West, or even upon members of one's own community when necessary. The revolution, Ndao seems to argue, will not transpire through reasoned discourse with the oppressor. In this he joins Frantz Fanon, a vocal critic of Senghor's *homme de culture* model of liberation, who wrote: "Challenging the colonial world is not a rational confrontation of viewpoints. It is not a discourse of the universal, but the impassioned claim by the colonized that their world is fundamentally different."[55] If the staged retelling of Lat Joor's story in Dakar served as a galvanizing symbol of African unity, the model of Fanon suggested the possibility of such unification facilitated, when required, by acts of violence.

✦

The reworkings of historical stage narratives that began with the theatrical creations of the William Ponty School, and which characterized much of the theatrical production of Francophone Africa in the years following political independence, proved highly useful to the Pan-African festivals discussed above. The political and cultural visions embodied and performed on stage varied considerably, showing that the epic style, like the Pan-African festivals themselves, could facilitate a range of ideological proposals. The key function of the historical epic in the festival context was to explore the place of culture in the work of the continent's men of state, the contemporary surrogates for the historical figures of African resistance. If an alternative form of statecraft was required of those expected to lead their newly independent countries, the stagecraft of the historical epic provided a means of exploring possible relations between these men of state, their history, culture, and people. The epic stage therefore proved just as useful to the vision of post-independence African statesmen as *hommes de culture* as it did to a view of Pan-Africanism that saw independence as an ongoing and often violent struggle.

In the decades following the World Festival of Negro Arts, the Daniel Sorano National Theater served as a platform for later developments and iterations of the epic theatrical style.[56] Such stage epics continued to play a role in official realms of culture and commemoration. Ferdinand de Jong and Vincent Foucher have noted the symbolic importance of a shortened performance of Aimé Césaire's *La Tragédie du Roi Christophe* at the inauguration of Senegalese president Abdoulaye Wade's controversial African Renaissance monument.[57] An attempted renewal of the historical epic has also marked certain occasions at Wade's Grand Théâtre National; this is an institutional project so similar to that of Senghor's Sorano Theater that it has fed criticisms according to which Wade was merely attempting to outdo his long political rival by taking on the same initiatives, but executing them on a larger scale.[58] These examples highlight the degree to which the epic form may serve not only revolutionary intentions but also the interests of politicians eager to use culture as a means of drawing, or at least symbolizing, popular support for their infrastructural *grands projets*.

Yet, while the Sorano Theater came to constitute a cultural landmark for the nation and continent, its appeal to a broader Senegalese audience proved limited from the start. The following three chapters will examine the reasons for such limitations by exploring the history and legacy of three cultural stage spaces—those of Sufi pageant plays, telefilms, and popular theater—that lie at the outskirts of Senegal's official theater history but which have, nonetheless, left indelible marks on the country's performance heritage. Whereas the sites of performance examined thus far have sought to use the Western stage space as a platform for political dialogue with a European colonial and cultural heritage, the "unofficial" stages studied in the second half of this book invite a thorough reworking of the very architecture and language of theatrical performance. They reimagine the forms of interaction the stage enables between performers and audience, and they reenvision the scope and meaning of crafting a decolonizing stage space in the post-independence era.

Chapter 4

✦

Staging Sufi Stories

The Religious Stage Space of *Bamba Mos Xam*

At performance sites such as the William Ponty School or the World Festival of Negro Arts, the dynamics of staged role-play proved a powerful tool for engaging with a global audience on the conditions of shared futures. As actors in a play, stage artists could step in and out of French and African roles to perform a meeting of civilizations and minds. The stage hosted a variegated fabric of modes of performance that included reenactments of myth and ritual, philosophical dialogues, and collective appeals to a new and rising sense of nationalism. Yet certain aspects of Senegal's cultural and historical heritage could not yet find their way into the confines of the performance stage as it emerged and developed from the Ponty School onward. It remained to be seen, for example, if the stage could host performed manifestations of the country's ubiquitous Sufi Muslim cultures of religious expression. More specifically, could theatrical role-play be used to stage the life stories of the country's venerated religious leaders and Sufi saints?

The scholastic stage that emerged in the years of the Ponty School presented itself as a fundamentally secular one. To attend a performance of ritual at Ponty or at the World Festival of Negro Arts was to do so not as a participant in the staged action but rather as a spectator-observer. The stage placed religious practices, historical reenactments, and myth upon the same platform, effectively homogenizing their mode of interaction with audience members. How might the same stage be appropriated and recrafted by a spiritual ontology with a sacred understanding of practices of representation and embodiment? Could the sacred reclaim the Western stage in the Senegalese context as a conduit for alternative forms of knowledge to those promoted by French theatrical culture? These questions lay at the heart of a post-independence touring theatrical production launched in 1968 by a group of stage artists hailing not from the cosmopolitan coastal urban areas but from the city of Kaolack in the inland region of Bawol. Here a deep connection to Senegal's history as a predominantly Sufi Muslim country meshed with a long-standing commitment to the preservation and promotion of

Figure 4.1. A Dakar street mural depicting Maam Shaykh Ibrahima Faal, Sëriñ Faliilu Mbakke, and Shaykh Amadu Bamba. Photograph by Gino Canella.

popular and traditional performance. The touring production, which went on to tour continuously throughout the country for over fifteen years, was called *Bamba Mos Xam* (a title that loosely translates from Wolof as "to taste Bamba is to know") and recounted the life and deeds of Shaykh Amadu Bamba, founder of the Sufi order of the Murids, or Muridiyya. In the course of its long production history, *Bamba Mos Xam* set the foundations of a religiously inspired use of the theatrical stage space.

Throughout urban and rural Senegal, one finds reproductions of the only known image of Amadu Bamba, a 1913 colonial photograph that has become the centerpiece of a rich and interactive culture of religious iconography among Murid devotees. As Allen and Mary Nooter Roberts have demonstrated in their book and exhibition *A Saint in the City: Sufi Arts of Urban Senegal*, the image of Bamba performs a crucial spiritual function through its multiple palimpsestic reproductions in the cityscape.[1] The visual manifestation of Bamba serves to transmit the saint's *baraka* (a term often translated as "charisma," but which the Roberts translate as "aura" and Fallou Ngom glosses as "spiritual earnings"), passing on spiritual blessings to onlookers as well as to those who facilitate the image's reproduction, circulation, and viewing. The image functions beyond the realm of metaphor. It does not "stand in" for another, implied meaning, but rather facilitates a relationship that brings the viewer into ocular contact with Bamba's spiritual essence. Given the prominence of such representational practices, any theater troupe eager to present a staged adaptation of Bamba's life could not do so without carefully considering the work of stagecraft required to render acceptable a staged embodiment of the saint that gave voice and movement to the sacred image. Could an actor's body on stage also take on a representational value beyond the metaphorical, assuming the essence of the Sufi saint in order to facilitate, through performance, a transmission of his *baraka*? How would Senegalese audiences react to, and interact with, such a stage conceit while respecting a sense of role-play that allowed actors to step into and out of the role of a religious figure?

Today there exists a large body of scholarship on the history, expressive practices, and belief system of the Muridiyya.[2] The facts of Bamba's life form the touchstones of what devotees celebrate as his path to sainthood through sacrifice, suffering, and forgiveness, or what Fallou Ngom has called the "pledge of suffering" at the heart of the Murid master narrative.[3] Born in 1853 in the inland village of Mbakke to a noted Islamic judge, or *qadi*, Bamba grew up to become a spiritual teacher, or what the French called a *marabout*, of great note. The movement he founded shunned worldly concerns in favor of a singular focus on drawing oneself closer to God. Bamba's masses of followers eventually threatened the status of other Sufi teachers while also testing the nerve of colonial authorities, who suspected the marabout of following in the footsteps of contemporaneous leaders of armed jihads in the region. The French responded by sending Bamba on the first of two long exiles in 1895. He spent seven years in captivity in Gabon and later an additional four years in forced exile in Mauritania. Upon his return, and once the colonizers came to understand that he had no intention of waging war, Bamba became an ally of the French. His pacific stance reflected the conviction that Islamic devotion must stand separate from and above all forms of earthly political concerns. His was what Cheikh Anta Babou has studied as the "greater jihad" of the soul, the *jihadu nafsi*, whereby a student does battle with the ego or carnal desires, a seemingly apolitical position until one recognizes, as does Babou, its use "as a tool to install Islamic values and shield people against the corrupting effects of negative traditional and French influences."[4]

The Murid order that Bamba founded (*murid* means "aspirant," or one who aspires to proximity with divine knowledge) has had a profound impact on Senegalese religious and expressive culture to the present day and remains the most visible of the country's four major Sufi brotherhoods.[5] Often described as Islamic mysticism, Sufism's rise in sub-Saharan Africa in the eighteenth century brought with it the practice of devoting oneself to a spiritual teacher, or *shaykh* ("cheikh" in the French orthography). Sufism offers followers a path, under the teacher's guidance, to becoming a friend of God, or *wali Allah*. The Sufi path includes the incorporation of arduously acquired forms of spiritual knowledge and leads the follower to become a living embodiment of that knowledge, or a "walking Qur'an."[6] The historian Rudolph Ware contextualizes the Sufi movement in West Africa as a means of transforming and channeling "a process of social change that was fundamentally driven by the claims for personal dignity of those previously held at arm's length from Islamic knowledge."[7] The Murid order's deconstruction of preceding social hierarchies, along with its focus on work and labor as a form of devotion equal to prayer, was in line with such a broader Sufi movement in the region and proved decisive in the order's rapid and enduring success.

Despite extensive scholarship on the Muridiyya, the order's use of theatrical performance has escaped scholarly attention. This chapter highlights the contribution of the Murid theatrical stage not only as a decisive factor in Murid and, by extension, Senegalese history, but also as a pivotal effort of stagecraft in Senegal's post-independence period. The troupe behind the Murid performance *Bamba Mos Xam* inherited the same stage space passed on through earlier experiments in French colonial education. However, it repurposed the stage to alter its secular mode of engagement, fitting it to the values and embodied forms of spiritual expression of a deeply religious population. The show proved radically decolonizing in its approach to stagecraft in that it engaged in a thorough reworking of the Western theatrical form, while also launching a vigorous critique of the forms of knowledge that had once facilitated the rule of the colonizer throughout French West Africa. The *Bamba Mos Xam* experience based itself on a different order of knowledge and pedagogy that resonated with a broader Sufi spiritual ontology. It called into question conventional secular and colonial understandings of what constitutes knowledge, the ends to which true knowledge may be used, and the means by which such knowledge must be acquired.

Locating the History and Impact of *Bamba Mos Xam*

My research on *Bamba Mos Xam* began in the early stages of interviews and fieldwork on Senegalese theatrical performance. My conversations about Senegalese stage practices tended to gravitate toward questions of cultural policy, disillusions with the notion of Francophonie, and the possibility of a theatrical aesthetic that could remain open to outside influences while maintaining the sense of a local Senegalese identity. Occasionally, Senegalese of a certain age category, roughly forty years of age or older at the time, recalled a long-closed Murid touring production on the life of Amadu Bamba.[8] The performance had left a lasting impression on its former spectators, who recounted a vibrant staging of Bamba's story attended by rapturous audiences from all walks of Senegalese life. Contemporary theater practitioners saw in the play a successful production model that they would like to see adopted by a new generation of stage artists. For the performers whose work I had been following, *Bamba Mos Xam* offered a heartening example of an independent troupe paving the way for an alternative approach to theatrical performance that would cater specifically to a Senegalese audience.

Mouhamadou Diol, director of the company Kàddu Yaraax, whose work I explore in my final chapter, shared my interest in the history and impact of the *Bamba Mos Xam* production. He vividly recalls having attended a performance of the show as a child in the early 1980s, when the troupe traveled to his neighborhood outside of Dakar. Like other former spectators, he retains the memory of an immersive experience designed specifically for a local audience that turned out for the performance in large numbers. In retrospect, Diol marvels at the troupe's resounding success in drawing a large public and prompting spectators not only to attend, but also to buy a ticket for the performance. (Diol's productions and those of countless contemporary theater troupes rely almost exclusively on sponsorships rather than on individual paying spectators.) Diol remarks that, by appealing to the common religious practices of almsgiving and bequeathing monetary gifts to one's spiritual teacher, *Bamba Mos Xam* created a financially sustainable model that allowed the troupe to tour the country for several years with a sizeable operating budget. He further contends that this made *Bamba Mos Xam* a successful traveling performance on an equal footing with the large-budget touring productions of Europe or America; proof, he added, that "theater is not just a European invention, but a Senegalese one as well!"[9]

Diol and I soon collaborated in researching the production's history, content, and contemporary legacy. In an attempt to measure the performance's reach, we began by informally surveying residents of the urban areas of Dakar, Pikine, Guédiawaye, and Thiès, where, we soon learned, the production had toured multiple times over its long history. Our conversations overwhelmingly confirmed the remarkable impact of *Bamba Mos Xam*, as scores of former spectators nostalgically recounted the impression the play made on them, as well as the effect it had on neighborhoods throughout the country. The reaction evoked by the mere mention of *Bamba Mos Xam* at the conference of a theater festival in Thiès, called FEST'RAIL, indicated the widespread popular memory of the show. Shortly after we announced our interest in the production and its history to the room of some fifty cultural actors and journalists, Baba Ndiaye, a painter and central figure of the Thiès arts scene, stood up to recall the national scope of the theatrical tour, which performed for all levels of Senegalese society while basing itself on a profoundly Senegalese history and hagiography. Ndiaye recalled to the audience the remarkable enthusiasm with which crowds received the traveling theatrical production each time it passed through town, adding: "You would actually see people fall into a trance during the show!"[10]

Since the only traces of the *Bamba Mos Xam* performance are the memories of those who saw it or were personally involved in it, we found ourselves collecting personal narratives, a process that led us to seek out contacts in the cultural and Murid milieus of Dakar, Touba, Thiès, Saint-Louis, Kaolack, and Pikine. We especially hoped to speak with those who might have direct knowledge of the production, people who were key cultural figures in the city of Kaolack at the time of its tour, or those sufficiently embedded in the Murid milieu to have knowledge of the play's reception among the religious community.[11] Early in our research we learned of the death of the play's director, Tamsir Ndiaye. Our interlocutors therefore led us to the director of the troupe, Cheikh Fall, whom we met at his place of work, the Hospital of Kaolack. A founding member of the troupe, Cheikh Fall had managed the logistics of touring and booking engagements and also performed several roles in the play. He described the production as the brainchild of the late Tamsir Ndiaye, who, he quickly pointed out, adhered to the Tijaniyya order rather than to the Muridiyya. For Cheikh Fall, this detail attested to the fundamentally theatrical nature of the performance which, although performed mostly by Murid devotees like himself, included performers from each of Senegal's main Sufi orders as well as Catholics and other non-Muslims.[12] In this first encounter, Fall wished to emphasize the fact that, despite the important role the production played in the Murid cultural imaginary of its day, it remained the work of professional performers who were able to take on roles outside of their own personal experience or religious beliefs.

The ambiguity between the performer's gesture of enactment and the audience's reception of what is taken to be an authentic personal form of religious expression recalls similar points of tension at work in the performances of the William Ponty School. Like the *pontins*, *Bamba Mos Xam* performers made ample use of the stage space's potential for ambiguity through the taking on of a role. Among Murid spectators, the production actively encouraged a reception of the staged enactment as a manifestation of Bamba's spiritual essence, or *baraka*. For non-Murid audience members, the production facilitated a cross-confessional engagement with the Bamba narrative by elevating the saint to the status of a national hero and situating his story within a landscape of regional Sufi saints and religious leaders. Although the *Bamba Mos Xam* stage shared with that of the Ponty School a desire to correct colonial narratives of the region's history, it also enacted a de-secularization in order to host expressions of religious experience lying far outside the scope of the Francophone notions of stage culture examined thus far.[13] Thus, within its performance space, it facilitated a collective and participatory celebration of regional and national identity through a cultural embrace of the country's Sufi religious heritage.

Crafting a Religiously Infused Stage Space

Our first meeting with Cheikh Fall led to a longer collaboration, which included several interviews during which Fall told us of the production's genesis late in the first decade of Senegal's independence and of its subsequent touring, which continued until the mid-1980s.[14] Fall also talked us through the play scene-by-scene, describing details related to costumes and staging, and reenacting each of the exchanges within the play, thus allowing us to reconstruct a rough script of the drama.[15] We first discussed the history of the production itself, which began during a period when the *Bamba Mos Xam* troupe was known as L'Amicale Sérère Colette Senghor; this was a way of paying homage to President Senghor by honoring his wife, a Frenchwoman named Colette. The name also reflected the historic Serer identity of the Kaolack region and, not incidentally, that of President Senghor himself. The choice of name further reflected an attempt to forge useful connections within the centralized state funding structures of the post-independence cultural landscape, although, despite its open praise of the state's leading *homme de culture*, the troupe remained mostly at the margins of emerging models of financial support for the arts.

The "amicale" had once traveled to Dakar as the Centre Culturel de Kaolack to perform concurrently with Senghor's 1966 World Festival of Negro Arts with an original creation called *Les Derniers Jours de Maba Diakhou Bâ* (*The Last Days of Maba Jaxu Ba*). The play, which is currently unpublished and unavailable, appears to have aligned itself with the "Ponty" style and approach of Cissé Dia's stage piece on Lat Joor by recounting the story of an important resistance leader of the country's past. However, the troupe never enjoyed the success or visibility granted to Cissé Dia's production, whose author, a former *pontin* and well-connected figure of national politics, had easier access to funding from national cultural institutions. This disappointing experience in Dakar inspired the troupe's members, and especially its artistic director, Tamsir Ndiaye, to change strategies by considering the theatrical potential of the spiritual narratives of the founders of the country's Sufi religious communities. Ndiaye contended that, by delving into the history and sources of local religious life, the troupe could offer populations underserved by Senghor's highly centralized approach to cultural policy a localized reflection of the country's cultural values. Above all, the troupe envisioned a stage culture untethered to notions of cultural globalism or Francophonie and thus freer to embrace a vision of artistic representation closer to the Murids' participative representational practices.

The troupe's audacious choice of subject matter tested the limits of acceptability for the Murid religious authorities. Rendering the saint's hagiography translatable to the stage necessitated an act of adaptation, which raised fears that the troupe might go so far as to take liberties with certain aspects of Murid history and doctrine.[16] To their great advantage, the company found itself in search of the required authorization, or *ndigal*, for the performance while the Murid order was still under the leadership of Sëriñ Faliilu Mbakke, and indeed during the last year of the immensely popular caliph's life, in 1968. Mbakke's favorable legacy, which continues to this day, stems in part from his strategically permissive approach to forms of cultural expression used as a means of voicing and transmitting a religious message. One important example in the realm of the performing arts was the practice of *diwaan*, a vigorous form of public storytelling recounting the history of the Murid order and the great deeds of its leaders. Performances of *diwaan*, which flourished in the 1950s and '60s thanks to the approval of Sëriñ Faliilu, often spontaneously erupted in the public spaces of Murid communities, and its practitioners, called *diwaankat*, frequently declared their love and admiration for the Murid caliph as part of their routine.[17] The widespread popularity of such a practice set the stage for further adaptations of the Murid master narrative. The *Bamba Mos Xam* troupe no doubt traveled to the Murid capital of Touba well aware of Sëriñ Faliilu's favorable view of the uses of performance for religious purposes. In seeking out his *ndigal*, which represents both a form of permission and an implicit endorsement, they also sought to associate the leader's name with their theatrical efforts. As Cheikh Fall recalls, the company managed, upon their arrival in Touba, to gain an audience with Sëriñ Faliilu, for whom they performed the show. When the Sëriñ asked for the show's title, troupe members simply replied "Bamba," to which he added the words "Mos Xam," thus giving the performance both his approval and its name: "Bamba mos xam," or "to taste Bamba is to know"[18]

The Sëriñ's official authorization proved all the more essential given that the performance placed an actor in the role of Shaykh Amadu Bamba, a gesture which, though seemingly tolerable in the exceptional circumstances of the performance of *Les Derniers Jours de Lat Dior* at the 1966 festival in Dakar, risked a far more hostile reception in the Senegalese countryside. Unlike in Cissé Dia's play, in *Bamba Mos Xam* the saint was the main subject of the staged narrative, which made ample use of the more dramatic elements of Bamba's life. The troupe defended its project first by striving for strict factual accuracy in its portrayal. Their stage adaptation drew from the authoritative source on Bamba's life, the first canonical work of the Senegalese poet Muusaa Ka, titled *Jasaa u sakóor bu yoonu géej gi* (*Reward of the Grateful of the Odyssey by Sea*) and originally composed in a form of Ajami called Wolofal, or Wolof-language text transcribed in Arabic characters.[19] By remaining faithful to the order's accepted hagiography, the play presented itself less as an adaptation than as a means of transmission of Bamba's story. Troupe members committed themselves to performing for an audience that might not otherwise have had access to Murid writings, given the limited availability of print publications at the time and the highly erudite nature of the texts themselves. Thus, *Bamba Mos Xam* took part in a broader effort, under the guidance of Sëriñ Faliilu, to popularize forms of Murid pedagogy and religious expression in the new national context of political independence.

The Bamba Mos Xam *Experience*

As Baba Ndiaye indicated in his recollection of the event, a central part of the *Bamba Mos Xam* production was the strong emotional reaction it elicited from attendees, especially those affiliated with the Murid order. In the middle of a performance a sensation of ecstatic rapture often came over spectators. Some of our interlocutors described the phenomenon as one of a collective fervor, even fanaticism, that surrounded the event, but they affirmed that even for those who did not share in such trance-like states, a lively interactive element contributed greatly to the overall spectacle that made the performance so memorable. In our interviews with former *Bamba Mos Xam* spectators, interlocutors consistently evoked the performance's ability to move Senegalese audiences to forms of embodied participation in the story of Bamba's life. A number of former audience members recalled the most potent moment for such reactions as the first time Bamba, known to Murid devotees as Sëriñ Touba (the "master of Touba"), appeared on stage and lifted his arms to the air to declaim the beginning of the Shahada or Muslim statement of faith, "There is no God but Allah." The sight and sound of the Sufi saint in the flesh ignited a stir in the form of cries and exclamations of joy and reverence.[20]

The hefty responsibility of portraying Sëriñ Touba fell on the troupe's lead actor, Demba Ndiaye, and placed him at the foreground of the production's engagement with representational practices in Murid culture. All personal recollections of the performance included commentary on the striking resemblance that Ndiaye bore to Shaykh Amadu Bamba.[21] One former spectator, Soukaye Ndiaye of Touba, echoed the clear consensus among former *Bamba Mos Xam* audience members in saying: "To see him [Demba Ndiaye] was to see Sëriñ Touba. To listen to him was to listen to Sëriñ Touba speak. Even the way he said 'Allah' was just like the Shaykh!"[22] Demba Ndiaye passed away around the time of the production's closure. My discussions with the show's former spectators and affiliates turned up widely circulated rumors suggesting that the act of standing in for Bamba on stage and thus serving as an embodied vehicle for the saint's *baraka* had proven too demanding for anyone to bear. This reflected the strength of the Sëriñ's aura, as well as the great spiritual burden—the pledge of suffering—that Bamba takes on through the course of the Murid narrative. For many former spectators, both the blessings and the burden of the Bamba story must have been brought to bear on the actor who had the courage, and perhaps the temerity, to embody Sëriñ Touba and to speak as if by the teacher's own voice.

Second only to Ndiaye's portrayal of Bamba, former *Bamba Mos Xam* spectators most fondly recalled the role of Sëriñ Touba's chief disciple, Maam Shaykh Ibrahima Faal. Known for expressing his devotion to Bamba through acts of excessive obedience and eccentric and expansive physical behavior, Ibra Faal, as he is also known, was the founder of the Murid order's most visible subgroup, the Baay Faal (Wolof for "Father Faal"). Today, one can often identify Baay Faal devotees throughout Senegal by their dress and appearance; this is often a form of patchwork, or *njaxas* in Wolof, combined with dreadlocks or amulets signaling the individual's adherence to the Baay Faal philosophy. Within the Murid master narrative, the figure of Ibra Faal represents a worldly complement to the esoteric, inward-looking spiritualism of Amadu Bamba. Ibra Faal's concerns lay within the exoteric domain of the visible, earthly realm. He enforced discipline in the teacher's religious school, or *daara*, and committed himself fully to a life of work in devotion to his marabout, a choice that, within the Murid order, exempted him from the obligation to pray five times daily or to fast during the month of Ramadan. Contemporary Murids retain from the figure of Maam Shaykh Ibrahima Faal an idealized example of the devoted disciple living in a state of pure submission to his teacher. He thus personifies the perfected act of submission (*jébbalu* in Wolof) that is so central to the order and philosophy of the Sufi *daara*. In Murid narratives his acts of obedience stand out for their sheer excess, characterized by an unquestioning execution of Bamba's every request and a relentless discipline imposed on his fellow disciples, along with intrepid bravery in his willingness to protect Bamba from all potentially hostile individuals, especially the French. [23]

Bamba Mos Xam placed a strong emphasis on the role of Maam Shaykh Ibrahima Faal and depicted the Murid order as only taking on its true form with Faal's integration into Bamba's *daara*. The two meet in a moment of profound destiny when, in the city of Tayba Daqar, Faal first lays eyes on Bamba and runs to him declaring: "I have sought you out by sea and by land."[24] Faal the truth-seeker has found his teacher but also foreshadows, in his poetic declaration, Bamba's exile, first by sea in the exile to Gabon and then by land in the subsequent period of exile in Mauritania. Ibra Faal's statement here also provides a moment of intertextuality with Ka's epic poems on the Bamba story, titled *Odyssey by Sea* and *Odyssey by Land*. Following his encounter with Bamba and immediately upon becoming his disciple, Faal antagonizes his fellow followers, or *taalibe*, by using violence to discipline peers he judges as lacking in rigor or devotion. Indeed, in the play, when first asked his name by Bamba, Ibra Faal replies "*yab sa xánc*," a succinct and allegorical declaration referring to the need to use a tough cord in order to bind the bundle of wood that one gathers. For, as Faal elaborates, large though your bundle may be, without the cord you will not be able to return home with it. This characteristically terse and enigmatic response reflects something of the Baay Faal philosophy, which flouts conventional means of knowledge and learning in either the Islamic or Western sense.

From a theatrical perspective, a figure like the founder of the Baay Faal offered a wealth of scenic possibilities. Former spectators often cited the eccentricities and gyrations of the stage version of Ibra Faal in *Bamba Mos Xam*, remarking that the actor who played him proved particularly adept at capturing the attention and imagination of young and impressionable audience members. A number of our interlocutors who had seen the performance as young children recalled first and foremost the commanding presence of Ibra Faal within the show.[25] More than one spectator recalled for us their impression of a scene where Faal stares down a roaring lion to protect Bamba. The lion holds considerable weight in Wolof culture as a symbol of masculinity, strength, and courage. Moreover, as the lion is the national symbol of

Figure 4.2. Maam Shaykh Ibrahima Faal (left) in *Bamba Mos Xam*. Image from *Bamba, the Taste of Knowledge*, directed by Gino Canella and Brian Valente-Quinn. Performance photograph courtesy of Cheikh Ibrahima Fall (pictured at right).

Senegal as well as a traditional symbol of kingly authority, its submission to Faal and, by extension, to Bamba, had a lasting impact on young spectators. It allowed them to witness firsthand, through stage performance, the Murid leader's otherworldly ability to overcome all levels of worldly authority.

The multi-generational aspect of the performance helped it to reach a broader audience and also explains its long life as a touring production. Moreover, the performance helped to define for a post-independence generation of Senegalese, many of whom devoted themselves to the Murid way after their contact with the play, the model behavior of one who is completely devoted to a religious and spiritual life. The renowned artist and Murid devotee Yelimane Fall first saw the performance in his native Saint-Louis and credits *Bamba Mos Xam* with initiating him to Muridism. Fall, a national authority on the Baay Faal movement, confirmed through the course of several interviews that *Bamba Mos Xam* played a central role in what proved to be a period of great expansion for the Murid order throughout Senegal. "Most of the people who became Murids in my generation converted after they saw *Bamba Mos Xam*," he asserts.[26] Although it is not possible to verify Fall's claim, his assertion does suggest, as do the echoes and popularity of the performance, a generational phenomenon wherein a group of young Senegalese in the decades following independence were able to see in *Bamba Mos Xam* the kind of nationalist stage expression with mass appeal that the Daniel Sorano National Theater sought to provide. By adopting different cultural landmarks tied to the country's Sufi religious heritage, and by proposing a fundamental rewriting of the stage space and the rules by which it operated, the Murid theater of *Bamba Mos Xam* created a powerful alternative approach to that of Senegal's national theatrical institutions.

Through its participative nature, *Bamba Mos Xam* both reaped the benefits of and fell victim to its own success. Financially, the participative aspect of the performance inspired many Murid devotees to contribute ostentatiously, often walking forward in the middle of a performance to place bills on the stage. Such financial donations resonated with the practice of *hadiyya*, or giving to one's spiritual teacher as an expression of gratitude, a participative gesture toward the community and a means of drawing to oneself the blessings of a charismatic spiritual guide.[27] The proffering of gifts from audience members became a part of the show, ensuring for the troupe a robust budget that covered the performers' salaries and the costs involved in maintaining a continuous long-term tour. However, the staged embodiment of Bamba, which called the viewer into a participative relationship as might a visual representation of his 1913 image, created certain obstacles that were particular to the stage. Breaking with the merely symbolic representational conventions of theater meant that the troupe frequently ran into the challenge of spectators running onstage to chide or physically attack characters who insulted or threatened Bamba or his Murid followers. The troupe had to respond to these dangers, which sprang, in director Cheikh Fall's view, from a misunderstanding of the nature of theatrical role-play. Such difficulties arose particularly in the depiction of the colonial authorities of Saint-Louis, who conspired to send Bamba into his fateful seven-year exile in Gabon. Physical barriers and protective measures, such as hired security guards, prevented audience members from running onstage to mete out justice to Bamba's oppressors in the middle of the performance. Such measures served as a means of habituating audiences to a new form of interaction with Bamba's story, permitting participation through verbal responses, financial gifts, or through an experience of rapturous trance, but preventing spectators from launching a physical intervention.[28]

Although the troupe was most accustomed to performing in a bustling, popular environment, the play did appear on several occasions in larger venues, including performances for which the company rented the Daniel Sorano National Theater; this fact required verification from a number of interviewees, including Cheikh Fall himself, as well as the former Sorano director Massamba Guèye, given that there appears to be no written record of the troupe's Sorano performances.[29] Remarkably, just as Senghor stood at the height of his power and influence, and throughout his volumes of writing on Senegalese and African culture, the poet-president never turned his scholarly attention to what proved to be the most successful and perennial touring performance in the country's history. Among the possible explanations for Senghor's silence on the performance—which again surprises, given that the troupe once called itself the Amicale Sérère Colette Senghor—one may infer a concern, central to Senegalese politics, to appear to respect all forms of religious identity while favoring none. The state's approach to religious institutions here constitutes a particular form of secularism, distinct from that of the French, whereby governmental heads acknowledge and exchange with religious leaders as equal partners in state authority.[30] As such, the state powers must strike a balance of equidistance among the various Sufi orders and religious institutions, one that praise of a performance like *Bamba Mos Xam* might have risked disrupting.

Another potential hypothesis regarding the lack of commentary from Senghor on *Bamba Mos Xam* may be drawn based on the production's depiction of its own form of cultural development which took Touba and Murid belief as the center of its worldview, rather than subscribing to notions of Francophonie. The focus on Touba as a holy city is reflected through the figure of Lamp Faal, another name for Bamba's first disciple, who is said to illuminate the Murid way forged by Bamba's teaching. Lamp Faal is often depicted as a light emanating from the minaret of the Great Mosque of Touba.[31] The notion of Ibra Faal serving as a guiding light to all Murids—"Lamp" here indeed derives from the French *lampe,* or "light"—suggests a radiation of Bamba's message, which is understood as a call to all Murids.

In its alternative theatrical approach, *Bamba Mos Xam* situated itself at the interstices of "official," or national theatrical production; of popular cultural works, as typified by the troupe's earlier stage experiences; and of preexisting Sufi narratives that provided a trove of theatrical material and resources. In the next section, I examine these canonical Sufi texts and how the *Bamba Mos Xam* troupe staged them to craft a new stage space in the Senegalese theatrical landscape.

Staging Murid Textuality

Bamba Mos Xam appealed to what performers and audience members perceived as a more locally inspired experience of stage performance. It also referred to and built upon a broader, transnational Sufi philosophy, most notably in its treatment of alternative ontologies and models of knowledge and knowledge transmission. Such questions lie at the heart of recent scholarship on the use of secular forms to convey sacred messages. These expressive forms are more than examples of a cultural bricolage, and constitute the articulation and defense of different ways of knowing. Joseph Hill frames the issue in relation to Talal Asad's notion of Islam functioning as a discursive tradition, discussing the practice of Islamic authority as "founded not just in discourse—especially in reference to foundational texts—but in multiple complementary principles of knowing and demonstration."[32] Oludamini Ogunnaike, in his work on the use of music videos among the Taalibe Baay, or followers of the Sufi teacher Ibrahima Ñas, points out that scholarship on West African Sufism tends to neglect regional engagements with a broader tradition of key Sufi symbols and themes. In this vein, the theatrical representation of Sëriñ Touba can be considered a staged "symbol" only so long as the symbol is conceived within a Sufi framework, meaning that the symbol is "not an arbitrary signifier linked to its signified through convention, but is rather ontologically continuous with that which it symbolizes."[33] The symbol, in this sense, transmits knowledge according to a philosophy of transmission whereby the learner actually tastes, taking in knowledge via a direct experience linked to the senses.

The title "Bamba Mos Xam" employs a Wolof idiomatic expression that is not necessarily associated with Sufi or religious doctrine in its everyday use. The phrase "*mos xam*" ("to tase is to know") signifies that one must literally taste, or more figuratively, experience, a given thing in order to know it. Inversely, it also implies that one cannot but know the thing once one has tasted it. The common expression can be used to refer to something one tastes, such as a dish, or to something one experiences, such as an event or a piece of music. However, the expression also resonates with a Sufi proverb stating "He who tastes, knows," or inversely, "He who tastes not, knows not."[34] The proverb indicates, on the one hand, the inadequacy of words to transmit true knowledge of the Sufi way and, on the other, the centrality of wordless, embodied experience and sensation as the sole means whereby one may hope to know certain spiritual truths. As a spectacle of the senses and of sensations, *Bamba Mos Xam* met the expectations set by its title and provided spectators with a theatrical work that one had to experience, or taste, in order to understand. It also engaged with the deeper meaning of the Sufi proverb to which it indirectly referred. The play did not present itself simply as a story or a succession of facts, but rather as an immersive spiritual experience of the knowledge conveyed by Sëriñ Touba's story.

Building on Ajami Pedagogies

In order to render their performance as faithful as possible to Bamba's hagiography and the spiritual knowledge contained therein, the *Bamba Mos Xam* troupe based their adaptation on the epic poetry of Mussaa Ka. Ka's canonical work on Bamba's life, *Jasaa u sakóor bu yoonu géej gi* (*Reward of the Grateful of the Odyssey by Sea*), recounts the Murid founder's first period of French-imposed exile for seven years in Gabon and is followed by another epic poem on Bamba's four-year exile in Mauritania, called the *Odyssey by Land* (*Yoonu jéeri ji*). A contemporary of Amadu Bamba, Muusaa Ka stands as one of the most emblematic authors of the region's Ajami literature, or African-language literatures transcribed in Arabic script.[35] Although Bamba wrote extensively, he did so exclusively in Arabic. For this reason, he instructed his poet student, Muusaa Ka, to write about the Murid movement in Wolofal—or Wolof-based Ajami—so that Ka's work might speak directly to its audience in their own language. Bamba's injunction led to a vast corpus of writings by Ka, much of it verse poetry, on the life and example of the founder of the Muridiyya, along with commentaries on the spiritual life of the era. In his study of West African Ajami literature, the linguist Fallou Ngom points out the central role these texts played as a means of communication and a vehicle for spreading the Murid tradition. This deeply imbricated Ajami literary traditions within Murid history and, for the *Bamba Mos Xam* troupe, made Ka's epic poem a fitting textual foundation from which to adapt a new, immersive, and theatrical means of communicating Bamba's story.

As Ka recounts, many of Bamba's hardships were brought on by his determination to distance local politics and power struggles from his spiritual practice. In his refusal to pledge allegiance to local chiefs or to engage in any outright political resistance against French domination in the region, Bamba placed himself in opposition to many of the conflictual power dynamics of the day. As students flocked to Bamba's *daara*, the rising movement ran afoul of previously established chiefs and Muslim teachers. Some of these conspired to denounce Bamba to the French by stoking rumors that the new teacher planned to launch a jihad against the colonizers, as other Muslim figures like Samory Ture and Maba Jaxu Ba had done before him. These accusations ultimately led to Bamba's first exile, which began in 1895 and lasted until his return to Dakar in 1902. Within the Murid narrative, Bamba's exile represents the apotheosis of his saintly path and destiny. Ka's poem explains that Bamba implored, at the moment of his exile, that his forced odyssey stand in as a pilgrimage for all those impeded from making the hajj on their own, and that it serve as an act of redemption for all sinners.[36] Ka points out that this gesture on Bamba's part motivates his followers to commemorate his exile every year during the Grand Magal celebration, in which millions of Murids from throughout the world converge on the city of Touba.

Ka immerses his writing deeply within a pedagogical spirit, a choice made evident from the poem's opening. Composed in rhyming couplets that mix Wolof and Arabic, the text opens in Arabic with a reference to Muusaa, the poem's author, who evokes Bamba's departure from his home of Mbakke-Baari in the month of Safar of the Islamic calendar and the year 1313 (1895 CE). Then begins the first of many exchanges between the author and his imagined interlocutor, a performative technique that facilitates the poem's public recitation. "If you listen to me today I will bring you back to awakening, so that those who sleep may rediscover their faith."[37] The poem exhorts listeners out of ignorance and toward the light offered by Bamba's story: "You, the blind, are before one who sees, so you must stay silent, I know not the excuse of the ignorant one who fails to learn from one who knows."[38] Ka's text adapts itself to the framework in which the poem might be performed; that is, through the voice of a learned reciter standing before a group of interlocutors, calling out to them in an attempt to grab their attention. The text serves as a form of historical witnessing by virtue of the narrator's position of authority—which he claims for himself throughout the text—as well as through citations of other Ajami works and Bamba's spiritual poetry in Arabic.

Aside from foregrounding Bamba's otherworldly ability to endure suffering without complaint—a highly valued quality in Wolof tradition—Ka's text also highlights the spirit of forgiveness that animates Bamba's actions. Once the teacher's persecutors are faced with the unjust nature of their acts, they repent and seek to redeem themselves by either pledging allegiance in the case of the Senegalese or, in the case of the French, building alliances. The saintly *baraka* connected with Bamba does not allow for motives of revenge or lower forms of worldly justice. In Ka's telling, those who oppose Bamba earn their just rewards through divine means, while those who come to him in aid soon find themselves rewarded. Ka provides two important examples of this; the first is the figure of Duudu Mambay, a colonial administrator who tormented Bamba during the Sufi master's incarceration. As a result, the narrator implies, Mambay later lost his post and career and eventually died anonymous and in poverty. This contrasts with the case of Blaise, who the reader/listener understands to be Blaise Diagne, the first Black African elected to the French Assembly, who showed kindness toward Bamba during the latter's imprisonment. Ka's narrator remarks that Diagne's electoral victory in 1914 resulted from his kindness toward Bamba in 1895. Although these examples do suggest a form of spiritual justice, in fact, as Ka tells it, each figure in the master narrative acted according to the will of God. Even the French, who might be seen as Bamba's primary oppressors, merely served unwittingly as a means to an end in Bamba's path to spiritual greatness, which required him to pay the price of great suffering. This important distinction helps to situate the colonial role as a central factor within the story, but not the determining one. The crux of the story remains Bamba's exceptional decision to accept God's challenge to him in the aim of ultimately attaining the status of an *Ahl al-Badr*, or one of the soldiers who fought for the cause of Islam in the legendary Battle of Badr. Beyond this decision, the French serve effectively as pawns in Bamba's quest, as Ka points out when he has Bamba say that "those who hoped to harm me by transporting me across the ocean have only brought me closer to God."[39]

Defining Knowledge by Opposition

In the same way that Muusaa Ka sought to infuse his poetry with a pedagogical spirit, *Bamba Mos Xam* aimed to spread knowledge about the Murid order and the story of its founder. The play had the additional ambition of appealing to a broader national identity by including a range of hero figures from throughout the region, both Muslim and non-Muslim. The performance began not with a leading figure of the Murid order, but rather with the travels of Al Hajj Umar Taal, an Islamic scholar, political leader, and major figure of the Tijani brotherhood in West Africa.[40] Taal appears in the play's first scene as he takes leave of his disciple Maba Jaxu Ba, who will next go on, outside the world of the play and with Taal's authorization, to conquer the kingdom of Saalum, forcibly converting the population to Islam. Taal cautions Ba against trying to expand his reign to the neighboring Siin region, where he will indeed be defeated and killed by an army of resisters to Islam's spread. Taal's warning, which predicts Ba's defeat and thus a defeat for Islam's influence in the region, is voiced out of a sense of kinship with the non-Muslim Serer population of Siin, whom he calls our brethren, or "*sunuy gàmmu*." The term *gàmmu* refers to the phenomenon of joking relationships, whereby pairs of certain family names maintain cordial relations through a culturally structured practice of joking or light-hearted mockery. More broadly, the term can also refer to a familial or ethnic tie between two groups or individuals that forbids conflict. On the *Bamba Mos Xam* stage, the foregrounding of such ties as potentially superseding any jihad-related imperative to convert populations played an important mediating function. It served to overlay, on the history of a turbulent period, a post-independence ethical framework of non-conflict highlighted both for its mediating value as well as for its consistency with the message professed by Bamba throughout his path to sainthood.

Taal next encounters Amadu Bamba's parents as he travels through Poroxaan. First, he meets Bamba's mother, Maam Jaara Buso, who is today a figure of devotion in the Murid order and whose home city has become a site of pilgrimage. After receiving Maam Jaara Buso's hospitality, Taal moves on to Bamba's ancestral city of Mbakke Bawol, where he meets Bamba's father, Maam Mor Anta Sali. As the two men converse, Taal reveals to Sali that, throughout his journey, he has been following a light, which led him on his current peregrination. The light, a symbol of the saintly figure to emerge in the form of Sali's son, allows Taal to make a number of predictions regarding the future history of the Murid order. He instructs Sali to treat his future son not as a child but as his teacher and to leave the spiritual path of the Qadiriyya, to which Sali adheres, upon the son's arrival in order to follow him. Taal then explains to Sali that his son will go into the savanna where he will establish a city and where the entire world will converge to find him, a reference to the founding of the city of Touba and the annual Murid pilgrimage for the Magal holiday. This staged exchange reflects a popular myth according to which Umar Taal once sought out the city of Touba before its founding and announced Bamba's imminent appearance. These first scenes in the *Bamba Mos Xam* play served to render the production relevant for a Senegalese audience of many religious and regional identities, particularly in the production's home region, which has a long historical tie to the Tijaniyya and a sizeable Serer population. *Bamba Mos Xam*'s broad view of the country's religious heritage, which framed Bamba's story beyond the confines of a strictly Murid or Wolof heritage, allowed the full range of the Senegalese population to attend and appreciate the show publicly alongside Murid compatriots.

Invested in the mission of an experiential, sensorial, and immediate contact with the knowledge contained within Bamba's life story, *Bamba Mos Xam* repeatedly returned to questions of what constituted knowledge in both the exoteric and esoteric sense. In the exoteric realm, the play foregrounded the historical conflict between a denouncer and a defender of Bamba in the figures of Mbaaxaan Jóob, the provincial chief of Bawol, and Kumba Ndoofeen Faa Ndeb Juuf, the Buur Siin, or king of the Siin kingdom. In the Murid narrative, Mbaaxaan Jóob plays a central role in Bamba's second exile by falsely reporting to French officials that the teacher had concealed a stockpile of arms and planned to launch an armed revolt against the colonial army. Jóob was a young and ambitious province chief at the time of his accusation and had arrived at his post after having studied at L'École des Fils de Chefs (School for Sons of Chiefs), as well as at the French colonial school in Tunis. Jóob's accusations led to Bamba's summoning to answer to the colonial governor of Saint-Louis. *Bamba Mos Xam*'s staging of the ensuing confrontation sheds light on where Jóob's loyalties lie. While other chiefs in attendance address the governor in Wolof through an interpreter, Jóob, the province chief, makes his case against Bamba before the governor in an accusatory French. He declares to the audience, as an erudite and trustworthy witness, that he stands by the contents of a letter he had written and sent to the colonial administration warning that Bamba intended to lead a revolt. His testimony appears to convince the governor until another attendee, Buur Siin Kumba Ndóofeen, speaks up to contest the charges against Bamba. Not himself a Muslim, Kumba Ndóofeen nonetheless speaks as a representative of the Serer culture of his native region, which places great importance on honesty and courage, the very values that drive Ndóofeen to come forward in Bamba's defense.

In the play, the Siin king offers his entire territory as a guarantee of Bamba's peaceful intentions. This intervention elicits a vituperative reaction from Jóob, who berates the Buur Siin, in Wolof this time, calling him an unlearned and an illiterate, "*Buur bu jàngul amul xam-xam*" ("A ruler without education is without knowledge").[41] This insult reflects the authority that Jóob grants, in this context, to the colonial school and learning then prized by an elite class of Senegalese leaders who were working as intermediaries for the French. Indeed, Kumba Ndóofeen offers a stark contrast to the forms of knowledge acquired through French colonial schooling. His claim to authority is rooted in his commitment to acquiring the local knowledge necessary to run the country, as he responds confidently: "*Mbaaxaan ba mu demee di jàng lékkol, man maa ngi jàng na ñuy yore réew*" ("While Mbaaxaan was off studying at the [colonial] school, I was learning how to run a country").[42] This claim to an alternative, implicitly anticolonial form of knowledge would have resonated in the decades after political independence. The heated words reflect not only a dispute over Amadu Bamba's activities, but also contrasting views of the acquisition and application of knowledge. The staging of such an exchange invited Senegalese audiences to consider the country's colonial history in a different light, with more attention to historical narratives that valorized the actions of regional leaders, rather than focusing on the work of political and cultural intermediaries for the French.

Senegalese audience members would also know that Kumba Ndóofeen later converted to Islam and devoted himself to Bamba, opening the way for the very Islamization of the Serer population of the Siin region first sought out by Maba Jaxu Ba, but by peaceful means. The play thus helped to activate notions of what could be viewed as an emerging, unified national identity with Bamba as an important galvanizing figure. This proves an important point of contrast with the staging of Bamba in *Les Derniers Jours de Lat Dior*, which focused on the jihad of Lat Joor. Indeed, more important is the way in which *Bamba Mos Xam* suggests not only an alternative nationalist model for the new Senegalese nation, but also an alternative vision of the kind of knowledge upon which such a nation should be constructed. Favoring the anticolonial tenor of Kumba Ndóofeen's gesture over a Francophone-centered educational or cultural model, *Bamba Mos Xam* offered a counter vision to those associated with cultural institutions and approaches being implemented during the golden age of Negritude.

As a character in the play, and indeed in Muusaa Ka's poem, Amadu Bamba does not implicate himself in the debate of the two models of knowledge and learning represented by Jóob and Ndóofeen. He does not articulate a clearly anti- or pro-French stance, but concerns himself exclusively with spiritual matters, thereby highlighting the esoteric realm of knowledge to which the play's title ultimately gestures. If Jóob and Ndóofeen find themselves interlocked, as do the French, in the conflicts of worldly interests and concerns, both forms of knowledge eventually concede to that of Bamba. As Ka points out in his poem in an episode that does not appear in the *Bamba Mos Xam* performance, Jóob, like Ndóofeen, will eventually submit himself to Bamba following a long period of suffering and abandonment. Thus, in the conflict between the two knowledge regimes, the hidden spiritual truth of Bamba triumphs. If to taste Bamba is to know him—that is, if to experience the Sufi master narrative in a live and immersive sense grants immediate knowledge of Bamba's essence—then this posits a form of knowledge that can be acquired in a more immediate fashion, in the moment of the spiritual experience, in contrast with Mbaaxaan Jóob's many years of colonial schooling or Buur Siin's knowledge gained through long political experience. One therefore finds inscribed in the play's dealing with texts of Murid knowledge an appeal for the immediate, experiential, and immersive form of knowledge transmission the production aimed to provide.

Legacies of Bamba Mos Xam

After over fifteen years of touring through the country and performing nightly to full audiences, the *Bamba Mos Xam* adventure came to an end. The mystery surrounding the successful troupe's closure has long fed speculation over a possible interdiction from the Murid leadership in Touba. Many of our interlocutors had heard that the show simply began earning too much money from the story of Sëriñ Touba—and in effect from selling it. Others suggested the production had garnered a level of autonomy and influence which was judged excessive by the leaders of the Murid order, or that it had crossed a line in the doctrinal limits of representing Sëriñ Touba. The exact reasons behind the closure of the performance remain unclear. Cheikh Fall insists that the performance was halted due to the complexity of passing on the torch to a younger generation, since Sëriñ Faliilu's *ndigal* granted permission to perform, but not to pass on that authorization to others. However, interviews with Murid figures, including at the Murid University in Touba, included veiled references to an intervention on behalf of the Murid leadership, although no one in a position of authority was willing or able to offer any specifics. If the exact circumstances surrounding the production's closure could not be determined in the framework of my research, what is certain is that popular rumors about the performance being subject to a formal interdiction sufficed to discourage later generations from mounting a similar effort.

In terms of religious pedagogy, *Bamba Mos Xam* responded to a need for a new means of dissemination for Sufi stories. Today's Murid order has at its disposal a vast media toolkit to take its place. Senegal's primary cultural export, its music, and particularly the form developed by the international star Youssou N'Dour, called *mballax*, has a long affiliation with Muridism. N'Dour, a best-selling singer and leading figure in "world music," has become a spokesman not only for the Senegalese nation, but also for artistic expressions of Murid devotion. His songs make frequent references to Bamba, including a number of his internationally released recordings.[43] In terms of the dissemination of the Murid message and Bamba's teachings, today's Murids also make ample use of the Internet to provide a range of online pedagogical materials, blogs, and social media sites to promote and encourage Murid gatherings in Senegal and abroad.[44] The ethnomusicologist Christine Thu Nhi Dang has explored the processes by which expatriate Murid communities employ various technologies to make Touba present in a diasporic context through the recording and sharing of religious chants and sermons.[45] For the purposes of religious education these media are, in a sense, carrying the torch once brandished by the *Bamba Mos Xam* troupe. The visual artist

Yelimane Fall also maintains a pedagogical view of his own work, seeing in it a continuation of the mission of *Bamba Mos Xam* in that its main purpose is to spread awareness of Bamba and the Murid master narrative. Fall points out that the pedagogical aspect of his paintings serves to forge a close link between his work and the *Bamba Mos Xam* initiative in that both aspire to pass on a Murid history to a younger generation.[46]

✦

The successful use of the theatrical stage in *Bamba Mos Xam* created a stage space upon which new forms of engagement with culture and religion could emerge. However, the troupe's innovative stage intervention cannot be reduced to having merely forged a path for a new type of "religious theater." In fact, the performance allowed for the inclusion of multiple narratives associated with the country's deeply religious culture, but not exclusively tied to it. *Bamba Mos Xam* looked beyond the national scope to tie its work to a broader Sufi philosophy engaged with exploring alternative forms of knowledge and transmission. The performance also allowed performers and audience members to interpret the play as something other than a strictly spiritual experience. The narrative's place within a broader regional history projected a possible nationalist and anticolonial reading for a post-independence audience that was highly receptive to the impulse to reframe, restage, and renarrate the relationship maintained by regional kings and religious leaders with the former colonizers. It did so while maintaining a broader philosophical lens that questioned strictly Cartesian or utilitarian notions of knowledge and learning to indicate more sensorial, immediate, and esoteric understandings of what it means to know.

The testimony of *Bamba Mos Xam* troupe director Cheikh Fall points out how the company, which reflected Senegal's religious diversity in its membership, operated without any proselytizing imperative. They rather saw their endeavor as an artistic one in which actors could step into and out of stage roles, as one might in any play. Popular theater artists, such as Fall and my research collaborator Mouhamadou Diol, see above all in the *Bamba Mos Xam* history an example of theatrical innovation originating from, and significantly altering, Senegal's own cultural and religious heritage. In one discussion, while reflecting on our research together, Diol, who is not himself a Murid devotee, remarked, speaking for all Senegalese stage artists, "We should be proud of what *Bamba Mos Xam* did. We should be proud that it was theater that made such a contribution to the spread of Shaykh Amadu Bamba's message."[47] In the remaining two chapters, I explore two additional stage spaces that constitute post-independence Senegalese theatrical inventions, looking first at the vibrant form of Senegalese televised drama and satire, and finally the forms of popular theater from which *Bamba Mos Xam* and Diol's own work have emerged.

Chapter 5

✦

From Stage to Screen

The Rise of Senegalese Television

In the late 1990s, Senegal's theatrical community underwent a period of active institutional soul-searching. At the heart of their discussions was the future of the state-sponsored system for the arts implemented during the early years of independence, of which the Daniel Sorano National Theater stood as an important symbol. By the end of Senghor's presidency in 1980, funding for the arts had fallen significantly from the generous levels first allocated in the 1960s.[1] National institutions endured drastic cuts throughout the reign of the country's second president, Abdou Diouf, who found himself forced to contend with the demands of structural adjustment programs imposed by the International Monetary Fund and the World Bank aiming to hoist the country out of an economic crisis.[2] The lasting effects of steep budget reductions under Diouf's reign earned him a reputation among the country's theater-makers as a negligent steward of his predecessor's vision of large national budgets for culture working in concert, not in competition, with the prioritization of economic development.[3] The leaner subsidies also undercut the economic model on which the Sorano Theater had been built. With three resident troupes employing full-time, salaried artists out of a large, centrally located building that required considerable funds for its maintenance, the National Theater quickly used up its annual budget on basic operational costs alone.[4] Although the permanent closure of Sorano never seemed to surface as a possible solution, no doubt due to the institution's sheer symbolic heft, by the 1990s its financial sustainability had come under serious question.

The decline of Sorano's activities following the years of Senghor's rule intersected with the debates and controversies over the effects of liberalizing reform programs implemented throughout the 1980s and '90s. Often associated with the years of Abdou Diouf's presidency, which began in 1981 and ended in 2000, the structural adjustment programs that hobbled much of the country's public sector were designed to reform a model of governance which had its roots in Senghor's attempts to establish an "African socialism." As the sociologist Momar-Coumba Diop writes, by the time of Diouf's inauguration, this model had, in fact, already come up against its "objective limit."[5] Senghor himself intimated as much at the end of his twenty years in power, warning the country in his final speech as president: "*la fête africaine est finie*" ("the African party is over").[6] His pronouncement marked the end of a period of spectacular Pan-African celebrations of the independent state at events such as the 1966 festival in Dakar. It also foreshadowed the consequences of years of a de facto single-party state—since Senghor did not begin authorizing political parties other than his own until 1974—and heavy government spending designed primarily to centralize power and foster a sense of national unity. Thus, the Diouf administration ushered in an era of conditions that were difficult to digest for cultural actors of the day, one in which foreign technocrats and consultants with no democratic or political mandate played a central role in policy-making decisions that had a profound and lasting impact on the social and political life of the country.[7]

By the end of Diouf's presidency, the Sorano Theater, once the crown jewel of the state's ambitious cultural policies, found itself without resources to pursue new creations, extend its outreach initiatives into remote areas of the country, or foster the growth and training of a new generation of theater artists. As a result, the theater gradually diminished in stature and importance as a cultural reference for both audiences and artists. In the culture pages of a 1997 issue of the national newspaper *Le Soleil*, Abdoulaye Diop Dany, director of the theatrical troupe, evoked the troupe's meager budget, which, he said, did not even cover contractual salary obligations for its *pensionnaires*, or full-time resident actors.[8] He remarked on the Sorano Theater's struggle to reach a broad national audience while facing regular drops in attendance rates. He attributed these shrinking audiences to several factors, including the degraded physical state of the theater itself. The newspaper's editorial staff offered another hypothesis as to the cause of the National Theater's decline in a headline on the following page that read: "La Faute à la Télé?" ("Is Television to Blame?"). It seemed that Senegalese people could no longer justify spending their time and money on transportation and tickets to support a theater ensconced in the compact, labyrinthine streets of the upper-class neighborhood of Plateau. Instead, the masses largely preferred the comfort of their own homes, where they could now enjoy the televised programming that constituted the Sorano Theater's most recent and formidable competitor.

The period that saw Sorano's star fade coincided with the sudden rise of television as a form of home entertainment in Senegal, a correlation that frequently led theater-makers to suggest that the relatively new medium killed the national theatrical stage by stealing its middle- and upper-class urban audience. Against this view of a direct causal relation, I argue in this chapter that the same liberalizing economic factors that led to the collapse of the national state-funded cultural model created an overwhelming demand for the kind of social and moral critique that television was uniquely suited to provide. If the Sorano stage offered an apt space of creation for a newly independent nation in the midst of its "African party," television became the stage space for the subsequent neoliberal era, when the thrill of independence gave way to a sense of disillusionment over the country's governance, as well as its ever-shrinking place in the global economy.[9] The years of the Diouf administration are often described as corresponding to a period of crisis—of values and of confidence—among the Senegalese middle class. As Momar-Coumba Diop points out, "The 'heirs' of the 'fathers' of independence favored the promotion of a culture of corruption, whose consequences were devastating on the administrative machinery and on society."[10] The private, domestic stage space crafted by the home television set provided an effective platform for criticizing this culture of corruption and for lamenting publicly its effects on Senegalese society at large.

Technology, Infrastructure, and a New Stage for the Masses

The rise of Senegalese television during the period of neoliberal reform reflects, in part, the role of broadcasting and the mass media in facilitating new forms of collective assembly and community formation. In the wake of structural adjustment programs that laid waste to many of the large, infrastructural ambitions of national cultural institutions like the Sorano Theater, the television airwaves provided a viable means of transmitting new works of stagecraft for viewing in private, domestic spaces. Scholarship on television and screen media in Africa has illustrated the generative role of this communications infrastructure, not merely as enabling hardware but also as part of symbolic systems of meaning.[11] In this vein, Brian Larkin theorizes the mass media as a form of "infrastructure," a term he defines broadly as the "totality of both technical and cultural systems that create institutionalized structures whereby goods of all sorts circulate, connecting and binding people into collectivities."[12] Unlike the state-driven cultural initiatives of early post-independence, television in Senegal never became an instrument of specifically nationalist energies.[13] First implemented and conceived as a potentially effective pedagogical tool, the medium owed its survival and eventual propagation to strong and persistent public demand, particularly among the urban middle class. Although the national television channel briefly experimented with broadcasting recordings of Sorano performances, this programming generated far less interest than the telefilms and series of drama and social satire that soon served the very role that Sorano once aspired to play, that of a mirror of the country's social and national consciousness.

The infrastructure necessary to make television a viable means of collectivity formation emerged through a series of initiatives funded in collaboration with international partners. Long among the best-equipped countries of the region in information and communication technology, Senegal launched its first initiative to bring television to the masses in the early 1960s, with the signing of a development initiative that was led by UNESCO and funded through an agreement with the governments of France and Canada.[14] Two transmitters, one in Dakar and the other in Thiès, were used to broadcast programming that focused mainly on educational themes related to literacy and public health. The initiative was discontinued in 1969 due to the limited range of the emitted signal and the high cost of providing enough television sets to create a critical mass of viewers. However, popular interest in the 1972 Olympic Games in Munich, for which a number of public viewing stations were installed, helped generate enough pressure from the elite and expatriate communities to launch a second national initiative, this time with transmitters provided by Thomson-CSF, which became the sole provider of television sets. Despite persistent obstacles of cost, the initiative took hold successfully, and in 1973 the government inaugurated the national audiovisual agency called the ORTS (Office Radiodiffusion Télévision du Sénégal), later renamed the RTS under Abdou Diouf.

The success of Senegalese television also owed much to the later advent of video technology, which enabled the widespread sale and distribution of movies on videocassettes. The informal sales networks and commercial infrastructure that grew from this technology revolutionized the West African region's television and film industries, most famously in Nigeria, which saw an explosion in demand for "Nollywood" films. In Senegal, video circulation did not generate a similar cottage film industry, but it did help to promote the televised miniseries and telefilms then gaining in popularity nationally. In the 1980s and '90s, Tuesday evenings, *le mardi soir*, became synonymous in households with the locally and independently produced dramas broadcast by RTS. Viewers tuned in weekly to watch Wolof-language dramatizations of the kinds of domestic crises, acts of corporate corruption, and failures of governmental oversight that were seen as characteristic of a period steeped in economic and moral decline. The thriving informal economy which supported the sale of recorded telefilms was indeed a by-product of this era of lost faith in public institutions. Daaray Kocc, the television troupe whose work I explore in this chapter, took advantage of this informal economy in response to what it saw as a flawed national distribution system that put performers at a considerable financial disadvantage. Dissatisfied with their arrangement with the RTS station, which provided a one-time buyout to television troupes but not royalties, Daaray Kocc took the initiative of selling its work directly to an eager national audience through the informal market for videocassettes. Internationally, an agreement with the independent video distributor Africassette allowed them to export their telefilms to the Senegalese diaspora. Such informal sales practices, which were the cause of a drawn-out legal battle between Daaray Kocc and RTS, dramatically increased the television troupes' visibility and continued into the early twenty-first century through the informal sale of DVDs.

While originally targeting a well-heeled middle-class audience, the televised "stage" quickly became the preferred site of creation for leaders of a popular, community-based theatrical movement, as evidenced by public debates of the late 1990s around the role of television as a broadly consumed form of popular theater. The Sorano Theater often found itself cited as a foil in this regard, as was the case in a 2000 *Sud Quotidien* interview with Macodou Mbengue, a graduate of the country's national conservatory and the founder of the popular independent troupe "Les Gueules Tapées."[15] In his portrayal of the theater scene at the time, Mbengue dismissed the Sorano Theater's capacity to serve properly in its artistic function, stating: "The elitism in which this theater has confined itself proves that it is no theater for the masses." Sorano would hardly find a more sympathetic voice in the premier playwright of the epic history plays that constituted its trademark. Reflecting on the inactivity of Sorano's large, state-funded performance troupes, Cheikh Aliou Ndao argued in an interview with *Le Soleil* that the institution's key failure lay in its inability to speak directly to its national audience and in its own language.[16] Regarding a cultural institution born of globalist ambitions, Ndao insisted that any theater must first learn to speak to its own public before hoping to travel beyond its borders. Sorano's irrelevance among the masses created an opportunity, according to Ndao, for smaller competitors, such as the immensely popular television productions, to outdo the national institution by taking for their primary material the realities of contemporary life. "These shortcomings of a society in a state of uneasiness," Ndao said, "are so obvious that one need only to point them out for all to chuckle." As a mirror of society's foibles, dreams, and ambitions, television had superseded Sorano in its mission by addressing the population's concerns at the dawn of the neoliberal era. Citing the most successful television troupes of the day, Ndao concluded: "Judging by the popularity of troupes like Daaray Kocc, Libidor, Jamonoy Tey, Radio St-Louis, we can say that the public has not been fooled. It recognizes its theater."

The creative movement sparked by locally produced television of the 1980s and '90s further reflected the liberalizing reforms of the era in that its key figures did not receive any official form of artistic training from national cultural institutions. Instead, most performers learned their trade by competing in the yearly *nawetaan* tournaments (discussed in chapter 2) or at popular "youth week" festivals called the "Semaines de la Jeunesse." The majority of television actors of this period, even those who became the country's most recognizable small-screen celebrities, maintained parallel careers in professions of the same bureaucratic milieus their work so frequently lampooned. One notable example is the actor Makhouredia Guèye, who became one of Senegal's most prominent performers after starring as the protagonist of Ousmane Sembène's film *The Money Order*. Guèye originally trained as an accountant before rising to fame in a highly popular radio comedy of the 1960s titled *Makhouredia Guèye, chauffeur de taxi*, in which he played a taxi driver newly arrived in Dakar from the countryside. The popular Medina neighborhood of downtown Dakar proved an important hub, producing two major companies, first Jamonoy Tey, and then Daaray Kocc, which formed as a splinter group of the former. These two companies and the Saint-Louis-based troupe Bara Yeggo formed the triumvirate of high-profile creators of televised content, whose work could be seen on alternate weeks during the regular Tuesday evening time slot.

The popular television movement's reach and success come across clearly in the optimism expressed in a 2000 article in *Sud Quotidien*, which asked stage artists to reflect upon the end of the Diouf regime as the country prepared to inaugurate its third president, Abdoulaye Wade. Representatives of a fledgling private theater movement (discussed further in the next chapter) fretted over their own survival and decried the lack of state support. Actors from the Sorano Theater expressed similar concerns and also took issue with the lack of dedicated housing for the theater's resident performers, an omission that symbolized, in their view, the state's larger neglect of cultural institutions. For popular artists in television, however, the future seemed limitless. The only thing they looked to acquire from the state was adequate airtime so that their already popular productions might reach their national viewership with greater ease. Referring to the work of television troupes, Daouda Guissé, leader of the Bara Yeggo troupe from Saint-Louis, declared in an interview: "There is no longer a shadow of a doubt as to the success of these theatrical productions. If we are given easier access to shooting and the small screen, we can fill the time slots now taken up by the foreign films that have invaded Senegalese television."[17] Cheikh Tidjane Diop, the director of Daaray Kocc, saw a bright future for television, which, he argued, should rely on the valuable resource of the widespread networks of popular theater practitioners, rather than on national cultural institutions which had proven incapable of thriving in the post-Senghor era: "The popular theater movement should be standing in for theatrical training. By supporting the ASC and the neighborhood troupes, we can cure Senegalese theater of what ails it: the lack of actors. Television's tricks and special effects are often there just to hide the shortcomings of the performers."[18]

Lessons from the School of Kocc

The words of Cheikh Tidjane Diop, screenwriter, director, and chemist by training, held considerable weight at the time. His troupe Daaray Kocc was a pioneer in television drama and satire and set the gold standard in local telefilm quality for Senegalese audiences. The troupe's name means "School of Kocc," a reference to the seventeenth-century philosopher Kocc Barma Faal, whose writings and maxims are still well known in Senegal and offer commentary on the political and domestic contexts of his day.[19] Barma is remembered as a great sage, and his wit and wisdom are closely associated with notions of the national Senegalese character and the need to combine respect for tradition with a sense of pragmatism. The figure of Kocc Barma thus provided a fitting symbol for a troupe that wished to present a mirror to Senegalese society in the decades following independence, highlighting its ills not only as a form of entertainment but also as a public service, inciting a national audience to consider some of the contradictions and absurdities at the root of their own lived experience.[20]

Some examples of Daaray Kocc's numerous productions include an early telefilm titled *Tere-tere mu të*, known popularly as *Opération Xamb*, with both titles referring to the storage in Senegalese households of sacred objects used in rituals. The telefilm effectively revisits the narrative of "Sarzan," the short story by Birago Diop that was once adapted for the Théâtre du Palais in Dakar (as discussed in chapter 2).[21] It examines the foibles of a newly appointed and ambitious, state-employed hygiene inspector, played by Makhouredia Guèye, who applies an excess of zeal to his job. The inspector eventually forbids in the name of hygiene the domestic storage of sacred alters, or *xamb*, which are used in the Lebu cleansing ritual of the *ndëp*. The spirits, or *rab*, associated with the *xamb* soon have their revenge, however, causing the inspector to go mad to the point of needing his own *ndëp* by the end of the film. Another of the troupe's most popular telefilms, *Ibra Italien*, depicts the misdeeds of a Senegalese Don Juan whose game of seduction includes passing for a migrant recently returned from an affluent life in Italy. The film's title signifies to this day the practice of appearing as more than one is in order to attract a spouse, especially by flaunting fictive connections with the El Dorados of the West. The lasting resonance of Daaray Kocc's films, as well as their entry into the popular vocabulary even of those too young to have watched them on television, are a testament to the troupe's success in speaking directly to its audience, thus accomplishing what Cheikh Aliou Ndao argued must be the first goal of any "national" theater.

Exploring Space and Media through So Long a Letter

One of Daaray Kocc's early accomplishments as a troupe was a televised adaptation in Wolof of the French-language epistolary novel *Une si longue lettre* (*So Long a Letter*), by Senegalese author Mariama Bâ. The telefilm stood out at the time given that most television troupes tended to work exclusively in comedy and satire.[22] The novel on which the adaptation was based also stands out when considered against a broader Francophone African literary canon. Now considered an indisputable "classic" of African literature, a status it has held since its designation as the 1980 winner of the Noma Award for Publishing in Africa, Bâ's novel is a pioneering work in several regards. In his reading of *Letter*, the Francophone scholar Christopher Miller indicates how the novel carved out a space for women's writing within the male-dominated canon of Francophone African literature.[23] Miller analyzes *Letter* as a doubly marginalized work, one that gives voice to the lived experience of women in Senegalese society through a genre, that of the epistolary novel, that is typically associated with a Western literary tradition.[24] And yet, the novel does not follow the typical conventions of the epistolary form. It does not include an actual exchange of letters, but rather gives a long testimony in the form of several letters written in the notebook, or *cahier*, of Ramatoulaye. This protagonist maintains a unidirectional exchange with her childhood friend now living abroad, Aïssatou, whose response the reader never sees but who, as an addressee, facilitates the voicing of a personal story with deep connections to the seemingly disappointing outcome of a particularly hopeful period of political and social reform.

Daaray Kocc's televised version of *So Long a Letter* shares with the novel an attempt to break ground in an unfamiliar genre, that of the epistolary Francophone African novel for Bâ, and that of the dramatic literary adaptation for television in the case of Daaray Kocc. In its adaptation, the troupe foregrounds not only the narrative content of Bâ's novel but also the epistolary means by which the tale is communicated, as well as the value granted to such literary gestures as a potential form of social commentary. Making use of the visual tools of its medium, the telefilm makes a fully invested image-sign of the performative act of taking up pen and paper to produce a sense of literary interiority that also serves as a figurative space of political expression. Moreover, Daaray Kocc's adaptation of the tale integrates the sites and visual signs that resonate in the national consciousness with the remembrance and longing that animate Bâ's novel. The visual cues at work in the telefilm parallel the work of the novel by tracing the doubts and regrets of a specific generation in the nation's history, the one called upon to lead the country to prosperity and modernity, but whose lives were largely undercut by the era's failure to produce the kind of society once promised in the exhilarating moment of independence.

In Bâ's novel, Ramatoulaye's story begins in a state of immense grief. The protagonist first writes to her friend following the sudden death of her husband, Modou, a government official who has suffered a heart attack at work. Ramatoulaye's sorrow inspires her to summon, through the process of writing, her memories of the school years of the two women and their respective husbands, four close companions who were once bright and ambitious students in the era leading up to independence. Ramatoulaye calls out to "the salt of remembrance," by writing: "I conjure you up. The past is reborn, along with its procession of emotions. I close my eyes. Ebb and tide of feeling: heat and dazzlement, the woodfires, the sharp green mango, bitten into in turns, a delicacy in our greedy mouths."[25] Her summoning of the past through the senses stirs up memories of a period full of hope whose recollection is now inevitably overshadowed by two parallel events that have marked both women's lives: "Yesterday you were divorced. Today I am a widow" (1).

Her subsequent letters to Aïssatou recall a period of courtship with Modou that includes a daring rejection of traditional expectations, since Ramatoulaye's mother had asked the young woman to consider another suitor. Ramatoulaye's decision to marry Modou against her mother's wishes, along with the growing solidarity of the four friends, all highly educated members of a rising urban professional class, symbolize in Ramatoulaye's memory a bold embrace of the country's new future as a "modern" nation on the verge of redefining its own social and gender norms. Following her husband's funeral, and as she writes during the period of four months and ten days during which Muslim widows must by custom remain secluded, Ramatoulaye faces the challenges of accepting her new widowhood. Of particular weight among her grievances is her husband's decision to exercise his right by Senegalese law to take another wife, followed by her own decision to remain with him in a polygamous arrangement. Ramatoulaye's choice differs from that of her friend Aïssatou who, when faced with the same imposition, left the country and created a new life for herself and her children as an interpreter for the United Nations in New York.

In its adaptation of *Letter*, the Daaray Kocc troupe offers a locally inspired critical response to Bâ's narrative that both prefigures and resonates with later scholarly engagement with the novel, especially in its association of Ramatoulaye's story with the sloping arc of nationalist sentiment from the late colonial to the postcolonial periods. The literary scholar Mildred Mortimer has pointed out in her study of domestic spaces in Francophone literature how "Bâ uses her characters as metaphors for disillusionment with her society."[26] Susan Andrade, in her consideration of the role of women's writing in forms of postcolonial nation-building, explores Bâ's interweaving of personal stories of domesticity with the lived experience of a failed political and social project. Thus, for Andrade, the novel's poignancy as a narrative of betrayal "stems from the story's self-understanding as a failed romance, that story standing in for the failure of social transformation once hoped of the decolonization process and national independence."[27] Critical interpretations of *Letter* have also contended with its status as a work of women's writing, with responses that range from framing writing as a tool for enfranchisement, to mixed views on the possibilities of writing as a means of liberation, to assessments of Bâ's engagement with femininity as opposed to feminism, along with some outlying denunciations of the story's protagonist as a member of a bourgeois class prone to an Enlightenment-based view of the postcolonial world's supposed need for salvation through a mimicry of European culture and values.[28] Scholarly readings have frequently framed *Letter* as an indictment of the continued practice of polygyny (commonly referred to as polygamy in Senegal), although the narrative never actually suggests a clear stance on the matter. In his study of *Letter* and its status as a work of "world literature," Tobias Warner underscores the assumption among many scholars and readers that the work carries an anti-polygamist message. Warner then considers how "the widespread investment in framing the novel in these ways is deeply revealing of the terms through which postcolonial literatures become legible to a world literary public."[29] While, for a Senegalese reader, the author's nuanced stance regarding the practice of polygamy might be more apparent, the interpretive frames of a world readership required a more direct affiliation with Western models of women's writing and feminism.

Bâ's audience indeed seems to have primarily consisted of such a "world" readership rather than a national, Senegalese one. The book, as Miller argues, represented the promise, if not the actuality, of a women's Francophone African literary canon to come. However, as Andrade points out, the novel seems to have had only a limited reach in the decades since its publication (1979) in inspiring analogous literary explorations among Francophone African women authors.[30] If the existence or lack of a broad national readership for Bâ's tale proves a point of tension, its audience was all but assured in the televised adaptation by the Daaray Kocc troupe, which likely constitutes *Letter*'s main point of contact with the Senegalese public. Daaray Kocc takes up a number of the themes later addressed in critical discussions of the work, starting with the exploration of national territories and the narratives that animate them. The telefilm's long opening sequence takes the viewer from the narrative present of Ramatoulaye mourning the loss of her husband to the nostalgic visions of the past conjured up by her memories, or what the novel calls the "salt of remembrance." Sites of national significance and collective memory occupy a central place in Daaray Kocc's adaptation, beginning with Ramatoulaye's taxi trip from her home to the hospital in the downtown neighborhood of Plateau. The taxi exits the residential area of Ramatoulaye's villa-strewn neighborhood, eventually driving south along the Corniche, the picturesque seaside thoroughfare that Senghor once envisioned as a promenade of cultural attractions set against the scenic backdrop of Africa's westernmost coastline. Ramatoulaye's taxi then enters the downtown area via the roundabout that faces the imposing National Assembly, and whose center then hosted the statue of "Demba and Dupont" commemorating African participation in the European wars of the twentieth century.[31] This visual itinerary at the beginning of the film reminds viewers of the nation's prominent place in world history as well as its optimistic post-independence commitment to become a bastion of commerce, cultural exchange, and democracy. It also sets the tale in motion by engaging in what Shaun Irlam has called a "praxis of memory" central to the novel, calling to visual consciousness key sites that recall "an idyllic space of lost completeness" left in the memories of both the nation and the story's protagonist.[32]

After a hasty navigation of the hospital's long corridors, Ramatoulaye arrives at the room where Modou's corpse lies. Upon seeing the body of her deceased husband, she finds herself overcome by a wave of emotions and memory, a sensation conveyed in the telefilm through a flashback effect. Ramatoulaye looks ahead beyond the camera, as the image slowly fades to a nostalgic haze, eventually refocusing on a couple the viewer soon discovers to be a young Ramatoulaye and Modou, seated at a beachside café. As a waiter serves them soft drinks, Modou gallantly imposes a reversal of traditional gender roles, insisting "Chérie, c'est moi qui te sers" ("Let me serve *you*, dear"). After the couple take a drink, Modou begins a long speech that situates the scene in the national memoryscape. The young students are seated near the Gorée Island campus of the famous William Ponty School. Modou articulates a view of the Ponty institution's historical legacy that projects even further into the past the nostalgic gaze originally cast by Ramatoulaye at the hospital. Filled with excitement, he voices his admiration for their shared school. "You know, here the École William Ponty is like a meeting place for people from all over Africa. You have people from Guinea, from Côte d'Ivoire, Central Africa, from Chad, from all over." Ramatoulaye adds approvingly: "From all of Africa!" Modou comes to his point by arguing that their experience at the Ponty School will form the basis of an African unity that will serve to bring together the future leaders of the continent.

Modou's evocation of the Ponty School represents, on the part of the Daaray Kocc troupe, a form of ahistorical remembrance of the institution, which only served the French colonies of West Africa, not Central Africa or Chad. Modou's vision of the school as a springboard for Africa's first leaders and the basis for a subsequent Pan-African unity also clashes with the colonial nature of the Ponty School. Having sought, as discussed in the first chapter, to enroot students in a sense of African otherness, the school was far from aiming to foster any kind of profound political or intellectual enfranchisement among its students. This scene in the telefilm does not appear in Bâ's novel, but resonates with one of Ramatoulaye's letters in which she recalls to her friend their shared experience at a French colonial school she calls "Ponty-Ville."[33] Ramatoulaye mentions a competitive entrance exam and a culturally vibrant ambience similar to those of the École William Ponty. Her memory of the women's school reveals a view of the country's post-independence history that laments the fragmentation of the sense of Pan-African unity that had begun to emerge as a by-product of colonial institutions, and which should have been preserved by the post-independence elite. Ramatoulaye describes the former territory of French West Africa as "now broken up into autonomous republics," and she insists on the political and cultural possibilities of the coherence once fostered through the colonial school, explaining: "Nothing differentiated us, apart from specific racial features, the Fon girl from Dahomey and the Malinke one from Guinea. Friendships were made that have endured the test of time and distance. We were true sisters, destined for the same mission of emancipation."[34]

As scholars have pointed out, Bâ no doubt bases her character's romanticized view of her education on her own experience as a student at the normal school in Rufisque, which was conceived as a women's equivalent of the William Ponty School.[35] Only men were admitted to Ponty, a fact which highlights another piece of ahistorical reconstruction in Daaray Kocc's adaptation, since Ramatoulaye could not have been a student there with Modou. However, Daaray Kocc's substitution of the William Ponty School for the novel's vaguely defined "Ponty-Ville" places the historical referent—colonial education for the elite of French West Africa—more squarely in the limelight, situating it in space for the telefilm's national audience. In Daaray Kocc's film such nostalgic reworkings of the past take on a primary role, preceding all later action in the plot. The enmeshment of two modes of distant recollection, that of Ramatoulaye looking into her past to understand the present and that of a national imaginary seeking in colonial institutions the seeds of a later Pan-African unity, foregrounds the act of remembering in Bâ's tale, as well as the deformations that come with it.

Through visual means, Daaray Kocc explores the impact of Bâ's novel as a work of, and about, women's writing, particularly through a recurring image that serves to interrogate the medium of the telefilm and its relationship to a budding post-independence national literature. Long scenes in which the only image is the seated protagonist engrossed in the act of writing are interspersed in the telefilm, serving as a technique for exposition, but also performing the literary gesture of self-expression portrayed, and carried out, through Bâ's novel. Over the image, Ramatoulaye voices, in French (a stark contrast with the Wolof dialogue of the film), excerpts from one of the letters as written in the original novel. In their reworking of the story, Daaray Kocc thus interrogates the possibility of medial translation and adaptation by establishing a visual sign to suggest the literality that the novel had come to represent.

As Warner has argued, the novel implicitly raises the question of translation in both the language and form it employs.[36] Any translation effort, whether to another target language, as in the case of the later Wolof translation by Maam Yunus Dieng and Arame Fal, or to another medium as in the work of Daaray Kocc, must contend with an inherent tension linked to the existence or lack of a reliable readership.[37] In literary terms, this concern imposes itself particularly in the complexities of translating works of literature with roots in Western literary tradition into African languages. For Daaray Kocc, the question at hand was whether they should merely set Bâ's novel along a coherent linear plot for television or integrate the notions of literality that are inevitably tied in with the novel. The troupe opted for the latter approach by demonstrating the force of its own medium, which is capable of integrating expressions of the visual, the oral (through Ramatoulaye's voice-over), and the literary (through a staging of the literary-sign).

Daaray Kocc's televised version of *So Long a Letter*, once watched by a large national audience and now accessible online via multiple video-sharing platforms that are popular with an increasingly connected Senegalese public, represents a critical translation of the novel not only to a more accessible language (as concerns the dialogue in Wolof), but also to a more accessible medium and form. In subsuming the act of self-writing within the visual medium of television, the telefilm also sublimates the sign of literality for its audience. The literary gesture driving the story expresses a form of interiorizing self-expression that interweaves nostalgic remembrance with the practice of social and political criticism. Daaray Kocc's memorable image of Ramatoulaye and her letter thus constitutes a powerful form of literary adaptation and transmedial stagecraft.

The durability of this particular image positing self-expressive letter-writing as a form of both personal and political expression testifies to the ambitions of Daaray Kocc's work as a creator of popular meaning. Notably, the visual trope of solitary writing reappears in the Senegalese director Rama Thiaw's 2016 film *The Revolution Won't Be Televised*. This is a documentary film on the rap movement Y'en a Marre (Fed Up), which contested Abdoulaye Wade's controversial and ultimately failed attempt to win a third presidential term in 2012.[38] Thiaw's film opens with a close-up shot of the Senegalese writer and filmmaker Khady Sylla who, from a room of her own, lights a cigarette and assumes the role of Ramatoulaye's surrogate, picking up a pen to write her thoughts in a notebook. Sylla's act marks the beginning of a highly political film that documents the efforts of an activist group, and especially those of its most visible musician, Thiat. The film more broadly expresses the grievances of a generation of young Senegalese committed to opposing an unconstitutional seizure of power by the autocratic figure of Wade. Sylla's image is interspersed throughout the film. Her letter-testimony, which she addresses directly to Thiat as she speaks to the camera, reflects the concerns of an older generation and denounces a rampant consumerism Sylla describes as overwhelming any sense of civic engagement or responsibility. If the content and the message, as well as the means of address, have changed, the visual trope once proposed by Daaray Kocc has provided an effective means of cross-generational reflection on the broken promises of a nation, expressed through the form of on-screen literary self-expression.

On Corporate Corruption: One Cultural Value Can Overcome Another

The impact of corruption and clientelism constitutes a central theme in considerations of the post-Senghor era. In their study of Senegalese society in the years of Abdou Diouf's administration, Momar-Coumba Diop and Mamadou Diouf explore how, following the first two decades of independence, the economic imperatives of the country were superseded by the needs of a ruling class and its clientele, which sought to secure their status while the structures of Senghor's African socialism were dismantled. As Diop and Diouf write, "The political practices induced by neopatrimonialism favored the creation, consolidation, and enrichment of groups and networks able to bargain their way into the reproduction of the social and political order. These networks and their overseers, parasitic staff and clientelism, largely benefited from the expansion and centralization of the State."[39] Such networks also constitute the focus of much of the social satire addressing this particular period of Senegalese history, when authors and artists took aim at the moral consequences of complex systems of graft that allowed those in power to protect their own interests at the expense of the public good.

In their best-known reckoning with the extent of the clientelist practices described by Diop and Diouf, Daaray Kocc distinguished themselves as leaders in the use of such social satire. Their 1989 televised miniseries *Un DG peut en cacher un autre* (*One Director General Can Hide Another*) tells of the difficulties encountered by a young and ambitious upper-level manager named Alassane Fall—played by Daaray Kocc founding member Moustapha Diop—as he takes on the graft and moral rot that have set in at the nationalized company SONAC, or La Société Nationale des Céréales (National Cereals Firm). As Fall will discover, an embezzlement scheme between SONAC's employees and cereal merchants has drained its coffers and pushed the publicly funded institution to the brink of collapse. The scheme involves all levels of the company, with several staff members taking regular payouts in exchange for their complicity or silence. Fraudulent bookkeeping by the in-house accountant, called "Maley comptable," has managed to conceal the illegal activity, and the staff's union representative is in the pockets of the perpetrators. Meanwhile, the former corrupt Director General, or "DG," Monsieur Diakhaté, played by Makhouredia Guèye, works from the outside to sabotage the newly arrived DG's efforts to set the company on the path of fiscal responsibility.

DG Alassane Fall, the product of a virtuous upbringing that has taught him the value of humility and hard work, steps into the role of the protagonist-hero who is determined to implement the highest standards of transparency and professionalism at SONAC. His arrival strikes fear in the hearts of those entangled in the corrupt system in place. Fall meets with intense forms of resistance that include slanderous attacks on him and his family, an elaborate public smear campaign, and even multiple attempts to cast spells on him through traditional acts of mysticism. Fall's trials stem from the multiple obstacles he encounters as he strives to save the company from its own unethical practices, which many of the personnel justify by citing culturally specific Senegalese values. Fall, who ultimately succeeds in his quest, rejects this view of Senegalese society, positing by his own example that, when correctly observed, traditional values should encourage the success of a national firm such as SONAC, rather than precipitating its demise.

The choice of the cereals sector for the miniseries' setting reflects one of the key economic stakes in Senegalese society at the time: self-sufficiency in the production and sale of rice, a staple of the Senegalese diet.[40] The title of the miniseries, *One Director General Can Hide Another*, refers to the concealed forces of high-level corruption that can work to impede such an evidently worthy objective. The title's wording derives from a warning commonly displayed in French train stations alerting foot traffic that oncoming trains may be hidden by standing ones. In a more figurative sense, the expression conveys the idea that appearances can prove deceitful, and underlying forces may be at work below the surface without one's knowledge. The warning prefigures Fall's difficulties throughout the series, while also offering an assessment of Senegalese society at a time when matters of the highest national importance lay in the hands of a corrupt leadership class, alongside an ultimately unaccountable group of external decision-makers seated at the World Bank and the IMF.

An early exchange between Fall and one of the company's most corrupt figures illustrates the conflict at hand through an acrimonious wielding of terms understood as inherent to the Senegalese value system. In one of his first actions as DG, Fall organizes a meeting with his assistant director, Mbengue. Fall opens the discussion on a conciliatory note, stating that he will not aim to single out guilty parties, but making it clear that the company's current practices cannot continue given the firm's catastrophic state. "It's true that any worker looks out for his own interest," Fall states, "but we mustn't, in any case, forget the company that's employed us: SONAC. Its best interest is our own. Its good image [*sutura*] is our own." Mbengue replies to Fall's assessment with a personal appeal. Whatever reforms Fall imposes, he asks that he do so with patience and flexibility, and manage the company "Senegalese style" (*à la sénégalaise*). When a surprised Fall asks for clarification, Mbengue cites the importance of *sutura* (discretion), *kersa* (deference, restraint), *muñ* (patience), and *maslaa* (civility). Fall dismisses Mbengue's request, insisting that he will set the company straight through the only effective and universal means, that of work. Although he diminishes the importance of the value terms cited by Mbengue, recourse to (and misuse of) these four concepts will present some of the most stubborn obstacles to his success.

Scholarship on these value terms and their uses has highlighted their place within a cultural system that aims to indicate for various categories of class and gender the correct course of action for a virtuous life that favors sustained social harmony. Direct translation of the terms proves difficult because they refer not only to a specific comportment, but also to the effect that comportment is expected to have on society at large. In a study that takes *sutura*, usually translated as "discretion," as its central theme, Ivy Mills glosses the term contextually, pointing out that "the virtuous practices and states that *sutura* indexes include discretion, modesty, privacy, protection, and the happiness that the previous terms are said to ensure."[41] In Mbengue's request, the term *sutura* constitutes an appeal to discretion that would avoid naming plainly the company's rampant corruption. However, when used by Fall moments earlier, the term indicates the desired outcome of a virtuous discretion that reflects positively on the reputation of an individual or group, setting the foundation for its public degree of integrity.

Such double readings of these value terms' significance and desired impact have led to varying interpretations of concepts such as *maslaa*, which suggests a respect for established hierarchies in order to maintain peace, or alternately a cultural obstacle to economic development, or a means of establishing lasting social harmony through a respect for tradition and social institutions.[42] Similar mixed interpretations can be offered for the values of *muñ*, or the ability to endure hardship with a sense of patient stoicism, and *kersa*, which emphasizes a form of restraint that, as Joseph Hill suggests, "demands a degree of interiority of both men and women, requiring them not to put themselves 'out there,' for example, through speaking too loudly or dressing immodestly."[43] If these Senegalese cultural values have an undeniable impact on society and its norms, how they are cited to justify one's actions highlights the discursive nature of their practice. While the term *sutura* may be used to describe the course of action taken by both Fall and Mbengue, their examples in the telefilm serve to contrast a socially desirable view of *sutura*, *kersa*, *muñ*, and *masala,* one that aims toward the collective and public good, with an interpretation that serves only to protect individual interests. By appearing to criticize Senegalese value terms and their negative impact on the nation and its post-independence modernization, Daaray Kocc in fact salvages the terms for what they have to offer to a society in need of a value system compatible with the global economy in which it must now participate.

In the face of moral ambiguity, the character of Fall, whose close relationship with his religiously devout parents serves as a moral compass throughout the series, represents the equally important Senegalese virtues of *fit* (courage) and *jom* (dignity). These Wolof concepts offer an antidote to the corrupting practices that have taken root in the firm and, by extension, in the Senegalese economy, civil society, and the political realm. In his first speech as the DG of SONAC, Fall cites *fit* and *jom* as the driving principles of the work he plans to undertake. His first action as DG will be to implement a strict transparency measure by which all orders and transactions must pass through his office, a decision that sends a wave of panic through the firm. Fall's stance of *fit* and *jom* in the face of a corrupt culture puts him at loggerheads with fellow cadres like Mbengue, who is eventually sent on mission by Fall to the remote city of Tambacounda following an argument over the place of prayer in the workplace. Mbengue demands the firm continue its practice of stopping work for prayer and allocating an office as a prayer room. Fall plans to implement a corporate sense of temporality, allowing for prayer in the workplace, but only if the workers' busy schedules permit it.

After a series of failed rebellions and conspiracies hatched by the more corrupt elements among the personnel, Fall ultimately succeeds in reforming the company's culture. His employees follow the example he sets, and even Mbengue returns to Dakar as a reformed and respectful collaborator. The firm increases its productivity and becomes one of the best-performing companies in the country. However, Fall's rise and SONAC's salvation take up only the first half of the series, since the DG's success earns him an appointment to a ministerial post. Upon his departure, the firm is taken over by Mbengue, who immediately reinstates the company's previous embezzlement schemes but, unlike his model, the former DG Diakhaté, he does not succeed in quelling a rebellion from a restive workers' union. Mbengue's lack of *fit* and *jom* has dragged SONAC back to the brink of collapse by the end of the series.

Un DG peut en cacher un autre concludes with a direct address to the camera by an everyday "woman-on-the-street" character who typifies Daaray Kocc's view of its own role as a creator of satire. In a discussion at the end of the seventh and final episode between two observers of SONAC's demise, both wonder at the company's fate and that of its corrupt DG. One of the unnamed characters asks: "Since one DG always hides another, what will the next one bring?" Her interlocutor's response ends with a pointed interrogation addressed directly to the camera and the viewer at home: "Now there's a question to follow, and very closely!" The statement punctuates the series' intention to entertain, but also to offer Senegalese households a subtle reflection of the real-life economic and cultural challenges faced during this particular period. A new stage space was indeed needed, and one which Daaray Kocc skillfully provided for a Senegalese population that witnessed the increased centralization of political and economic power, the spread of systemic corruption, and a profound loss of faith in public institutions. These factors contributed to the rise of a now-ubiquitous informal economic sector. On a more intangible level, they also fostered a deep disenchantment among the Senegalese middle class as it grew increasingly frustrated by the non-arrival of the bourgeois life once promised, first in the midst of the Pan-African enthusiasm of political independence, and later in the form of liberalizing programs which sought to dynamize the economy.

On Television in the Digital Media Age

Today, television enjoys a greater reach than ever in Senegal thanks to the advent of online video-sharing platforms.[44] As with the installation of television transmitters and the subsequent use of videocassette technology, the growing availability of high-speed, wireless Internet connections, combined with the flooding of the Senegalese market with inexpensive smartphones, has created new opportunities to facilitate the kinds of collectivity formation that Larkin describes as key to the function of media as a form of communal infrastructure. In both private and public spaces, from the home to all forms of public transportation, the Senegalese have become avid consumers of the many independently produced television series that have emerged to meet the public's growing demand. A number of informally managed video-sharing platforms have combined with more familiar, international sites such as YouTube to provide a Senegalese viewership with a digital archive of television offerings. Available series include those of the early decades of Senegalese television, published by independent accounts without the cooperation or permission of the actors or television stations. While in no way remunerative to members of the early television troupes, the availability of these videos has revived interest in the work of "*les anciens*," or the leaders of a certain golden age of Senegalese television. In talk show interviews with former Daaray Kocc members, discussions often circulate around the quality of their troupe's work in comparison with the more slapstick or melodramatic approach of contemporary productions.[45]

A basic Internet search of "*théâtre sénégalais*" highlights the features of today's television industry in Senegal, beginning with the sheer number of popular theater troupes promoting their work online, very few of which benefit from any distribution on the country's now broader range of public and privately owned television channels.[46] The Internet has become the favored means of distribution for television programming, a fact that has presented a number of advantages to both small-scale actors and producers of larger-budget series benefiting from access to televised airtime and a cast of national celebrities. The payment structures for those who manage to work professionally have not changed since the days of Daaray Kocc. Actors continue to receive one-time buyouts rather than royalties, and so have responded to the lack of reliable income by producing a far greater volume of episodes. A single season of a television series can count as many as fifty episodes, a quantity made possible by shorter episode lengths, the flexibility afforded by digital technology, which dramatically cuts the cost of filming, and the use of everyday sets rather than the professionally crafted ones of a television studio. For small companies, this format has provided a wider range of opportunities to break through in the industry.[47]

For larger companies, the prevalence of Internet distribution has fed ambitions, once held by Daaray Kocc but never realized, of selling their work to a broader international, and especially African, audience. One prominent example is that of Marodi TV, a Senegalese production company that has released a number of highly popular series. In its subject matter, Marodi's series take inspiration from the current success of North American shows, focusing on dramas of domestic intrigue, crime, and political scandal. The company has also taken advantage of contemporary digital technology to create a sophisticated website whose interface resembles those of today's most popular international paid streaming platforms, but which makes its content available free of charge. The Marodi website even guides navigators to select series that can be viewed with French subtitles, a feature made available through the YouTube platform, thus rendering the company's Wolof-language content accessible to a broad, Francophone audience. This strategy has paid off tremendously, and the YouTube channel to which the company's website directs viewers counts as of this writing more than 2,500,000 subscribers.

Figure 5.1. From the series *Maîtresse d'un homme marié*, by Marodi Productions.

If Marodi's offerings have enjoyed considerable success and visibility nationally, the release of its most popular series to date, *Maîtresse d'un homme marié* (*Mistress of a Married Man*), has solidified the production company's place as the industry's best hope for breaking through to an international audience. The series focuses on the lives of a group of independent working women living in Dakar and has demonstrated television's ability to create controversy by broaching societal issues and cultural taboos. The depiction of its female protagonist, Marème, who is the mistress of a wealthy businessman and soon aspires to become her lover's second wife, has sparked a wave of criticism and calls for censorship from the country's religious organizations.[48] Marème's open defiance of the norms of *sutura* (discretion) that are often imposed on women caused the greatest shock. In one scene, she declares to her friend in the privacy of their shared apartment that her "thing," and here she points between her legs to eliminate any ambiguity, is hers alone to give to whomever she pleases. Shortly after the episode, which appeared early in the show's first season, the Muslim NGO Jamra filed a complaint that went before the country's National Audiovisual Regulatory

Council (Conseil National de Régulation Audiovisuelle), resulting in a stern warning to the company. Polygamy again finds itself at the core of the story's controversy. However, Marème's ambition is to use the Muslim custom of taking a second wife to her advantage, ultimately using the institution to justify behavior otherwise judged as immoral by the country's religious standards. Complicating the plot even further is the fact that Marème is not a female character in a position of inferiority seeking to secure a stable life for herself. She has a successful career, drives an impeccable SUV through the city, and lives in a luxury apartment building in one of the capital's affluent neighborhoods. The series' depiction of successful and outspoken women living among a rising class of affluent professionals has earned the show an international reputation as the *Sex and the City* of West Africa.

Although this TV series differs considerably from the work of the first decades of Senegalese television, its storytelling similarly reflects the economic concerns of a contemporary national audience, most notably in the inclusion of the radical changes underway in the capital's urban landscape. A number of the central characters of *Maîtresse* work for the international construction firm Senegindia, which has invested heavily in luxury homes for the newly built site of Diamniadio. This "new city" built from scratch some thirty kilometers inland from Dakar is part of the current president Macky Sall's Emerging Senegal Plan, which aims to relieve some of the congestion of the capital. Since the first foundations were lain, Diamniadio has seen the construction of an International Conference Center, a sports stadium, and a series of high-rise luxury apartments and villas currently being sold aggressively to professionals as an opportunity to secure a place in the city of tomorrow. Many of the *Maîtresse* scenes take place in such villas and display their stylish modern architecture. In several scenes, Marème's lover Cheikh, a successful real estate developer, vaunts the luxurious amenities of Senegindia's offerings. More than a compelling drama, the series also offers Senegalese of all classes an opportunity to imagine themselves in the homes of a new Senegalese bourgeoisie on which the nation will soon rely to turn the government's dream of a prosperous city in the bush of Diamniadio into a reality. Perhaps more aspirational than earlier depictions of such a rising professional class, the series nonetheless takes as its subject the lives of an affluent bourgeoisie whose failure to emerge fully and to drive economic growth nationally has proven one of the nation's most formidable challenges from the post-independence period to the present day.

✦

In a period when official theatrical structures began fading from relevance for the country's audiences and aspiring theater-makers, television has provided a framework in Senegal for mounting an alternative and highly visible form of stage that aims to hold up a mirror to Senegalese society. In the first decades of television, and especially through the 1980s and early 1990s, the small screen's most prominent works offered youth and community theater groups the opportunity to take the stage to express the general disillusionment of an urban class that once eagerly anticipated its promised role as the rising bourgeoisie driving the economic growth of a newly independent and prosperous country. The televised narratives produced and consumed by this urban class highlight the non-arrival of such a *nouvelle bourgeoisie*. They call to question the widespread nationalist optimism that followed independence, and underscore the failures of those charged with running the independent economy now overseen by international organizations with no political mandate. For its staged social commentary on a growing sense of disillusionment, and for lack of an adequate response from struggling cultural institutions like the Daniel Sorano National Theater, the Senegalese public turned largely to the newly available small screen.

The digital platforms and filming technology of today's media landscape have all but ensured the durability of television in the homes and collective imagination of the Senegalese people. The small screen today gives the most complete picture of the range of backgrounds and trajectories that bring people to the craft of theater-making in this country. The television industry has maintained strong ties with popular theater organizations, which are often enlisted to promote a given series to their home neighborhoods. One also finds certain *pensionnaires* of the Sorano Theater who have decided, not without reservations in many cases, to take part in the medium which has the greatest promise for reaching a national audience. As such, Senegalese television has shown remarkable adaptability as it finds new ways to speak directly to its public, a characteristic it shares with the movement that provides the focus of the next chapter: that of popular theater.

Chapter 6

Stagecraft and Popular Theater

Although it is by far the primary point of interaction between theatrical performance and the Senegalese public, popular theater in Senegal, as in many African contexts, remains a category whose characteristics and limits prove difficult to define. In the histories of Senegalese stagecraft explored thus far, the spirit of "popular theater" has inspired an array of cultural movements and initiatives, including the community-based *nawetaan* competitions, the religiously inspired Sufi stage space, the mass consumption of telefilm satires and dramas, and even the broad popular engagement in Cissé Dia's *Les Derniers Jours de Lat Dior* at the World Festival of Negro Arts. While the many evocations and manifestations of popular theater have produced a variety of stage spaces, a common feature appears in their artists' commitment to using theatrical performance as a tool to speak directly to the collectively imagined Senegalese masses, rather than to an audience of elites. The anthropologist Karin Barber highlights, in her study of popular theater in western Nigeria, popular theater's summoning of crowds of spectators not as an audience but rather as a "public," which she describes as "a horizon of address composed of anonymous and, in principle, interchangeable individuals, of potentially indefinite extent."[1] The language and spirit of the Senegalese popular theater movement adopts a similar view in its address to the non-elite "masses." Today's popular theater approach is articulated largely in contrast to nearly a century of Senegalese dramaturgy in French, which the playwright and scholar Marouba Fall evokes in pointing out that "from the days of theatrical performance at the William Ponty School until today one question has stuck with the Black African playwright who writes in French. For whom, in truth, does he write?"[2] In its recrafting of the stage space, the Senegalese popular theater movement responds by insisting that popular theater-making must produce a stage that is accessible to all and capable of mobilizing to action the masses to which it speaks.

The stage director Alioune Oumy Diop describes, in his book *Le Théâtre traditionnel au Sénégal* (*Traditional Theater in Senegal*), the objectives of a Senegalese popular theater movement in search of an alternative to the country's national cultural institutions, which he judged as rooted in a bourgeois, elitist aesthetic. Calling for a complete reworking of the African stage space, Oumy Diop argues that theater in Black African contexts must situate its work within an activist political framework. "Black African popular theater," he writes,

> must convince as much as it entertains, incite groundbreaking action among the masses to which it speaks. In order to fulfill its social function completely, modern Black African popular theater must imperatively be spoken in Black African languages. Alongside and in connection with the creation of new plays, the techniques of theatrical architecture, direction, stage management, set design, sound and light design, makeup and so on, must be thoroughly revamped. Instead of understanding these techniques from a borrowed European framework, we must design new techniques that make an optimal contribution to the language of the theatrical work.[3]

Oumy Diop's insistence on the use of African languages represents a thinly veiled criticism of the Daniel Sorano National Theater, which tends to present stage works in French. Yet he extends the long-debated language question of African cultural production to the stage language inherent to any theatrical performance. It will not suffice, Oumy Diop points out, to perform in African languages while retaining all the other conventions of Western performance. For theater-makers like Oumy Diop, a decolonizing stage must be fully reconceptualized in order to allow performers to do theater differently. Reflecting a Fanonian view of the need for a national culture that, if it is to be truly national, will respond dynamically and actively to its own political context, Oumy Diop criticizes the place of traditional theater and folklore in the country's national institutions and even in many "popular" settings: "Theater's content must not be commercial folklore set to dance and music. It must serve as a transformative instrument for society through direct action upon society. Its sources must dig into ancient or modern myth, as well as present-day reality, in order to awaken people's consciousness."[4]

The goal of radically transforming the relationship between theater artists and the masses has long animated the Senegalese popular theater movement. This movement became institutionalized in 1965 with the creation of the Senegalese Federation of Popular Theater, and continues to dominate today's theatrical landscape with countless popular theater troupes, most of them amateur but some professionalized. Despite the movement's undeniable success, even its most prominent figures often struggle to describe with precision what, exactly, the term "popular theater" represents in today's Senegalese context. Mouhamadou Diol, director of the forum theater company Kàddu Yaraax (which is Wolof for "Voice of Yarakh," Diol's neighborhood just outside of Dakar), is very familiar with the principles of popular theater laid out by Oumy Diop. Diol's troupe has made a name for itself by working in the spirit of popular theater, although, as he points out, it is a term that often confounds as much as it inspires. "I'm the treasurer of the Federation of Popular Theater and I still don't know what 'popular theater' means," he says. "It doesn't mean anything anymore. People talk about popular theater as opposed to professional theater, classical theater, or elitist theater. They talk about popular theater to refer to the masses!" Diol adds with a laugh, "which basically means people like us, the poor losers who have nothing."[5]

In this chapter, I use a field-based approach to explore the creative acts of stagecraft by which contemporary popular theater artists like Diol contextualize, theorize, and implement the decolonizing principles behind the popular theater movement in Senegal.[6] In addressing the uses and reworkings of the notion of "popular" on the theatrical stage, I look to build on scholarship addressing the shifting parameters of the popular arts in Africa. I refer here especially to the work of Karin Barber, who asserts that, despite the slipperiness of the term "popular" as an artistic category, the popular arts must be studied, and on their own terms, due to "their sheer undeniable presence as social facts."[7] As Barber points out, the popular arts impose themselves as a focus of study all the more because they "loudly proclaim their own importance in the lives of a large number of African people."[8] This chapter's first section explores the emergence of such a popular theater movement in Senegal through the major events, documents, and institutions that have defined its overarching principles. The movement's success resonates with Gaurav Desai's observation that popular theater cannot be conceived of as a monolithic form, but is "best thought of as a normative discursive practice that engages in dialogues with other theatrical practices of society."[9] The popular theater movement in Senegal indeed found its voice by way of a similar form of dialogue with other theatrical groups and institutions.

In the second section, I examine the implementation of the popular frame through a case study of one of the country's leading popular theater companies, Diol's Kàddu Yaraax. Drawing from thirteen months of fieldwork carried out over a period of four years, I consider the artistic and logistical decisions and accommodations imposed on companies when their attempts to embrace the popular approach meet local material demands and cultural expectations. In order to subsist, popular theater companies must find their way in a world of scarce funding opportunities and commissions. The required maneuvering does not tend to sit well with critical frameworks assessing the degree to which companies succeed or fail to align their work with the decolonizing and democratizing ideals of popular theater and theater activism in the Global South.[10] Through my case study, I argue that even in their "failures" to live up to the ideals of the popular theater movement, troupes like Diol's create a space for critical discourse through the multifaceted work of stagecraft constituted by the producing, rehearsing, performing, and framing of the popular event.

The Emergence of the Popular Stage Space in Senegal

The tenets and institutions of the popular theater movement emerged out of the cultural debates that took place in the decade following Senegal's independence in 1960. Popular theater artists generated momentum for the movement by creating institutional affiliations with youth and community organizations rather than with more centralized arts funders like the Ministry of Culture. In 1969 the Senegalese Federation of Popular Theater, which had been founded four years earlier and received its funding from the Ministry of Youth and Sports, drafted a manifesto laying out the key principles of Senegalese popular theater. The manifesto outlined the discussions of an event that same year called the Festival of Popular Theater, where a colloquium titled "Functions and Perspectives of Popular Theater" had included a host of premier cultural figures, including the Senegalese playwrights Cheikh Aliou Ndao and Thierno Bâ, the Haitian poet Jean Brierre, and the Senegalese theater scholar Bakary Traoré. The participants sought to define a theatrical movement they saw as running counter to the artistic forms and practices found in national institutions like the Sorano Theater. The Federation of Popular Theater's leaders called the widely circulated, though never officially published, manifesto that resulted from their discussions "Les Options fondamentales pour le théâtre populaire" ("Fundamental Choices for Popular Theater").

One of the first tenets laid out in the cultural manifesto highlighted the movement's departure from the notion of Francophonie then being promoted by President Senghor. The manifesto states that a theater truly for the people must imperatively be performed in the people's language. For actors and organizers in popular theater at the time, this condition drew an important distinction between their work and that of the official theater seen on national stages. The use of African languages proved all the more essential for a performance practice that was envisioned as providing a form of civic education through engagement with youth culture and local political movements. When, in the 1970s, the regional networks of the Associations Sportives et Culturelles paired annual soccer tournaments with competitions of popular theater (as discussed in chapter 2), they also effectively established a means of engagement and potential protest in the political sphere for large groups of young Senegalese men and women. This mode of political activism through culture inscribed itself within the popular theater movement's civic mission, enabling youth to participate in and act upon the public sphere in new ways.

Another key tenet of the popular theater manifesto reflected the organizers' desire to restructure what they called the stage's theatrical architecture. The participants aspired to break away from what they saw as a mimicry of the European proscenium-style stage space in favor of a layout inspired by precolonial African performance forms. The most bitingly critical section of the popular theater manifesto was a characterization of the European model of theater, according to which

> the word "theater" brings to mind a room split into two parts; on one side, women and men stuffed into the most outmoded costumes imaginable, speaking in a language increasingly unintelligible to the people and making gestures from a long-gone society all under ten-to-twenty kilowatt lighting; on the other side you have ladies and gentlemen dressed according to the latest fashion, sitting still in perfect silence and in complete darkness.[11]

For these artists, the layout favored by European-inspired stage spaces impeded the kind of civic education and local engagement that popular theater sought to facilitate. Meanwhile, they argued, performers had at their disposal alternatives to the proscenium that did not separate theater artists from their public. Chief among these was the *géew*, a Wolof term for the circle formed in the public square to make room for the West African griot, or storyteller. This local form of theatrical architecture enabled the kind of direct interaction between performers and spectators that was needed for theater to serve as both a tool of civic education and a mirror of social consciousness, to return to Bakary Traoré's definition of theater's primary social function.

In the same year that the Senegalese Federation of Popular Theater held its seminal colloquium, the limitations of the state's approach to national performance cultures were beginning to come to light. In 1969, the dramatic arts section of the School of Arts of Senegal found that its graduates could no longer join the now full roster of the Sorano Theater's troupe. The school had been founded after independence to meet the training demands of a national arts policy seeking to develop and promote the country's many forms of expressive culture.[12] But when the 1969 graduates in drama learned that they would not be offered a place as resident artists at the National Theater, they responded by launching Senegal's first private theater troupe, called Les Tréteaux Sénégalais (The Senegalese Stageboards). Although the leaders of the private theater movement first tried to align themselves with the principles laid out by the budding popular theater movement, what eventually emerged from their efforts was a third cultural approach that became known as Senegal's "contemporary" theater. What set private, contemporary troupes apart from their popular theater peers was an ambition to produce stage works that could be performed both locally and abroad. They thus sought to take advantage of opportunities presented by a transnational, cultural form of globalization, offering a globally focused, market-based response to the gradual decline of nationally funded arts institutions.[13]

Whereas the Sorano Theater had made a name for itself by staging large-scale productions, which were often epically inflected plays on African royalty, or adaptations of Western canonical plays, such undertakings were far beyond the means of the newly emerging private companies. The fledgling companies instead decided to reduce their numbers and focus on small productions that could be sent on tour. One of the pioneers of the contemporary movement, Oumar Ndao, describes an early period in which private companies outperformed their national counterparts:

> There was a transitional period, between 1987 and '92 more or less, just before the devaluation of the franc CFA, when the private theater experiment completely wiped out historical theater. It was because we had understood the international context, which required very basic sets, with basic costumes, almost like street clothes, and a small number of actors on stage. And it's tough to perform an epic with just 2 or 3 actors.[14]

Ndao describes this success as both a blessing and a curse. Having never expected the support of the state, companies developed a suppleness in their work that allowed them to outpace the Sorano troupe and book far more traveling dates nationally, as well as throughout the Francophone world.

However, the primary funder for the arts became, regrettably in Ndao's view, the contemporary network of French cultural centers that was established by the French government shortly after independence. These new *centres culturels français*, which continue to exist and were recently rebranded simply as the Institut Français (French Institute), have since served as a key tool of cultural dipolomacy for France. The structures seek, among other things, to participate in the widespread promotion of African contemporary creation. Their initiatives therefore include the funding of tours and performance dates both locally and throughout their vast network. The trouble with this model, for Ndao, was that the directors of the cultural centers imposed a restrictive view of African theater, an imposition that left an indelible mark on contemporary theater practices. As Ndao explains, "Everyone wanted tales. At one point they wanted dance, and when we arrived in France, they asked us 'where are the *djembes*?' [The *djembe* is a West African drum.] They asked us for folklore. They asked for *djembes*, for dance, for tales. And then they said 'now *that's* African theater.' "[15] The rising "contemporary" performance style by Senegalese artists thus became, in effect, a co-creation resulting from the interaction of theater practitioners in search of touring dates and commissions from French cultural organizations.[16] The interstitial position of private theater—existing within a global avant-garde that, in turn, projected upon it images of a timeless, traditional African culture—proved untenable from a market standpoint, particularly as these companies began to note an increasing distance between themselves and their local and national audiences. However, the rise of private theater brought with it a generation of stage directors, like Oumar Ndao, who became skilled at merging the traditional, the social, and the avant-garde in original performance works that were designed to appeal to both national and international audiences.

One such theater-maker was the dancer and choreographer Mamadou Diop, who led the first private company, Les Tréteaux Sénégalais, and whose formative years included a long period of study at the Moscow Art Theater. To mark the company's beginnings, Les Tréteaux made the astute choice of staging for their inaugural performance the poem *Chaka* by none other than Léopold Sédar Senghor. The strategic decision earned the company a sizeable state subsidy that was later renewed by President Abdou Diouf.[17] The early success of the company paved the way for a handful of notable successors in following decades. These included Le Nouveau Toucan, which was formed in 1976 under the direction of Seyba Traoré and named in honor of Jean-Marie Serreau's Compagnie du Toucan, which had staged the original production of *La Tragédie du Roi Christophe* featuring Douta Seck. After Le Nouveau Toucan came Les Gueules Tapées, a company directed by Macodou Mbengue and launched with the support of the Belgian Development Cooperation initiative.[18]

Looking back at the rise of private theater companies, Mamadou Diop saw the movement as part of a larger attempt to revitalize theatrical creation, with a focus on forms such as the *géew*, and a more participatory approach to theatrical performance.[19] In this sense, as Diop pointed out in an interview, the private theater companies were very much inspired by the spirit of the popular theater movement. However, the performers' affiliation with the School of Arts of Senegal, where Diop, Traoré, and Mbengue all trained or taught under the European conservatory model, created a certain distance from their peers working with the country's popular theater organizations. Furthermore, the leading figures in private theater maintained an international profile that led some critics to see them as too deeply influenced by their formal dramatic training and tied to a Europeanized, cosmopolitan aesthetic. Again, this artistic divergence is reflected at the administrative level in that, while the popular movement remained affiliated with the Ministry of Youth and Sports, private theater companies sought support mainly from the Ministry of Culture. This administrative parsing-out of theatrical approaches remains in place today and represents, for Marouba Fall, a form of exclusion of popular theater artists from the cultural field.[20] Yet it did not prevent popular theater from gaining the upper hand over contemporary approaches. In an interview, Ndao attributed the eventual decline of contemporary theater to two factors. The first was linguistic, given that Senegalese performers were generally less at ease in French than many of their Francophone African counterparts.[21] Second, through its affiliation with the Ministry of Youth and Sports, the popular theater movement became deeply involved with regional and national politics. The movement soon formed well-organized networks capable of launcing powerful forms of political demonstration or resistance.[22]

Although popular theater is often framed as a means of giving a voice to the less powerful and articulating a community-based response to social and political injustices, popular theater companies have also been hired by politicians to promote a campaign or to spread a strategically designed political message. One recent example of this was when Abdoulaye Wade informally commissioned popular theater troupes in his ultimately unsuccessful 2012 campaign for a third presidential term. Popular theater's availability as a means of staged communication between "the powerful" and "the people" has also been readily employed by NGOs in Senegal to implement campaigns on a wide range of topics, from education to family planning, to public health and hygiene. Indeed, one factor driving popular theater's prominence is a patronage model slightly different from those of either contemporary or "official," national forms of theater. Unlike the spectators in an audience, members of the "masses" do not typically purchase tickets to watch popular theater performances. This marks an important ideological and practical difference from institutions such as the Sorano Theater or the French cultural centers, where, notwithstanding numerous public outreach initiatives, performances operate along the logic of the individual spectator-consumer.

Popular theater is framed as a form of address to the masses, in the public sphere, and is free for all to see and hear. Its patronage comes from institutions wishing to stage a dialogue, or merely to transmit a targeted message. Thus, popular theater can indeed be appropriated to serve, seemingly against its own tenets, as a mouthpiece for a range of political and/or nongovernmental organizations rather than as a form of political and artistic expression emerging "from below." However, between this practice and the ideal of performance serving as a "mirror for social consciousness," one finds a diverse array of popular stage artists who are well aware of the nature of the compromises and alliances they make while attempting to strike a balance between professionalization and the defense of their own sense of artistic integrity and independence.

Kàddu Yaraax and the Practice of Popular Theater

Today popular theater troupes proliferate in Senegal, especially in and around the country's urban areas. Typically formed by young people whose first experience with performance takes place in the context of *nawetaan* youth competitions, popular theater companies address a wide range of objectives and themes. Some focus on local issues and organize their performances solely around the life of a community. Others aspire to professionalize and offer their services to governmental and institutional funders that use the theatrical stage for educational purposes. The Kàddu Yaraax company has developed a hybrid approach to appealing to funders and, in its two decades of existence, has become known as one of the country's leading forum theater groups.

Each of the troupe's founding members hails from the small fishing village of Yarakh, located just outside of Dakar and wedged between the congested Route de Rufisque and the densely polluted Hann Bay. The area's elevated poverty levels and its peripheral location, which leaves it caught between the city center and the populous suburbs, have forced the local population to contend with a number of pressing social and economic issues. Kàddu Yaraax has responded to these with theatrical creations that seek to foster dialogue between authorities and local communities. One of its better-known pieces, *La Baie de Hann n'est pas une poubelle* (*Hann Bay Is Not a Garbage Can*), called large industries to task for their contamination of the neighborhood's water and air. The play also called attention to domestic practices that contribute to this contamination, such as the common practice of disposing of used water by throwing it into the bay. Another of the troupe's landmark performances, *Partir, ne pas partir* (*To Leave or Not to Leave*), addressed the factors that push thousands of Senegalese to attempt to emigrate clandestinely to Spain via the Canary Islands by departing from Yarakh in Hann Bay on small wooden fishing boats called *pirogues*. The performance depicted the many dangers that awaited the would-be émigrés, many of whom drown at sea, while also giving voice to the sense of hopelessness and desperation that drives them to leave despite the enormous risks.

Diol and the founding members of Kàddu Yaraax had their first encounter with theater while representing their neighborhood in the local *nawetaan* theater competitions in the 1990s. The group complemented its artistic work by becoming a vocal presence in local political and social debates. They were very visible participants in the Set-setal movement, which encouraged young people of urban areas to organize cleaning campaigns for the public spaces of their neighborhoods. This movement also represented an important instance, in the late 1980s and early 1990s, in which the youth of the nation sought to assert their own political influence and presence in the urban landscape. The historian Mamadou Diouf contextualizes the Set-setal movement in relation to the years of Abdou Diouf's presidency, when the reduction of public funds led to an inevitable degradation of infrastructure and public services.[23] A new political and cultural context required theater-makers and community organizers to operate with an increased level of autonomy. Performers largely responded by highlighting theater's role in matters of civic education, and Kàddu Yaraax thus dedicated its work to civic-minded thematic shows on questions of community and individual responsibility.

In 1998, the troupe discovered "forum theater" at a training workshop offered at the French cultural center (now the Institut Français) in Dakar and run by the Burkinabe performing artist Prosper Kampaoré, founder of the Atelier Théâtre Burkinabé. Forum theater is a performance form originally developed by the Brazilian stage director Augusto Boal as part of his larger vision of a "Theater of the Oppressed," a concept inspired by the Brazilian educator Paulo Freire's book *Pedagogy of the Oppressed*.[24] Since its

Figure 6.1. Leïty Kane runs the forum at the Senegalese Forum Theater Festival. Photograph by La Compagnie Kàddu Yaraax.

development, Boal's method of using theater as a tool for political activism and social dialogue has spread throughout the globe, and today a network of performers and activists works to promote forum theater as a means of political expression.[25] Throughout much of Africa, the writings of both Freire and Boal served as a critical point of departure for imagining alternative, postcolonial models to what Freire called the "banking model" of colonialist education supported by an oppressive "culture of silence."[26] In his book *Theater of the Oppressed*, Boal extended Freire's theories to the practice of theater, elaborating on the structure and phases of forum theater which, in the vein of Bertolt Brecht's "V-effekt," seeks to countervail Aristotelian processes of dramatic catharsis.[27] Taking Brecht's position of anti-empathetic distance one step further, Boal advocated a theater in which spectators, or as he called them, "spect-actors," are invited to act immediately onstage to embody the type of social or behavioral changes necessary to address a given problem. To begin, actors present a short scenario in which a person or group is the victim of a form of oppression. Once the actors have performed their scene, a "joker" intervenes to solicit reactions from the audience. When the spectators have affirmed that what has taken place onstage could be improved upon toward a more equitable end, the troupe encourages them to take on the status of "spect-actor," that is, to step on stage themselves to replace one of the actors and modify the scene's outcome.

From the moment of this initial contact with forum theater, Kàddu Yaraax decided to dedicate their work to that form. However, the troupe maintains a level of flexibility in its approach that allows it to bend the rules set out by Boal. In fact, much of the forum theater produced throughout Senegal has departed from the Boal playbook, and the term is frequently used to describe any short-form performance with a social message. These performances often omit the forum altogether or use it more as a free-spirited means of interaction with spectators. In the clearest departure from the form's original Freirean principles, the forum is even used rather frequently as a tool for propaganda, allowing actors to steer audience members toward a particular conclusion, or even to encourage support for a particular political movement or candidate. In the case of Kàddu Yaraax, the troupe has refused to engage in such political endorsements, but the NGO-funded recourse to the forum can certainly be called into question as a propagandistic use of a form that was intended to facilitate dialogue with oppressed populations, not as a tool for nongovernmental agencies to sway public opinion.

At the time of our first meeting in December 2012, when the core members of the company agreed to meet for an interview at their headquarters, I had learned about Kàddu Yaraax's work through online news stories and hoped to discuss their artistic approach, as well as their own position within what I conceived as a broader Senegalese stage heritage. I received a warm welcome and, at the end of a series of interviews, Mouhamadou Diol and the association's vice president and founding member, Leïty Kane, invited me to return to follow the troupe's work more closely and regularly. In the ensuing four years I returned for a total of six stays and became a direct collaborator on two occasions, first as a performer and then as a production assistant for the company's annual Senegalese Forum Theater Festival. This experience highlighted the multiple levels of stagecraft involved in such theatrical work, as well as the need to study these stagings not only through the content presented in performance, but also through the myriad entanglements of power dynamics embedded in popular theater practices.

Political Entanglements of the Popular Stage

The beginning of my fieldwork with Kàddu Yaraax in 2012 coincided with the end of a politically turbulent time in Senegal following an election in which Abdoulaye Wade had attempted to win a third presidential term in violation of a constitutional amendment of his own making. The clear power grab sparked an energetic "*tout sauf Wade*" ("anything but Wade") movement that handed victory to Wade's opponent Macky Sall in the second round of voting. A major factor in the election was the impact of artists and musicians calling for Wade's defeat. The most prominent of these was an association of activist rappers and musicians that came to be known as "Y'en a marre" ("Fed up").[28] As part of their political messaging, the group made a full-throated call for *un nouveau type de sénégalais*, or new type of Senegalese, whom they described as a person with a sustained and active commitment to the civic life of the country. The term gained traction during the electoral campaign and could be seen on posters and T-shirts throughout the country. Although Kàddu Yaraax was not affiliated with the Y'en a marre organization, the troupe used its work to criticize Wade's abuses of power, especially in a 2011 performance called *C'est simple comme Mbane* (*It's as Easy as Mbane*), which toured the country denouncing Wade's antidemocratic decision to install a special delegation in the locality of Mbane to offset the political damage in a region where he had just lost representatives in local elections. The show put the company at odds with a number of its peers, who at the same time were accepting commissions from the government to stage popular theater performances touting the accomplishments of Wade and his party.

Nearly one year after the election, Kàddu Yaraax was asked to perform in an event organized by the Senegalese nonprofit organization COMEVA (Collectif en Mouvement pour l'Équité, les Valeurs et l'Action, or Collective in Motion for Equity, Values, and Action), which was concerned with public health. COMEVA planned to mark its one-year anniversary in a daylong celebration at the recently completed Grand Théâtre National. The grandiose building was one of the "seven marvels" of an urban renewal plan launched by Wade and the only one to reach completion during his mandate. COMEVA had thrown its support behind the presidential candidacy of Macky Sall, and its founder Awa Marie Coll Seck, a medical doctor and former executive director of the Roll Back Malaria Partnership, was named minister of health following Sall's election. The minister would be in attendance at the rally, as would the president. Upon receiving the request, Kàddu Yaraax first balked at the overtly political nature of the event. However, after some reflection the company's vice president, Leïty Kane, accepted the commission, deciding in the absence of Diol (who was in Johannesburg for an artistic residency) that the performance would serve as an opportunity to let the country's new leaders know that they would be held to their electoral promises.

The troupe quickly got to work, under the direction of founding member and stage director Seydou Ndiaye, on a piece responding to the event's theme, "*Un nouveau type de citoyenneté*" ("A new type of citizenship"). This variation on one of the presidential campaign's most familiar phrases suggests an attempt to tap into some of the subsiding activist energy that had put Macky Sall into office. The Kàddu Yaraax performers sought to highlight, through their piece, the need for greater accountability at the level of political leadership. The troupe works with an evolving roster of actors composed of young people from the Yarakh neighborhood, as well as more seasoned performers recruited by Diol. The cast for this performance, which aimed to represent "the masses" for an audience of COMEVA members and supporters, included five men and four women who hailed from a variety of backgrounds and professions and whose ages ranged from the early twenties to the fifties. The performers from the Yarakh community tend to be students, laborers, mechanics, itinerant vendors, or market workers. The company also regularly employs a small number of performer-journeymen, including the seasoned popular theater actor Malick Mbaye, who lives in Saint-Louis but travels regularly between cities to perform with various companies and in television productions.[29] The troupe prepares its pieces through a collaborative process, first selecting a number of themes for performers to work on individually. In the case of the COMEVA performance, the actors considered the themes of equality, mutual respect, and the importance of a strong work ethic. At the group rehearsal, each member presented his or her idea and the director Ndiaye worked these into a coherent, ten-minute piece which included four vignettes, each with a chorus that often spoke in unison, conveying a staged sense of popular opinion. The use of such a chorus is a common technique among popular theater troupes and has the advantage of making lines clearly audible in any venue. Much of the rehearsal is spent syncing these group recitals in rhythm with a responding actor who presents a counterpoint to the crowd's opinion.

Two days later, Kàddu Yaraax departed from their headquarters by bus to the Grand Théâtre National, located just outside of the congested city center. Upon our arrival, we found that the ambience was more that of a political rally than a cultural event. Indeed, while the Grand Théâtre boasts a state-of-the-art stage and sound system, the building's size and architecture has made it difficult for theater artists to find a home there. The structure far exceeds the Sorano Theater in audience capacity; this is just one of the many aspects in which Wade was intent on outdoing his long predecessor and political opponent Senghor. The building's architectural style clearly reflects the influence of the Chinese government, which provided funding for the theater's construction. The theater was, moreover, built by a Chinese firm and was called by many, in half jest, *le théâtre chinois* upon its opening. Its angular facade, high-ceiling foyer, and capacious performance space are far better suited to political rallies and concerts than to intimate theatrical performances.

Stepping into this brand-new building for the first time, the troupe members were in awe of its soaring marble walls and shiny surfaces. Inside the crowded foyer, the organizers told them that they would be one of several troupes performing and informed them that Macky Sall would not be in attendance as initially planned. Disappointed on both accounts, the troupe reported to the theater's large dressing room and awaited their cue. The political nature of the event was unmistakable. The celebration began with a live performance, to the enthusiastic applause of the capacity audience, of Macky Sall's presidential campaign rally song. After the musical introduction and a few speeches came the theatrical performances, most of which consisted of comedic sketches loosely addressing issues of women's health and rights. When Kàddu Yaraax finally stepped onto the stage, they struggled to hold the audience's attention due to the deafening noise in the theater. A few of their statements struck a chord with some sections of the house, earning short bursts of applause. But in the end, the ambience was too chaotic, and at the conclusion of their presentation the crestfallen performers quickly gathered their things and left the theater to return to Yarakh.

The post-performance discussion at the company headquarters reflected the difficulty artists face in trying to maintain a critical distance from political organizations while also agreeing to work with them when useful. Though originally attracted to the idea of performing in front of the new president in such an official setting, the troupe found its efforts thwarted by the absence of Sall and by the tone and architecture of the event. Such a piece could only have worked, the company's vice president, Kane, opined, had the association allowed them to follow up on the performance with a forum, as Kàddu Yaraax had originally proposed. Upon his return from South Africa, Diol let it be known that he would have preferred that the troupe turn down the commission altogether. Arguing that the event had pulled them too deeply into national electoral politics, he added that the style of the show, which he called *monothéâtre*, where a chorus reflects public opinion in unison, was problematic in relation to the kind of direction they were trying to take as a company. This form, he argued, is too focused on presenting a moral and is too easily manipulated by those who would use this kind of theater for propagandistic purposes. Diol's assessment highlights the difficulty of distancing oneself from the myriad political alliances and commissions that tend to be the lifeblood of the performing arts in the absence of a single, centralized patron in the form of the state. In response, companies like Kàddu Yaraax must carefully choose their path, not only in deciding with whom to align and to what extent, but also in developing a theatrical style that reflects their own political position, inside or outside the fray of electoral politics.

School Lessons of the Forum

Clearly, Kàddu Yaraax's refusal to use theater to promote the message of specific politicians has not saved the company from potential compromises or unwanted appropriations of their work. However, in instances where the troupe's performances are not purely dialogical in a Freirean sense, their approach often stages the effects of a failed encounter with their diverse publics which can, in fact, serve to highlight certain forms of social, political, or global inequality. One example of this occurred when the company was contacted by one of the expensive private schools in the capital, located in the residential, upper-middle-class neighborhood of Amitié 3. Looking for a show to complement a daylong outdoor event for their students, the school's administration called on Kàddu Yaraax to perform a short piece on the problem of pollution in Dakar and the ubiquity of discarded plastic bags throughout the city.[30] In the piece, actors perform examples of irresponsible behavior, such as throwing away trash in the street, or discarding kitchen

Figure 6.2. A festival performance in the streets of Yarakh. Photograph by La Compagnie Kàddu Yaraax.

refuse in the ocean. The characters are taken from all walks of life, and the show culminates in the sudden entrance of a performer who incarnates all city pollution and is covered with plastic bags from head to toe. The actor yells loudly on stage and engages in erratic movements that are meant to frighten and amuse the children. The stage effect concludes with the masked actor exhorting audience members to take responsibility for their own garbage and their impact on the urban environment.

At the school, the show was well-received and the children reacted enthusiastically to the appearance of the man covered in city trash. During the forum, however, the children behaved in ways that belied any possibility for an open civic exchange among equals. The interactions lay bare the fact that the Kàddu Yaraax members and the young students of this affluent private school were of very different socioeconomic backgrounds. As the students stepped onto the stage to offer alternatives to the characters' behavior, their enacted proposals quickly turned to moralizing and then to outright berating, especially of the housewives in the performance, for being, as the students said, so dirty and poor. Their remarks sparked a heated exchange with one of the actors playing a housewife, Maty, who, in French, yelled back, "I'm not like you. I don't have money! What can I do?" She further pointed out that, unlike the more prosperous residential neighborhoods of Dakar, in Yarakh and the congested outer suburbs there was no convenient way to dispose of household trash due to the narrow streets and infrastructural neglect.[31] As it turned to the slightly confrontational, the performance was brought to a close before further societal rifts were exposed. The show was intended to encourage an equal dialogue on a shared civic responsibility, but the forum quickly tore at the imagined communal fabric of Senegalese urban society. This suggested that the performers and spect-actors could not engage in dialogue to find shared solutions without first addressing the inequalities inherent to the event itself. In this case these manifested themselves linguistically, since the students' preference to speak in French was a testament to their social setting, as well as economically, a fact highlighted by the stark differences in clothing between the well-heeled students and the performers. According to Diol, social and class inequalities within Senegalese society turn out to be a major theme whenever the troupe carries out the forum in the wealthier neighborhoods of Dakar, where performances often end with the company reasserting to an upper-class audience: "But we are all Senegalese!"[32]

The Senegalese Forum Theater Festival

While from September to May Kàddu Yaraax members are often busy fulfilling one-time commissions like the ones described above, the summer is fully dedicated to the troupe's yearly flagship event: the Senegalese Forum Theater Festival. The festival first ran in 2005 and has continued annually ever since. For the company, the event has served three main intersecting functions. First, it allows Kàddu Yaraax and its local affiliates to focus exclusively on the kind of activist work that inspired their beginnings. Diol and other troupe members have described the festival as the closest affirmation of their vision of an independent theatrical organization acting to foster open dialogue among local community members. Indeed, the troupe has managed to maintain a certain level of independence by operating with minimal, and often only nominal support from national structures such as the Ministry of Culture. While Diol first saw the paucity of funding from national organizations as an obstacle, he now presents it as one of the festival's major strengths, since governmental involvement would risk pulling the event into the concerns of local or national politics. Instead, Kàddu Yaraax has relied on a network of local contacts for logistical support, while obtaining its main operational funding from the Dakar office of the Rosa Luxemburg Foundation. This affiliation, combined with support from the local municipality (La Commune de Bel-Air) and the local, foreign-funded cultural center Kër Thiossane, has allowed Kàddu Yaraax to bypass national funding schemes, thereby bringing the local into direct conversation with international structures and participants. Although by no means free of the need to accommodate their donors to a certain extent by making their participation visible and by holding some festival events at their respective headquarters, the company has found a satisfactory arrangement in its diversity of funders, all of whom have agreed to participate without imposing strict conditions on the festival's content.

The second key function of the festival is that it has allowed Kàddu Yaraax to secure a place for itself within the cultural landscape, both locally and nationwide. The festival's logistics are managed by a tightly knit local community which sees the yearly event as a key part of the Yarakh neighborhood's identity. The local school offers its facilities for a modest fee so that the troupe can lodge festival participants in small classrooms lined with foam mattresses. Audience members come from throughout the neighborhood as well as from the nearby suburbs to attend performances in the public squares of Yarakh. During the day, festival participants take part in workshops and public discussions on issues of social and global justice. The festival has also garnered favorable attention nationwide, not the least because Diol has always invited theater companies from throughout the country. This includes affiliated companies from the southern region of Casamance, which is often isolated culturally as well as geographically, given the difficulty of the trip from this region to Dakar, which requires one to pass either through or around neighboring Gambia. The festival offers an opportunity for aspiring theater troupes from Dakar, Thiès, Kaolack, Ziguinchor, and elsewhere to convene in Yarakh and present their work to a group of peers. Furthermore, the daily workshops of the festival, which are often run by established teachers from Europe or the United States, have turned the event into a training opportunity for those who wish to professionalize.[33]

Lastly, the festival has allowed the company to develop an extensive international network through long-term relationships with theater companies from France, Spain, Brazil, and the United States, as well as with companies from Mauritania, Guinea-Bissau, Guinea-Conakry, and Mali. The festival's international profile differs from those of the contemporary theater movement described earlier in this chapter because it stems from a commitment to practice theater strictly in an activist vein. So while Diol and Kàddu Yaraax have carried out tours and artistic residencies in Europe, South Africa, the United Kingdom, and Brazil, this has scarcely affected public perceptions of their role as a local activist troupe. In this respect, Kàddu Yaraax has succeeded in maintaining an international network without being subjected to the kind of criticism once targeted at "contemporary" companies. Moreover, Kàddu Yaraax has, in a sense, reversed the "contemporary" paradigm that sent companies in search of performance dates abroad by regularly attracting international participants to their festival event at home, which takes place not in the pristine halls of the National Theater, but in the dusty streets of Yarakh. The convening of theater artists and teachers from around the world for this shoestring-budget festival symbolizes, for both local audiences and nationwide onlookers, a renewed respect for Senegalese cultural forms.

While the reputation of the Senegalese Forum Theater Festival rests on its ability to bring together a wide range of cultural actors, its strength lies in an articulated and contextualized understanding of culture and performance. Forum theater is the federating theme of the festival, but understandings of the forum and its uses differ greatly among the participants, who arrive with a variety of goals and expectations. For the international attendees of the festival, the event implicitly represents an affirmation, from below, of the power of the performance form and approach developed by Augusto Boal. Their participation in the festival, and their travel to Dakar at their own expense, often reflects a desire to validate their activist work at home through a discovery of successful illustrations of the forum in action in a Global South context. The local Senegalese companies, however, tend to view the festival as a networking opportunity, as well as a chance to assert their place among a small group of professional popular theater troupes. Most African companies at the festival do not actually use the forum in their performances but rather specialize in what Diol calls "monotheater," where groups speak in unison as a chorus transmitting a moral or civic lesson. In this case, "forum theater" is simply taken as another term for popular theater.

Discussions between the international and African participants quickly lay bare these differing, often rival expectations. Corralling these onto a single, accommodating stage space constitutes Diol's primary challenge during the festival. An illustrative example of the tentative acts of stagecraft required to bring members of the event together within the same conceptual framework took place during the 2014 edition, with the participation of the Barcelona-based forum theater company La Xixa Teatre. La Xixa is a regular presence at the festival and has found a creative way to respond to the challenges of intercultural communication and collaboration. Every year, in the weeks leading up to the festival, the company's members travel to the Casamance region where they meet with the forum theater company La Noumec to work on a play that they will then present for festival attendees in Yarakh. In 2014, the two companies choose to address the violence that often springs from separatist causes, such as those of Casamance independence groups or the ETA in the Basque region of Spain. The yearly collaboration between the two groups has led to new artistic partnerships and friendships and represents one of the most fruitful affiliations to emerge from the festival. And yet, the performance's staging can present a considerable challenge.

In this particular year, Diol decided to include the two companies' collaborative piece in the festival's opening ceremony. This ceremony is where Diol is obliged to invite the "who's who" of Senegalese theater, since not to do so would reflect poorly on his own commitment to Senegalese culture and would suggest ingratitude toward his predecessors and fellow theater artists. However, this ceremony is also where the festival event melds with the customs of the Senegalese *xew*, or special occasion, to which the most important guests traditionally arrive last and very late. Thus, in the middle of the ceremony and during a performance by a young Senegalese troupe, audience members were surprised by the arrival of the ceremony's guest of honor, Leyti Fall, a prominent Senegalese screen actor and president of a branch of a popular theater artists' association called ARCOTS (L'Association des Artistes Comédiens du Théâtre Sénégalais, or the Association of Stage Actors of Senegalese Theater).

Fall arrived with an entourage, all dressed in spectacular, voluminous *boubous* to fit their prominent role at the event. They moved through the crowd, dislodging seated spectators, festival participants, and neighborhood children in order to take their place at the front of the audience. The Senegalese spectators recognized this practice as conforming to norms of deference and respect toward an esteemed guest. However, the visiting forum theater practitioners stood aghast as the powerful and prominent appeared to relegate others to the back of the hall in a scene that reinforced the same uneven power dynamics that the forum was designed to deconstruct. Shortly afterward, La Xixa and Noumec took the stage. However, minutes into their performance, the kitchen announced that juices and donuts were being served, and pandemonium ensued as half of the crowd rushed to the serving counter. The performance continued for the benefit of a handful of foreign participants who had managed to move their way toward the stage. The forum was cut short for lack of attentive spectators. Visibly upset by the disregard of their efforts and those of their Senegalese collaborators, the director of La Xixa nonetheless reacted with admirable restraint, smiling, taking a bow with his fellow performers, and quickly walking off stage. The foreign participants were left frustrated and confused, while the Senegalese participants socialized in the audience or congregated around the snack counter.

In a subsequent conversation, Diol admitted to dreading this particular opening ceremony for fear that such a scene might take place. While the festival may regularly succeed in attracting a diverse array of attendees and participants, their respective conceptual frameworks often lead to the coexistence of seemingly disparate events, one experienced by Senegalese participants and the other by European and American attendees. And yet, the festival continues to thrive despite the regularity of such scenes. In fact, the apparent chaos of the festival is also reflective of one of its key strategies. Instead of attempting to model a centralized notion of the relationship between culture and society or politics, the festival allows for numerous articulations of the forum theater paradigm, along with a wide range of expectations as to what, exactly, forum theater is and what it is supposed to do. Although it took place on a very different scale, the 1966 World Festival of Negro Arts serves as an illuminating foil. Notwithstanding the diversity of voices at the festival, the framing of that international event was centered around Senghor's model of Negritude as an aesthetic and political concept. The Senegalese Forum Theater Festival, by contrast, adopts a far broader ideological lens and seeks to facilitate an open dialogue on the uses of forum, or simply "popular," theater within a range of cultural and political contexts. Diol has admitted that this open and articulated approach has run the company afoul of more militant forum practitioners. However, it has also allowed a wide range of participants to find their own interests within the event, leading to a fluid understanding of the relationship between culture, activism, and performance.

Reviving the Ethnographic Stage

In May 2014, I became an object of stage reading myself as a performer in one of Kàddu Yaraax's pieces. While I was sitting at the troupe's headquarters, the stage director Ndiaye informed me that he would be putting together a commissioned performance and they needed me to play a part in the show. I was to report to rehearsal the following day in the courtyard of the school adjacent to the Kàddu Yaraax office. The next day at rehearsal, after the troupe's routine warm-up based on Augusto Boal's handbook *Games for Actors and Non-Actors*, we broke into groups and Ndiaye came to explain my role and dialogue. In my scene, which was the opening part of a series of tableaus on motherhood and family life, I would be in the bedroom of a young woman as she prepared for her wedding. My relationship to her was that of a friend, and I was to take pictures of her as she rushed to get ready. The nature of the staged relationship between myself and the other actor seemed stubbornly ambiguous to me, since every time I asked why I would realistically be in such a position Ndiaye explained that I was her friend, and perhaps something more. I asked if that meant I should be jealous, to which Ndiaye, now assisted by the rest of the troupe in his explanations, responded that, on the contrary, I should show that I was very happy for her and curious to see how the wedding would unfold. Since I seemed to be the only person struggling to understand the relationship, I abandoned my questions and decided to simply do as I was told. Seeing that I was perplexed, Ndiaye sought to reassure me by saying that, in exchange for my participation, I would get to keep all of the photos I was instructed to take of the nuptial traditions during the performance.

At this point I had been interacting with the company for over a year, following along on tours and sitting through many rehearsals and long discussions. I had nearly always brought a camera with me—a habit I eventually lost—so I could well understand, and in fact had contributed to, the notion that photographic documentation must form a sort of currency for white outsiders. However, my inability to comprehend my role and relationships within the play, as I later came to understand, was due to the fact that I had become a functional signifier on stage, an incarnation of "whiteness," whose characteristics were not only unfamiliar, but needed to be explained and explicitly demonstrated to me by my Senegalese collaborators. As I took photos of my stage partner as she rehearsed getting ready for a traditional wedding, Ndiaye egged me on, repeating, "You can go ahead," "Don't be afraid," "Have at it!" When these directions were met by me with confused looks, Ndiaye took the camera to demonstrate what he wanted—which was for me to jump around the room, asking intrusive, personal questions, and generally irritating my stage partner as she tried to put on her outfit and veil. My partner's irate reactions to my prying created a comedic effect, as would, Ndiaye calculated (correctly), my boisterous, impromptu singing of the ceremonial Wolof song that traditionally precedes a wedding.

Ndiaye's stage directions to me were worded in such a way as to suggest that I was perhaps holding back from how I might wish to behave, or that he was demonstrating a form of comportment that should come to me naturally. As I struggled to understand his meaning, and to recognize myself in the character I was meant to be "naturally" incarnating on stage, I experienced a keen sense of alienation from my own subjecthood, a distance between my sense of self and the image of whiteness and white behavior that I was expected to project on stage. My experience recalled that of the self-alienating performing students of the William Ponty School. Beyond a mere individual sensation, these processes of alienation are, I contend, a key feature of the stage upon which the Kàddu Yaraax actors perform. They attest to a stage heritage that began with the performance of "authentic" African customs by the students of French colonial schools for young African teachers, doctors, and administrators. Although a creative work, our thematic piece on various stages of motherhood in traditional Senegalese society in fact hinted less at a scripted scene than at an imagined collective remembering of an event where we would all have behaved in ways that came to us naturally. These natural behaviors are of course learned and reinforced through our stage performance, and once I finally learned how to behave "white" in the ways expected of me, I found myself interacting on stage with ease with similarly prototypical figures such as the Senegalese girlfriend, the family patriarch, and the intermediary and interpreter who repeatedly fooled me into handing over fistfuls of bills in exchange for false information. The ensemble constituted a skillfully enacted constellation of folkloric roles, with the crafty addition of the outsider's gaze, in this case my own, as well as one of the key instruments (the camera) with which such roles are documented and solidified by the Western "expert."

Mine was not the only experience of alienation in this performance, and my participation responded to some purely practical concerns for the troupe. The performance was commissioned by the international NGO Amref Health Africa, which planned to hold a fund-raising gala dinner at the King Fahd Palace, a five-star luxury hotel in the Almadies neighborhood of Dakar. As there would be foreign dignitaries and non-Wolophones in attendance, it was necessary to provide a way for these spectators to follow the action onstage, and my role as the outsider to whom the action had to be explained in French proved useful. The need to include French text within the show reflected the attendance of a certain upper-class Senegalese audience for whom French was more appropriate than Wolof. This was made evident in Kane and Ndiaye's interactions with the NGO representatives who, though Senegalese, often communicated with the troupe in French. These same representatives came to attend one of our rehearsals and to give Ndiaye a number of phrases for inclusion in the show. Their contributions included statistics related to the NGO's work throughout Africa, as well as the show's concluding line: "*Soutenons la candidature des sages-femmes africaines au Prix Nobel de la Paix 2015!*" ("Let's support African midwives' candidacy for the 2015 Nobel

Peace Prize!"). This unwieldy line, which was better suited for a conference presentation or flyer than for a stage play, caused some trepidation among the performers, most of whom had only a tenuous fluency in French. After some group discussion, the concluding line was assigned to one of the senior members, Séga, who had a relatively strong command of French but who nonetheless required a long stretch of rehearsal time before he could consistently achieve the appropriate levels of diction, fluency, and enthusiasm.

The gala organizers gave us a warm welcome upon our arrival at the hotel on the day of the performance. The troupe members were starstruck as they pointed out television actors in attendance, as well as the musician Carlou D, who performed his song "Sama Yaay," written in honor of his mother. The gala attendees received our piece with great enthusiasm and read my own presence onstage with perfect ease. That I should be there and behaving in such a manner appeared perfectly comprehensible and was even met with knowing interjections by the audience, while my singing in Wolof ignited an explosion of laughter. Our piece went on to stage a traditional Senegalese wedding, with the father handing his hat to the bride to indicate that she should not return home and now belonged to her husband. This was followed by the performed chaos of a hospital delivery room, where actors portraying nurses pointed out the lack of resources and governmental support available for Senegalese midwives.

After a series of performed happy births in trying circumstances, our designated actor stepped forward to deliver his dreaded line and found that he could not get it out properly. Following some misstarts and misplaced prepositions, the sympathetic audience quickly recognized his struggle, laughed forgivingly and, in unison, began to applaud over the voice of the nervous actor, allowing us to conclude on a high note and relieving him of his duty to complete the line. The sympathetic silencing of the actor was an act of generosity on the part of the audience, but it also reflected a spontaneous and unsettling recognition of the immense economic and educational gap between the elite attending the gala and the outer city troupe brought in to perform. The actor's struggle with his line highlighted the linguistic estrangement experienced by a large part of the urban population as a result of the preponderant role of the French language in the upper echelons of Senegalese society. The performance of identity hit too close to home for our worldly spectators, who responded by cutting the piece short in a gesture of warm approval that also revealed their discomfort at being faced with their own status as seen against the country's drastic social and economic inequalities.

✦

What characterizes popular theater as a successful strategy in the context of Senegalese culture is its halfway stance between a series of categories. These are categories that continue to hold currency in the world of performance commissions, artistic training, and scholarship on performance in Africa. However, their parameters are ever-shifting, making them apt material for the crafting of new stage spaces and practices. Companies like Kàddu Yaraax publicly situate themselves on the middle ground of binaries such as professional and amateur, politics versus the arts, local or global activism, and public versus private arts funding. They are able to prioritize one category over the other when needed, and this facilitation of mobile and dynamic articulations of performance culture lies at the heart of their craft. It also allows companies to develop their own sense of working as an independent, publicly engaged organization while responding to a broad range of commissions and requests from local, national, and international funding structures. Such a modus operandi is symptomatic of a long process of public disengagement from the arts, an oft-lamented phenomenon in the cultural world not just in Africa. However, popular theater companies in the early twenty-first century have managed to find a relatively effective survival strategy, and one that has allowed them to outlast a number of co-emergent approaches to theatrical performance. For this reason, it is unclear to what extent popular theater companies share in older generations' nostalgia for the golden age of national culture under Senghor, especially in a context where close affiliation with national politics might compromise a group's eligibility for commissions from NGOs known to be wary of direct collaboration with the state.

Field observations of the work of popular theater companies like Kàddu Yaraax tend to lead to two initial deductions that require further problematizing if such work is to be approached on its own terms. First, popular theater is difficult to grasp or to categorize as a form. While popular theater's existence as a "form" is instantiated by the work of formalized institutions such as the Senegalese Federation of Popular Theater, in fact it is best thought of as a practice. Furthermore, although popular theater employs discursive techniques to secure a place for itself in the cultural landscape, it is through embodied acts of innovation, accommodation, and craft that it creates its performance space. Second, popular theater is often seen as falling short of the political and social convictions laid out in documents such as the popular theater manifesto. Indeed, the illustrations given here of Kàddu Yaraax's work can be interpreted as four instances of failed encounters, where the popular or forum approach fell apart when tested against political and social realities on the ground. But in fact, to frame such experimentations as failures would be to impose a specific notion of success, as defined by external criteria. These failed encounters can also enact a critically productive laying-bare of forms of inequality, or forge mutually beneficial artistic affiliations that would not be possible within a more ideologically driven framework of cultural production.

Conclusion

✦

Theater as a Senegalese Invention

One evening as we walked through the streets of Yarakh, Mouhamadou Diol recounted to me the discussions of a colloquium he had recently attended where participants examined at length "the state" of Senegalese theater today. Much of the event covered familiar topics such as the shortage of funding and the need for more democratic forms of local organization to support neighborhood troupes. But it was the participants' ahistorical view of Senegalese theater that most stuck with Diol, who recalled how one speaker, to give context to his overall remarks, described theater as an invention of ancient Greece that was later handed down to the Senegalese by the French. The Senegalese speaker's wrap-up of the region's theater history suggested no significant Senegalese contribution, formalistic or otherwise, subsequent to the transmission of theatrical performance in the context of French colonialism. Unable to intervene at the time, an indignant Diol later declared: "Our theater has got *nothing* to do with the Greeks!" He has long insisted on the need for a decolonizing approach to theater in Senegal, both in its creation and its reception. Against a worldview that sees Europeans as the inventors of formal theatrical performance, Diol points out the many performance forms that existed in Africa long before any contact with Europeans, or even before they were "invented" by the West. The mask, dance, total theater, theater in the round: all hold a prominent place in histories of avant-garde theatrical movements of Europe, but in African contexts they have been described as emerging out of timeless forms of traditional performance practices.

Diol's criticism of Eurocentric theater histories is borne out by the reception of the colonial-era sites of stagecraft explored in this book. Performers of the Ponty School interwove multiple modes of stage performance to craft new and hybrid stage spaces that were designed to reassess narratives of colonial conquest. The stage experiments of later decades, most notably at the French cultural centers but also among a budding professional theater scene, benefited from the erudition of a multicultural generation of writers, community leaders, and performers. These theater-makers used fluid notions of traditional culture and customs to participate in transnational debates that were exploring post-empire models of citizenship at the time. The close association, from the Ponty School onward, of theatrical practice with political and social engagement turned stagecraft into a functional tool of the statecraft later taken up by the leaders of the newly independent African nations. Yet, despite their lasting political and cultural influence, the stage spaces created by African performers were seen not as sites of experimental and political performance but rather as ones of fateful encounter, defined by the melding of Western culture and pedagogy with African performance traditions.

Diol's objection to historical timelines that place the "beginnings" of theater at the time of the ancient Greeks has more to do with the present than with the past. His call to decolonize readings of the stage demands an acceptance, in the present, of Senegalese and other Global South creators as inventors and innovators of experimental forms rather than as inheritors of traditions or practices imported from the West. Part of the work of stagecraft as a conceptual framework, as I have employed it throughout this book, is to serve as a reminder that, whatever may be "transmitted" through forms of cross-cultural or colonial influence, live stage spaces, in order to exist and to function, must be reimagined, reembodied, and recrafted with each manifestation. I argue that in the process of making and remaking the stage, Senegalese artists ranging from the Ponty performers to Diol's own company have established a decolonizing ethos as a constitutive aesthetic and political element of their work.

The ambitions and terms of such decolonizing efforts vary greatly across contexts and time periods. Although it may seem anachronistic to attribute decolonizing intentions to figures like the *pontins*, their student performances established what would become an enduring decolonizing stage practice. The *pontins* took the stage to enter into explicit dialogue with colonial society, stating grievances and articulating demands that prefigured the later unraveling of France's colonial project in the region. Even after political independence, decolonizing stages proliferated to contend with the legacy of colonial domination. Theater artists crafted such stages to address the corruption that existed at the highest levels of the Senegalese government (as seen in the work of television troupes), as well as the marginal status of religious and spiritual forms of cultural practice in models of Francophonie (most memorably in the touring production *Bamba Mos Xam*), or the place of independent Senegalese performers in activist movements of the Global South (as in the work of Kàddu Yaraax). Each of these dynamic and contextual stage spaces has sought to redefine the terms and adjust the focus of a fundamentally decolonizing framework.

And yet these stage spaces tend to escape the critical or scholarly attention paid to contemporary or avant-garde forms of theatrical innovation. The critical blind spots about certain stage spaces both past and present in African contexts reveal an overreliance on Western criteria of theater-making, and especially that of written and published plays. In the case of Francophone

African theater, site-based studies that also engage in aesthetically oriented readings of performances remain rare. From a literary standpoint, the major playwrights who have written in French and hail from the former African colonies of France or Belgium—Tchicaya U Tam'si, Sony Labou Tansi, and Werewere Liking, to name but a few—represent an important movement in experimental theater-making in the postcolonial era. Given the increased scholarly attention to playwrights of subsequent generations (Koffi Kwahulé and Kossi Efoui, for example), as well as the renewed efforts and initiatives of generative venues like the radio play contest of Radio France Internationale, there is every reason to expect that Francophone African playwrights will continue to contribute to critical frameworks of experimental approaches to the stage. However, the work and reception of these playwrights provide only a partial and potentially misleading idea of the uses of theatrical performance in Francophone African contexts. The scarcity of studies exploring African theater in African contexts in dialogue with forms of experimental performance practices begs the question of where, in scholarly models, theatrical experimentalism can be seen as taking place. To what extent does the predominance of anthropological approaches to the study of contemporary theater-making in Francophone Africa suggest a continuation of the modes of reception in place at the time of the Ponty performances, and according to which artistic experimentation happens in Europe, whereas Africa transmits its performance practices or adapts the ones it is given?

My focus throughout this book—the creation and use of stage spaces and performance practices in Senegalese contexts—has led me to engage in a sited analysis that considers simultaneously the constituting of stage spaces, the summoning of audiences, and the creation of new forms of aesthetic content and audience address. This multidisciplinary approach serves to highlight innovations and movements that are often situated just beyond and between the scopes of strictly literary or field-based methods. It also facilitates a much-needed provincializing of Western performance forms and traditions of theater-making and stagecraft. A broad, multisciplinary outlook on the constituting and work of the theatrical stage proves essential in order to include Global South stages and performance practices in discussions of theatrical experimentalism and innovation. Articulated through this broader framework of sited theater-making, a study of Senegal's multiple stage experiments and innovations should allow the reader/observer to join my research collaborator Diol in declaring emphatically that theater is indeed *also* a Senegalese invention.

NOTES

Introduction

1. Guinea was the first of the French West African colonies to declare its independence and did so in 1958. The remaining seven colonies declared their independence (with Senegal and French Sudan, today's Mali, as part of a short-lived Mali Federation) in 1960.

2. Bakary Traoré, *Le Théâtre négro-africain et ses fonctions sociales* (Paris: Présence Africaine, 1958), 9.

3. One notable exception to this exclusion is Bojana Coulibaly's study of recent Wolof-language performances at the Daniel Sorano National Theater. Coulibaly, "Senegalese Theater Unabashed: Wolof Drama and Cultural Liberation," *Alif: Journal of Comparative Poetics*, no. 39 (2019): 123–48.

4. For a sited approach to the visual arts scene in Dakar, see Joanna Grabski, *Art World City: The Creative Economy of Artists and Urban Life in Dakar* (Bloomington: Indiana University Press, 2017).

5. Ngũgĩ wa Thiong'o, *Penpoints, Gunpoints, and Dreams* (Oxford: Oxford University Press, 1998), 41.

6. Thiong'o, *Penpoints*, 40.

7. Jesse Weaver Shipley writes that strands of performance theory "tend to presuppose the universality of performance as public enactment and what it does. There is a tendency to underestimate the contextually specific nature of performativity itself and its relationship to subject formation." Shipley, *Trickster Theatre: The Poetics of Freedom in Urban Africa* (Bloomington: Indiana University Press, 2015), 15.

8. In his recent book on Senegalese literature, Tobias Warner productively poses a similar question with regard to the production of literary culture. Warner, *The Tongue-Tied Imagination: Decolonizing Literary Modernity in Senegal* (New York: Fordham University Press, 2019), 8.

9. Some recent notable exceptions have provided valuable perspectives and analyses regarding the conditions of theater-making in Francophone West Africa. See Christophe Konkobo, *La Pratique du théâtre moderne au Burkina Faso* (Paris: L'Harmattan, 2017); Pierre Médéhouégnon, *Le Théâtre francophone de l'Afrique de l'Ouest: Des origines à nos jours: Historique et analyse de la dramaturgie en Côte d'Ivoire, au Burkina Faso, au Togo et au Bénin* (Jéricho-Cotonou: CAAREC, 2010); Fernand Nouwligbèto, *Théâtre béninois: Logiques marchandes et enjeux esthétiques* (Benin: CIREF Éditions, 2016); and Alain Cyr Pangop Kameni, *Rires des crises postcoloniales: Le Discours intermédiatique du théâtre comique populaire et la fictionnalisation de la politique linguistique au Cameroun* (Berlin: Lit Verlag, 2009).

10. Sylvie Chalaye, “Contemporary Francophone Drama: Between Detours and Deviations,” *Yale French Studies* 112 (2007): 149.

11. Sylvie Chalaye, *Afrique noire et dramaturgies contemporaines: Le Syndrome Frankenstein* (Paris: Éditions Théâtrales, 2004), 14.

12. On the RFI radio play competition, which was reinstated in 2014 as the Prix RFI Théâtre and now accepts submissions from the broader Francophone world, see Sélom Komlan Gbanou, “De la planche à la bande: Les Voies modernes de l’oralité africaine: De la scène à la cassette,” *Matatu. Journal for African Culture and Society* 31–32, no. 1 (August 2005): 43–60; Françoise Ligier, “Le Concours théâtral interafricain,” *Recherche, Pédagogie, et Culture* 33 (1978): 58–59; and Alain Ricard, “The ORTF and African Literature,” *Research in African Literatures* 4, no. 2 (Autumn 1973): 189–91. On the archival traces of the competition, see Céline Gahungu, “Le Concours théâtral interafricain: Quelles archives? Quels usages?” *Continents Manuscrits* no. 13 (2019), online.

13. Judith G. Miller, “Is There a Specifically Francophone African Stage Textuality?” *Yale French Studies* 112 (2007): 133.

14. Valentin Mudimbe, *The Invention of Africa: Gnosis, Philosophy and the Order of Knowledge* (Bloomington: Indiana University Press, 1988), x.

15. Miller, “Is There a Specifically Francophone African Stage Textuality?” 143.

16. John Conteh-Morgan, *Theatre and Drama in Francophone Africa: A Critical Introduction* (Cambridge: Cambridge University Press, 1994), 221.

17. Aimé Césaire, *La Tragédie du Roi Christophe* (Paris: Présence Africaine, 1963), 31 (translations mine).

18. Césaire, *La Tragédie,* 33.

19. See Jean-Philippe Dedieu, “L’Impérialisme de la voix: Théâtre français en Afrique et comédiens africains en France,” in *L’Esclavage, la colonisation, et après . . . ,* ed. Stéphane Dufoix and Patrick Weil (Paris: Presses Universitaires de France, 2005), 323–56. For a brief history of French cultural initiatives and influence on the African continent, see Altaïr Despres, *Se faire contemporain* (Paris: Publications de la Sorbonne, 2016), 22–39.

20. One *coopérant*, in this case a highly qualified one, stage actor Raymond Hermantier, became a central figure in the halls of the Daniel Sorano National Theater and the most prominent director of Senegalese stage productions. His oeuvre included the productions of *Macbeth* and *The Imaginary Invalid* sent on tour in France in 1969. On Hermantier’s life and work, see Marie Pasquini, “Raymond Hermantier, un parcours: Du théâtre populaire au dialogue des cultures,” Mémoire de maîtrise (master’s thesis), Université Paris III Sorbonne Nouvelle, 2006.

21. See Robert Cornevin, *Le Théâtre en Afrique noire et à Madagascar* (Paris: Le Livre Africain, 1970); and Jacques Scherer, *Le Théâtre en Afrique noire francophone* (Paris: Presses Universitaires de France, 1992). Reviewing Scherer’s work, which was commissioned by the French Ministry of Cooperation, the Cameroonian stage director Hansel Ndumbe Eyoh describes the project as “a marvelous celebration of French paternalism.” Eyoh, review of *Le Théâtre en Afrique noire francophone*, by Jacques Scherer, *Research in African Literatures* 26, no. 1 (Spring 1995): 141.

22. James Clifford, *Routes: Travel and Translation in the Late Twentieth Century* (Cambridge, MA: Harvard University Press, 1997), 8.

23. Shalini Puri, "Finding the Field: Notes on Caribbean Cultural Criticism, Area Studies, and the Forms of Engagement," *Small Axe* 17, no. 2 (July 2013): 70.

24. For example, in exploring the work of the Algerian playwright Abdelkader Alloula in tandem with his own performance experience with an activist street theater troupe in India, Neil Doshi seeks "to trace how direct experience of place and audience in performance can shape both notions of textuality and the reading practices that one might bring to the dramatic text." Doshi, "Absent Performances: Distant Fieldwork on Social Movement Theater of Algeria and India," in *Theorizing Fieldwork in the Humanities: Methods, Reflections, and Approaches to the Global South*, ed. Debra A. Castillo and Shalini Puri (New York: Palgrave Macmillan, 2016), 115.

25. Dwight Conquergood, "Rethinking Ethnography: Towards a Critical Cultural Politics," *Communication Monographs* 58, no. 2 (June 1991): 187.

26. Conquergood, "Rethinking Ethnography," 190.

27. Conquergood, "Rethinking Ethnography," 179.

28. See Johannes Fabian, *Time and the Other: How Anthropology Makes Its Object* (New York: Columbia University Press, 2014). Fabian has also explored the scholar's place specifically in research on theatrical production in Africa, most notably in *Power and Performance: Ethnographic Explorations through Proverbial Wisdom and Theater in Shaba, Zaire* (Madison: University of Wisconsin Press, 1990).

29. Margaret Thompson Drewal, "The State of Research on Performance in Africa," *African Studies Review* 34, no. 3 (December 1991): 32.

30. Drewal, "The State of Research," 33.

31. Catherine Cole, *Ghana's Concert Party Theatre* (Bloomington: Indiana University Press, 2001), 2.

32. Maëline Le Lay, *La Parole construit le pays: Théâtre, langues et didactisme au Katanga (République Démocratique du Congo)* (Paris: Honoré Champion, 2014), 11.

33. Hélène Neveu Kringelbach, *Dance Circles: Movement, Morality and Self-Fashioning in Urban Senegal* (Oxford: Berghahn, 2013), 148.

34. Ricard is primarily responding to Richard Schechner's *Public Domain: Essays on the Theatre* (Indianapolis, IN: Bobbs-Merrill, 1969).

35. Alain Ricard, *L'Invention du théâtre: Le Théâtre et les comédiens en Afrique noire* (Lausanne: L'Age d'Homme, 1986), 24.

36. Christopher Balme, *Decolonizing the Stage: Theatrical Syncretism and Post-Colonial Drama* (Oxford: Clarendon, 1999).

37. Balme, *Decolonizing the Stage,* 66.

38. Anne Ubersfeld, *Lire le théâtre* (Paris: Éditions Sociales, 1977).

39. What Bakhtin describes as dialogism in the novel is the ability of the novelistic voice to represent the multi-vocality of discourse, incorporating the infinite voices of the social reality in which an utterance came about. This approach takes into account the imprint of a social sphere on literary creation: "The living utterance, having taken meaning and shape at a particular moment in a socially specific environment, cannot fail to brush up against thousands of living dialogical threads, woven by socio-ideological consciousness." Mikhail Bakhtin, *The Dialogic Imagination: Four Essays*, trans. Caryl Emerson and Michael Holquist (Austin: University of Texas Press, 2010), 276.

40. Bakhtin, *The Dialogic Imagination*, 266.

41. Almuth Grésillon and Jean-Marie Thomasseau, "Scènes de genèses théâtrales," *Genesis (Manuscrits—Recherche—Invention)* 26 (2005): 31.

42. Grésillon and Thomasseau, "Scènes de genèses théâtrales," 21.

43. Karin Barber, *The Anthropology of Texts, Persons and Publics* (Cambridge: Cambridge University Press, 2009), 22.

44. Barber, *The Anthropology of Texts,* 29.

45. Referring to the relevance of Barber's theory of textuality to the study of African theater, Maëline Le Lay writes: "If this approach proves so relevant to understanding the texts that we extract from the field, it is because the very nature of the theatrical text almost naturally lends itself to it." Le Lay, "Du chiffonnier à l'anthropologue: Statut du texte et positionnement du chercheur sur un terrain littéraire et théâtral," *Continents Manuscrits* no. 13 (2019), para. 13.

46. Diana Taylor, *The Archive and the Repertoire: Performing Cultural Memory in the Americas* (Durham, NC: Duke University Press, 2003), 13.

47. For a study on these questions in France, see Sylvie Chalaye, *Du noir au nègre: L'Image du noir au théâtre (1550–1960)* (Paris: L'Harmattan, 1998).

48. Karin Barber, "Preliminary Notes on Audiences in Africa," *Africa* 67, no. 3 (1997): 353–54.

49. This research process also produced a short documentary on *Bamba Mos Xam*, titled *Bamba, the Taste of Knowledge* (co-directed with Gino Canella).

Chapter 1

1. Maurice Sonar Senghor, *Souvenirs de théâtres d'Afrique et d'Outre-Afrique: Pour que lève la semence* (Paris: L'Harmattan, 2004), 18. Sonar Senghor's idea of the place of this school's theater in a larger national heritage was seconded in an interview with the Senegalese stage director Seyba Traoré, who asserts: "Our theater comes from the École Normale William Ponty . . . It was at Ponty that our first dramatists distinguished themselves, our first actors and our first stage directors." See Myriam Odile Blin and Moustapha Tamba, *50 ans de cultures noires au Sénégal, 1960–2010* (Paris: L'Harmattan, 2014), 234.

2. The William Ponty School enrolled several future presidents, including Félix Houphouët-Boigny (Côte d'Ivoire), Modibo Keïta (Mali), Hubert Maga and Emile Zinsou (both of Benin), and Abdoulaye Wade (Senegal). Other highly prominent figures include Paul Hazoumé, Ousmane Socé Diop, Bernard Dadié, and Mamadou Dia.

3. Bernard Dadié, "Mon pays et son théâtre," *Le Théâtre Indigène et la Culture Franco-Africaine, Numéro Spécial de L'Éducation Africaine* (1937): 61.

4. Dadié, "Mon pays," 62.

5. Dadié, "Mon pays," 63.

6. For more scholarship dealing directly and indirectly with the Ponty theater, see Joshua Cohen, "Stages in Transition: Les Ballets Africains and Independence, 1959–1960," *Journal of Black Studies* 43, no. 1 (January 2012): 11–48; Unionmwan Edebiri, "The Development of the Theatre in French-Speaking West Africa," *Theatre Research International* 9, no. 3 (Autumn 1984): 168–80; Jean-Hervé Jézéquel, "Le 'Théâtre des instituteurs' en AOF (1930–1950): Pratique socio-culturelle et vecteur de cristallisation de nouvelles identités urbaines," in *Fêtes urbaines en Afrique: Espaces, identités et pouvoirs*, ed. Odile Goerg (Paris:

Karthala, 1999), 181–200; Ben Jukpor, "Le Rôle de l'École William Ponty dans le développement du théâtre ouest-africain francophone," *Présence Francophone* 24 (1982): 47–64; Bernard Mouralis, "William Ponty Drama," in *European-Language Writing in Sub-Saharan Africa*, ed. Albert S. Gérard (Budapest: Akadémiai Kiadó, 1986), 130–40; Peggy Sabatier, "African Culture and Colonial Education: The William Ponty School Cahiers and Theater," *Journal of African Studies* 7, no. 1 (1980): 2–10; and Gary Warner, "The Use of Historical Sources in Francophone African Theatre," *Theatre Research International* 9, no. 3 (Autumn 1984): 180–94.

7. Traoré, *Le Théâtre négro-africain*.

8. Cornevin, *Le Théâtre en Afrique*, 44–50; François-Joseph Amon d'Aby, *Le Théâtre en Côte d'Ivoire des origines à 1960: Suivi de Kwao Adjoba et de la Couronne aux Enchères* (Abidjan: Éditions CEDA, 1988), 15–17.

9. Wole Soyinka analyzes the Ponty theatrical productions as a derivation of colonial society rather than a reflection of traditional African theater: "The community represented by William Ponty was an artificial one. It was distanced from the society whose cultural board it rifled both in qualitative thought and material product." Soyinka, "Theatre in African Traditional Cultures: Survival Patterns," in *Modern African Drama: Backgrounds and Criticism*, ed. Biyodun Jeyifo (New York: Norton, 2002), 431.

10. Jukpor, "Le Rôle de l'École William Ponty," 54–55.

11. Jézéquel, "Le 'Théâtre des instituteurs,' " 181; Harry Gamble, *Contesting French West Africa: Battles over Schools and the Colonial Order, 1900–1950* (Lincoln: University of Nebraska Press, 2017), 116.

12. The colonies of French West Africa were Senegal, French Sudan (now Mali), Mauritania, French Guinea, Upper Volta (now Burkina Faso), Côte d'Ivoire, Dahomey (now Benin), and Niger.

13. For more on this school, see Kelly Duke Bryant, *Education as Politics: Colonial Schooling and Political Debate in Senegal, 1850s–1914* (Madison: University of Wisconsin Press, 2015), 93–116; and Yves Hazemann, "Un outil de la conquête coloniale: L'École des Ôtages de Saint-Louis (1855–1871; 1892–1903)," *Cahiers du CRA 5* (1987): 135–59.

14. In Boubacar Ly, *Les Instituteurs au Sénégal de 1903 à 1945: La Formation au métier d'instituteur, Vol. 3* (Paris: L'Harmattan, 2009), 103.

15. The actual role of Gorée Island in the history of the slave trade has been a matter of debate. UNESCO has nonetheless declared the site an "*île-mémoire*," or memory island. For a discussion of the island's role at the intersection of "history and memory scapes," see Paulla Ebron, "Tourists as Pilgrims: Commercial Fashioning of Transatlantic Politics," *American Ethnologist* 26, no. 4 (November 1999): 910–32. On the island's place in fiction and narrative, see Charles Forsdick, "*Cette île n'est pas une île*: Locating Gorée," in *At the Limits of Memory: Legacies of Slavery in the Francophone World*, ed. Nicola Frith and Kate Hodgson (Liverpool, UK: Liverpool University Press, 2015), 131–53.

16. Mamadou Diouf, "The French Colonial Policy of Assimilation and Civility of the Originaires of the Four Communes (Senegal): A Nineteenth-Century Globalization Project," *Development and Change* 29, no. 4 (October 1988): 671–96; Hilary Jones, *The Métis of Senegal: Urban Life and Politics in French West Africa* (Bloomington: Indiana University Press, 2013).

17. "L'École William Ponty, pépinière d'une élite africaine," Institut Fondamental d'Afrique Noire, Saint-Louis, Senegal, n.d.

18. In interviews about their experience on the later Sébikotane campus, former president Abdoulaye Wade and former minister Assane Seck emphasized above all the bucolic setting, which was conducive to study, as well as the vibrant cultural life of the school. Assane Seck, in discussion with the author, July 5, 2012; Abdoulaye Wade, in discussion with the author, July 4, 2012.

19. Ly points out the occasional episodes of protest on the part of students or their African *moniteurs*. Ly, *Les Instituteurs au Sénégal*, 362.

20. Jean-Hervé Jézéquel, "Les Enseignants comme élite politique en AOF (1930–1945): Des 'meneurs de galopins' dans l'arène politique," *Cahiers d'Études Africaines* 178 (2005): 519–43.

21. Among the most prominent visitors to the school were the French writers Georges Duhamel and André Gillois, as well as the Fourth Republic French president Vincent Auriol.

22. As Jézéquel points out, colonial categories such as the *élites lettrés* and the *évolués* were not, in fact, rigid social signifiers, but rather emerging colonial roles that African students attempted to fulfill or resist to their own benefit. Jézéquel, "Grammaire de la distinction coloniale: L'Organisation des cadres de l'enseignement en Afrique occidentale française (1903–fin des années 1930)," *Genèse* 69 (December 2007): 4–25.

23. "Théâtre et chants indigènes: Compte-rendu de la fête de l'École William Ponty," *L'Éducation Africaine: Bulletin de l'Enseignement de l'A.O.F.* (April–September 1935): 180.

24. "Théâtre et chants indigènes."

25. The irony of French instructors aspiring to enroot young native students in African culture is not unique to French colonial education, and was also the practice at the Achimota School in the Gold Coast. See Cati Coe, "Educating an African Leadership: Achimota and the Teaching of African Culture in the Gold Coast," *Africa Today* 49, no. 3 (Autumn 2002): 23–44.

26. Jézéquel, "Les Enseignants comme élites politiques," para. 12.

27. Bernard Dadié, *Climbié* (Paris: Seghers, 1956), 84.

28. See Raymond F. Betts, *Assimilation and Association in French Colonial Theory, 1890–1914* (Lincoln: University of Nebraska Press, 2005).

29. For a comparative reading of Saussure's notion with the thought of his more famous brother, Ferdinand, see Robert J. C. Young, "Race and Language in the Two Saussures," in *Philosophies of Race and Ethnicity*, ed. Peter Osborne and Stella Sanford (New York: Continuum Books, 2002), 63–78.

30. Albert Sarraut, *La Mise en valeur des colonies françaises* (Paris: Payot & Cie, 1923).

31. On historical variations and the repurposing of French republicanism in the colonies, see Alice Conklin, *A Mission to Civilize: The Republican Idea of Empire in France and West Africa, 1895–1930* (Palo Alto, CA: Stanford University Press, 1997).

32. On the colonial humanists, see Jean-Loup Amselle, *Branchements: Anthropologie de l'universalité des cultures* (Paris: Flammarion, 2003), 32–34; and Brent Hayes Edwards, *The Practice of Diaspora: Literature, Translation and the Rise of Black Internationalism* (Cambridge, MA: Harvard University Press, 2003), 73–77.

33. Gary Wilder, *The French Imperial Nation-State: Negritude and Colonial Humanism between the Two World Wars* (Chicago: University of Chicago Press, 2005), 124.

34. Wilder, *French Imperial Nation-State,* 124.

35. Wilder, *French Imperial Nation-State,* 5.

36. M. Michel, "La Colonisation: L'Action sociale," *L'Éducation Africaine, Bulletin de l'Enseignement de l'A.O.F.* 93 (1936): 6.

37. On the conditions surrounding the school's transfer and the Sébikotane site, see Ferdinand De Jong and Brian Quinn, "Ruines d'utopies: L'École William Ponty et l'Université du Futur Africain," trans. Jean-Nicolas Bach, *Politique Africaine* 135 (2014): 71–93; and Gamble, *Contesting French West Africa*, 118–24.

38. For an extensive study of the role of this journal and other writings by African *instituteurs*, see Céline Labrune-Badiane and Etienne Smith, *Les Hussards noirs de la colonie: Instituteurs africains et "petites patries" en AOF (1913–1960)* (Paris: Karthala, 2018).

39. Charles Béart, "Le Théâtre indigène et la culture franco-africaine," *Le Théâtre Indigène et la Culture Franco-Africaine, Numéro Spécial de L'Éducation Africaine* (1937): 12.

40. Stephen Bulman, "A School for Epic? The 'École William Ponty' and the Evolution of the Sunjata Epic, 1913– c. 1960," in *Epic Adventures: Heroic Narrative in the Oral Performance Traditions of Four Continents*, ed. Jean Jansen and Hans M. J. Maier (Münster: Lit Verlag, 2004), 34–45.

41. In this, educators were influenced by, and commented on, the early writings of Lucien Lévy-Bruhl, especially *La Mentalité primitive* (Paris: Félix Alcan, 1925).

42. Warner, *Tongue-Tied Imagination*, 64. See also Tobias Warner, "Para-Literary Ethnography and Colonial Self-Writing: The Student Notebooks of the William Ponty School," *Research in African Literatures* 47, no. 1 (Spring 2016): 1–20.

43. Sabatier, "African Culture and Colonial Education."

44. Bernard Dadié, "Assémien Déhylé, Roi du Sanwi," *Le Théâtre Indigène et la Culture Franco-Africaine, Numéro Spécial de L'Éducation Africaine* (1937): 29–40.

45. Charles Béart, introduction to "Assémien Déhylé, Roi du Sanwi," by Bernard Dadié, *Le Théâtre Indigène et la Culture Franco-Africaine, Numéro Spécial de L'Éducation Africaine* (1937): 23–28.

46. Charles Béart, "Les Origines du théâtre dans le monde, position du théâtre africain," *Comptes Rendus Mensuels de l'Académie des Sciences d'Outre-Mer* 22 (1962): 156.

47. "Entrevue de Samory et du Capitaine Péroz," *Le Théâtre Indigène et la Culture Franco-Africaine, Numéro Spécial de L'Éducation Africaine* (1937): 42.

48. Jay Straker, *Youth, Nationalism, and the Guinean Revolution* (Bloomington: Indiana University Press, 2009), 89–91.

49. Here Straker refers to oral-historical accounts compiled by J.-M. Touré in "Mobiliser, informer, éduquer un instrument efficace: Le Théâtre," *Notre Librairie* 88/89 (1987): 86–96.

50. Labrune-Badiane and Smith, *Les Hussards noirs de la colonie*, 508.

51. François-Joseph Amon d'Aby, one of the ten Ivorian students to embark on the Paris tour, lists the *pontins*' theatrical program as consisting of *Assémien*

Dehylé and *Les Prétendants rivaux* (both by the Ivorian students), *Sokamé* (Dahomey), and *La Ruse de Diégué* (French Sudan). Amon d'Aby, *Le Théâtre en Côte d'Ivoire*, 27. In a footnote, Labrune-Badiane and Smith point out that Paule Brasseur asserts that the revised version was performed in Dakar, not Paris. Brasseur, "Le Bâton et le caïman ou Fily Dabo Sissoko et la France," in *Études africaines offertes à Henri Brunschwig* (Paris: Éditions de l'École des Hautes Études en Sciences Sociales, 1982), 399–409; quoted in *Les Hussards noirs de la colonie*, 508, n. 213.

52. See Bocar Cissé, *Instituteur des sables: Témoin du Mali du XXe siècle* (Brinon-sur-Sauldre: Grandveaux, 2014), 111; Labrune-Badiane and Smith, *Les Hussards noirs de la colonie*, 511–14; Bernard Salvaing, "Les 'Ailleurs' d'un instituteur africain, Bocar Cissé (1944–1945)," in *L'Ailleurs de l'autre, récits de voyageurs extra-européens*, ed. Claudine Le Blanc and Jacques Weber (Rennes: Presses Universitaires de Rennes, 2009), 219–33.

53. Labrune-Badiane and Smith, *Les Hussards noirs de la colonie*, 514.

54. Abiola Irele, "In Praise of Alienation," in *African Literature: An Anthology of Criticism and Theory*, ed. Tejumola Olaniyan and Ato Quayson (Malden, MA: Blackwell, 2007), 601.

55. "A Dakar, de jeunes acteurs noirs ont joué des pièces inspirées des coutumes et du folklore indigènes," news article, n.d., Series O 138 (31), Archives Nationales du Sénégal, Dakar, Senegal.

56. Robert Delavignette, "Le Théâtre de Gorée et la culture franco-africaine," *Afrique Française* 10 (1937): 471.

57. Denis Moran, "Les Élèves d'une école normale africaine donnent, à Dakar, un spectacle d'art indigene," *Le Théâtre Indigène et la Culture Franco-Africaine, Numéro Spécial de L'Éducation Africaine* (1937): 59.

58. Amon d'Aby, *Le Théâtre en Côte d'Ivoire*, 26.

59. On the exoticized colonial representations of Africa and Africans on the Parisian stage at the time, see Chalaye, *Du noir au nègre*, 256–318.

60. Delavignette, "Le Théâtre de Gorée," 471.

61. Albert Charton, letter replying to the governor-general, Jules Brévié, January 5, 1937, Series O 587 (31), Archives Nationales du Sénégal, Dakar, Senegal.

62. Delavignette, "Le Théâtre de Gorée," 472.

63. Delavignette, "Le Théâtre de Gorée," 472.

Chapter 2

1. According to Frederick Cooper, the French Union portrayed itself, however misleadingly, "as a voluntary assemblage of different peoples, all of whom were now considered to be French citizens enjoying the same rights." Cooper, "Alternatives to Empire: France and Africa after World War II," in *The State of Sovereignty: Territories, Laws, Populations*, ed. Douglas Howland and Luise White (Bloomington: Indiana University Press, 2008), 100.

2. On the legal and legislative debates of this interstitial period, see Frederick Cooper, *Citizenship between Empire and Nation: Remaking France and French Africa, 1945–1960* (Princeton, NJ: Princeton University Press, 2014).

3. On postwar educational reforms in French West Africa, see Harry Gamble, "The Education of African 'Citizens': Struggles over Integration," in *Contesting French West Africa*, 211–41.

4. Former *pontin* Assane Seck confirmed the importance of this grievance to former students of the Ponty School, several of whom wished to pursue an education in France. Assane Seck, in discussion with the author, July 5, 2012.

5. Among the few explorations of the cultural centers as sites of cultural and theatrical production are Robert Cornevin, *Le Théâtre en Afrique noire*, 104–20; Despres, *Se faire contemporain*; Bruno Gnaoulé-Oupoh, *La Littérature ivoirienne* (Paris: Karthala, 2000), 135; Konkobo, *La Pratique du théâtre moderne*, 41–59; and Alioune Mbaye, "Le Théâtre des centres culturels en AOF: 1948–1958, 'Du casque colonial au béret tropical,'" *Ethiopiques* no. 76 (2006). The playwright Marouba Fall also points out the scant attention paid to this period in theatrical production, in *Théâtre et tradition en Afrique noire francophone: Exemple du théâtre sénégalais de langue française* (Dakar: L'Harmattan-Sénégal, 2019), 280.

6. Nicolas Bancel explores this concern in his study of the centers: "Les Centres Culturels en A.O.F. (1953–1960): Un projet de contrôle sociopolitique des jeunes élites," in *Lieux de sociabilité urbaine en Afrique*, ed. Laurent Fourchard, Odile Goerg, and Muriel Gomez-Perez (Paris: L'Harmattan, 2009), 109–34. Konkobo points out how the need to pacify a young, potentially restive political class was also a driving motive in the centers' activities, in *La Pratique du théâtre moderne*, 45.

7. Bernard Cornut-Gentille, "Les Centres Culturels, foyers d'amitié," *Traits d'Union* no. 7 (March–April 1955): 3.

8. Cornut-Gentille, "Les Centres Culturels," 3.

9. As Bancel points out: "Participation in these activities functioned for this urban elite as the sign of a reciprocal acknowledgement. This reality is all the more significant in that it goes against the view and recommendations of the High Commissioner." Bancel, "Les Centres Culturels en A.O.F.," 125.

10. Lompolo Koné, "Nos Activités!" *Traits d'Union* no. 7 (March–April 1955): 5.

11. Lompolo Koné, "Hésitations," *Traits d'Union* no. 8 (May–June 1955): 4.

12. Lompolo Koné, "M. Lompolo Koné est chargé des fonctions de rédacteur en chef de 'Traits d'Union,'" *Traits d'Union* no. 1 (1953): 5.

13. Koné, "Hésitations," 3.

14. Amon d'Aby, *Le Théâtre en Côte d'Ivoire*, 102.

15. Bernard Cornut-Gentille, "Organisation d'un Grand Concours artistique et théâtral," *Traits d'Union* no. 5 (1955): 3.

16. On the early years of Sonar Senghor's life, see *Souvenirs de théâtres*, 7–46.

17. Published as "Sarzan, un conte de Birago Diop, adapté par Lamine Diakhaté," *Traits d'Union* no. 7 (March–April 1955): 48–65. The original short story is published in Birago Diop, *Les Contes d'Amadou Koumba* (Paris: Présence Africaine, 1969).

18. Diakhaté, "Sarzan," 52.

19. Sonar Senghor's reports are kept in the National Archives of Senegal, Series O 677 (31).

20. L. Dale Byam, *Community in Motion: Theatre for Development in Africa* (Westport, CT: Bergin and Garvey, 1999), 5.

21. Konkobo, *La Pratique du théâtre moderne*, 54–59.

22. Robert Delavignette, *Les Paysans noirs* (Saint-Étienne: Publications de l'Université de Saint-Étienne, 2011).

23. Michèle Dacher, "Une épopée gouin: *Les Paysans noirs* à Banfora aujourd'hui," in *Robert Delavignette, savant et politique (1897–1976)*, ed. Bernard Mouralis and Anne Piriou with Romuald Fonkoua (Paris: Karthala): 61–72.

24. Letter from Governor Etcheber of Upper Volta to the High Commissioner of French West Africa, January 17, 1956, Archives Nationales du Sénégal, Series O 677 (31).

25. The same group had been instrumental in forming, in 1938, a troupe called Théâtre Indigène de la Côte d'Ivoire (shortly after their studies at Ponty) as a club of young bureaucrats waiting for the administration to make good on the promise of attractive administrative positions. Amon d'Aby, *Le Théâtre en Côte d'Ivoire*, 33–50.

26. Mathieu Ekra, "Première de Kwao Adjoba, Drame de J.F. (sic.) Amon d'Aby," *Traits d'Union* no. 5 (1955): 74.

27. Amon d'Aby, *Le Théâtre en Côte d'Ivoire*, 64.

28. Amon d'Aby, *Le Théâtre en Côte d'Ivoire*, 148.

29. Amon d'Aby, *Le Théâtre en Côte d'Ivoire*, 157.

30. Sylvie Chalaye describes a rupture in the clichés that once surrounded the staged figure of the African in France, most notably after the Second World War. See "L'Après-Guerre: Vers l'éclatement de la chrysalide (1945–1960)," in *Du noir au nègre*, 367–91.

31. On Cornut-Gentille, Sonar Senghor writes: "When the high commissioner left Dakar in the early rainy season of 1956, he left behind a theatrical movement of which he had laid the foundations." Sonar Senghor, *Souvenirs de théâtres*, 69.

32. On the Theater of Nations festival, see Odette Aslan, *Paris, capitale mondiale du théâtre* (Paris: Gallimard, 2009); and Daniela Peslin, *Le Théâtre des Nations: Une aventure théâtrale à découvrir* (Paris: L'Harmattan, 2009).

33. For a consideration of the festival's interaction with Cold War politics, see Christian Wenkel, "Le Théâtre des Nations—Un théâtre de la guerre froide?," in *La France en guerre froide, nouvelles questions*, ed. Sylvie Le Clech and Michel Hastings (Dijon: Éditions Universitaires de Dijon, 2015), 181–89.

34. Aslan, *Paris, capitale mondiale du théâtre*, 7.

35. Aslan, *Paris, capitale mondiale du théâtre*, 8.

36. See James M. Harding and John Rouse, "Introduction," in *Not the Other Avant-Garde: The Transnational Foundations of Avant-Garde Performance*, ed. James M. Harding and John Rouse (Ann Arbor: University of Michigan Press, 2006), 1–17.

37. Planson was indeed an early proponent of total theater in France, where the total theater approach was closely associated with the writings of Antonin Artaud. Artaud's vision of a nonrepresentational theater had a strong influence on the work of many French directors, particularly that of Jean-Louis Barrault, who became the director of the Theater of Nations festival in 1965. On the development of total theater in Barrault's work, see Christopher Innes, "Primitive, Ritual and Ceremony," in *Holy Theatre: Ritual and the Avant-Garde* (Cambridge: Cambridge University Press, 1981), 111–58.

38. Artaud's seminal text *Le Théâtre et son double* (Paris: Gallimard, 1938) famously takes the non-Western form of Balinese dance as his inspiration in a search for a theater that went beyond the limited scope of a theater of words.

39. Claude Planson, "Théâtre noir" debate at the Théâtre des Nations, March 23, 1960, Fonds Centre Français du Théâtre, Paris, Société d'Histoire du Théâtre (quoted in Peslin, *Le Théâtre des Nations*, 181).

40. Charles Béart, "Théâtre noir" debate at the Théâtre des Nations, March 23, 1960, Fonds Centre Français du Théâtre, Paris, Société d'Histoire du Théâtre (quoted in Peslin, *Le Théâtre des Nations*, 178).

41. Bakary Traoré, "Le Théâtre noir," *Le Théâtre dans le Monde* 9, no. 1 (1960): 345.

42. As Aslan explains, at the time of the event, "[Planson] does not want to hear about folklore or the westernization of African practices. For him, the griots' tales are theater and so are the songs and dances." Aslan, *Paris, capitale mondiale du théâtre*, 126

43. From Cissé Dia's correspondence with Raymond Hermantier, in Pasquini, "Raymond Hermantier, un parcours," annex.

44. Praise Zenenga, "The Total Theatre Aesthetic Paradigm in African Theatre," in *The Oxford Handbook of Dance and Theatre*, ed. Nadine George-Graves (Oxford: Oxford University Press, 2015), 246.

45. Zenenga, "The Total Theatre Aesthetic Paradigm," 241.

46. For the development and formalization of the ASC, see Susann Baller, "Urban Football Performances: Playing for the Neighbourhood in Senegal, 1950s–2000s," *Africa: The Journal of the International African Institute* 84, no. 1 (February 2014): 17–35.

47. Susann Baller, "Youth, Theatre and Sports: Creating 'Conscious' Citizens within the Senegalese Nawetaan Movement," *African Insight* 37, no. 3 (2007): 380.

48. Neveu Kringelbach describes how the privately produced televised event of the "Oscars" actually made use of the already existing ASC competitions. Neveu Kringelbach, *Dance Circles*, 103–6.

49. Papa Samba Sow, "Théâtre Nawetaan, théâtre des valeurs," in *De l'instinct théâtral: Le Théâtre se ressource en Afrique*, ed. Julius Effenberger (Paris: L'Harmattan, 2004), 45–66.

50. Alioune Diakhaté Mbaye focuses primarily on the role of soccer to explore the *nawetaan* phenomenon as a syncretic cultural space that emphasizes and produces local and African cultural identities. Mbaye, *Les Sports Navétanes au Sénégal* (Dakar: L'Harmattan-Sénégal, 2017).

51. Oumar Ndao, in discussion with the author, July 3, 2012.

Chapter 3

An earlier version of this chapter appeared in "Staging Culture: Senghor, Malraux and the Theatre Programme at the First World Festival of Negro Arts," in *The First World Festival of Negro Arts, Dakar 1966*, ed. David Murphy (Liverpool, UK: Liverpool University Press, 2016), 83–96.

1. Catherine Coquery-Vidrovitch, "Festan, Festac, Panaf," in *Une histoire des festivals, XXe–XXI1 siècle*, ed. Anaïs Fléchet et al. (Paris: Publications de la Sorbonne, 2013), 317–21.

2. Léopold Sédar Senghor, "Le Message de l'Afrique," in *Premier Festival Mondial des Arts Nègres* (festival program) (Paris: Impressions André Rousseau, 1966), 14.

3. Senghor, "Le Message," 14 (English translation in original).

4. Some of the event's most prominent international guests included Josephine Baker, Louis Armstrong, Langston Hughes, Emperor Haile Selassie of Ethiopia, French author Michel Leiris, Wole Soyinka, André Malraux, Katherine Dunham, and Aimé Césaire.

5. On Senegal's cultural policies, see Elizabeth Harney, *In Senghor's Shadow: Art, Politics, and the Avant-Garde in Senegal, 1960–1995* (Durham, NC: Duke University Press, 2004); and Tracy D. Snipe, *Arts and Politics in Senegal, 1960–1996* (Trenton, NJ: Africa World, 1998).

6. As Murphy and Neveu Kringelbach explain, tensions nonetheless abounded following the decision to appoint a white socialite named Virginia Inness-Brown as chair of the festival's U.S. committee. Suspicions of hidden intervention by the State Department suggest that underlying influences served to prevent the participation of more politically vocal African American artists who were fighting for the cause of civil rights at the time. See David Murphy, "The Performance of Pan-Africanism: Staging the African Renaissance at the First World Festival of Negro Arts," in *The First World Festival of Negro Arts, Dakar 1966, Contexts and Legacies,* ed. David Murphy (Liverpool, UK: Liverpool University Press, 2016), 29; and Hélène Neveu Kringelbach, "Dance at the 1966 World Festival of Negro Arts: Of 'Fabulous Dancers' and Negritude Undermined," in *The First World Festival of Negro Arts, Dakar 1966, Contexts and Legacies,* ed. David Murphy (Liverpool, UK: Liverpool University Press, 2016), 79.

7. Murphy, "Performancc of Pan-Africanism," 2.

8. Christina McMahon, *Recasting Transnationalism through Performance: Theatre Festivals in Cape Verde, Mozambique and Brazil* (New York: Palgrave Macmillan, 2014), 26.

9. On the Algiers festival, see Samuel D. Anderson, "'Negritude Is Dead': Performing the African Revolution at the First Pan-African Cultural Festival (Algiers, 1969)," in *The First World Festival of Negro Arts, Dakar, 1966, Contexts and Legacies,* ed. David Murphy (Liverpool, UK: Liverpool University Press, 2016), 133–50; and Mériem Khellas, *Le Premier Festival Culturel Panafricain, Algers, 1969: Une grande messe populaire* (Paris: L'Harmattan, 2014).

10. The Portuguese colonies of Angola, Mozambique, Guinea-Bissau, and Cabo Verde did not achieve their independence until after the 1974 Carnation Revolution in Portugal that saw the end of its dictatorship under António de Oliveira Salazar.

11. Andrew Apter, *The Pan-African Nation: Oil and the Spectacle of Culture in Nigeria* (Chicago: University of Chicago Press, 2005).

12. Apter, *The Pan-African Nation,* 70.

13. Dominique Malaquais and Cédric Vincent, "Panafest: A Festival Complex Revisited," in *The First World Festival of Negro Arts, Dakar 1966, Contexts and Legacies,* ed. David Murphy (Liverpool, UK: Liverpool University Press, 2016), 195.

14. Murphy, "Performance of Pan-Africanism," 35.

15. Lépold Sédar Senghor, *Ce que je crois* (Paris: Grasset & Fasquelle, 1988), 136.

16. Murphy, "Performance of Pan-Africanism," 35–37.

17. Sembène was awarded the *grand prix* for cinema, having presented his film *La Noire de . . .* (*Black Girl*). Soyinka earned a prize for drama, and Cheikh Anta

Diop was recognized, along with W. E. B. Du Bois, as an African thinker who had profoundly influenced the twentieth century.

18. Tsitsi Jaji, "'The Next Best Thing to Being There': Covering the 1966 Dakar Festival and Its Legacy in Black Popular Magazines," in *The First World Festival of Negro Arts, Dakar 1966, Contexts and Legacies*, ed. David Murphy (Liverpool, UK: Liverpool University Press, 2016), 113.

19. Neveu Kringelbach, "Dance at the 1966 World Festival of Negro Arts," 66.

20. Seen in William Klein, dir., *Festival Panafricain d'Alger*, 2010, Arte Éditions, 120 min.

21. Léopold Sédar Senghor, *Liberté I, négritude et humanisme* (Paris: Seuil, 1964), 288.

22. Souleymane Bachir Diagne, *African Art as Philosophy: Senghor, Bergson, and the Idea of Negritude*, trans. Chike Jeffers (Chicago: University of Chicago Press, 2011).

23. Gary Wilder, *Freedom Time: Negritude, Decolonization, and the Future of the World* (Durham, NC: Duke University Press, 2015), 1.

24. Wilder, *Freedom Time*, 59.

25. Wilder, *Freedom Time*, 135.

26. Frantz Fanon, "On National Culture," in *The Wretched of the Earth*, trans. Richard Philcox (New York: Grove, 2004), 224.

27. Joshua Cohen, "Locating Senghor's École de Dakar: International and Transnational Dimensions to Senegalese Modern Art, c. 1959–1980," *African Arts* 51, no. 3 (2018): 10–12.

28. Coquery-Vidrovitch, "Festan, Festac, Panaf," 321.

29. For an extensive study of the *françafrique* system, see François-Xavier Verschave, *La Françafrique: Le Plus Long Scandale de la République* (Paris: Stock, 1998).

30. Catherine Coquio, "Un intellectual 'accompagné': Malraux, de Gaulle, Foccart et le récit de la 'décolonisation,'" in *Malraux et l'Afrique*, ed. Rafael Lambal (Paris: Présence Africaine, 2013), 175.

31. Coquio, "Un intellectual 'accompagné,'" 178. Hannah Feldman has also written about the political stakes concealed by Malraux's de-historicized and universal notion of culture, permitting what she calls an "amnesiac aesthetic" as a form of response to France's failure in the wars of decolonization. Feldman, *From a Nation Torn: Decolonizing Art and Representation in France, 1945–1962* (Durham, NC: Duke University Press, 2014), 43.

32. Philippe Poirrier, *La Politique culturelle en débat: Anthologie, 1955–2012* (Paris: La Documentation Française, 2013), 305.

33. André Malraux, "Présentation du budget de la culture à l'Assemblée Nationale," October 27, 1966, http://www2.assemblee-nationale.fr/decouvrir-l-assemblee/histoire/grands-moments-d-eloquence/andre-malraux-27-octobre-1966.

34. Emile Biasini, *Sur Malraux, celui qui aimait les chats* (Paris: Odile Jacob, 1999); Marie-Ange Rauch, *Le Bonheur d'entreprendre: Les Administrateurs de la France d'outre-mer et la création du Ministère des Affaires Culturelles* (Paris: Comité d'Histoire du Ministère de la Culture, 1998).

35. Biasini, *Sur Malraux*, 14. See also Herman Lebovics, *Mona Lisa's Escort: André Malraux and the Reinvention of French Culture* (Durham, NC: Duke University Press, 1999), 98.

36. Rauch, *Le Bonheur d'entreprendre*, 65.
37. Lebovics, *Mona Lisa's Escort*, 82.
38. In August 1960 alone, Malraux participated as a guest of honor in the independence ceremonies of Chad, the Central African Republic, Congo, and Gabon.
39. André Malraux, *Le Miroir des Limbes II: La Corde et les souris* (Paris: Gallimard, 1976), 12.
40. André Malraux, "Discours prononcé à Dakar à la séance d'ouverture du colloque organisé à l'occasion du Festival Mondial des Arts Nègres le 30 mars 1966," http://www.assemblee-nationale.fr/histoire/andre-malraux/discours_politique_culture/discours_Dakar.asp.
41. André Paris, review of *Macbeth* by the Daniel Sorano Troupe at the Cultural Center of Uccle, Belgium, *Le Soir*, January 8, 1970, consulted in Series 4 SW 10811(2), La Collection du Département des Arts du Spectacle, Bibliothèque Nationale de France, Paris.
42. The French novelist Jean Dutourd offered the following assessment, which was characteristic of other reviewers at the time: "Nothing resembles savage Medieval Scotland more than this chivalrous and fabulous Africa full of strange rites, cruelty, and sounds of tam-tams and xylophones wherein [the play] was transposed." In "*Macbeth* noir: Une grande et belle leçon de théâtre," *France Soir*, December 14–15, 1969, Series 4 SW 10811(2), Bibliothèque Nationale de France, Paris.
43. Interview with Maurice Sonar Senghor, *Ouest-France*, November 6, 1969, Rennes, Series 4 SW 10811(2), Bibliothèque Nationale de France, Paris.
44. Ruth Bush, "Making History: Performances of the Past at the 1966 World Festival of Negro Arts," in *The First World Festival of Negro Arts, Dakar 1966, Contexts and Legacies*, ed. David Murphy (Liverpool, UK: Liverpool University Press, 2016), 103.
45. Senghor, *Souvenirs de théâtres*, 86.
46. Seyba Traoré, in discussion with the author, July 3, 2012.
47. Ferdinand De Jong, "Shining Lights: Self-Fashioning in the Lantern Festival of Saint-Louis, Senegal," *African Arts* 42, no. 4 (Winter 2009): 38–53. De Jong points out the importance of Faidherbe's image in the festivities of the popular "Fanal" event in Saint-Louis. However, the legacy of Faidherbe, whose statue stands prominently on the city's main square, has become a matter of intense debate and the target of a "Faidherbe Must Fall" movement pointing out atrocities committed in the course of the general's conquest of the West African region.
48. Amadou Cissé Dia, *Les Derniers Jours de Lat Dior: Drame en 5 actes; La Mort du Damel, pièce en 3 actes* (Paris: Présence Africaine, 1978), 26.
49. Allen F. Roberts and Mary Nooter Roberts, *A Saint in the City: Sufi Arts of Urban Senegal* (Los Angeles: Fowler Museum of Cultural History, 2003).
50. Although this meeting is often assumed to have taken place and to have had a profound impact on subsequent Murid history, Cheikh Anta Babou argues that the event is most likely a myth, in *Fighting the Greater Jihad: Amadu Bamba and the Founding of the Muridiyya of Senegal, 1853–1913* (Athens: Ohio University Press, 2007), 110.
51. Cheikh Aliou Ndao, *L'Exil d'Albouri, suivi de la décision; Le Fils de l'Almamy; La Case de l'homme* (Dakar: Nouvelles Éditions Africaines, 1985), 17.

52. Omar Mokhtari, ed., "Le Manifeste culturel panafricain," in *Alger 1969, Premier Festival Culturel Panafricain* (Algiers: Éditions Actualité Algérie, 1970), 5.

53. Mamadou Diouf, *Histoire du Sénégal: Le Modèle islamo-wolof et ses périphéries* (Paris: Maisonneuve & Larose, 2001), 159–60.

54. Conteh-Morgan, *Theatre and Drama in Francophone Africa*, 155.

55. Fanon, *Wretched of the Earth*, 6.

56. Some notable examples of later Senegalese history plays to receive productions at the Sorano Theater and elsewhere include Thierno Bâ, *Lat Dior, le chemin de l'honneur* (Dakar: Nouvelles Éditions Africaines, 1987); Marouba Fall, *Chaka, ou le roi visionnaire* (Dakar: Nouvelles Éditions Africaines, 1984); Mamadou Seyni M'Bengue, *Le Procès de Lat Dior* (Paris: ORTF-DAEC, 1972); and Ibrahima Sall, *Le Choix de Madior* (Dakar: Nouvelles Éditions Africaines, 1981).

57. Ferdinand De Jong and Vincent Foucher, "La Tragédie du Roi Abdoulaye? Néomodernisme et renaissance africaine dans le Sénégal contemporain," *Politique Africaine* 118 (2010): 187–204.

58. At the 2014 Sommet de la Francophonie in Dakar, the performance of a historical epic, *Le Légende du fusil*, by the Senegalese playwright Massèye Niang, was the capstone event in a production that reprised many of the themes of Cissé Dia's play on Lat Joor.

Chapter 4

Parts of this chapter appeared in "Sur les traces de *Bamba Mos Xam*: L'Invention du théâtre mouride," *Continents Manuscrits* no. 13 (2019).

1. Roberts and Roberts, *A Saint in the City*.

2. A non-exhaustive list of major works includes Babou, *Fighting the Greater Jihad*; Jean Copans, *Les Marabouts de l'arachide* (Paris: Le Sycomore, 1980); Donal Cruise O'Brien, *The Mourides of Senegal: The Political and Economic Organization of an Islamic Brotherhood in Senegal* (Oxford: Oxford University Press, 1971); and David Robinson, *Paths of Accommodation: Muslim Societies and French Colonial Authorities in Senegal and Mauritania, 1880–1920* (Athens: Ohio University Press, 2000).

3. Fallou Ngom, *Muslims beyond the Arab World: The Odyssey of ʿAjamī and the Muridiyya* (Oxford: Oxford University Press, 2016), 125.

4. Babou, *Fighting the Greater Jihad*, 5.

5. The other Sufi brotherhoods in Senegal are the Tijaniyya (the largest by number of devotees), the Qadiriyya, and the Layenniyya (founded among the Lebu community of Dakar). For Sufism in Senegal, see Khadim Mbacké, *Sufism and Religious Brotherhoods in Senegal*, trans. Eric Ross, ed. John Hunwick (Princeton, NJ: Markus Wiener, 2005).

6. Rudolph Ware, *The Walking Qur'an: Islamic Education, Embodied Knowledge, and History in West Africa* (Chapel Hill: University of North Carolina Press, 2014).

7. Ware, *The Walking Qur'an*, 164.

8. The show and its title were frequently cited during my fieldwork carried out on popular theater forms over a nine-month period in 2014.

9. Mouhamadou Diol (director of La Compagnie Kàddu Yaraax), in discussion with the author, December 20, 2016.

10. Baba Ndiaye, intervention at the FEST'RAIL conference titled "Théâtre, diversité culturelle, et développement durable," Thiès, Senegal, May 14, 2016.

11. Our principal interlocutors throughout this research were Cheikh Fall (former director of the troupe); Selbe Diagne and Abdoulaye Faye (former *Bamba Mos Xam* performers); Mor Sadio Niang (former director of the Kaolack cultural center); Oumar Thiam (an internationally renowned percussionist from Kaolack); Yelimane Fall (internationally renowned painter and a public figure of the Murid community); Fallou Fall Mbaor (grandson of Maam Shaykh Ibrahima Faal and a public figure of the Murid community); Cheikh Samb (grandson of the lead actor of *Bamba Mos Xam* and a journalist for several Murid media outlets in Touba); and Beug Fallou (former *diwaankat*, or professional storyteller from Touba). We also spoke with dozens of former spectators and benefited from invaluable research assistance by Ousmane Guèye of Touba and Pikine.

12. Cheikh Ibrahima Fall (former director of the *Bamba Mos Xam* troupe), in discussion with the author, May 15, 2016.

13. For studies of more recent sacred uses of secular cultural forms and spaces, see Joseph Hill, "'Baay Is the Spiritual Leader of the Rappers': Performing Islamic Reasoning in Senegalese Hip-Hop," *Contemporary Islam* 10, no. 2 (2016): 267–87; Fiona McLaughlin, "Islam and Popular Music in Senegal: The Emergence of a 'New Tradition,'" *Africa: Journal of the International African Institute* 67, no. 4 (1997): 560–81; and Abdoulaye Niang, "'Preaching Music' and Islam in Senegal: Can the Secular Mediate the Religious? The Case of Rap and *Mbalax* Music," *African Communication Research* 2, no. 1 (2009): 61–84.

14. Due to the lack of written records on the production and its countless performances, we were never able to establish with certainty the exact date or year of its closure.

15. Cheikh Fall, in discussion with the author, May 15 and 21, 2016. In transcribing the play, we benefited from the invaluable assistance of Abdoulaye Karel Dieng, of the Salon Africain des Langues et Cultures, and of linguist Paap Alsaan Sow.

16. Yelimane Fall also insisted on the importance, in any act of artistic adaptation dealing with Murid history, of complying with the brotherhood's accepted dogma. In discussion with the author, May 18, 2016.

17. Beug Fallou (former *diwaankat*), interview with the author, December 18, 2016. The aptly named "Beug Fallou," whose name means "love Faliilu," performed primarily in his home city of Touba.

18. Cheikh Ibrahima Fall, in discussion with the author, May 15, 2016.

19. Moussa Ka, *L'Épopée de Cheikh Amadou Bamba de Serigne Moussa Ka*, ed. Bassirou Dieng and Diaô Faye (Dakar: Presses Universitaires de Dakar, 2006).

20. Beug Fallou recalled the impact of Demba Ndiaye's appearance and vocalization of Sëriñ Touba on audiences in Touba. In discussion with the author, December 17, 2016.

21. Ndiaye's grandson, Cheikh Samb, corroborated the special status that playing Bamba conveyed on his grandfather in the Murid community. In discussion with the author, December 17, 2016.

22. Soukaye Ndiaye (Touba street vendor), in discussion with the author, December 17, 2016.

23. As Fallou Ngom points out, the popular and stereotypical image of Ibra Faal, which *Bamba Mos Xam* no doubt played some role in disseminating, appears to have little to do with the actual historical figure. Murid records indicate that Faal was "a highly educated mystic with extraordinary inner strength who had the same preoccupations as Bamba and who was exceptionally committed to the ethical ideas of the Muridiyya." Ngom, *Muslims beyond the Arab World*, 97.

24. Transcription of *Bamba Mos Xam* play, compiled with former troupe director Cheikh Ibrahima Fall, in the author's possession.

25. The former spectator Leïty Kane of Yarakh spoke of the impression made on him by the actor portraying Ibra Faal and reenacted some of the performer's vigorous and expansive gestures. In discussion with the author, December 23, 2016.

26. Yelimane Fall, in discussion with the author, May 18, 2016.

27. Babou, *Fighting the Greater Jihad*, 93.

28. Such forms of intervention are common in other circumstances. One example is the banning of *Karmen Geï*, a film by the Senegalese filmmaker Joseph Gaï Ramaka, for superimposing a religious song associated with Sëriñ Touba onto an intimate scene between two female characters. See Steve Nelson, "Karmen Geï: Sex, the State, and Censorship in Dakar," *African Arts* 44, no. 1 (Spring 2011): 74–81.

29. Massamba Guèye, "Intervention du Directeur de Sorano Massamba Guèye: Le Théâtre, une réussite face à l'interdit," website of La Compagnie du Théâtre National du Sénégal Daniel Sorano, November 11, 2013, http://compagnietheatresorano.com/rubriques.php?rub=article.php&id_article=62.

30. The political scientist Alfred Stepan describes a range of "rituals of respect" involved in the delicate balance between religious institutions and the state that characterizes the so-called "Senegalese exception." Stepan, "Rituals of Respect: Sufis and Secularists in Senegal in Comparative Perspective," *Comparative Politics* 44, no. 4 (July 2012): 379–401.

31. On the history and significance of the Murid capital of Touba in religious and cultural terms, see Cheikh Guèye, *Touba, la capitale des Mourides* (Paris: Karthala, 2002); and Eric Ross, *Sufi City: Urban Design and Archetypes in Touba* (Rochester, NY: University of Rochester Press, 2002).

32. Hill, "Baay Is the Spiritual Leader," 276.

33. Oludamini Ogunnaike, "Performing Realization: The Sufi Music Videos of the Taalibe Baye of Dakar," *African Arts* 51, no. 3 (2018): 29.

34. Idries Shah, *The Sufis* (London: Idries Shah Foundation, 2015), 35.

35. Sana Camara, "*A'jami* Literature in Senegal: The Example of Sëriñ Muusaa Ka, Poet and Biographer," *Research in African Literatures* 28, no. 3 (Autumn 1997): 163–82; Ngom, *Muslims beyond the Arab World*.

36. Ka, *L'Épopée de Cheikh Amadou Bamba*, 69, v. 219–20.

37. Ka, *L'Épopée,* 37, v. 6 (English translations my own).

38. Ka, *L'Épopée,* 37, v. 8.

39. Ka, *L'Épopée*, 71, v. 231.

40. For a transcription of the opening sequence of scenes in Wolof, English, and French, see Brian Valente-Quinn, "Sur les traces de *Bamba Mos Xam*: L'Invention du théâtre mouride," *Continents Manuscrits* no. 13 (2019).

41. Transcription of *Bamba Mos Xam* play.
42. Transcription of *Bamba Mos Xam* play.
43. One notable example is N'Dour's song "Bamba," whose English lyrics reflect a common desire among Bamba's devotees to disseminate the Murid message well beyond the borders of Senegal.
44. The popular website www.majalis.org is designed as a virtual Murid university. Bichri.tv, based out of Denver, Colorado, also offers open access to educational videos and has streamed events live from Touba during the Murid celebration of the Grand Magal.
45. See Christine Thu Nhi Dang, "Pilgrimage through Poetry: Sung Journeys within the Murid Spiritual Diaspora," *Islamic Africa* 4, no. 1 (Spring 2013): 69–101.
46. Yelimane Fall, in discussion with the author, May 18, 2016.
47. Mouhamadou Diol, in discussion with the author, December 20, 2016.

Chapter 5

1. On the generational effects of these funding cuts on the art world, see Hélène Neveu Kringelbach, "Choreographic Performance: Generations and the Art of Life in Post-Colonial Dakar," *Africa* 81, no. 1 (February 2014): 36–54.
2. On the structural adjustment reforms and their failure to address the challenges faced by the Senegalese economy, see Momar-Coumba Diop, "Réformes économiques et recompositions sociales," in *La Construction de l'état au Sénégal*, ed. Donal Cruise O'Brien et al. (Paris: Karthala, 2002), 64–82.
3. Resentment of Diouf was a recurring theme in interviews with an older generation of theater-makers and forms a contrast with the glowing reputation of Senghor. See Francesca Castaldi, *Choreographies of African Identities* (Urbana: University of Illinois Press, 2006), 197–204.
4. In an interview during his final year as director of the Sorano Theater, Ousmane Diakhaté pointed out the excessive operational costs involved in running such an institution. He cited as a major challenge of his early tenure the acquisition of funds from the state to repair the air-conditioning system, without which the theater becomes intolerably hot during the summer. Discussion with the author, June 27, 2012, Dakar.
5. Momar-Coumba Diop, "Le Sénégal à la croisée des chemins," *Politique Africaine* no. 104 (2006): 106.
6. Quoted in Diop, "Le Sénégal à la croisée des chemins," 107.
7. As Diop writes: "The structural adjustment programs were overseen primarily by consultants and experts at the technical ministries, the local, technocratic clientele of the funders. This group therefore operated outside any political mandate, although the reforms it required had a considerable social and political impact." Diop, "Le Sénégal à la croisée des chemins," 107.
8. "Le Théâtre se meurt mais ne se rend pas," *Le Soleil*, February 6, 1997, 8.
9. Fatoumata Seck explores the broad implications of such economic anxieties through the immensely popular comic book character Goorgoorlou, which was also turned into a successful television series. Seck, "Goorgoorlou, the Neoliberal *Homo Senegalensis*: Comics and Economics in Postcolonial Senegal," *Journal of African Cultural Studies* 30, no. 3 (May 2017): 263–78.
10. Diop, "Le Sénégal à la croisée des chemins," 110.

11. On the impact of innovations in communications and media technology on African television and video production, see Carmela Garritano, *African Video Movies and Global Desires* (Athens: Ohio University Press, 2013); and Boukary Sawadogo, *West African Screen Media: Comedy, TV Series, and Transnationalization* (East Lansing: Michigan State University Press, 2019).

12. Brian Larkin, *Signal and Noise: Media, Infrastructure, and Urban Culture in Nigeria* (Durham, NC: Duke University Press, 2008), 6.

13. Jo Ellen Fair points out the driving force of notions of Francophonie, rather than nationalism, in television's rise. See Fair, "*Francophonie* and the National Airwaves: A History of Television in Senegal," in *Planet TV: A Global Television Reader*, ed. Shanti Kumar and Lisa Parks (New York: NYU Press, 2002), 189–210.

14. Gaye Daffé and Mamadou Dansokho, "Les Nouvelles Technologies de l'information et de la communication: Défis et opportunités pour l'économie sénégalaise," in *Le Sénégal à l'heure de l'information: Technologies et société*, ed. Momar-Coumba Diop (Paris: Karthala, 2002), 50; André-Jean Tudesq, *L'Afrique noire et ses télévisions* (Paris: Anthropos INA, 1992), 51–53.

15. A. B. Dièye, "Les Comédiens interpellent le nouveau pouvoir," *Sud Quotidien*, March 29, 2000.

16. Cheikh Aliou Ndao, "Éthique et esthétique dans le théâtre sénégalais," *Le Soleil*, July 27, 1998.

17. Dieye, "Les Comédiens."

18. Dieye, "Les Comédiens."

19. Kocc Barma's maxims are situated within the political tensions and conflicts of the time of the Jolof kingdom ("A king is not a relative"), but they also provide memorable insights on handling the intricacies of Wolof family structures ("A child from the first bed [a previous marriage] is not a child, but an internal war") as well as gender roles ("Love your wife but do not trust her").

20. Ivy Mills uses the prism of the Wolof value term *sutura* (discretion) to explore gender in Daaray Kocc's work as well as the troupe's interrogation of popular Wolof wisdom and morality. Mills, "Sutura: Gendered Honor, Social Death, and the Politics of Exposure in Senegalese Literature and Popular Culture," Ph.D. dissertation, UC Berkeley, 2011, 82–117.

21. Cheikh M. S. Diop, "Tradition théâtrale et identités sénégalaises: Contributions sur la pratique dramatique au Sénégal: Approche historique et analytique," Africultures, July 22, 2004, http://africultures.com/tradition-theatrale-et-identite-senegalaises-3464/.

22. In contrast, the very popular group Jamonoy Tey worked mainly in comedic sketches.

23. Christopher L. Miller, "Senegalese Women Writers, Silence, and Letters: Before the Canon's Roar," in *Theories of Africans* (Chicago: University of Chicago Press, 1993), 246–94.

24. Miller, "Senegalese Women Writers," 278.

25. Mariama Bâ, *Une si longue lettre* (Dakar: Les Nouvelles Éditions Africaines du Sénégal, 1979); citations from Mariama Bâ, *So Long a Letter*, trans. Modupé Bodé-Thomas (London: Heinemann, 1981), 1.

26. Mildred Mortimer, *Writing from the Hearth: Public, Domestic, and Imaginative Space in Francophone Women's Fiction of Africa and the Caribbean* (Lanham, MD: Lexington Books, 2007), 75.

27. Susan Andrade, *The Nation Writ Small: African Fictions and Feminisms, 1958–1988* (Durham, NC: Duke University Press, 2011), 76.

28. Nicki Hitchcott examines Bâ's "negative" reading of feminism in favor of feminity, in "'Confidently Feminine'? Sexual Role-Play in the Novels of Mariama Bâ," in *African Francophone Writing: A Critical Introduction*, ed. Laïla Ibnlfassi and Nicki Hitchcott (Washington, DC: Berg, 1996), 139–52. For a critique of Bâ's feminism as a phenomenon of the West, see Femi Ojo-Ade, "Still a Victim? Mariama Bâ's *Une si longue lettre*," *African Literature Today* no. 12 (1982): 71–87.

29. Tobias Warner, *Tongue-Tied Imagination*, 181.

30. Andrade, *The Nation Writ Small*. Andrade writes: "As of 2009, I know of no literary texts that *Lettre* has inspired, as either epigone or antagonistic interlocutor" (73). This statement may hold true in the case of Francophone authors, but it overlooks Maam Yunus Dieng's literary response to Bâ in *Aawo Bi* (Dakar: IFAN Cheikh Anta Diop, 1991). For a reading of Dieng's novel in dialogue with *Lettre*, see Warner, *Tongue-Tied Imagination*, 198–202.

31. For a study of commemorative practices tied to the "Demba et Dupont" monument in Dakar, see Ferdinand De Jong, "Recycling Recognition: The Monument as *Objet Trouvé* of the Postcolony," *Journal of Material Culture* 13, no. 2 (July 2008): 195–214.

32. Shaun Irlam, "Mariama Bâ's *Une si longue lettre*: The Vocation of Memory and the Space of Writing," *Research in African Literatures* 29, no. 2 (Summer 1998): 78.

33. Bâ, *So Long a Letter*, 13.

34. Bâ, *So Long a Letter*, 15.

35. Mortimer, *Writing from the Hearth*, 85–87. Pascale Barthélémy offers an extensive study of the conditions and framings of young women's education in French West Africa, in *Africaines et diplômées à l'époque coloniale (1918–1957)* (Rennes: Presses Universitaires de Rennes, 2010).

36. Warner teases out the complexities of translation in relation to a text's public by pointing out that "a text's public is not a function of books nor even of readers, but rather of being presumable and reflexive—of being able to presume both that readers exist and that they will identify themselves as your addressees." Warner, *Tongue-Tied Imagination*, 198.

37. Mariama Bâ, *Bataaxal bu gudde nii*, trans. Maam Yunus Dieng and Arame Fal (Dakar: Les Nouvelles Éditions Africaines du Sénégal, 2007).

38. Rama Thiaw, dir., *The Revolution Won't Be Televised*, 2016, Boul Fallé Images, 110 min.

39. Momar-Coumba Diop and Mamadou Diouf, *Le Sénégal sous Abdou Diouf* (Paris: Karthala, 1990), 11.

40. Momar-Coumba Diop, "Du 'socialisme' au 'libéralisme': Les Légitimités de l'état," in *Sénégal: Trajectoires d'un état*, ed. Momar-Coumba Diop (Dakar: Codesria, 1992), 28.

41. Mills, "Sutura," 2–3. *Sutura* appears as an important concept in analyses of private financial transactions: Beth Buggenhagen, *Muslim Families in Global Senegal: Money Takes Care of Shame* (Bloomington: Indiana University Press, 2012); in marabouts' preaching practices: Fiona McLaughlin and Babacar Mboup, "Mediation and the Performance of Religious Authority in Senegal," *Islamic*

Africa 1, no. 1 (Spring 2010): 39–61; in women's dance and their maintenance of gender roles: Neveu Kringelbach, *Dance Circles*, 84; as well as in the strategies of queer women: Loes Oudenhuijsen, "Quietly Queer in Senegal," Africa Is a Country, July 15, 2019, https://africasacountry.com/2019/07/quietly-queer-in-senegal.

42. This is described as a culturally rooted obstacle to development by Rosnert Ludovic Alissoutin in *Les Défis du développement local au Sénégal* (Dakar: Codesria, 2008), 56. *Maslaa* has also been described as a way of focusing on the positive, which can present a challenge to certain public health and awareness initiatives, as explored in Fatou Leïty Mbodj, "'On ne se dévêt pas devant n'importe qui': Le Témoignage des personnes vivant avec le VIH au Sénégal," *Cahiers d'Études Africaines* 55, no. 217 (2015): 133–62.

43. Joseph Hill, "'All Women Are Guides': Sufi Leadership and Womanhood among the Taalibe Baay in Senegal," *Journal of Religion in Africa* 40 (2010): 382–83. Fallou Ngom explores *muñ* as a celebration of perseverance and thus a central value in Sufi religiosity, in *Muslims beyond the Arab World*, 116.

44. Boukary Sawadogo points out how digital and web technologies have facilitated a new era in Francophone African television series. Sawadogo, "Are Sitcoms the Future of Francophone West African Cinema?" *CineAction* 94 (2014): 40–44.

45. Following the death of Cheikh Tidjane Diop, there was a schism in the leadership of the Daaray Kocc troupe; this troupe still exists today but has not managed to maintain the same level of prominence as the company's founding generation.

46. In the Nigerian context, Anouk Batard applies a Certeaudian framework to discuss the "*arts de faire*" of local film productions emerging from similarly popular milieus. In "Système D, marginalisation et émancipation dans le cinéma nigérian: Arts de 'faire avec' une accumulation d'intermédiaires," *Politique Africaine* 153 (2019): 29–58.

47. The month of Ramadan, when people use slapstick entertainment to endure the long wait to sunset when they can break the fast, sees a yearly proliferation of such independent troupes and their low-budget series.

48. See Marame Gueye, "Senegal's Fear of Outspoken Women," Africa Is a Country, April 1, 2019, https://africasacountry.com/2019/04/senegals-fear-of-outspoken-women; and Julie Turkewitz, "Bold Women, Scandalized Viewers: It's 'Sex and the City,' Senegal Style," *New York Times*, August 22, 2019, https://www.nytimes.com/2019/08/22/world/africa/senegal-mistress-of-a-married-man.html.

Chapter 6

An earlier version of this chapter appeared in "Crafting the Popular Stage Space in Urban Senegal," *Research in African Literatures* 51, no. 2 (2020), 168–86.

1. Karin Barber, *The Generation of Plays: Yorùbá Popular Life in Theater* (Bloomington: Indiana University Press, 2000), 225.

2. Fall, *Théâtre et tradition*, 258.

3. Alioune Oumy Diop, *Le Théâtre traditionnel au Sénégal* (Dakar: Nouvelles Éditions Africaines du Sénégal, 1990), 44–45.

4. Oumy Diop, *Le Théâtre traditionnel*, 47.

5. Mouhamadou Diol, in discussion with the author, December 3, 2012.

6. By approaching contemporary performance groups in urban Africa through fieldwork, I aim to interact with scholarship based on similar approaches, primarily in the fields of anthropology and performance studies, especially David Donkor, *Spiders of the Market: Ghanaian Trickster Performance in a Web of Neoliberalism* (Bloomington: Indiana University Press, 2016); Shipley, *Trickster Theatre*; Neveu Kringelbach, *Dance Circles*; Laura Edmondson, *Performance and Politics in Tanzania: The Nation on Stage* (Bloomington: Indiana University Press, 2007); and Cole, *Ghana's Concert Party Theatre*.

7. Karin Barber, "Popular Arts in Africa," *African Studies Review* 30, no. 3 (September 1987): 1.

8. Barber, "Popular Arts in Africa."

9. Gaurav Desai, "Theater as Praxis: Discursive Practice in African Popular Theater," *African Studies Review* 33, no. 1 (April 1990): 68.

10. One important example is the clear-eyed critique, from the perspective of theater-for-development practitioners, of the uses of Freirean theory in an African context in Ross Kidd and Krishna Kumar, "Co-Opting Freire: A Critical Analysis of Pseudo-Freirian Adult Education," *Economic and Political Weekly* 16, no. 1/2 (January 3–10, 1981): 27–36; and Ross Kidd and Martin Byram, "Demystifying Pseudo-Freirian Development: The Case of Laedza Batanani," *Community Development Journal* 17, no. 2 (April 1982): 91–105.

11. "Options fondamentales du théâtre populaire," unpublished manifesto, personal archives of Magette Thiam, Thiès, 1970, 10–11.

12. On the history of the school, which at independence was named the House of Arts of Mali before becoming the School of Arts of Senegal and then, in 1972, the National Institute of Arts of Senegal and finally, in 1995, the National School of Arts of Senegal, see Ibrahima Wane, "The School of Arts and the Music Scene of Senegal," in *Music Education in Africa: Concept, Process, and Practice*, ed. Emily Achieng' Akuno (New York: Routledge, 2019), 126–34.

13. For a discussion of manifestations of the "contemporary" in the context of African dance, see Despres, *Se faire contemporain*.

14. Oumar Ndao, in discussion with the author, July 3, 2012.

15. Oumar Ndao, in discussion with the author, July 3, 2012.

16. This resonates with the experience of Senegalese contemporary dance as observed by Hélène Neveu Kringelbach (*Dance Circles*, 149–54).

17. Mamadou Diop, in discussion with the author, December 9, 2012.

18. Diop, "Tradition théâtrale et identités sénégalaises"; Oumar Ndao, "Le Théâtre privé au Sénégal," Wootico, July 12, 2008, http://festart.over-blog.com/article-21185531.html.

19. Mamadou Diop, in discussion with the author, April 17, 2013.

20. Fall, *Théâtre et tradition*, 293.

21. On the politics of "Wolofization" in Senegal, see Donal Cruise O'Brien, "The Shadow-Politics of Wolofisation," *Journal of Modern African Studies* 36, no. 1 (1998): 25–46; and Fiona McLaughlin, "Senegal: The Emergence of a National Lingua Franca," in *Language and National Identity in Africa*, ed. Andrew Simpson (Oxford: Oxford University Press, 2008), 79–97.

22. On the youth movement under President Diouf and beyond, see Mamadou Diouf, "Urban Youth and Senegalese Politics: Dakar 1988–1994," *Public Culture* 8, no. 2 (1996): 225–49; and Mamadou Diouf, "Engaging Postcolonial Cultures:

African Youth and Public Space," *African Studies Review* 46, no. 2 (September 2003): 1–12. Today the Senegalese Popular Theater Federation is attached to the Ministry of Youth.

23. Mamadou Diouf, "Fresques murales et écriture de l'histoire: Le *Set/Setal* à Dakar," *Politique Africaine* 46 (1992): 43.

24. Augusto Boal, *Theatre of the Oppressed*, trans. Charles McBride (New York: Urizen Books, 1979); Paulo Freire, *Pedagogy of the Oppressed*, trans. Myra Bergman Ramos (New York: Seabury, 1970).

25. The Centro de Teatro do Oprimido in Rio de Janeiro continues to play an important role in this regard.

26. Byam, *Community in Motion*, 18.

27. Bertolt Brecht, *Brecht on Theatre: The Development of an Aesthetic*, ed. Steve Giles et al., trans. John Willett (London: Eyre Methuen, 1964), 91–99.

28. On the contentious 2012 presidential election and resulting forms of cultural resistance, see Devin Bryson and Molly Enz, "Fed Up: Creating a New Type of Senegal through the Arts," *African Studies Quarterly* 14, no. 3 (2014): 1–12.

29. Mbaye has made a trademark of his short size and high-pitched voice and is regularly recognized on the street.

30. A subsequent law, implemented in January 2016, banned these small plastic bags in an attempt to mitigate their overwhelming impact on city pollution.

31. Since the performance, large sections of Yarakh have been rebuilt as part of an EU-funded development project that will broaden the neighborhood's roads in order to facilitate regular garbage collection. Rosalind Fredericks explores how such "infrastructures in postcolonial cities codify government prerogatives and unequal citizenship across the urban landscape." Fredericks, "Vital Infrastructures of Trash in Dakar," *Comparative Studies of South Africa, Asia and the Middle East* 34, no. 3 (2014): 535. See also Rosalind Fredericks, *Garbage Citizenship: Vital Infrastructures of Labor in Dakar, Senegal* (Durham, NC: Duke University Press, 2018).

32. For a similar case of unequal power dynamics between audience and performers in Kàddu Yaraax's work, see Brian Quinn, "De-Centering Theatrical Heritage: Forum Theater in Contemporary Senegal," *African Studies Quarterly* 14, no. 3 (2014): 75–88.

33. The workshops can range from discussions of local topics such as how to establish one's troupe as a legal administrative entity, to more globally focused topics, such as a tremendously popular and well-attended workshop given by visiting instructor Brent Blair, head of the Theatre and Social Change program at the University of Southern California.

BIBLIOGRAPHY

Alissoutin, Rosnert Ludovic. *Les Défis du développement local au Sénégal*. Dakar: Codesria, 2008.

Amon d'Aby, François-Joseph. *Le Théâtre en Côte d'Ivoire des origines à 1960: Suivi de Kwao Adjoba et de la Couronne aux Enchères*. Abidjan: Éditions CEDA, 1988.

Amselle, Jean-Loup. *Branchements: Anthropologie de l'universalité des cultures*. Paris: Flammarion, 2003.

Anderson, Samuel D. "'Negritude Is Dead': Performing the African Revolution at the First Pan-African Cultural Festival (Algiers, 1969)." In *The First World Festival of Negro Arts, Dakar 1966, Contexts and Legacies*, edited by David Murphy, 133–50. Liverpool, UK: Liverpool University Press, 2016.

Andrade, Susan. *The Nation Writ Small: African Fictions and Feminisms, 1958–1988*. Durham, NC: Duke University Press, 2011.

Apter, Andrew. *The Pan-African Nation: Oil and the Spectacle of Culture in Nigeria*. Chicago: University of Chicago Press, 2005.

Artaud, Antonin. *Le Théâtre et son double*. Paris: Gallimard, 1938.

Aslan, Odette. *Paris, capitale mondiale du théâtre*. Paris: Gallimard, 2009.

Bâ, Mariama. *Bataaxal bu gudde nii*. Translated by Maam Yunus Dieng and Arame Fal. Dakar: Les Nouvelles Éditions Africaines du Sénégal, 2007.

———. *Une si longue lettre*. Dakar: Les Nouvelles Éditions Africaines du Sénégal, 1979. Translated by Modupé Bodé-Thomas as *So Long a Letter*. London: Heinemann, 1981.

Bâ, Thierno. *Lat Dior, le chemin de l'honneur*. Dakar: Nouvelles Éditions Africaines, 1987.

Babou, Cheikh Anta. *Fighting the Greater Jihad: Amadu Bamba and the Founding of the Muridiyya of Senegal, 1853–1913*. Athens: Ohio University Press, 2007.

Bakhtin, Mikhail Mikhailovich. *The Dialogic Imagination: Four Essays*. Translated by Caryl Emerson and Michael Holquist. Austin: University of Texas Press, 2010.

Baller, Susann. "Urban Football Performances: Playing for the Neighbourhood in Senegal, 1950s–2000s." *Africa: The Journal of the International African Institute* 84, no. 1 (February 2014): 17–35.

———. "Youth, Theatre and Sports: Creating 'Conscious' Citizens within the Senegalese Nawetaan Movement." *African Insight* 37, no. 3 (2007): 376–87.

Balme, Christopher. *Decolonizing the Stage: Theatrical Syncretism and Post-Colonial Drama*. Oxford: Clarendon, 1999.

Bancel, Nicolas. "Les Centres Culturels en A.O.F. (1953–1960): Un projet de contrôle sociopolitique des jeunes élites." In *Lieux de sociabilité urbaine en*

Afrique, edited by Laurent Fourchard, Odile Goerg, and Muriel Gomez-Perez, 109–34. Paris: L'Harmattan, 2009.

Barber, Karin. *The Anthropology of Texts, Persons and Publics*. Cambridge: Cambridge University Press, 2009.

———. *The Generation of Plays: Yorùbá Popular Life in Theater*. Bloomington: Indiana University Press, 2000.

———. "Popular Arts in Africa." *African Studies Review* 30, no. 3 (September 1987): 1–78.

———. "Preliminary Notes on Audiences in Africa." *Africa* 67, no. 3 (1997): 347–62.

Barthélémy, Pascale. *Africaines et diplômées à l'époque coloniale (1918–1957)*. Rennes: Presses Universitaires de Rennes, 2010.

Batard, Anouk. "Système D, marginalisation et émancipation dans le cinéma nigérian: Arts de 'faire avec' une accumulation d'intermédiaires." *Politique Africaine* 153 (2019): 29–58.

Béart, Charles. "Les Origines du théâtre dans le monde, position du théâtre africain." *Comptes Rendus Mensuels de l'Académie des Sciences d'Outre-Mer* 22 (1962): 156.

———. "Le Théâtre indigène et la culture franco-africaine." *Le Théâtre Indigène et la Culture Franco-Africaine, Numéro Spécial de L'Éducation Africaine* (1937): 3–14.

Betts, Raymond F. *Assimilation and Association in French Colonial Theory, 1890–1914*. Lincoln: University of Nebraska Press, 2005.

Biasini, Émile. *Sur Malraux, celui qui aimait les chats*. Paris: Odile Jacob, 1999.

Blin, Myriam Odile, and Moustapha Tamba. *50 ans de cultures noires au Sénégal, 1960–2010*. Paris: L'Harmattan, 2014.

Boal, Augusto. *Theatre of the Oppressed*. Translated by Charles McBride. New York: Urizen Books, 1979.

Brasseur, Paule. "Le Bâton et le caïman ou Fily Dabo Sissoko et la France." In *Études africaines offertes à Henri Brunschwig*, 399–409. Paris: Éditions de l'École des Hautes Études en Sciences Sociales, 1982.

Brecht, Bertolt. *Brecht on Theatre: The Development of an Aesthetic*. Edited by Steve Giles et al., translated by John Willett. London: Eyre Methuen, 1964.

Bryson, Devin, and Molly Enz. "Fed Up: Creating a New Type of Senegal through the Arts." *African Studies Quarterly* 14, no. 3 (2014): 1–12.

Buggenhagen, Beth. *Muslim Families in Global Senegal: Money Takes Care of Shame*. Bloomington: Indiana University Press, 2012.

Bulman, Stephen. "A School for Epic? The 'École William Ponty' and the Evolution of the Sunjata Epic, 1913–c. 1960." In *Epic Adventures: Heroic Narrative in the Oral Performance Traditions of Four Continents*, edited by Jean Jansen and Hans M. J. Maier, 34–45. Münster: Lit Verlag, 2004.

Bush, Ruth. "Making History: Performances of the Past at the 1966 World Festival of Negro Arts." In *The First World Festival of Negro Arts, Dakar 1966, Contexts and Legacies,* edited by David Murphy, 97–112. Liverpool, UK: Liverpool University Press, 2016.

Byam, L. Dale. *Community in Motion: Theatre for Development in Africa*. Westport, CT: Bergin and Garvey, 1999.

Camara, Sanaa. "*A'jami* Literature in Senegal: The Example of Sëriñ Muusaa Ka, Poet and Biographer." *Research in African Literatures* 28, no. 3 (Autumn 1997): 163–82.

Castaldi, Francesca. *Choreographies of African Identities*. Urbana: University of Illinois Press, 2006.

Césaire, Aimé. *La Tragédie du Roi Christophe*. Paris: Présence Africaine, 1963.

Chalaye, Sylvie. *Afrique noire et dramaturgies contemporaines: Le Syndrome Frankenstein*. Paris: Éditions Théâtrales, 2004.

———. "Contemporary Francophone Drama: Between Detours and Deviations." *Yale French Studies* 112 (2007): 145–56.

———. *Du noir au nègre: L'Image du noir au théâtre (1550–1960)*. Paris: L'Harmattan, 1998.

Cissé, Bocar. *Instituteur des sables: Témoin du Mali du XXe siècle*. Brinon-sur-Sauldre: Grandveaux, 2014.

Clifford, James. *Routes: Travel and Translation in the Late Twentieth Century*. Cambridge, MA: Harvard University Press, 1997.

Coe, Cati. "Educating an African Leadership: Achimota and the Teaching of African Culture in the Gold Coast." *Africa Today* 49, no. 3 (Autumn 2002): 23–44.

Cohen, Joshua. "Locating Senghor's École de Dakar: International and Transnational Dimensions to Senegalese Modern Art, c. 1959–1980." *African Arts* 51, no. 3 (2018): 10–25.

———. "Stages in Transition: Les Ballets Africains and Independence, 1959–1960." *Journal of Black Studies* 43, no. 1 (January 2012): 11–48.

Cole, Catherine. *Ghana's Concert Party Theatre*. Bloomington: Indiana University Press, 2001.

Conklin, Alice. *A Mission to Civilize: The Republican Idea of Empire in France and West Africa, 1895–1930*. Palo Alto, CA: Stanford University Press, 1997.

Conquergood, Dwight. "Rethinking Ethnography: Towards a Critical Cultural Politics." *Communication Monographs* 58, no. 2 (June 1991): 179–94.

Conteh-Morgan, John. *Theatre and Drama in Francophone Africa: A Critical Introduction*. Cambridge: Cambridge University Press, 1994.

Cooper, Frederick. "Alternatives to Empire: France and Africa after World War II." In *The State of Sovereignty: Territories, Laws, Populations*, edited by Douglas Howland and Luise White, 94–123. Bloomington: Indiana University Press, 2008.

———. *Citizenship between Empire and Nation: Remaking France and French Africa, 1945–1960*. Princeton, NJ: Princeton University Press, 2014.

Copans, Jean. *Les Marabouts de l'arachide*. Paris: Le Sycomore, 1980.

Coquery-Vidrovitch, Catherine. "Festan, Festac, Panaf." In *Une histoire des festivals, XXe–XXI1 siècle*, edited by Anaïs Fléchet et al., 317–21. Paris: Publications de la Sorbonne, 2013.

Coquio, Catherine. "Un intellectual 'accompagné': Malraux, de Gaulle, Foccart et le récit de la 'décolonisation.'" In *Malraux et l'Afrique*, edited by Rafael Lambal, 169–201. Paris: Présence Africaine, 2013.

Cornevin, Robert. *Le Théâtre en Afrique noire et à Madagascar*. Paris: Le Livre Africain, 1970.

Cornut-Gentille, Bernard. "Les Centres Culturels, foyers d'amitié." *Traits d'Union,* no. 7 (March–April 1955): 3.

———. "Organisation d'un Grand Concours artistique et théâtral." *Traits d'Union*, no. 5 (1955): 3.

Coulibaly, Bojana. "Senegalese Theater Unabashed: Wolof Drama and Cultural Liberation." *Alif: Journal of Comparative Poetics*, no. 39 (2019): 123–48.

Cruise O'Brien, Donal. *The Mourides of Senegal: The Political and Economic Organization of an Islamic Brotherhood in Senegal*. Oxford: Oxford University Press, 1971.

———. "The Shadow-Politics of Wolofisation." *Journal of Modern African Studies* 36, no. 1 (1998): 25–46.

Dacher, Michèle. "Une épopée gouin: *Les Paysans noirs* à Banfora aujourd'hui." In *Robert Delavignette, savant et politique (1897–1976)*, edited by Bernard Mouralis and Anne Piriou with Romuald Fonkoua, 61–72. Paris: Karthala.

Dadié, Bernard. "Assémien Déhylé, Roi du Sanwi." *Le Théâtre Indigène et la Culture Franco-Africaine, Numéro Spécial de L'Éducation Africaine* (1937): 29–40.

———. *Climbié*. Paris: Seghers, 1956.

———. "Mon pays et son théâtre." *Le Théâtre Indigène et la Culture Franco-Africaine, Numéro Spécial de L'Éducation Africaine* (1937): 61–63.

Daffé, Gaye, and Mamadou Dansokho. "Les Nouvelles Technologies de l'information et de la communication: Défis et opportunités pour l'économie sénégalaise." In *Le Sénégal à l'heure de l'information: Technologies et société*, edited by Momar-Coumba Diop, 45–96. Paris: Karthala, 2002.

Dang, Christine Thu Nhi. "Pilgrimage through Poetry: Sung Journeys within the Murid Spiritual Diaspora." *Islamic Africa* 4, no. 1 (Spring 2013): 69–101.

De Jong, Ferdinand. "Recycling Recognition: The Monument as *Objet Trouvé* of the Postcolony." *Journal of Material Culture* 13, no. 2 (July 2008): 195–214.

———. "Shining Lights: Self-Fashioning in the Lantern Festival of Saint-Louis, Senegal." *African Arts* 42, no. 4 (Winter 2009): 38–53.

De Jong, Ferdinand, and Vincent Foucher. "La Tragédie du Roi Abdoulaye? Néomodernisme et renaissance africaine dans le Sénégal contemporain." *Politique Africaine* 118 (2010): 187–204.

De Jong, Ferdinand, and Brian Quinn. "Ruines d'utopies: L'École William Ponty et l'Université du Futur Africain." Translated by Jean-Nicolas Bach. *Politique Africaine* 135 (2014): 71–93.

Dedieu, Jean-Philippe. "L'Impérialisme de la voix: Théâtre français en Afrique et comédiens africains en France." In *L'Esclavage, la colonisation, et après . . .*, edited by Stéphane Dufoix and Patrick Weil, 323–56. Paris: Presses Universitaires de France, 2005.

Delavignette, Robert. "Le Théâtre de Gorée et la culture franco-africaine." *Afrique Française* 10 (1937): 471–72.

———. *Les Paysans noirs*. Saint-Étienne: Publications de l'Université de Saint-Étienne, 2011.

Desai, Gaurav. "Theater as Praxis: Discursive Practice in African Popular Theater." *African Studies Review* 33, no. 1 (April 1990): 65–92.

Despres, Altaïr. *Se faire contemporain*. Paris: Publications de la Sorbonne, 2016.

Dia, Amadou Cissé. *Les Derniers Jours de Lat Dior: Drame en 5 actes; La Mort du Damel, pièce en 3 actes*. Paris: Présence Africaine, 1978.

Diagne, Souleymane Bachir. *African Art as Philosophy: Senghor, Bergson and the Idea of Negritude*. Translated by Chike Jeffers. Chicago: University of Chicago Press, 2011.

Diakhaté, Ousmane (director of the Daniel Sorano National Theater). In discussion with the author, June 27, 2012.

Dieng, Bassirou, and Diaô Faye, eds. *L'Épopée de Cheikh Ahmadou Bamba de Serigne Moussa Ka: Jasaa u sakóor u géej gi-jasaa u sakóor u jéeri ji*. Dakar: Presses Universitaires de Dakar, 2006.

Dieng, Maam Yunus. *Aawo Bi*. Dakar: IFAN Cheikh Anta Diop, 1991.

Dièye, A. B. "Les Comédiens interpellent le nouveau pouvoir." *Sud Quotidien*, March 29, 2000.

Diol, Mouhamadou (director of La Compagnie Kàddu Yaraax). In discussion with the author, December 3, 2012, and December 20, 2016.

Diop, Alioune Oumy. *Le Théâtre traditionnel au Sénégal*. Dakar: Nouvelles Éditions Africaines du Sénégal, 1990.

Diop, Birago. *Les Contes d'Amadou Koumba*. Paris: Présence Africaine, 1969.

Diop, Cheikh M. S. "Tradition théâtrale et identités sénégalaises: Contributions sur la pratique dramatique au Sénégal. Approche historique et analytique." Africultures, July 22, 2004. http://africultures.com/tradition-theatrale-et-identite-senegalaises-3464/.

Diop, Mamadou (stage director and choreographer, teacher at the École Nationale des Arts du Sénégal). In discussion with the author, December 9, 2012, and April 17, 2013.

Diop, Momar-Coumba. "Du 'socialisme' au 'libéralisme': Les Légitimités de l'état." In *Sénégal: Trajectoires d'un état*, edited by Momar-Coumba Diop, 13–38. Dakar: Codesria, 1992.

———. "Le Sénégal à la croisée des Chemins." *Politique Africaine* 104 (2006): 103–26.

———. "Réformes économiques et recompositions sociales." In *La Construction de l'état au Sénégal*, edited by Donal Cruise O'Brien et al., 64–82. Paris: Karthala, 2002.

Diop, Momar-Coumba, and Mamadou Diouf. *Le Sénégal sous Abdou Diouf*. Paris: Karthala, 1990.

Diouf, Mamadou. "Engaging Postcolonial Cultures: African Youth and Public Space." *African Studies Review* 46, no. 2 (September 2003): 1–12.

———. "The French Colonial Policy of Assimilation and Civility of the Originaires of the Four Communes (Senegal): A Nineteenth-Century Globalization Project." *Development and Change* 29, no. 4 (October 1988): 671–96.

———. "Fresques murales et écriture de l'histoire: Le *Set/Setal* à Dakar." *Politique Africaine* 46 (1992): 41–54.

———. *Histoire du Sénégal: Le Modèle islamo-wolof et ses périphéries*. Paris: Maisonneuve & Larose, 2001.

———. "Urban Youth and Senegalese Politics: Dakar 1988–1994." *Public Culture* 8, no. 2 (1996): 225–49.

Donkor, David. *Spiders of the Market: Ghanaian Trickster Performance in a Web of Neoliberalism*. Bloomington: Indiana University Press, 2016.

Doshi, Neil. "Absent Performances: Distant Fieldwork on Social Movement Theater of Algeria and India." In *Theorizing Fieldwork in the Humanities:*

Methods, Reflections, and Approaches to the Global South, edited by Debra A. Castillo and Shalini Puri, 109–29. New York: Palgrave Macmillan, 2016.

Drewal, Margaret Thompson. "The State of Research on Performance in Africa." *African Studies Review* 34, no. 3 (December 1991): 1–64.

Duke Bryant, Kelly. *Education as Politics: Colonial Schooling and Political Debate in Senegal, 1850s–1914*. Madison: University of Wisconsin Press, 2015.

Ebron, Paulla. "Tourists as Pilgrims: Commercial Fashioning of Transatlantic Politics." *American Ethnologist* 26, no. 4 (November 1999): 910–32.

Edebiri, Unionmwan. "The Development of the Theatre in French-Speaking West Africa." *Theatre Research International* 9, no. 3 (Autumn 1984): 168–80.

Edmondson, Laura. *Performance and Politics in Tanzania: The Nation on Stage*. Bloomington: Indiana University Press, 2007.

Edwards, Brent Hayes. *The Practice of Diaspora: Literature, Translation and the Rise of Black Internationalism*. Cambridge, MA: Harvard University Press, 2003.

Ekra, Mathieu. "Première de Kwao Adjoba, Drame de J.F. (sic.) Amon d'Aby." *Traits d'Union* no. 5 (1955): 74.

"Entrevue de Samory et du Capitaine Péroz." *Le Théâtre Indigène et la Culture Franco-Africaine, Numéro Spécial de L'Éducation Africaine* (1937): 41–46.

Eyoh, Hansel Ndumbe. Review of *Le Théâtre en Afrique noire francophone*, by Jacques Scherer. *Research in African Literatures* 26, no. 1 (Spring 1995): 141.

Fabian, Johannes. *Power and Performance: Ethnographic Explorations through Proverbial Wisdom and Theater in Shaba, Zaire*. Madison: University of Wisconsin Press, 1990.

———. *Time and the Other: How Anthropology Makes Its Object*. New York: Columbia University Press, 2014.

Fair, Jo Ellen. "*Francophonie* and the National Airwaves: A History of Television in Senegal." In *Planet TV: A Global Television Reader*, edited by Shanti Kumar and Lisa Parks, 189–210. New York: NYU Press, 2002.

Fall, Cheikh Ibrahima (director of the *Bamba Mos Xam* troupe). In discussion with the author, May 15 and 21, 2016.

Fall, Marouba. *Chaka, ou le roi visionnaire*. Dakar: Nouvelles Éditions Africaines, 1984.

———. *Théâtre et tradition en Afrique noire francophone: Exemple du théâtre sénégalais de langue française*. Dakar: L'Harmattan-Sénégal, 2019.

Fall, Yelimane (painter). In discussion with the author, May 18, 2016.

Fallou, Beug (former *diwaankaat*, or professional Murid storyteller). In discussion with the author, December 17, 2016.

Fanon, Frantz. "On National Culture." In *The Wretched of the Earth*, translated by Richard Philcox. New York: Grove, 2004.

Feldman, Hannah. *From a Nation Torn: Decolonizing Art and Representation in France, 1945–1962*. Durham, NC: Duke University Press, 2014.

Forsdick, Charles. "*Cette île n'est pas une île*: Locating Gorée." In *At the Limits of Memory: Legacies of Slavery in the Francophone World*, edited by Nicola Frith and Kate Hodgson, 131–53. Liverpool, UK: Liverpool University Press, 2015.

Fredericks, Rosalind. *Garbage Citizenship: Vital Infrastructures of Labor in Dakar, Senegal*. Durham, NC: Duke University Press, 2018.

———. "Vital Infrastructures of Trash in Dakar." *Comparative Studies of South Africa, Asia and the Middle East* 34, no. 3 (2014): 532–48.

Freire, Paulo. *Pedagogy of the Oppressed.* Translated by Myra Bergman Ramos. New York: Seabury, 1970.

Gahungu, Céline. "Le Concours théâtral interafricain: Quelles archives? Quels usages?" *Continents Manuscrits,* no. 13 (2019), online.

Gamble, Harry. *Contesting French West Africa: Battles over Schools and the Colonial Order, 1900–1950.* Lincoln: University of Nebraska Press, 2017.

Garritano, Carmela. *African Video Movies and Global Desires.* Athens: Ohio University Press, 2013.

Gbanou, Sélom Komlan. "De la planche à la bande: Les Voies modernes de l'oralité africaine: De la scène à la cassette." *Matatu: Journal for African Culture and Society* 31–32, no. 1 (August 2005): 43–60.

Gnaoulé-Oupoh, Bruno. *La Littérature ivoirienne.* Paris: Karthala, 2000.

Grabski, Joanna. *Art World City: The Creative Economy of Artists and Urban Life in Dakar.* Bloomington: Indiana University Press, 2017.

Grésillon, Almuth, and Jean-Marie Thomasseau. "Scènes de genèses théâtrales." *Genesis (Manuscrits—Recherche—Invention)* 26 (2005): 19–34.

Guèye, Cheikh. *Touba, la capitale des Mourides.* Paris: Karthala, 2002.

Gueye, Marame. "Senegal's Fear of Outspoken Women." Africa Is a Country, April 1, 2019, https://africasacountry.com/2019/04/senegals-fear-of-outspoken-women.

Guèye, Massamba. "Intervention du directeur de Sorano Massamba Guèye: Le Théâtre, une réussite face à l'interdit." Website of La Compagnie du Théâtre National du Sénégal Daniel Sorano, November 11, 2013, http://compagnietheatresorano.com/rubriques.php?rub=article.php&id_article=62.

Harding, James M., and John Rouse, eds. *Not the Other Avant-Garde: The Transnational Foundations of Avant-Garde Performance.* Ann Arbor: University of Michigan Press, 2006.

Harney, Elizabeth. *In Senghor's Shadow: Art, Politics, and the Avant-Garde in Senegal, 1960–1995.* Durham, NC: Duke University Press, 2004.

Hazemann, Yves. "Un outil de la conquête coloniale: L'École des Ôtages de Saint-Louis (1855–1871; 1892–1903)." *Cahiers du CRA* 5 (1987): 135–59.

Hill, Joseph. "'All Women Are Guides': Sufi Leadership and Womanhood among the Taalibe Baay in Senegal." *Journal of Religion in Africa* 40 (2010): 375–412.

———. "'Baay Is the Spiritual Leader of the Rappers': Performing Islamic Reasoning in Senegalese Hip-Hop." *Contemporary Islam* 10, no. 2 (May 2016): 267–87.

Hitchcott, Nicki. "'Confidently Feminine'? Sexual Role-Play in the Novels of Mariama Bâ." In *African Francophone Writing: A Critical Introduction*, edited by Laïla Ibnlfassi and Nicki Hitchcott, 139–52. Washington, DC: Berg, 1996.

Innes, Christopher. "Primitive, Ritual and Ceremony." In *Holy Theatre: Ritual and the Avant-Garde*, 111–58. Cambridge: Cambridge University Press, 1981.

Irele, Abiola. "In Praise of Alienation." In *African Literature: An Anthology of Criticism and Theory*, edited by Tejumola Olaniyan and Ato Quayson, 599–607. Malden, MA: Blackwell, 2007.

Irlam, Shaun. "Mariama Bâ's *Une si longue lettre*: The Vocation of Memory and the Space of Writing." *Research in African Literatures* 29, no. 2 (Summer 1998): 76–93.

Jaji, Tsitsi. "'The Next Best Thing to Being There': Covering the 1966 Dakar Festival and Its Legacy in Black Popular Magazines." In *The First World Festival of Negro Arts, Dakar 1966, Contexts and Legacies*, edited by David Murphy, 113–29. Liverpool, UK: Liverpool University Press, 2016.

Jézéquel, Jean-Hervé. "Grammaire de la distinction coloniale: L'Organisation des cadres de l'enseignement en Afrique occidentale française (1903–fin des années 1930)." *Genèse* 69 (December 2007): 4–25.

———. "Le 'théâtre des instituteurs' en AOF (1930–1950): Pratique socio-culturelle et vecteur de cristallisation de nouvelles identités urbaines." In *Fêtes urbaines en Afrique: Espaces, identités et pouvoirs*, edited by Odile Goerg, 181–200. Paris: Karthala, 1994.

———. "Les Enseignants comme élite politique en AOF (1930–1945): Des 'meneurs de galopins' dans l'arène politique." *Cahiers d'Études Africaines* 178 (2005): 519–43.

Jones, Hilary. *The Métis of Senegal: Urban Life and Politics in French West Africa*. Bloomington: Indiana University Press, 2013.

Jukpor, Ben. "Le Rôle de l'École William Ponty dans le développement du théâtre ouest-africain francophone." *Présence Francophone* 24 (1982): 47–64.

Kane, Leïty (president of La Compagnie Kàddu Yaraax). In discussion with the author, December 23, 2016.

Khellas, Mériem. *Le Premier Festival Culturel Panafricain, Algers, 1969: Une grande messe populaire*. Paris: L'Harmattan, 2014.

Kidd, Ross, and Martin Byram. "Demystifying Pseudo-Freirian Development: The Case of Laedza Batanani." *Community Development Journal* 17, no. 2 (April 1982): 91–105.

Kidd, Ross, and Krishna Kumar. "Co-opting Freire: A Critical Analysis of Pseudo-Freirian Adult Education." *Economic and Political Weekly* 16, no. 1/2 (January 3–10, 1981): 27–36.

Klein, William, dir. *Festival Panafricain d'Alger*. 2010. Arte Éditions, 120 min.

Koné, Lompolo. "Hésitations." *Traits d'Union* no. 8 (May–June 1955): 4.

———. "M. Lompolo Koné est chargé des fonctions de rédacteur en chef de 'Traits d'Union.'" *Traits d'Union* no. 1 (1953): 5.

———. "Nos Activités!" *Traits d'Union* no. 7 (March–April 1955): 5.

Konkobo, Christophe. *La Pratique du théâtre moderne au Burkina Faso*. Paris: L'Harmattan, 2017.

Labrune-Badiane, Céline, and Etienne Smith. *Les Hussards noirs de la colonie, instituteurs africains et 'petites patries' en AOF (1913–1960)*. Paris: Karthala, 2018.

Larkin, Brian. *Signal and Noise: Media, Infrastructure, and Urban Culture in Nigeria*. Durham, NC: Duke University Press, 2008.

Le Lay, Maëline. *La Parole construit le pays: Théâtre, langues et didactisme au Katanga (République Démocratique du Congo)*. Paris: Honoré Champion, 2014.

"Le Théâtre se meurt mais ne se rend pas." *Le Soleil*, February 6, 1997, 8.

Lebovics, Herman. *Mona Lisa's Escort: André Malraux and the Reinvention of French Culture*. Durham, NC: Duke University Press, 1999.

Lévy-Bruhl, Lucien. *La Mentalité primitive*. Paris: Félix Alcan, 1925.

Ligier, Françoise. "Le Concours théâtral interafricain." *Recherche, Pédagogie et Culture* 33 (1978): 58–59.

Ly, Boubacar. *Les Instituteurs au Sénégal de 1903 à 1945: La Formation au métier d'instituteur, Vol. 3*. Paris: L'Harmattan, 2009.

Malaquais, Dominique, and Cédric Vincent. "Panafest: A Festival Complex Revisited." In *The First World Festival of Negro Arts, Dakar 1966, Contexts and Legacies*, edited by David Murphy, 194–202. Liverpool, UK: Liverpool University Press, 2016.

Malraux, André. *Le Miroir des Limbes II: La Corde et les souris*. Paris: Gallimard, 1976.

Mbacké, Khadim. *Sufism and Religious Brotherhoods in Senegal*. Translated by Eric Ross, edited by John Hunwick. Princeton, NJ: Markus Wiener, 2005.

Mbaye, Alioune. "Le Théâtre des centres culturels en AOF: 1948–1958, 'Du casque colonial au béret tropical.'" *Ethiopiques* no. 76 (2006).

Mbaye, Alioune Diakhaté. *Les Sports Navétanes au Sénégal*. Dakar: L'Harmattan-Sénégal, 2017.

M'Bengue, Mamadou Seyni. *Le Procès de Lat Dior*. Paris: ORTF-DAEC, 1972.

Mbodj, Fatou Leïty. "'On ne se dévêt pas devant n'importe qui': Le Témoignage des personnes vivant avec le VIH au Sénégal." *Cahiers d'Études Africaines* 55, no. 217 (2015): 133–62.

McLaughlin, Fiona. "Islam and Popular Music in Senegal: The Emergence of a 'New Tradition.'" *Africa: Journal of the International African Institute* 67, no. 4 (1997): 560–81.

———. "Senegal: The Emergence of a National Lingua Franca." In *Language and National Identity in Africa*, edited by Andrew Simpson, 79–97. Oxford: Oxford University Press, 2008.

McLaughlin, Fiona, and Babacar Mboup. "Mediation and the Performance of Religious Authority in Senegal." *Islamic Africa* 1, no. 1 (Spring 2010): 39–61.

McMahon, Christina. *Recasting Transnationalism through Performance: Theatre Festivals in Cape Verde, Mozambique and Brazil*. New York: Palgrave Macmillan, 2014.

Médéhouégnon, Pierre. *Le Théâtre francophone de l'Afrique de l'Ouest: Des origines à nos jours: Historique et analyse de la dramaturgie en Côte d'Ivoire, au Burkina Faso, au Togo et au Bénin*. Jéricho-Cotonou: CAAREC, 2010.

Michel, M. "La Colonisation: L'Action sociale." *L'Éducation Africaine, Bulletin de l'Enseignement de l'A.O.F.* 93 (1936): 6–8.

Miller, Christopher L. *Theories of Africans*. Chicago: University of Chicago Press, 1993.

Miller, Judith G. "Is There a Specifically Francophone African Stage Textuality?" *Yale French Studies* 112 (2007): 131–44.

Mills, Ivy. "Sutura: Gendered Honor, Social Death, and the Politics of Exposure in Senegalese Literature and Popular Culture." Ph.D. dissertation, University of California at Berkeley, 2011.

Mokhtari, Omar, ed. *Alger 1969, Premier Festival Culturel Panafricain*. Algiers: Éditions Actualité Algérie, 1970.

Moran, Denise. "Les Élèves d'une école normale africaine donnent, à Dakar, un spectacle d'art indigene." *Le Théâtre Indigène et la Culture Franco-Africaine, Numéro Spécial de L'Éducation Africaine* (1937): 59–60.

Mortimer, Mildred. *Writing from the Hearth: Public, Domestic, and Imaginative Space in Francophone Women's Fiction of Africa and the Caribbean*. Lanham, MD: Lexington Books, 2007.

Mouralis, Bernard. "William Ponty Drama." In *European-Language Writing in Sub-Saharan Africa*, edited by Albert S. Gérard, 130–40. Budapest: Akadémiai Kiadó, 1986.

Mudimbe, Valentin. *The Invention of Africa: Gnosis, Philosophy, and the Order of Knowledge*. Bloomington: Indiana University Press, 1988.

Murphy, David. "The Performance of Pan-Africanism: Staging the African Renaissance at the First World Festival of Negro Arts." In *The First World Festival of Negro Arts, Dakar 1966, Contexts and Legacies*, edited by David Murphy, 1–42. Liverpool, UK: Liverpool University Press, 2016.

Ndao, Cheikh Aliou. "Éthique et esthétique dans le théâtre sénégalais." *Le Soleil*, July 27, 1998.

———. *L'Exil d'Albouri, suivi de la décision; Le Fils de l'Almamy; La Case de l'homme*. Dakar: Nouvelles Éditions Africaines, 1985.

Ndao, Oumar. In discussion with the author, July 3, 2012.

———. "Le Théâtre privé au Sénégal." Wootico, July 12, 2008. http://festart.over-blog.com/article-21185531.html.

Ndiaye, Soukaye (Touba resident). In discussion with the author, December 17, 2016.

Nelson, Steve. "Karmen Geï: Sex, the State, and Censorship in Dakar." *African Arts* 44, no. 1 (Spring 2011): 74–81.

Neveu Kringelbach, Hélène. "Choreographic Performance: Generations and the Art of Life in Post-Colonial Dakar." *Africa* 81, no. 1 (February 2014): 36–54.

———. "Dance at the 1966 World Festival of Negro Arts: Of 'Fabulous Dancers' and Negritude Undermined." In *The First World Festival of Negro Arts, Dakar 1966, Contexts and Legacies*, edited by David Murphy, 64–82. Liverpool, UK: Liverpool University Press, 2016.

———. *Dance Circles: Movement, Morality, and Self-Fashioning in Urban Senegal*. Oxford: Berghahn, 2013.

Ngom, Fallou. *Muslims beyond the Arab World: The Odyssey of ʿAjamī and the Muridiyya*. Oxford: Oxford University Press, 2016.

Ngũgĩ wa Thiong'o. *Penpoints, Gunpoints, and Dreams*. Oxford: Oxford University Press, 1998.

Niang, Abdoulaye. "'Preaching Music' and Islam in Senegal: Can the Secular Mediate the Religious? The Case of Rap and *Mbalax* Music." *African Communication Research* 2, no. 1 (2009): 61–84.

Niang, Massèye. *Le Légende du fusil*. Paris: L'Harmattan, 2015.

Nouwligbèto, Fernand. *Théâtre béninois: Logiques marchandes et enjeux esthétiques*. Benin: CIREF Éditions, 2016.

Ogunnaike, Oludamini. "Performing Realization: The Sufi Music Videos of the Taalibe Baye of Dakar." *African Arts* 51, no. 3 (Autumn 2018): 26–39.

Ojo-Ade, Femi. "Still a Victim? Mariama Bâ's *Une si longue lettre*." *African Literature Today* no. 12 (1982): 71–87.

Oudenhuijsen, Loes. "Quietly Queer in Senegal." Africa Is a Country, July 15, 2019. https://africasacountry.com/2019/07/quietly-queer-in-senegal.

Pangop Kameni, Alain Cyr. *Rires des crises postcoloniales: Le Discours intermédiatique du théâtre comique populaire et la fictionnalisation de la politique linguistique au Cameroun*. Berlin: Lit Verlag, 2009.

Pasquini, Marie. "Raymond Hermantier, un parcours: Du théâtre populaire au dialogue des cultures." Mémoire de maîtrise (master's thesis), Université Paris III Sorbonne Nouvelle, 2006.

Peslin, Daniela. *Le Théâtre des Nations: Une aventure théâtrale à découvrir*. Paris: L'Harmattan, 2009.

Poirrier, Philippe. *La Politique culturelle en débat: Anthologie, 1955–2012*. Paris: La Documentation Française, 2013.

Puri, Shalini. "Finding the Field: Notes on Caribbean Cultural Criticism, Area Studies, and the Forms of Engagement." *Small Axe* 17, no. 2 (July 2013): 58–73.

Quinn, Brian. "De-Centering Theatrical Heritage: Forum Theater in Contemporary Senegal." *African Studies Quarterly* 14, no. 3 (2014): 75–88.

Rauch, Marie-Ange. *Le Bonheur d'entreprendre: Les Administrateurs de la France d'outre-mer et la création du Ministère des Affaires Culturelles*. Paris: Comité d'Histoire du Ministère de la Culture, 1998.

Ricard, Alain. *L'Invention du théâtre: Le Théâtre et les comédiens en Afrique noire*. Lausanne: L'Age d'Homme, 1986.

———. "The ORTF and African Literature." *Research in African Literatures* 4, no. 2 (Autumn 1973): 189 91.

Roberts, Allen F., and Mary Nooter Roberts. *A Saint in the City: Sufi Arts of Urban Senegal*. Los Angeles: Fowler Museum of Cultural History, 2003.

Robinson, David. *Paths of Accommodation: Muslim Societies and French Colonial Authorities in Senegal and Mauritania, 1880–1920*. Athens: Ohio University Press, 2000.

Ross, Eric. *Sufi City: Urban Design and Archetypes in Touba*. Rochester, NY: University of Rochester Press, 2002.

Sabatier, Peggy. "African Culture and Colonial Education: The William Ponty School Cahiers and Theater." *Journal of African Studies* 7, no. 1 (1980): 2–10.

Sall, Ibrahima. *Le Choix de Madior*. Dakar: Nouvelles Éditions Africaines, 1981.

Salvaing, Bernard. "Les 'Ailleurs' d'un instituteur africain: Bocar Cissé (1944–1945)." In *L'Ailleurs de l'autre, récits de voyageurs extra-européens*, edited by Claudine Le Blanc and Jacques Weber, 219–33. Rennes: Presses Universitaires de Rennes, 2009.

Samb, Cheikh (journalist, grandson of the lead actor in *Bamba Mos Xam*). In discussion with the author, December 17, 2016.

Sarraut, Albert. *La Mise en valeur des colonies françaises*. Paris: Payot & Cie, 1923.

Sawadogo, Boukary. "Are Sitcoms the Future of Francophone West African Cinema?" *CineAction* 94 (2014): 40–44.

———. *West African Screen Media: Comedy, TV Series, and Transnationalization*. East Lansing: Michigan State University Press, 2019.

Schechner, Richard. *Public Domain: Essays on the Theatre*. Indianapolis, IN: Bobbs-Merrill, 1969.

Scherer, Jacques. *Le Théâtre en Afrique noire francophone*. Paris: Presses Universitaires de France, 1992.

Seck, Assane. In discussion with the author, July 5, 2012.

Seck, Fatoumata. "Goorgoorlou, the Neoliberal *Homo Senegalensis*: Comics and Economics in Postcolonial Senegal." *Journal of African Cultural Studies* 30, no. 3 (May 2017): 263–78.

Senghor, Léopold Sédar. "Le Message de l'Afrique." In *Premier Festival Mondial des Arts Nègres* (festival program). Paris: Impressions André Rousseau, 1966.

———. *Liberté I, négritude et humanisme*. Paris: Seuil, 1964.

Senghor, Maurice Sonar. *Souvenirs de théâtres d'Afrique et d'Outre-Afrique: Pour que lève la semence*. Paris: L'Harmattan, 2004.

Shah, Idries. *The Sufis*. London: Idries Shah Foundation, 2015.

Shipley, Jesse Weaver. *Trickster Theatre: The Poetics of Freedom in Urban Africa*. Bloomington: Indiana University Press, 2015.

Snipe, Tracy D. *Arts and Politics in Senegal, 1960–1996*. Trenton, NJ: Africa World, 1998.

Sow, Papa Samba. "Théâtre Nawetaan, théâtre des valeurs." In *De l'instinct théâtral: Le Théâtre se ressource en Afrique*, edited by Julius Effenberger, 45–66. Paris: L'Harmattan, 2004.

Soyinka, Wole. "Theatre in African Traditional Cultures: Survival Patterns." In *Modern African Drama: Backgrounds and Criticism*, edited by Biyodun Jeyifo, 421–33. New York: Norton, 2002.

Stepan, Alfred. "Rituals of Respect: Sufis and Secularists in Senegal in Comparative Perspective." *Comparative Politics* 44, no. 4 (July 2012): 379–401.

Straker, Jay. *Youth, Nationalism, and the Guinean Revolution*. Bloomington: Indiana University Press, 2009.

Taylor, Diana. *The Archive and the Repertoire: Performing Cultural Memory in the Americas*. Durham, NC: Duke University Press, 2003.

"Théâtre et chants indigènes: Compte-rendu de la fête de l'École William-Ponty." *L'Éducation Africaine, Bulletin de l'Enseignement de l'A.O.F.* 90–91 (April–September 1935): 177–99.

Thiaw, Rama, dir. *The Revolution Won't Be Televised*. 2016. Boul Fallé Images, 110 min.

Touré, J.-M. "Mobiliser, informer, éduquer un instrument efficace: Le Théâtre." *Notre Librairie* 88/89 (1987): 86–96.

Traoré, Bakary. *Le Théâtre négro-africain et ses fonctions sociales*. Paris: Présence Africaine, 1958.

Traoré, Seyba. In discussion with the author, July 3, 2012.

Tudesq, André-Jean. *L'Afrique noire et ses télévisions*. Paris: Anthropos INA, 1992.

Turkewitz, Julie. "Bold Women, Scandalized Viewers: It's 'Sex and the City,' Senegal Style." *New York Times*, August 22, 2019, https://www.nytimes.com/2019/08/22/world/africa/senegal-mistress-of-a-married-man.html.

Ubersfeld, Anne. *Lire le théâtre*. Paris: Éditions Sociales, 1977.

Verschave, François-Xavier. *La Françafrique: Le Plus Long Scandale de la République*. Paris: Stock, 1998.

Wade, Abdoulaye. In discussion with the author, July 4, 2012.

Wane, Ibrahima. "The School of Arts and the Music Scene of Senegal." In *Music Education in Africa: Concept, Process, and Practice*, edited by Emily Achieng' Akuno, 126–34. New York: Routledge, 2019.

Ware, Rudolph. *The Walking Qur'an: Islamic Education, Embodied Knowledge, and History in West Africa.* Chapel Hill: University of North Carolina Press, 2014.

Warner, Gary. "The Use of Historical Sources in Francophone African Theatre." *Theatre Research International* 9, no. 3 (Autumn 1984): 180–94.

Warner, Tobias. "Para-Literary Ethnography and Colonial Self-Writing: The Student Notebooks of the William Ponty School." *Research in African Literatures* 47, no. 1 (Spring 2016): 1–20.

———. *The Tongue-Tied Imagination: Decolonizing Literary Modernity in Senegal.* New York: Fordham University Press, 2019.

Wenkel, Christian. "Le Théâtre des Nations—Un théâtre de la guerre froide?" In *La France en guerre froide, nouvelles questions*, edited by Sylvie Le Clech and Michel Hastings, 181–89. Dijon: Éditions Universitaires de Dijon, 2015.

Wilder, Gary. *Freedom Time: Negritude, Decolonization, and the Future of the World.* Durham, NC: Duke University Press, 2015.

———. *The French Imperial Nation-State: Negritude and Colonial Humanism between the Two World Wars.* Chicago: University of Chicago Press, 2005.

Young, Robert J. C. "Race and Language in the Two Saussures." In *Philosophies of Race and Ethnicity*, edited by Peter Osborne and Stella Sanford, 63–78. New York: Continuum Books, 2002.

Zenenga, Praise. "The Total Theatre Aesthetic Paradigm in African Theatre." In *The Oxford Handbook of Dance and Theatre*, edited by Nadine George-Graves, 236–51. Oxford: Oxford University Press, 2015.

INDEX

Page numbers in *italic* refer to illustrations.